ST. MARTIN'S

MINOTAUR
MYSTERIES

The Cold Blue Blood

A BERGER & MITRY MYSTERY

DAVID HANDLER

St. Martin's Paperbacks

THE COLD BLUE BLOOD

Library of Congress Catalog Card Number: 2001041804

ISBN: 0-312-98610-6

Printed in the United States of America

St. Martin's Press hardcover edition / October 2001
St. Martin's Paperbacks edition / October 2002

St. Martin's Paperbacks are published by St. Martin's Press, 175 Fifth Avenue, New
York, NY 10010.

10 9 8 7 6 5 4 3 2 1

ACKNOWLEDGMENTS

I am extremely grateful to Elaine M. Pagliaro of the Connecticut State Police Forensic Science Laboratory for generously sharing her expertise with me; Susan Stephenson, Jerry Weiss, and Peter Zallinger, gifted artists and teachers all, for showing me the world through their eyes; Judy Friday, who offered me her insights into rescuers; William Goldman, who encouraged me when I really needed it the most; Ruth Cavin, who believed in me; and Diane L. Drake, who gave me the Fibonacci series and way, way more.

PROLOGUE

APRIL 18

HE CALLED HIMSELF STAN, although Torry was pretty sure that Stan wasn't his real name. There was something about the way it seemed to catch in his throat the first time he said it. Plus he was real nervous. His eyes kept flicking around the bar as if he were afraid someone might recognize him.

Not that he seemed like the kind of guy who ever hung out with the kind of guys who hung out at the Purple Pup.

Stan wasn't fat. Stan wasn't loud. Stan didn't reek of bad cologne. He was classy and soft-spoken. He said "thank you" when Torry brought him his draft beer—Beck's, which was a dollar more than Miller. And pretty good-looking for an older guy, too. Tall and trimly built, with nice Ralph Lauren clothes. Torry, who was not good with ages, figured he was somewhere around fifty. And a real curiosity. Because she didn't see his type around the Pup too often. Hardly at all, actually. Stan's type belonged in a country club in Farmington.

The Purple Pup was a scruffy roadhouse next to Kwik Lube on Highway 66—just west of Middletown on the way to Meriden. Middletown was known for Wesleyan University and for the big mental hospital that was there, Connecticut Valley Hospital. Meriden wasn't known for anything except the inadequacy of its storm drains. Residents of the neighboring towns knew to steer clear of Meriden whenever more than a quarter-inch of rain fell. As a consequence, Meriden was not considered a good place to own and operate a small business. Still, the Purple Pup managed to do well on the weekends when the weather was good. It was very popular with the bikers—the middle-aged firemen and postal workers who liked to toodle around in the sunshine on their vintage Harleys. It was a thing they all did, like playing golf or going bowling. They'd pull in by the dozens, drink and laugh and listen to oldies on the jukebox. It was fun when the bikers came, and Torry could make fifty bucks a shift in tips. She was a big, meaty woman, large through the breasts and hips. Not fashion magazine material—but she went over well with the Purple Pup crowd.

Torry had been slinging drinks there for almost two years. For the past year, she had been a blonde.

When it was cold and rainy, the Pup was deserted. Particularly on weeknights. A few young guys who worked odd jobs and still lived with their folks would hang there, nursing a couple of beers and watching the games on the dish. Lousy tippers, to a man. And their advances toward her were crude and smirky. Not to mention unsuccessful. Curt, who owned the place and tended bar, barely broke even on such nights.

That was the kind of night it was when Stan first came in. It had been raining, a cold March rain. The parking lot out front was under four inches of water.

He drank two Beck's, seated there by himself in the shadows at a small corner table. When she asked him if he would like another one he asked her if she would like to go for a drive someplace after work. She said, "Where?" He said, "We'll find someplace nice." She said, "Why not?" Someplace nice turned out to be Wadsworth Falls, where they made out in the front seat of his mud-splattered Range Rover and listened to the rain beat down. Stan was a total gentleman. He even asked Torry for her permission before he unhooked her bra, marveling over the size and beauty of her breasts as he tongued them gently. He treated her like she was a prized figurine. She did not even have to ask him to use a condom. He was prepared. He was solicitous. He was as gentle as a lamb.

Afterward, he asked Torry how she made ends meet.

"I do what I have to do," she replied matter-of-factly.

"And how does that work?"

"Not real well." Not that she was complaining. Or had her hand out.

2

Still, when he dropped her off back at her car, Stan slipped her fifty dollars. And asked her when he could see her again.

"Whenever you'd like, Stan."

Torry was not a hooker. She was simply someone who did what she had to do in order to get by in life. And there was no crime or shame in that. She was making it on her own. She wasn't on welfare—even though she was a twenty-three-year-old single mother who had no high school diploma and got no child support from Stevie's father, Tyrone, who was still in jail in North Carolina for armed robbery. She hadn't seen Tyrone in four years and did not expect she ever would again. In spite of this, her parents had refused to have anything to do with her since she became pregnant with Stevie. They could not deal with Tyrone being black.

Torry worked thirty hours a week at an Ames discount store in Waterbury for not much more than minimum wage, although she did get a 20 percent discount on toys. Evenings and weekends she worked at the Pup. She and Stevie lived on Meriden Road in a twelve-unit apartment court with fake brick facing. Stevie got the bedroom. She slept on a convertible sofa in the living room. The walls were paper thin. She could hear everybody else's toilets flushing and phones ringing. She could hear their love moans and their sneezes. She could hear the trucks rolling by at night as she lay there, her feet throbbing from so many hours on the job. It wasn't much. But it was theirs.

Stevie was a sturdy, clear-eyed boy of five. Her true love, her best friend, her everything. She hated that she had to be away from him so much. Luckily, her next-door neighbor, a widow named Laura, was home watching TV virtually day and night and was happy to baby-sit for her. Laura would accept no payment for this. As thanks, Torry would bring her a bottle of good bourbon every week from the Pup's back room. Curt would let Torry take this bourbon in the belief that he would one day soon be collecting a blow job from her in that same back room. Of which there was zero chance. But this was how much of Torry's life worked. The invisible economy that kept her afloat. She had no health insurance. No retirement plan. A total beater of an Isuzu that needed new brakes. And no man to take care of her. Curt wanted a piece of her. So did Wade, her assistant manager at Ames. But she was not about to give herself up without getting something in return. Sex, in her opinion, was a transaction. Marriage was a transaction.

Life was a transaction.

So when a man like Stan came along, Torry went along. He was her third such steady gentleman. She never allowed herself to be involved with more than one of them at a time. And she never gave them more than two evenings a week. Al, who was a member of the state legislature from Waterbury, had been her first. He liked to come over to the apartment to watch adult movies on the VCR and frolic with her in the sofa bed. He was overweight and homely, but he filled her freezer with steaks, her closet with clothes and shoes. He even bought her a new sofa bed—her old one was giving him back trouble. Al had lasted for about six months. Right up until his wife found out and threatened to divorce him. After Al there was Dominick, who was an executive with Jolly Rubbish in Middletown. Dominick drove a flashy vintage Corvette and liked to drive her in it to the big Mohegan Sun Casino on the Indian reservation in Uncasville, where they would check into the hotel and order bottle upon bottle of champagne from room service. He would pour it over Torry's bare feet and lick it off of her toes. Dominick had a thing for her toes. Afterward, he would give her a stack of chips to gamble with, most of which she would quietly cash in and pocket. The thing with Dominick lasted for three months. He just stopped calling her.

When Stan came along, there was no one. She started seeing him two evenings a week. He gave her fifty dollars in cash after every evening. He never asked to spend the night with her. Which was how she knew for certain that he, too, was married. Not that she'd ever doubted it. Or cared. Four hundred a month tax-free was damned good money for pleasant part-time employment. It meant she could think about getting health insurance for Stevie.

She would meet Stan at either Wadsworth Falls or Laurel Brook

Reservoir. Both were deserted at this time of year. She would bring a blanket. If the weather were good they would spread it out on the grass and do it there. If it were bad they would do it in his car. Sometimes he pulled up in the Range Rover. Sometimes a pickup truck. Once he came in a minivan. She thought he might possibly run a car dealership. Or might be a building contractor of some kind—his hands knew hard work. They were large and surprisingly strong. But he told her nothing about himself. Stan was a bit unusual that way—most men, in Torry's experience, could not stop bragging about themselves. Not Stan. He was modest. And extremely private. He never once came to her apartment. He never came to the Purple Pup again. And he never gave her his phone number. He would simply call her at the Pup and tell her where and when to meet him.

The lovemaking was not particularly inspired. Not as far as Torry was concerned. But it was quick and it was harmless, except for that time she got poison ivy all over her in a place where she couldn't exactly scratch it. Only once did Stan ask her to do something that bordered on the slightly kinky. But Torry didn't mind. In fact, it was kind of fun checking into that hotel all by herself. Playacting. Wearing that wig. Being all mysterious and sultry. Every man in the place had eyes for her. And the intrigue sure seemed to excite him. When he knocked on her door he was so hot he came the instant he got inside of her.

That was the only time she ever met Stan somewhere other than in the woods.

Torry was not someone who permitted herself to dream big, like those people who were always buying Lotto tickets. Still, she did allow herself to fantasize what it would be like if Stan ever divorced his wife and the two of them got together for real. They would have a home with a backyard on a tree-lined street somewhere. An investment portfolio. A college fund for Stevie. Sure, she dreamt about it. She was human, wasn't she?

And then one night he wanted to end it.

He seemed very tense and preoccupied when they got out of their cars. Didn't say a word as they strolled down the trail for a ways by the light of his flashlight. She carried the blanket. When they reached a nice little clearing she stopped and spread it out on the cool, wet spring grass in the moonlight. She knelt on it, her arms held out to him. Stan just stood there, motionless.

"What is it, honey?" she asked.

"This has to be the last time, Torry," he said, his voice choking.

"Your wife getting suspicious?"

"H-How did you know?"

Torry shrugged her soft shoulders. "It happens," she said, wondering why it always had to happen to her.

"No hard feelings, kid?"

Kid. He had never called her that before. "Of course not, Stan."

"You're very mature."

"That's me, all right. I'm a big girl now."

They fell into silence. Suddenly, there was very little left to say.

She took a deep breath and released it slowly. "Listen, Stan, you're a real nice guy. I like you. If things ever change, call me, okay? Maybe we can pick up where we left off or something."

He let out a strangled sob. "I-I don't think that's ever going to happen." That was when he reached inside his jacket and pulled out the .38 caliber revolver and aimed it right at her head. His gun hand was shaking so badly that when he fired it the first shot merely glanced off her forehead, stunning her. Torry did try to grasp what was happening to her. Did try to react, to move, to *do* something. But she could not. Because none of this was happening. It could not be happening. Although it did occur to Torry, in the final seconds of her life, that she should never have trusted any man, even one who had nice manners.

And then the second shot caught Torry directly over her left eye and pitched her back over onto the blanket and she was gone.

THREE WEEKS LATER

CHAPTER 1

MITCH BERGER WAS SPRAWLED on his living room sofa at two in the afternoon watching *The Manchurian Candidate* and devouring his fourth Krispy Kreme honey-dipped of the day when the woman he worked for buzzed his apartment.

For Mitch to be home in the middle of the day watching an old movie on TV was not unusual. He was the lead film critic of the most prestigious—and therefore the lowest paying—of the three New York City daily newspapers. And while he did have a desk in midtown alongside of the paper's other eminent culture vultures, he generally worked at home. His books were here. His VCR was here. His lair was here.

But for his editor to show up at his apartment unannounced was most unusual indeed. Shocking, even.

Lacy Mickerson was a tall, edgy tuning fork of a woman in her late fifties, an immaculate dresser who favored gray flannel pants suits and claimed to have bedded Irwin Shaw, Mickey Mantle and Nelson Rockefeller in her youth. As the paper's arts editor, she was one of the most influential cultural arbiters in New York, if not the whole country. It was Lacy who decided which shows and films merited extra attention. It was Lacy who had hired Mitch away from a scholarly film journal the year before when the man who had been the paper's reigning film critic since Truman was in the White House finally agreed to hang up his flashlight pen. Mitch was young for such a heavyweight job, thirty-two. The same age William Holden had been when he played Joe Gillis in *Sunset Boulevard*. But he was uncommonly knowledgeable when it came to films. In fact, Lacy believed Mitch had seen virtually every film that had ever been made. He hadn't, although he had written two highly authoritative and entertaining film reference guides, *It Came from Beneath the Sink* and *Shoot My Wife, Please*, which catalogued and critiqued the worlds of horror and crime films, respectively. As a critic, Mitch was considered witty, informative and enthusiastic. As a person he was considered unusually modest. He did not have a swelled head. He did not think his opinion mattered more than anyone else's did. In fact, he still could not believe that someone was actually paying him to go to the movies.

The day she hired him, Lacy predicted that Mitch would win a Pulitzer before he was forty.

Right now she stood there looking around at his living room with keen disapproval. Mitch had a very desirable parlor floor-through in a turn-of-the-century brownstone on Gansevoort in the West Village's meat-packing district. Hanging over the fireplace was a framed poster made from a rare Sid Avery black-and-white group photograph featuring all of the cast members of *Ocean's Eleven*. When Maisie was living with him it had been a photograph of Georgia O'Keeffe that hung there. When Maisie was living with him it had been spotless, too. Now it was dingy and cluttered. Books and videos and magazines were heaped on every available surface. Clothes and food wrappers were strewn all over. The sky-blue Fender Stratocaster that Mitch had recently bought to ease his pain was propped against the monster-sized stack that went with it—a pair of Fender twin reverb amps, piled one atop the other, with a signal splitter on top and two foot pedals, a wa-wa and an Ibanez tube screamer. He could blow out all of the windows on the street if he wanted to. Every tenant in his building had been sure to let Mitch know they hated him for buying it.

There had been a cat, but Mitch had given it away. He could not bear to look at it after Maisie was gone.

Mitch reached for his remote control and stopped the tape of *The Manchurian Candidate*, even though it was right in the middle of the landmark garden club scene. He cleared space for Lacy on the love seat. He offered her a doughnut. She accepted one. Krispy Kreme doughnuts were considered a great delicacy among New York foodies. Lacy was a consummate New York foodie.

"Would you like a glass of chocolate milk with that?" he asked her, opening the shutters to let in some of the midday sunlight. "They go very well with chocolate milk, I've discovered."

She gazed at him curiously a moment. He did not look great. Mitch knew this. He was still in his bathrobe. He was unshaven, his curly black hair uncombed. "All right," she said finally.

He padded into the kitchen and came back with two cold glasses and handed her one and sat down.

"What are we working on?" She bit into her doughnut.

"A Sunday piece on Laurence Harvey," Mitch replied, sipping his milk. "He's amazing in this movie. Positively oozes with self-loathing. I don't think I ever appreciated how good an actor he was before. I just finished watching *Room at the Top* and *Darling* and now I'm trying to track down *Expresso Bongo*, a British cult film he made with Cliff Richard. I thought I'd give him his due, because the sad truth is that no one under thirty even knows who he was."

"I am loving this, Mitch!" Lacy said excitedly. Lacy was very good at being excited. It was one of her greatest gifts as an editor. "Only, now you're making me wonder who else we've forgotten about."

He frowned at her thoughtfully. "Oskar Werner . . . ?"

"Definitely!"

"Of course," he pointed out hastily, "for every one of them you've got your Michael Saracens and your Richard Beymers. Performers who make you wonder how they ever landed the starring role in a major Hollywood film."

"There might be a Sunday piece in that, too," Lacy suggested, wagging a long, manicured finger at him. "Coupled with a 'where-are-they-now' sidebar. I could put a reporter on it."

Mitch peered at her for a moment in silence. "We're not talking about what you came here to talk about." And when she said nothing to that he said, "Lacy, why are you here?"

"I have some news for you, Mitch," Lacy replied, uneasily. "I don't know whether you'll be disappointed or relieved, but . . . I came to tell you that you're not going to Cannes this year. I'm sending Karen instead."

He was relieved, actually. Usually, he looked forward to Cannes. It was France. It was fun. But he hadn't wanted to go—to Cannes or anywhere else. He did not want to see anyone. He did not want to talk to anyone.

"It'll be good experience for her," he said encouragingly. Karen was the paper's new second-string critic. Very raw. Her precedessor, an Oxford-trained classical scholar, had left just after Christmas to write the new Jackie Chan movie. "Although I should warn you that it's a bit of a meat market. You might lose her to another paper."

Lacy fell silent. She wasn't done. Mitch could tell by the determined set of her jaw. "You're headed somewhere else, Mitch," she added in a firm, quiet voice.

A sudden wave of panic washed over him. Here it was—his worst nightmare. She was banishing him to the L.A. bureau. A fate which he regarded as worse than death. Within a week he would become a character straight out of *The Day of the Locust*. Living in a run-down bungalow court. Hanging around with tormented midgets, broken-down cowboys and baby-faced, brain-dead blondes. He would quit the paper, that's what he'd do. He would have to quit.

Yeah, right. And do what?

Mitch breathed in and out, watching Lacy intently now. And waiting.

"I've wangled you a weekend getaway piece for the Sunday travel section."

He heaved a huge, inward sigh of relief. "And where am I getting away to?"

"Dorset."

"Where?"

"It's on the Connecticut shoreline, out near Rhode Island."

"What am I going to . . . Wait, isn't that the place that had the outbreak of killer mosquitoes last summer?" demanded Mitch, whose natural habitat was a darkened movie theater, preferably below Fourteenth Street.

"It's the jewel of the Gold Coast," she said crisply. "Serious old money—more millionaires to the square mile than East Hampton. It's also charming and unspoiled and way New Englandy. Artists have been drawn to it for years. The Dorset Academy of Fine Arts is there. You've heard of it, surely."

"Vaguely," Mitch grunted.

Lacy managed a tight smile. "Hell, I wish I were going."

"So why don't you? I'll stay here and work on my Laurence Harvey piece."

"It's *a perk*, Mitch. A freebie. Only columnists and chief correspondents are supposed to get them."

"So how did I get so lucky?"

"I thought you could stand to get out of the house for a change," she replied.

She was right. Mitch knew this. And she was trying to help him the only way she knew how. Mitch knew this, too. He was becoming a recluse. Whole days went by when he spoke to no one. If he didn't watch out he might turn into Jack Nicholson in *As Good As It Gets*. He needed to take charge of his life again. He needed to heal. He knew this. Healing was right up there near the top of his list of things to do—pick up shirts at cleaners, punch out Oliver Stone, play shooting guard for the Knicks, heal. It was right up there. But knowing it and doing it were two vastly different things. Especially when it was so much more comforting to sit watching old movies for days at a time in wounded, Olestra-free isolation.

"Go to Dorset," Lacy commanded him. "Write about what you see. And don't think about anything else for a couple of days, okay? Look, I don't do the nurturing mother thing particularly well. I know this about myself . . ." Like all self-absorbed New York media people, Lacy turned every conversation about somebody else's feelings into a conversation about her own feelings. "But this is what is known in the trade as a wake-up call. Your work hasn't been up to your usual high standards lately. In fact, your Adam Sandler review was downright hostile."

"Okay, time out," Mitch objected defensively. "That movie was total crap."

"Everyone else at the paper thought it was hilarious. The scene in the elevator? I wet my pants."

"So did he!"

"Frankly, Mitch," she shot back scoldingly, "you no longer seem able to comprehend the concept of comedy."

Mitch didn't disagree. He could smile from time to time, but he did not know how to laugh anymore.

"Naturally, I've understood," Lacy added tactfully. "We all have. But when you get back we need to talk about where your life is headed."

The West Coast, if he didn't watch out. Oblivion.

"The getaway is for two," Lacy added gamely. "Why don't you take someone?"

"Now why didn't I think of that?"

He took his Power Book, in the hope that he might at long last get rolling on his new reference book on Westerns. He had a ton of notes and raw material on floppy disks, but he couldn't seem to get started on the actual writing. And it was rapidly becoming overdue. The computer rode next to him on the passenger seat, along with a generous bag of goodies from the Cupcake Café, as Mitch reluctantly piloted his rental Toyota out of Manhattan, his hands gripping the wheel tightly. Mitch Berger was a true child of the pavement—a product of Stuyvesant Town, Stuyvesant High and Columbia. Being a native New Yorker, he almost never drove. And driving in Manhattan, with its cab drivers, potholes, delivery trucks, bike messengers and pedestrians, was no easy task. Particularly during rush hour on a muggy Friday afternoon in May.

He had stowed his weekend bag in the backseat. Maisie had tried in vain to pep up his semi-shlumpy wardrobe, having once described his look as two-parts teddy bear and one-part tornado. Now that she was gone, he had reverted to what he had always worn—wrinkled button-down collar shirts, roomy V-neck sweaters and rumpled khakis. He owned two sport coats: an olive corduroy and a navy blazer. He had brought along the corduroy in case it was required in the dining room of the inn where he was staying. He did not bring a tie. He did not own a tie. He was very proud of this fact.

As he drove, Mitch's thoughts drifted back to the last weekend getaway he had taken. *They* had taken. It had been one year ago almost exactly. They had driven up to Mohonk Mountain House to hike and snuggle and not think about the test results that were due on Monday. Maisie had been incredibly gay and cheerful on the way up. Mostly, she kept going on and on about some damned thing called the Fibonacci Series.

"For weeks we have been absolutely wracking our brains for the iteration of our planting plan," she had declared excitedly. The planting plan was for the Hillview Reservoir. The city of New York was capping it against airborne contamination, which was a polite way of saying bird shit. Her firm had been hired to make it look nice. "And guess who thought of the Fibonacci Series—moi!"

"Congratulations!" he had exclaimed. "Maisie . . . ?"

"Yes, my sweet baboo?"

"What *is* the Fibonacci Series?" The influence of German Expressionism on the noir films of Robert Siodmak Mitch understood. Maisie's work he never did.

"Why, it's a variation of the Golden Section."

"Which is . . . ?"

"A basic mathematical system of proportion dating back to the Greek temple structures. Le Corbusier based his Modular system on it. It's defined geometrically as a line that is divided such that the lesser portion is to the greater as the greater is to the whole."

"And the Fibonacci Series . . . ?"

"Is a variation using whole numbers. Each representing the sum of the two preceding numbers. So instead of counting out *one, two, three, four, five,* you count out *one, one, two, three, five, eight, thirteen* and so on. Just *imagine* it as a planting pattern of grasses spanning some two hundred acres. *Imagine* it from the air." Maisie sighed. "If only one were a bird."

"If only."

Maisie Lawrenson was in a landscape architecture firm down on Duane Street with four other young women, all of them Harvard Graduate School of Design alums. All of them were smart, which was not necessarily synonymous with being a Harvard graduate. All of them were pretty, although in Mitch's opinion Maisie was far and away the prettiest. She was a tall, slender blonde who dressed in loosely flowing linen and silk things and was in a perpetual hurry.

He had met her on Fire Island at the Fair Harbor dock. The first words he said to her were, "Are you waiting for the ferry?" The first words she said to him were, "You're not supposed to call them that anymore—they prefer to be known as alternative water craft." Within three weeks they had moved in together. They had been married nearly two years when they went away to Mohonk that weekend. They did not believe each other to be perfect. She felt he was among the socially lost, a brooder, a screening-room rat, a slob. He felt she could be impulsive and rash—Polyanna in Arche sandals. But she was his Maisie.

Until that Monday morning when they got back from Mohonk and he found out he was going to lose her. It was ovarian cancer. The silent killer, they called it, because there were no early warning signs. First they removed her ovaries. Then they put her on chemo. When her lovely blond hair fell out Mitch bought her a Yankee cap to wear. To this day whenever he saw a kid on the street wearing a Yankee cap he would start crying. She was gone in six months. She was thirty years old.

Mitch had a sister in Denver, parents in Florida, colleagues, pals. He had nobody. It was Maisie who had brought him out of his shell. She was his lifeline. Without her, he was achingly, crushingly alone.

Some mornings, he could barely will himself to get out of bed. The future terrified him. On several occasions, he had awakened with a gasp in the night, his heart racing and fluttering out of control. His doctor had diagnosed it as anxiety. He advised Mitch to seek counseling. Which Mitch had. His counselor had advised Mitch to find some way to relax. That was how he'd ended up with the Stratocaster. He had taken up the guitar in high school, briefly, in the hope that it would enable him to meet girls. Another fervid illusion shattered. But he had enjoyed the playing.

As he inched his way now over the Triborough Bridge onto the Bruckner Expressway, Mitch helped himself to a cupcake and glanced at the travel kit he'd been given. His destination was the historic Frederick House Inn in historic Dorset, which was situated on the Long Island Sound at the mouth of the historic Connecticut River.

It does not take very long, Mitch reflected grumpily, for the word *historic* to get *old*.

It started to drizzle when he was crawling along outside of swank Greenwich on I-95. By the time he had made it to Westport he had managed to figure out how to work his windshield wipers, which was a good thing because it was pouring now. And the temperature had dropped markedly. Beyond Fairfield, upscale suburbia gave way to the downscale rust belt of Bridgeport and New Haven, where he ran out of cupcakes. Then Mitch crossed the Quinnipiac River and officially entered Southern New England. The foliage got thicker, the traffic thinner. It was getting dark by the time he reached Exit 69, which was the last exit before the Connecticut River. He wanted Exit 70, but he got in the wrong lane and instead of crossing the river he somehow ended up on Route 9, heading due north toward Hartford. He was halfway to East Haddam before he figured out what he'd done and managed to double back. As a result, it was pitch black by the time he finally set eyes on Dorset.

The town was utterly asleep. Mitch had a funny feeling it would look exactly the same when it was wide awake.

A stand of trees shielded the Frederick House Inn from the road. A broad circular driveway led to the front door of the three-story house, which had been built in 1756. There were eleven rooms, each furnished with antiques. There was a fireplace in the dining room.

Chilled, Mitch warmed himself in front of the fire with a generous jolt of Bushmill. He was too late for dinner. In fact, the dining room was technically closed. But the innkeeper managed to assemble a plate of cold sausages, lentil salad and rolls for him.

Afterward, he went upstairs to his snug little room and drew a bubble bath for himself in the claw-footed tub. As it filled Mitch stripped off his clothes and gazed at himself in the mirror. He was not terrible-looking. He was not bald. He was not short. His weight generally fluctuated between burly and pudgy, depending on his intake of sweets. Right now, pudgy was winning out. Still, he was not in bad shape for someone who spent most of his waking hours sitting in a dark room on his butt. He sucked in his stomach and puffed out his chest and flexed his tattooed right bicep in the mirror. His tattoo said: *Rocky Dies Yellow*. He grinned at his reflection, a brave, jaunty grin reminiscent of Errol Flynn in *Captain Blood*. This was something he had taken to doing lately. His way of assuring himself that he was going to be okay.

I am laughing in the face of danger.

After his bath Mitch burrowed into his canopied bed with a collection of Manny Farber's film columns from the fifties. Briefly, he was absorbed by the cranky iconoclast's brilliant dissection of the films of Budd Boetticher. But before long Mitch found his mind drifting and he set the volume aside and lay there listening to the rain and thinking the same thing he thought every night as he lay in bed alone:

I am so glad I do not own a gun for my personal protection. Because if I had one I would shoot myself.

CHAPTER 2

SCARY SPICE WOKE UP Des at 3:59 A.M. It had taken the little vixen less than a week to master the subtle complexities of the textbook head-butt technique: First, climb directly onto human target's chest. Next, knead said human's chest firmly and insistently with front paws. Purr. Then tickle target's face with whiskers. And, finally, butt heads until target groans.

Des groaned, feeling as if her own head had only just hit the pillow. It had. She'd worked late and squeezed in only four hours of sleep. Maybe she was too wedded to her job. Maybe there was no maybe about it. Yawning hugely, she fumbled for her horn-rimmed glasses and flicked on the nightstand light, blinking at the rest of the original Spice Girls—Ginger, Sporty, Posh and Baby. Tabby short-hairs, all of them. Predominately gray. Three months old. And maddeningly perky and bright-eyed, considering the hour. She and Bella had rescued them from the parking lot of an Outback Steakhouse in Shelton two weeks ago. Within days they had become snug muffins.

There was no man in her bed. No man in her life. Des Mitry was off men right now, having concluded that they were vastly overrated as a species. They required huge outlays of attention, care, feeding and patience and all you got back in return from them was a full laundry hamper, an empty refrigerator and a bladder infection. Nothing good came of them. Not one thing. So Des was going it alone for the foreseeable future. She was not looking for a relationship. In fact, she was the happiest she'd ever been, even though absolutely no one believed her. Single women were not supposed to be happy. That was one of the bedrock myths of modern American society, right up there with the invincibility of four-wheel drive, the great taste of lite beer and the guarantee of equal justice for all.

She did not make the bed. After four years at West Point, Des took great, sinful pleasure in having a sloppy, unmade bed. For her it was a feeling comparable to that of sinking into a hot bubble bath with a flute of cold Moët and Robert Cray crying his heart out on her stereo. She stretched her lower back and touched her toes, her dreadlocks brushing the floor. She stripped off her T-shirt and hung it on the back of the master bathroom door. She dressed in sweatpants and a New York Giants jersey.

Barefoot, she padded downstairs and into the kitchen to put the coffee on, the Spice Girls meowing in harmony as they tripped over her ankles and one another in starved, eager pursuit. The house was a three-bedroom raised ranch on a dead-end road in Woodbridge, a woodsy suburb of New Haven that was popular with Yale mathematicians and lab geeks, many of whom were Asian or Middle Eastern. The assorted cooking smells were unbelievable when Des managed to get in a jog at suppertime. It was a family neighborhood. Other than Bella, her next-door neighbor, Des was the only person on the block who lived alone.

Des also happened to be the only person on the block who was black.

She and Brandon bought the place right after they got married. They built themselves a redwood deck onto the back, complete with hot tub. Remodeled the kitchen. Refinished the oak floors. Invested in fine furniture of leather and teak. It was a home to be proud of when they were done with it. It was their Love Shack. And Des did think about unloading it after the bust-up, finding someplace smaller. It was certainly more house than she needed. But she'd have to pay a whopping tax bill if she did that, so why not keep it? The overhead was manageable. It was a half-hour drive from work. And she enjoyed taking care of it. Particularly the acre and a half of yard. She did all of the outdoor work herself. Des absolutely loved riding around on her mower. Actually, it was not natural how much

Des loved that Toro. She was starting to become convinced that in a previous life she had been an Iowa hog farmer.

She put down food for the girls while the coffee was brewing. Then she checked on the rest of her guests. Spinderella, Foxy Brown, Lil' Kim and Jam Master Jay were getting along just fine in her basement, one to a padded crate. Milli Vanilli—Fab and Rob— had the garage to themselves since they could only seem to get along with each other. Those two had been full-grown adults when Des rescued them. The adult feral strays were the hardest. It took time to earn their trust. It took patience and gentleness. A lot of her new arrivals had to be kept somewhere solitary and small, like her guest bathroom, for several weeks before they were ready to venture out. Right now, Big Bad Voodoo Daddy, a surly black strutter, was decompressing in her mud room. She went in and spent a couple of minutes with him on her knees, her hand stretched out to him, softly cooing, "Your father must be hydrogen, because you da bomb, Daddy." She said that to him every morning and night, and every morning and night he hissed and swatted at her outstretched hand. He would eat her food and drink her water but he would not let her near him.

This did not deter Des, who was partial to the ungrateful badasses. She regarded them as a challenge. She loved a challenge.

The average life span of a feral stray was less than two years. They battled starvation, disease, predators and one another. But in spite of this they managed to reproduce at such an appallingly high rate that the animal shelters were unable to keep up. It was a crisis. Crises called for action. And so Des and Bella were taking action. To date, they had rescued over forty feral strays. They took them straight to the local vet, Dr. John, who promptly checked them over for worms and ear mites and vaccinated them against distemper, rabies and feline leukemia. He also neutered them—all this free of charge. Dr. John applauded Des and Bella's concern. He was also partial to Des's form, especially when she was in her spandex running tights.

Right now, Des could hear Bella's garage door opening. It was time to move out. They'd gotten a tip: Donna in produce at the A & P on Amity Road had overheard her manager—a real dick—say that he was going to call the animal shelter people about the half-dozen adult strays that were hanging around the Dumpsters out back. The animal shelter was a kill facility. Consequently, such a pronouncement was akin to genocide.

Consequently, Des and Bella were on Dawn Patrol.

Des grabbed her coffee and headed on out into the predawn darkness with it. Bella was waiting for her behind the wheel of her Jeep Wrangler in her driveway, engine idling, the back crowded with cages, have-a-heart traps and food. The personalized license plate on Bella's Jeep read *CATS22*.

"Hey, girl," Des said as she hopped in.

"Hey back at you," Bella exclaimed brightly, her chubby fists gripping the wheel. "Desiree, how is it that you manage to look so gorgeous at five o'clock in the morning?"

"Um, okay, you forgot to put your contact lenses in again, Bella. I'd better drive."

"I mean it, Desiree," she insisted, handing her a shopping bag from her lap. "Stuffed cabbage. I made it last night. Just heat it and eat it."

"Bella, why do you keep feeding me?" Des objected, smiling at her.

"Because you're a healthy young girl and you need to eat. I don't want to see you turn into some little wasted thing like that Ally McBeal person."

"That I would pay to see," laughed Des, who was six-foot-one in her stockinged feet, broad-shouldered, high-rumped and cut with muscle.

Bella Tillis, on the other hand, was an inch under five feet tall and totally round, a feisty, silver-haired little bowling ball of a Brooklyn Jewish widow in her early seventies. Her late husband, Morris, had been on the Yale Medical School faculty. Bella had three kids scattered around the Northeast, eight grandchildren and nine million causes. Around Woodbridge she was known as the Queen of Petition drives. Lately, she had been harnessing her considerable energies toward raising money for a No Kill shelter.

"What's up with you today?" Des asked her as they went rocketing down the sleepy lane in the Jeep. Bella drove like a demon.

"Clothing drive over at the *shul* later this morning," Bella replied, chin thrust up into the air over the steering wheel. Her legs were so short that she had to shove her seat up right against it, practically squashing her breasts. "Have you got any old clothes?"

"Girl, I'm wearing them."

"What about Brandon—did he leave anything behind?"

Des let out a laugh. "Just ill will."

When Des was twenty-three, she and Brandon had been featured on the cover of *Connecticut* magazine under the headline: "Our State's Shining Future." She was a West Point graduate with almond-shaped pale green eyes, a wraparound smile and dimples that could melt titanium at a distance of a thousand feet. Brandon, just two years out of Yale Law School, was the state's top young district prosecutor. Only it turned out their future was in Washington, not Connecticut. Or at least his was. He went to work for the Justice Department looking into campaign fraud by several high-ranking senators. It was just a temporary assignment, he insisted. But one investigation led to another. And then he was signing a two-year lease on an apartment there without talking to her about it.

It was right around then that Des started rescuing cats with Bella. There is an old saying in pet connection circles: People who are trying to save stray animals are really trying to save themselves.

Des knew it was over when Aretha peed in Brandon's $395 Ferragamo loafers. Cats know about such things. That same night he told her there was another woman. For the record, she was not white. But she *was* the daughter of a wealthy Philadelphia congressman. Their affair had started when they were in law school together. And it had picked up heat again in D.C. In fact, it had never actually ended, not even after he married Des. Which had taught Des a most valuable lesson in life:

Don't ever trust lawyers.

"What you need," Bella counseled her as they drove along, "is a Jewish man."

"Is that right?" asked Des, raising an eyebrow at her.

"Absolutely," Bella replied with total conviction. "They don't drink to excess, they always come home at night and, oy-yoy, do they have low self-esteem."

"Why is that such a good thing?"

"It means they work harder to please you—morning, noon and night."

"Um, wait a second, are you saying Jewish men make better lovers?"

"I'm saying it."

Des let out a hoot. "Bella, you are baad."

"Now don't misunderstand me," Bella cautioned. "Stallions they are not."

"Been there, done one. Maybe two."

"But a good Jewish man won't sleep a wink until he is absolutely positive you are satisfied. And I mean fully. Even if it means he has to go to work in the morning with bags under his eyes and full-blown case of lockjaw."

"Yum, sounds totally off the hook."

"They also make excellent fathers."

"Whoa, let's not get ahead of ourselves." Des drained her coffee and put her empty cup in the bag at her feet. "But, listen up, I thought they only went out with their own kind."

"Not a problem. You're one of us."

"I am?"

"You forget, I've personally laid eyes on you climbing in and out of your hot tub," Bella replied, her eyes twinkling at her with mischief. "And there's no getting around it, Desiree—you are one of the chosen people."

Des grinned at her. "Girl, are you alluding to my bootay?"

"If bootay is another word for *tuchos* then the answer is yes. And you've got one to die for. Although what you do for a living might scare them."

"Hey, it scares me."

It was not yet dawn when they pulled up behind the darkened supermarket and unloaded their traps. Dog cages worked the best, they had found. They would tie a length of string to the cage door. Lure the cats inside with opened jars of Gerber's strained turkey. Then pull the cage door shut behind them.

They waited, strings in hand, huddled together by the Jeep in hopeful silence. As dawn came, the first to show was that black male with the white patch on his face and paws. Big Willie, Des had dubbed him. He was her kind of guy. Skinny. One ear bloodied. One eye, the left, half shut. She thought they might get him today. He actually crept to within two feet of the cage, the closest he'd come since they'd started staking out his Dumpster. And then he was just one foot from the cage. He was very hungry. Also very skittish and suspicious. His head was actually in the cage . . . Des tensed, poised to slam it shut behind him . . . But at the last minute he went skittering away into the brush and was gone. They waited an hour more but none of the others showed.

By 6:00 A.M. Des was back home in the spare bedroom that she had turned into her studio, seated before her easel with her 18-by-24-inch Strathmore 400 drawing pad and her sticks of soft vine charcoal. A pair of high-intensity desk lamps cast light on her subject, which was affixed to the easel at eye level with a bulldog clip. Not exactly ideal studio conditions. Natural light would have been vastly preferable. But Des had no choice. It was vital that she draw for at least an hour every morning before she left for work. The studio was Des's sanctuary. Here, she found wholeness and meaning. Here she found peace. These things she found nowhere else.

Always, she drew still lifes. Always, her subjects were taken from photographs.

Always, Desiree Mitry drew dead bodies.

They were crime scene photos. Gruesome photos. Horrifying

photos. They were photos of what she had seen on the job. Des had seen things that most people never do and never should have to. Des had seen too much.

And so she drew.

On this particular morning, her subject was one Torry Mordarski, a young single mother who had been found in the woods near Wadsworth Falls shot twice in the face. One shot had glanced off her forehead. The other had caught her over her left eye, which was submerged under a coating of congealed blood and brain matter. Her right eye was staring straight at the camera. Her lips were drawn back from her teeth in the frozen death rictus.

Draw what you see, not what you know.

Des drew, stroking boldly as she had been taught to. Although she did not handle the soft charcoal in the preferred manner. She gripped it tightly, not loosely, and she held it between her thumb and middle finger, digging the tip of her index finger into the side of the stick. But it worked for her. Her strokes were sure and precise, her passion boundless. Always, she kept in mind the rule that a drawing teacher had drummed into her years ago. For Des, it had become a mantra.

Draw what you see, not what you know.

Des drew what she saw. What she saw were lines and contours, shadows and highlights. Nothing more. She started Torry Mordarski's face very dark, then began to pull the light away from the shadows with swipes of her kneaded eraser. Finding Torry's features. Giving contour and value to the shadows, texture to the highlights. Line by line, shadow by shadow, highlight by highlight, Des deconstructed the image of Torry Mordarski from her memory. Expunging the visceral impact. Neutralizing the horror. Abstracting the painful reality—stretching it, contorting it, injecting it with fearsome emotional power. Until the image was no longer a photographic memory but a haunting, mesmerizing work of art.

Her drawings gave Des chills up and down her spine. They gave her comfort as well. When she drew, Des was alive and free. She was the person who she wanted to be. In a perfect world she would have quit her job and drawn full-time. But it wasn't a perfect world. So she brought copies of crime scene photos home. No one knew she did this. No one had ever seen her drawings. She did not display them. She did not talk about them. Once a drawing was completed, she would store it away in a folio book and never look at it again.

No one knew. Not even Bella.

When she was done she ate her breakfast of grapenuts, banana and skim milk. It was the same breakfast she ate every morning. She showered and dressed in a crisp white blouse and pressed gray gabardine slacks, blue blazer, polished cordovan loafers. She cleaned the charcoal smudges from her horn-rimmed glasses and put them back on. She applied a bit of purple lipstick. She wore no other makeup. Her hair burst forth in dreadlocks that tumbled wild and free halfway down her shoulders and back. A woman in East Hartford did them for her every three months. All Des had to do was keep them washed and oiled. Des's immediate higher-ups on the job, all of them white men, regarded her hair as some kind of a militant black feminist statement. They hated it. Des didn't care.

In fact, that was kind of the whole point.

Gazing at herself in the mirror, Des felt that she looked remarkably like a stylish, promising young minority quota executive at one of the insurance giants in Hartford.

Just as long as you didn't notice the top-of-the-line SIG-Sauer that she wore on her hip.

CHAPTER 3

THE STORM WAS GONE in the morning. The sky was blue, the birds were chirping and the air wafting through Mitch's window was scented with cherry blossoms and the tangy freshness of the sea. It was a cheerful, life-affirming sort of day. It was just the sort of day that made Mitch yearn for a darkened movie house, a Tod Browning double bill and an economy-sized tub of buttered popcorn.

But not today. Today he had a story to write.

After he had shaved and dressed he partook of the Frederick House's homemade scones with honey and coffee on the porch. Then, armed with his notepad and a local map, he headed out to tour the village on foot, blinking in the blinding sunlight and trying very hard not to bump into any sharp objects.

Quickly, Mitch found himself in the Dorset Street Historic District, which was lovingly restored, immaculate and straight out of Norman Rockwell. There was a marvelous white steepled Congregational church, a town hall, library, schoolhouse, general store. There were stately colonial mansions with picket fences and window boxes and flower gardens. There was a firehouse and a barber shop with an old Wildroot hair tonic sign hanging out front. The Dorset Academy that Lacy had referred to, which attracted painters and sculptors from all over the world, was located in the Gill House, circa 1817. There were huge, leafy maples and oaks everywhere. There was no graffiti, no trash, no traffic and no stress. An elderly woman who he passed on the sidewalk smiled and said, "Good morning." A boy rode by on a bike with a fishing pole, a sheepdog tailing after him, arfing happily.

"*Day One—Have found it,*" Mitch scribbled in his notepad. "*Have at long last discovered the land that time forgot. All is quiet—too quiet. Have queer feeling that someone, or something, is following me."*

He stopped in at the barber shop. Had himself the seven-dollar haircut and listened to some crusty locals make fun of each other's fishing prowess. All of it was good-natured—clearly they had known each other since they were boys. Mitch asked them how the fishing was this year and got three sharply different responses, all of them vigorously voiced. Freshly tonsored, he strolled over to the village's cemetery, where he discovered an exceptional slice of New England history. Sea captains who had lived in the 1600s. Family plots that dated from the present all the way back to before the Revolution. In one such plot he found a beloved Pembroke Corgi resting for eternity by its master's side. Mitch was so taken by the tiny headstone that he tore a sheet from his notebook and made a rubbing of it.

His appetite whetted by the fresh air and exercise, Mitch trudged back to the inn for a lunch of cold poached salmon, potato salad and baby greens. Then he climbed into his rental car and headed back out.

He found the village's business district on Big Brook Road. There was a market, a package store, hardware store, bank. Nothing noteworthy. Not until Mitch stopped at the gas station to fill up and discovered that a living, breathing attendant was on duty there to fill the tank for him and wash his windshield. He even offered to check Mitch's oil. It was a positively eerie experience. From there Mitch turned north onto Route 156 and headed up around a bend into Dorset's soft, rolling green hills. He was in moneyed farm country now. There were huge old colonial estates edged by stone fences, with lush meadows and forests and rushing streams. They had names, these estates. He passed a riding academy called Buttermilk Farms. He passed Gray Rocks, which bred champion Burmese Mountain dogs. He passed no place called Affordable Handyman Special or Dump Falling Down. He made notes . . . *Estimated median property value—north of 2 mil. Estimated number of For Sale signs observed—zero* . . . There was a working dairy farm,

Winston Farms, that had three silos and hundreds of acres of pasturage. Numerous spotted black and white cows with name tags around their necks were feeding at the troughs by the split-rail fence. Mitch got out and introduced himself to Lizzy and conducted a brief but trenchant interview on local political conditions.

From there he headed down Route 156 to the shore. There were bait and tackle shacks here. Boatyards where yachts and fishing boats were being readied for the summer. Beach colonies where the rental cottages were being spruced up. He turned off onto Old Shore Road, a narrow snaking country lane where the cottages got conspicuously more Laurenesque. Many had views of Long Island Sound. And vineyards. They had vineyards, these people.

Old Shore Road ended at the Peck's Point Nature Preserve, which was open from sunup till sundown, according to the hand-carved wooden sign. He followed the dirt road inside. The point was a windswept peninsula that jutted right out into the Sound at the mouth of the Connecticut River. There were footpaths along the bluffs, an observation deck, a meadow that tumbled down to the shifting tidal marshes, where, according to the signs, osprey, least terns and the highly endangered piping plover nested. Beyond the marshes was the Sound, where sailboats scudded through the sparkling blue water. On a clear day, it was possible to see all the way across to the north shore of Long Island. This was a clear day.

As Mitch sat there, gazing out his windshield, he felt a powerful tug. This would be the first summer in a long time that he wouldn't be renting a beach cottage. He couldn't go back to Fire Island. Too many ghosts. And he detested the Hamptons, which were strictly for show. Even the way people gardened there was relentlessly competitive and joyless. Peony envy, Maisie used to call it. So he had decided to stay in town this summer. Work on his book in air-conditioned solitude.

But sitting here now, he felt a pang of regret.

Near the southernmost tip of the Point, the dirt road ended at a barricaded bridge. It was a long, narrow wooden bridge that led a quarter-mile or so out over the swirling surf to a small island. He could make out a cluster of houses out there. Towering over them was a lovely old whitewashed lighthouse. A sign that was posted at the barricade said PRIVATE PROPERTY. ACCESS BY PERMISSION ONLY. VIOLATORS WILL BE PROSECUTED. The barricade was raised and lowered by inserting a coded card in an electronic sensor device, like in a private parking garage. Deliverymen and guests could gain access only by buzzing the residents, who were obviously very rich and very lucky.

Mitch consulted his map. The island was called Big Sister.

He was still sitting there gazing at it when someone pulled up behind him. Someone who wanted to cross this private bridge that Mitch was doing a very effective job of blocking. It was a woman in an ancient blue Mercedes diesel that rumbled and shook as it idled there, sending plumes of exhaust into the air. Before Mitch could move out of her way she got out and approached him.

She was in her late forties or early fifties, and she must have been quite beautiful when she was a girl. She was still an exceedingly lovely and well put-together woman. Tiny, no more than five feet two, and slender, with an air of innate class and elegance that reminded Mitch of Deborah Kerr at her most genteel and ladylike. She had porcelain blue eyes, delicate features, high cheekbones. She wore her silver blond hair cropped at her chin and parted on the side, like a boy. She was deeply tanned but her complexion was unlined and youthful. She wore no makeup. She wore a buttery yellow cashmere sweater, tailored gabardine slacks and pearls. A silk kerchief was knotted at her throat.

She smiled faintly at Mitch through his open window. "You're early—I wasn't expecting the ad to run until Tuesday." Her voice was very gentle and reserved.

"The ad?"

"You *have* come about the carriage house, haven't you?" she asked, flushing slightly.

"Yes, I have," Mitch said impulsively.

"If you'll lead me to my house—it's the cream-colored one—I should be happy to show it to you."

"And I should be happy to see it." He was here to write a getaway story. If his getaway happened to include a guided tour of a private island, so much the better. "I'm Mitch Berger, by the way."

"Pleased to meet you, Mr. Berger. I am Dolly Seymour." She inserted a plastic card into the security slot. The barricade in front of the bridge hummed and slowly began to rise. "Kindly lead on. I shall follow." She started back to her car.

Mitch eased his way slowly out over the choppy blue water on the spindly wooden bridge, trying to remember the last time he had heard someone use the word "shall" in ordinary conversation. The bridge was exceedingly loud, bumpy going. Also exceedingly narrow. Not much more than one car-width, with railings on either side, along with utility poles that carried the power and phone lines out there.

As he drew closer to Big Sister he began to realize that the houses were not clustered nearly so close together as they had seemed. Each of them was built on the rocky cliffs overlooking the Sound and distanced from its neighbor by acres of woods and green meadows. There was the cream-colored center chimney colonial that Dolly had referred to. It was at least two hundred years old, and quite grand. But not nearly so grand as the natural-shingled Victorian summer cottage next door. This place had wraparound balconies and turrets and sleeping porches and must have had at least ten or twelve bedrooms. Also a spectacular garden. There was a second Victorian summer cottage that was like a miniature version of the big one. There was a squat stone lighthouse-keeper's cottage house built in the shadow of the old lighthouse. A gravel driveway connected the houses, which were also joined by footpaths bursting with wild beach roses and bayberry. They had a tennis court out here, their own private beach and their own dock, where two yachts were presently moored.

It was, Mitch reflected, a hundred or so acres of pure paradise.

He told her so when he pulled up outside of her house and got out. It was at least five degrees cooler out here, thanks to the brisk breeze off of the water.

"Yes, it is quite lovely," she acknowledged wistfully. "Sometimes, I forget just how lovely."

"How did it get the name Big Sister?"

She squinted at him, as if she were regarding him from a great distance. "It's the tides. At low tide one can actually walk out here across the rocks and tide pools. That's how the animals get out here. The deer and so forth. But when the tide is high, such as it is now, the cross currents from the river are swift and treacherous. Swimming out here from the Point is unthinkable—one would be washed out to sea instantly. And there are rocks. That was why they built the light-house. It's been decommissioned for years, poor thing. But in its hey-day, it had a pair of thousand-watt lamps that could be detected from thirty-five miles away on a starry night. There was no bridge in the old days. We had our own little ferry boat to the Point. And once, during a terrible storm, my grandfather's older sister, Enid, capsized in it and drowned. That's why it's called Big Sister. It was simply known as Peck Island prior to that. That's also why we built the bridge. Hurricane Gloria totalled it in 1985," Dolly Seymour recalled, her chin raised with stubborn Yankee pride. "We rebuilt it."

Now she marched briskly down a path that led around to the back of her house. She pumped her arms vigorously as she walked, her small fists clenched. He had to speed up to stay with her. She had a formal ornamental garden back there. But that wasn't where they were heading. She was leading him in the direction of a sag-ging, unpainted old barn.

"They used to raise salt marsh hay on the island in the old days," Dolly continued. "There are about fifty good acres of land. They floated the oxen out here on flat barges." Beyond the barn there was a carriage house that had been converted into living quarters. "Well, here we are," she exclaimed. "What do you think?"

Mitch didn't know what to think. It was small. It was dilapidated. It was a wreck. One end of it appeared to be sinking down into the overgrown shrubbery. Then again, it was entirely possible that the shrubbery was actually holding it up. Its shingles were green with mildew and rot. Its windows were either broken or gone. It looked as if one good gust of wind would blow the whole place over.

"It used to be our caretaker's house," Dolly explained. "But we haven't had anyone full-time in years. And now that my Niles is gone I'm afraid that money is . . ." She broke off, her bright blue eyes widening with alarm. "Oh, dear, should I be telling you this? I suppose there's no harm. What I mean to say is that the income would be most welcome. That's why I've decided to rent it out."

"For the summer?"

"I *had* hoped year-round," she answered fretfully, "but I suppose if you're only interested in the summer we *could* work something out . . . Oh, dear, maybe I shouldn't have said that either, since you *are* the first person who has come. I didn't want to go through one of the agencies, you see. The Realtors out here are such busybodies. Frightful, nosy women. And it's none of their business, is it?"

"No, it's not," Mitch agreed, liking her. She was just the tiniest bit dizzy.

"My lawyer will want references and deposits and things," she added with a vague, helpless wave of her hand. "You're a New Yorker? I noticed the license plate."

"Yes, I am."

"And do you and Mrs. Berger have children? The reason I ask is because it's really quite ill-suited for a family."

"No, no. I'm a widower."

She considered this, her brow furrowing sympathetically. "How awful. She must have been frightfully young, poor thing."

Mitch said nothing, knowing his voice would catch if he did.

Dolly plunged hastily into the awkward silence. "Let's have a look inside, shall we? Now I should warn you—I've been using the downstairs for storage and it's, um, a bit . . ."

Filthy. It was filthy. There were cobwebs and mouse droppings everywhere, coupled with the pervasive smell of mold and disuse. A man's things had been heaped rather carelessly in the center of the bare floor. There were garment bags and suitcases stuffed to bursting with coats and suits and sweaters, cartons crammed with shoes, athletic trophies, old yearbooks, papers. There was a set of golf clubs, a bicycle, a stuffed and mounted warthog's head.

But in spite of this, Mitch was awestruck by what he saw. Because this was no ordinary outbuilding. It was a genuine antique post-and-beam carriage house with exposed beams of hand-hewn chestnut. The room, which was a good-sized one, had a big fieldstone fireplace at one end, wide-boarded oak floors and floor-to-ceiling windows that afforded a totally unobstructed view of the water in three different directions. It was a bit like being on the bridge of a ship at sea.

Standing there, Mitch felt a tingle of excitement. It had been Maisie's dream that they would one day find a little cottage for themselves. A place where they could curl up in front of the fire. Dig in the garden. A place to escape from everyone when they felt like it. *This* place. Mitch was sure of it. He had never been more sure of anything in his whole life.

"I haven't quite figured out what to do with his things," Dolly murmured apologetically. "Niles hasn't asked me for them—I suppose he's not settled yet. Mind you, I did consider taking all of it to the dump, but that would have been so petty, would it not?"

Evidently her husband had left her. Which Mitch found rather hard to imagine. Dolly was so attractive and classy and nice. Plus this island was so remarkable. Why would anyone ever want to leave?

"I'll move all of it out, of course," she went on. "And have it properly scrubbed and painted. The windows repaired and so forth. But we do tend to be a pretty self-sufficient lot out here. So it would help if whoever took it were handy. Are you?"

Mitch was not. His experience with handyman specials began and ended with *Mister Blandings Builds His Dream House*, which he considered a vastly overrated film. "Well, I'm certainly game," he said helpfully.

"Good, good! The roof is sound . . . Fairly sound, anyway. And it has its own oil furnace and septic and well."

"You said the caretaker used to live out here?"

"Yes, when I was a girl. I was raised on Big Sister. My maiden name is Peck, you see."

"As in Peck Point?"

"That's right. My family settled this area back in 1649. Saybrook was nothing more than a fort at that time, built by Lion Gardiner of

Dorset Regis. The rest of this area, hundreds of thousands of acres, was land granted to Malcolm and Matthew Peck for services rendered to the crown."

"What kind of services?"

"No one knows, but my own theory is that they were thieves and scoundrels," she answered with a smile.

There was a pullman kitchen and a bathroom with a scarred old tub. They weren't much, but they were adequate. There was a hinged trapdoor in the kitchen floor fitted with a brass transom catch that had a recessed pull ring. She raised it to show him what was down there. It was a dirt crawl space, very dark.

"There's no basement, I'm afraid," she apologized. "That means no washer-dryer. There *is* a laundromat in town . . ." She broke off, frowning prettily. "Of course, as it's just you, I should think you could use mine. And there are a few odd sticks of furniture collecting dust in the barn. Nothing grand, mind you."

A steep, narrow staircase led up to a loft above the living room. It had a peaked ceiling with exposed beams and skylights. It had a pair of dormered windows for light and ventilation. There was enough space for a bed up there but not much else.

"Dear God, would you believe I had my very first kiss up here?" Her eyes shone with schoolgirl longing. "I was twelve."

Mitch eyed her curiously. She seemed attached to this place. Also reluctant to part with it. "Are you sure you want to go through with this?"

A dark look crossed her face—and Dolly Seymour suddenly seemed someplace else. Someplace very far away. Someplace very unpleasant. It shook her. A shudder of pure animal revulsion seemed to shoot right through her entire body. But then, just as suddenly, she returned. "I'm quite sure I don't want to," she responded in a soft, thin voice. "But I must. I need the income. I have no marketable skills of any kind. None. And our property taxes are positively crippling. That's why we gave the Point to the Nature Conservancy. These houses out here are just about all we have left.

And we *can't* lose them. The trouble is that I'm on my own now, Mr. Berger."

"It's Mitch," he said quietly. "Not easy being alone, is it?"

"No, it's not. I guess you understand that, don't you?" She looked him over carefully, as if realizing for the first time that she knew virtually nothing about him. "What is it you do, Mitch?"

"I'm a film critic."

"How fascinating! I've always admired people who do creative things."

"The filmmakers are the ones doing the creating. I just write about it. But I have a new book to get done. And I need someplace quiet to work."

"Big Sister is definitely quiet. In fact, winters it's too quiet for some."

"I wouldn't mind that," said Mitch, imagining himself taking long walks on the snow-driven beach. Curling up with a good book in front of a roaring fire, the surf pounding outside his window. "I would want a vegetable garden."

"There's an old one out behind the barn that is just waiting for someone to bring it back to life. And I've garden tools aplenty and . . ." Dolly took a deep breath and blurted out, "I'm asking a thousand a month, Mitch. What do you say, shall I call my lawyer and tell him you want it?"

Mitch stood there a moment in stunned silence, realizing to his own astonishment that it had finally happened. One door was closing and another one was opening. Today was the day. *As of this moment, I am moving on.* Maisie would want him to do this. Change was healthy. Change was life. It was time to get on with his life. And so Mitch Berger smiled at Dolly Seymour and in a loud, clear voice said, "I would love for you to call him."

CHAPTER 4

THE CENTRAL DISTRICT HEADQUARTERS of the Connecticut State Police's Major Crime Squad was located in Meriden across from the Lewis Avenue Mall in what had once been a state-run reform school for boys.

A narrow, unmarked road snaked its way up a hill to the secluded and unexpectedly pastoral campus of gently aged red-brick dormitories and classrooms. The state's prestigious Forensic Science Laboratory had sprouted up here, under the guiding hand of its nationally eminent director, Dr. Henry Lee. The state's K-9 training center was headquartered here as well, providing a steady background chorus of barking German Shepherds. Des practically heard them in her sleep. And she had learned never to stroll too near any parked cruisers on her way inside—if a K-9 trainee happened to be stationed in the car, it would lunge at her through the partly open window.

Major Crimes operated out of the old headmaster's residence, a sober and dignified brick mansion with a slate mansard roof. The entry hall beneath the grand staircase had been converted into a reception area with a desk and mail slots. Also a bulletin board over which hung a crude, hand-lettered sign that read: WELCOME TO THE JUNGLE. The district commander's office was in the ornate dining room. The grand parlors and bedrooms had been partitioned into cubicles.

Des aggressively worked the room as she made her way toward hers, trading frisky, playful banter with her male colleagues. If a man was into pumping iron she remarked on how big his arms looked. If he was trying to take off a few pounds she told him he was looking buff. She admired their new neckties. She even laughed at their bad jokes. The squad room was the land of opportunity. Des was not above a little flirting if it meant she could find a loving home for a healthy, neutered male tabby. A number of the single guys had indeed fallen prey to her charms, adopting one of her strays in the tumid hope that Des would follow up with a visit. No chance. She did not do house calls. As for the happily married ones, they were afraid to so much as make eye contact with her. The word was out: Get too friendly with Desiree Mitry and you get stuck with a feral cat.

The hand-lettered sign that one of them had stuck on the wall of her cubicle said it all: CAT GIRL FROM HELL.

By eight Cat Girl was parked at her desk, hard at work. At age twenty-eight, Desiree Mitry was one of the youngest Major Crime Squad lieutenants in the state of Connecticut. And one of only three who were women. Of those three women, Des was the only one who also happened to be black. This made her the state police's prized poster girl, its great non-white hope. Des also had pull. She had major pull.

Des had the Deacon behind her.

This made her a magnet for resentment from some white officers. Up to and including her district commander, Capt. Carl Polito, who belonged to the so-called Waterbury Mafia—a tightly knit network of Italian American officers who'd been born and raised in the Brass City and who were, in many cases, related to each other. Capt. Polito's deputy commander, Lt. Angelo Tedone, was his brother-in-law as well as an academy classmate. And the muscle-bound little preener of a sergeant with whom Des had been saddled, Rico "Soave" Tedone, was Angelo's kid brother.

Soave was infinitely more loyal to the Mafia than he was to Des. There was no doubt in her mind that he believed she'd been handed her lieutenancy strictly because of her color and gender and pull. That he felt he'd deserved it more than she did. And that he would seize any opportunity he could to cut her long, fine legs out from under her. Anything negative about her that came along, Soave passed directly on to his big brother Angelo. Any slip. Any stumble.

Anything. She could not trust the little twerp. But she could not get him reassigned either—not without just cause. Otherwise, it would go down on her record that she couldn't get along with male subordinates. So she put up with him.

She put up with all of them. In many ways, they were just like a gang of little boys who had their own secret club, their own secret handshake and their own fort. And she, Des, was a g-i-r-l. But she could handle it. She *did* handle it—by routinely outperforming them. She'd cut her teeth on rape cases and bombings when she first joined the squad, but now her caseload consisted mostly of homicides. Homicides were her bread and butter. Captain Polito may not have been in her corner, but he was not an idiot. Every district commander was under constant pressure from Hartford to produce. And that's what Des did. She produced.

Besides, she did not want to go running to the Deacon. Not unless she absolutely had to.

From the moment she sat down at her desk, she was totally focused on her caseload. Nothing interrupted her concentration.

On this morning, Des was zoned in on the Torry Mordarski file. The shooting had attracted considerable media attention. When a young, attractive white woman was found shot to death in the woods, it inevitably did. And, just as inevitably, there was considerable pressure to find her shooter. It had been Des's top priority for several weeks. She, Soave and up to a dozen uniformed troopers had expended hundreds of man-hours on the search. But it had grown cold. And Des could not accept that.

So she pored over the ongoing investigative report one more time, sifting carefully through the details from beginning to end. The autopsy findings continued to puzzle her. In Des's experience, when a pretty girl died violently it was about sex. Always. But Torry was clean. No traces of semen. No vaginal secretions. No bruises or abrasions. No bites. No saliva. No scratches. No tissue or blood under her nails. No hairs not her own. No one else's fingerprints were found on her skin. There was no evidence of human contact whatsoever. When toxicology had come through a few days later, it showed no trace of drugs or alcohol in the dead girl's system.

A botched robbery attempt? Not a possibility. The first troopers on the scene had found her purse on the front seat of her 1987 Isuzu sedan, which had been parked nearby in a gravel parking area. There had been ninety-seven dollars and credit cards in her wallet. And no other discernible tire marks in the gravel.

No one had seen or heard a thing. The body had been discovered by a jogger early the following morning. Time of death was estimated to be between midnight and one A.M.

After a painstaking search of the primary crime scene, technicians had recovered one .38 caliber slug embedded in the base of a tree eight feet behind the victim. Based on the trajectory of the entrance and exit wounds—the shot had entered her frontal lobe from above, angled sharply downward through the temporal lobe and exited through the cerebellum—it appeared that she had been seated while the shooter had been standing. A laboratory examination of the twists on the slug yielded characteristics consistent with it having been fired by a Smith and Wesson .38 caliber revolver. No similar markings had been found on any .38 slugs recovered in any other major crimes listed in the computer's database. Nor was there a record of any killings of a similar nature that had gone unsolved in the state in the past three years.

A search through the victim's car revealed a few fibers caught in the wheel hub of the spare in her trunk. The fibers were a coarse wool-nylon blend typically used for inexpensive blankets. No blanket had been found at the scene, but a few matching blanket fibers were found snagged on twigs on the ground near the body. The underbrush and dead leaves adjacent to the body appeared to have been flattened, consistent with a blanket having been laid across them. It was Des's belief that Torry had come to the Reservoir with the intention of meeting a man she knew. She had carried the blanket from her car into the woods and stretched out on it. Instead of joining her, he had shot her. Then he had taken the blanket with him because it might contain traces of his hair or semen from previous trysts.

Her killer had been careful. But he had left one piece of transient evidence behind—a man's partial shoe print had been discovered in the damp earth next to Torry's body. A plaster cast of the impression had been made. The pattern of the sole was consistent with that of a Vibram sole used on work boots made by numerous manufacturers. The depth and length of the impression indicated that the wearer had weighed between 180 and 200 pounds and wore a size eleven or twelve shoe. Based on this information a common formula was applied to yield the wearer's probable height—in this case, six foot two. But Des had never placed much stock in this formula. She felt it misled an investigator just as often as it proved helpful. There were, after all, plenty of short men around who were overweight and had big feet.

She had not released the shoe print information to the media. Nor had she revealed that two of the primary crime scene technicians had come down with a vicious case of poison ivy. One of them had experienced such a severe outbreak that he'd gone to see his doctor, who had prescribed betamethasone dipropionate in cream form. On a hunch, Des had canvassed the area's clinics and drug stores for any adult males who might have sought similar treatment or medication in the days immediately following the murder. The search had proven fruitless.

Torry Mordarski had worked two jobs—cashier at an Ames in Waterbury and barmaid at the Purple Pup, a roadhouse on the outskirts of Meriden. She'd had male admirers at both places—the Purple Pup's owner, Curtis Wilkerson, and her immediate supervisor at Ames, Wade Stephenson. She had spurned both of them. However, each man could account for his whereabouts at the time of the shooting. Wilkerson was behind the bar at the Pup. Stephenson had gone to a microbrewery in Willimantic with three friends, where they remained until closing at 2:00 A.M. Wilkerson had a gun permit—for a Baretta .9 mm semi-automatic. Stephenson had none. Neither man had a police record.

The crime scene technicians had scoured Torry Mordarski's apartment for evidence, but the search had turned up nothing. No trace of a man was found there. Not even in the girl's vacuum cleaner bag. In fact, her apartment was uncommonly free of personal effects. She'd kept no address book, no letters, no photographs. There were no business cards, no scraps of paper with phone numbers scrawled on them. They did find bank statements and cancelled checks. She'd had a checking account with Fleet Bank that held a current balance of $271.16. No savings account. She'd had a Visa card that she used sparingly—to buy gasoline at the Amoco minimart down the street or toys and clothing at Ames, where she enjoyed an employee discount. She had never fallen behind on any of her payments. And currently owed nothing. Her wardrobe was modest and casual. She owned no furs and no jewelry of any value. In fact, she owned nothing that cost more than a hundred dollars. A check of her phone records revealed a handful of toll calls—to the Ames in Waterbury—but no long-distance calls whatsoever.

Des had started to think Torry Mordarski had had no life at all. Until she'd knocked on the door of Torry's next-door neighbor, Laura Burt, who turned out to be the dead woman's closest friend. And Des's most valuable source of information.

It was from Laura Burt that Des learned that Torry had dropped out of high school in New Britain when she'd gotten pregnant with Stevie. Torry's mother had not spoken to her since, according to Laura. Laura was reluctant to volunteer why—but one look at Stevie's dusky coloring gave Des a pretty good idea. She sent Soave to talk to the mother, figuring she'd be more candid with a white officer. She was. She told him that Torry's ex-husband, Tyrone Dionne, was "ghetto trash." Dionne's own family likewise had little use for him—he was presently serving time in North Carolina for armed robbery. Neither the Dionnes nor the Mordarskis would consider taking even temporary custody of the boy. It was, Des felt, quite deplorable. Only Laura Burt, who'd frequently baby-sat for him, seemed at all concerned about what would happen to him.

Des referred her to the Connecticut Department of Children and Families, the agency that would be charged with placing him in a foster home.

Whoever killed Torry Mordarski had also destroyed the life of an innocent child. That was one reason why the case bothered Des so much.

Soave had worked the North Carolina angle. There was a possibility that Torry's killing had been a reprisal by a criminal associate of her ex-husband's. Someone he had cheated out of money or ratted out in exchange for a reduced sentence. But neither the arresting officer nor the prosecuting attorney could offer any encouragement in that direction. Tyrone Dionne was not known to operate with a crew. He had not given evidence against anyone. There were no vultures circling him. He was a loner.

Des, meanwhile, had kept after Laura Burt. Even induced her to adopt Sir Mix-a-Lot, a long-haired adult male. It was Laura, with extreme reluctance, who finally turned Des on to the boyfriends. They were older men, married men. Laura suspected that some money had changed hands, although she insisted that Torry was not a prostitute. Torry had never had more than one of them at a time. And she had never told Laura their last names.

Laura knew them only as Al, Dominick and Stan.

Al and Dominick had been somewhat careful. Just not *real* careful. They had been worried about their wives, not the law. Al had bought Torry a new sofa bed. Laura, who was home during the day, had let in the deliverymen. They were from Bob's Discount Furniture, she recalled. By tracking down the delivery invoices and matching them to Torry's address, Des was able to determine that the sofa bed had been purchased by Albert Marducci, the embattled state legislator from Waterbury. Al Marducci was already under fire for having been stopped twice for DWI in the last six months, the second time after leaving a strip club. Des had shown the legislator the courtesy of questioning him at his office, rather than his home, so as not to humiliate him in front of his wife. Yet she still found him to be belligerent and deceitful. He claimed he had never heard of Torry Mordarski. He claimed he had never bought a sofa bed at Bob's. The man was pure sleaze. He had even busted a move on her—invited Des out on his boat for a little nude sunbathing some weekend.

"Since you have no connection to the case," Des had stated coolly, "you won't mind if I give this element of my investigation out to the press, will you?"

He was real cooperative after that. Admitted he'd known Torry. Claimed the relationship had ended two years prior. Gave Des a full accounting of his whereabouts the night of the murder. He could not have been more helpful. Although he did phone his old pal Carl Polito, her district commander, to complain about her insolent manner. Polito, in turn, had called her into his office to deliver a stinging lecture on the meaning of the word "professionalism." A rebuke she had suffered in smoldering silence. In the end, it had all been for naught. Al Marducci had been home with his wife and family the night of Torry's murder. Two neighbors had seen him out walking his dog at around midnight.

Dominick had been easier to find. On several occasions Laura had seen him pick Torry up at her apartment in his electric-blue vintage Corvette Stingray. The Viagramobile, Torry had called it. Laura had no trouble recalling his personalized license plate: *65 RAY*. Soave tracked the plate to Dominick Salerno, a principal partner of the Jolly Rubbish Company in Middletown. Yes, he had known Torry, Salerno admitted. But their affair had ended a year ago. He had been in Boca Raton the night it happened. And could prove it.

Neither man had expressed the slightest bit of sorrow over what had happened. Their only concern was in protecting their own reputations. To them, Torry Mordarski was a piece of human Kleenex. Someone to use up and discard.

This, too, Des found deplorable.

The trail led her to married boyfriend number three, Stan. But Stan had been much more careful than the others. He had never come to Torry's apartment. Laura had never seen him. Did not know what kind of car he drove. In fact, knew virtually nothing about him. The owner of the Purple Pup, Curtis Wilkerson, thought he might have seen Stan once, on a rainy night a month or so prior to the murder, but he was unable to give Des any description of him beyond the fact that he'd been white and middle-aged.

Des liked Stan for it. She liked him because he had gone out of his way to leave no traces of himself. It was almost as if he'd been *planning* to kill Torry. But why? And how on earth was she going to find him? Who was he? Where was he?

She was still poring over the report, looking for answers, when Soave came sauntering up to her desk with his morning coffee. At age twenty-eight Soave was, in Des's opinion, a man who simply could not outgrow being someone else's shorter, twerpier kid brother—no matter how hard he tried. And he did try. He had lifted so many weights to pump up his chest and arms that he bordered on reptilian. He had grown a scraggly moustache that he thought made him look older but actually made him look like a petulant little boy with fuzz on his lip. He dressed in dark suits that he thought whispered class but actually shouted low-rung and cheap. If Des had seen him on the street, she would have made him as a limo driver for a funeral parlor. He had picked up the nickname Soave from a Latino rap song by Gerardo that had been a hit back when he was coming up.

"Morning, loot," he grunted at her. Calling her loot—as opposed to Lieutenant—was his own little way of refusing to acknowledge her authority over him. Rico was not comfortable dealing with Des. She was not his mother. She was not his girlfriend. She was someone who filled a role in his life no woman had ever filled before.

"Back at you, wow man," she said. "How's Little Eva?"

"You mean Bridget? She hates me." He showed her the fresh set of cat scratches all over his hands.

"You've got to be more gentle with her, Rico," she informed him, not unkindly. Spoon-feeding was required with Soave. He was a work-in-progress, not unlike one of her strays. "A feral cat is like a woman. You work your way into her good graces and she will be loyal to you until the day she dies." Not that he understood a thing about women. He'd been dating the same girl since high school, a manicurist named Tawny. Here is how Des had described her to Bella: picture Lisa Kudrow, only dumb.

"You still wigging on the hooker?" he asked, glancing over her shoulder at the report. "It's ice cold."

"Torry was not a hooker, Rico."

"Well, she wasn't exactly Suzy Homemaker either."

"Um, okay, I'm thinking there must be like some kind of point to this," she said, an edge creeping into her voice. Sometimes Des ran out of patience.

Soave stuck out his lower lip, chastened. "No point, loot. No point at all." Red-faced, he returned to his desk.

Des went back to scanning the report, chewing on her own lower lip. Maybe he was right—maybe she was wigging on it. But with good reason. It wasn't just that Torry Mordarski was a young single mother who had fallen through the cracks and had paid dearly for it.

It was Stan. He frightened Des. He was calculating. He was careful. He was good.

And he was out there somewhere, roaming.

CHAPTER 5

"Frankly, I wish Dolly had rented the place to someone else," Kinsley Havenhurst declared flatly. "Nothing against you, Mitch. I just would rather have seen the carriage house go to someone we *know*."

Mitch was seated in Havenhurst's law office, where he had come to sign the lease and pass inspection. Which he clearly did not. When they'd shaken hands, Havenhurst had told him that everyone except his late mother called him Bud. It was the only cordial thing that Dolly Seymour's lawyer said to him. Bud Havenhurst was too well bred to be overtly hostile, but he was chilly. Clearly, he saw Mitch as the point man for an invading army of loud, pushy New Yorkers bearing cell phones. Clearly, he felt threatened by him.

His law office was over an art gallery in the center of Dorset's Historic District. The building had once been a grain and feed store. The office was quaintly old-fashioned, with a roll-top desk, potbellied stove and decidedly nautical air. There was an aged brass ship's barometer mounted on the wall. Also a number of maritime charts and architectural drawings of sailboats. Havenhurst's Yale Law School diploma hung in the outer office where his secretary sat. She evidently walked to work. There had been only one car in the rear lot where Mitch parked—a mud-splattered Range Rover.

"To be perfectly honest," Bud Havenhurst added, "I'd rather she simply hadn't rented it out at all."

Bud Havenhurst was in his early fifties and he struck Mitch as someone who had always been rich and good-looking and sure of himself. He was tall and tanned and sleekly built, with close-cropped salt and pepper hair, a long, patrician blade of a nose and a big, forward-thrusting chin. He wore a blue button-down shirt, striped tie, khakis and a pair of scuffed Topsider boating shoes. He had an air of privilege about him. Also an air of authority. He was Somebody in Dorset.

"She did seem a bit reluctant," Mitch allowed.

"Young fellow, it's important for you to understand the caliber of individual you're dealing with here. Dolly happens to be the product of an exceedingly distinguished American family."

"She told me about how the Pecks founded Dorset."

Bud sat back in his sea captain's chair, narrowing his gray eyes at Mitch. "Did she tell you that her father was the U.S. ambassador to Japan during the Carter Administration? That her grandfather, Harrison, was a U.S. senator from the state of Connecticut from 1948 until 1960? That her great-grandfather was chief justice of the state supreme court? That her great-great-great grandfather was a vice president of the United States under Benjamin Harrison?"

"Why, no. She didn't."

"My own family has been here since the early seventeen-hundreds," Bud pointed out loftily. "The Havenhursts came here to fell the white oaks. Milled them for barrels and boats and sent them back to England, where lumber was scarce. As the colonies grew, the Connecticut River became a major shipping artery. Dorset grew into a bustling port. General Washington slept here en route to New York after taking command of the American Army in April of 1776. And that's no joke. Lafayette marched through here with his troops. His men slept out on Peck's Point before they were ferried across the river." Bud got up out of his chair and went over to the window and looked out at the carefully preserved mansions lining Dorset Street. "Nowadays, this is a place for people who want to live somewhere lovely and quiet. Somewhere that isn't as trendy and touristy as Newport or the Hamptons. I happen to serve as town counsel. I've fought hard to preserve Dorset's small-town flavor. And, believe me, it has been a fight. We've had to keep out the condo developers, the hamburger franchises, drive-through windows, motels . . . Every day there's a new fight. And every day we take it on—because Dorset is a gem. And we want to keep it that way." Now he turned away from the window and stared down his long narrow nose at Mitch. "Dolly Seymour is a gem, too. And she's on her own now. And I don't want to see anyone take advantage of her."

"I gather that her husband left her," Mitch said.

"It was quite a blow to her," Bud confirmed. "She loved Niles. But nice ladies don't always have great taste in men, do they? It didn't last long—three years. It was a second marriage for her. Her first lasted twenty-four years. It was a good marriage to a local fellow from a good family—*me*, as it happens." He glanced at Mitch sharply. "I imagine you think it's odd that I represent my ex-wife's legal affairs."

Downright weird, actually. Also none of his business. "No, not at all."

"I've remarried myself," Bud explained, sitting back down. "Quite happily. Mandy and I live out on Big Sister, as a matter of fact. I took over the guest cottage as part of our divorce settlement. My mother lived there for the last ten years of her life and Dolly knew how attached I was to the place. We're still good friends. I'm like another brother to her. Hell, we started going around together when we were thirteen years old . . ." A fond glow came over his face now. "We used to call her Peanut in those days. She was the cutest little thing you ever saw. And I got her. I was the lucky one. And I still care for her. The feelings, they don't end just because the marriage ends."

"No, they don't."

"Actually, we're all family out on Big Sister. Evan, our son, lives in the old lighthouse-keeper's cottage with his friend Jamie. The two of them have an antique store up in Hadlyme. And the big summer cottage belongs to Dolly's brother Redfield and his wife, Bitsy. We're not used to having strangers out there. That's why I'd rather she had rented the carriage house to someone we know. But she accepted your deposit and your references check out, so here we are . . ."

"Yes, here we are." Mitch reached for a pen.

Bud hesitated, glancing uncertainly down at the lease on his desk. "Unless, that is, you wish to reconsider. Dolly would gladly refund your deposit."

"Not a chance." Mitch signed it with a happy flourish. He didn't give a damn whether Dolly Seymour's ex-husband wanted him there or not.

Bud let out a long sigh. "Well, I sincerely hope you won't have reason to regret this."

"Why would I?"

Bud Havenhurst didn't answer. And Mitch wondered why the man had said it. It was, he reflected, a very odd thing to say.

Dolly had assured Mitch the little house would be scrubbed and painted, and it was. A local handyman in overalls named Tuck Weems came out to do the work. Weems was a big, strapping man in his fifties with unruly blond hair and every appearance of a substance-abuse problem. He definitely had the shakes. Could not seem to shave without cutting himself. Bits of toilet paper were stuck to different parts of his chin and neck every morning. And his electric-blue eyes were lit by drugs or drink. He was not a friendly native. His face was a tight mask of anger. Twice Mitch tried to strike up a conversation with him. Twice the man walked away without responding. But Weems was a steady and capable worker. He repaired the windows, replaced the rotted shingles and sills, cut back the shrubbery that was threatening to engulf the little house. Within two weeks, it qualified as habitable.

Wheels were a necessity. Happily, Dolly had an old pickup she was willing to part with for a song provided Mitch was willing to make the occasional dump run for her. Not a problem, he assured her. As a result Mitch became the proud owner of a rust-free, plum-colored 1956 Studebaker half-ton with a V-8 engine and three-speed overdrive transmission. It was an uncommonly bulbous-looking vehicle compared to the aerodynamic styling of everything else on the road. And it did have 186,000 miles on it. But it ran like a champ. And he didn't intend to drive it back and forth to New York. Only as far as Old Saybrook, the neighboring town across the river, which had an Amtrak station.

He did drive it into the city once to gather up some things and put in an appearance at the paper. The Sunday Travel editor had been very happy with the Weekend Getaway piece Mitch had filed on Dorset. She'd especially liked Mitch's one-on-one interview with the cow. And Lacy took it as a very positive sign that he had rented himself a place there. Although she was a bit surprised.

"I have trouble picturing you there," she said, when he stopped by her elegantly appointed office to see her.

"Why is that?"

"Have you ever actually lived in a village before, Mitch?"

"Not unless you count Greenwich Village. Why?"

"Because I have. And it's way different, believe me."

"I'll say it is," Mitch exclaimed. "People smile at each other. They say please and thank you. They don't park in the handicapped spaces unless they are genuinely handicapped. It's utterly remarkable."

"And utterly fake," she argued. "They carry sharp knives, Mitch. Everyone is into everyone else's business. It's what they do for amusement. There's no privacy. And no secrets. Village life is one big soap opera."

"I have nothing against soap operas."

"You will when you discover you've become a character in one."

Since the advance screenings for the first big wave of summer film releases had already crested, Mitch informed Lacy that he intended to spend most of his summer out there. He would come in for any screenings as they arose but it figured to be pretty quiet until the studios started gearing up again for fall. She agreed that this would be fine, and wished him luck. There was no more talk from her about where Mitch's life was heading.

"I just want to be left alone to work on my book, Lacy," he explained.

"Good luck. But that won't happen, Mitch."

"Yes, it will," he insisted. "Why wouldn't it?"

He brought out the brown corduroy love seat that was crammed into the corner of his study, collecting newspapers and dust. He brought out his Stratocaster and stack, figuring he now had the perfect setup for playing as loudly as he wanted. He brought out two pieces of art, some dishes and pots and pans, bedding and linens, the stereo and television that they'd bought for Fire Island. Mitch's super gladly helped him load it all into the Study. He liked Mitch. Mitch was the only tenant who gave him free tickets to Broadway musicals.

Mitch needed a bed. He bought one from a mattress outlet in Westbrook. The rest he scavenged. He found a rocker and kitchen table in Dolly's barn. A beat-up little rowboat worked as a coffee table with a storm window fitted atop it. A steamer trunk served as a nightstand. He bought a comfortably worn armchair for ten dollars at a tag sale in town. Also a set of gallantly hideous bright yellow kitchen chairs.

At the town dump he found a fine old raised panel oak door which he mounted on sawhorses to serve as his desk. Actually, the dump was a picker's paradise. He almost always came back from there with more than he took in—a pair of shell-back aluminum garden chairs, lamps, bookcases. And he was generally in very good company. Mitch rubbed shoulders with a former mayor of New York City, a Tony Award–winning actress and a bestselling author of children's books at the dump. They, too, were picking.

He put in long, hard days outfitting his new cottage. For nourishment he feasted on prodigious quantities of his famous American Chop Suey. His recipe was a closely guarded secret: one large jar of Ragu, one pound of ground beef, one box of spaghetti, an onion, a green pepper and a package of frozen mixed vegetables. Garlic salt to taste. Maisie had pronounced it dog food and refused to eat it. Mitch could survive on it for several days straight. The nights were still cool on Big Sister. After dinner, he would make a fire in the fireplace and stretch out with a pint of Häagen-Dazs Vanilla Swiss Almond and a spoon, gazing at it. He would fall into bed early, lulled to sleep by the hard work and the rhythm of the water slapping gently against the rocks outside his little cottage. He had not slept so soundly in months. The bright morning sunlight would awaken him well before seven. The Fisher's Island Ferry was already making its return trip to New London. The fishermen and sailors were already out. He would stand at the living room window, breathing in the clean sea air and watching them, the slanted early-morning light on the water reminding him of Edward Hopper's Maine seacoast paintings.

He liked to walk the island's rocky little beach in the morning, particularly when the tide was out. He rolled up his pants and slogged his way barefoot through the tidal pools, marveling at the diversity of life forms to be found there. Sargassum, Irish moss, bright green sea lettuce. Crabs and oysters. Orange-beaked oyster catchers, terns and cormorants. Geese flew right overhead in V-formation, honking loudly.

And he liked to observe his fellow islanders as they went about their lives of vigorous and accomplished leisure. Frequently, as dusk approached, he would sit out on a lawn chair and watch them—competing on the island's tennis court or returning home to the dock from a sail, sunburned and exhilarated. For Mitch, watching from his front-row seat, these bluebloods were as exotic as the characters in a Merchant-Ivory movie. There was handsome young Evan, Dolly and Bud's son, who drove a Porsche 911 and shared the stone lighthouse-keeper's cottage with Jamie, an older man. Those two spent a lot of time together on their boat. There was Bud and his very hot young wife, Mandy, a tall, athletic blonde with good legs who drove a vintage MGA and regularly destroyed the lawyer on the tennis court. One afternoon, they had a croquet party on their lawn. Their guests arrived in white flannels. The men wore straw boaters on their heads. The sounds of laughter and the clinking of glasses wafted across the island toward Mitch like bubbles on a current of warm air. There was Dolly's mysterious brother, Redfield, who left for work before dawn and was regularly gone for days at a time. Mitch didn't know what he did for work, but he decided he had to be in the CIA. His wife, Bitsy, was a chubby *hausfrau* who spent endless hours in her garden, where she grew flowers and vegetables with spectacular success.

Mitch they utterly ignored. No one welcomed him. No one invited him over for a drink. He was sharing the island with them, but he was not one of them.

His sleeping loft was not wired for electricity. In order to read in bed, Mitch found it necessary to buy an oil lamp at the village's magnificently cluttered hardware store. Dennis, the jovial, apple-cheeked owner, assured him it would also come in plenty handy during hurricane season. Having established that Mitch was a new resident, Dennis insisted on opening an account for him. And when Mitch gave him his address he was treated to quite some reaction.

For one thing, the name Niles Seymour did not go down too well around the tubby shopkeeper. "He still owes me two hundred bucks, the cheap bastard," Dennis snarled, his round cheeks reddening. "You'd think he could settle his accounts with the poor local business people before he flies the coop on her." For another, the man seemed genuinely startled by the news that Dolly had rented out her carriage house. "You are a brave man moving into that place," he confided to Mitch over the counter in a low, husky voice. "Me, I don't think I'd have the nerve."

Dennis did not elaborate. And Mitch did not have the slightest idea what he meant. But he did wonder—same as he had wondered when Bud Havenhurst said he hoped Mitch wouldn't have any reason to feel sorry.

Mitch was toodling home on the Old Shore Road in his truck, puzzling over this, when a state trooper in a gray cruiser came up on his tail, flashing his lights at him. Mitch pulled over onto the shoulder and waited. Out climbed a tall, broad-shouldered figure in his fifties wearing a trimly tailored uniform and a wide-brimmed Smokey the Bear hat. His sideburns were a bristly gray, face square and leathery, posture erect, stomach flat. One look at him and Mitch immediately thought of Randolph Scott in *A Lawless Street*.

"Was I speeding?" Mitch asked him incredulously through his open window. "I didn't think I could even go fifty without a strong tail wind."

"No, sir, nothing like that," the trooper said politely. "I recognized the old truck. Didn't recognize the man behind the wheel. I figured you must be Mr. Berger."

"That's right . . ."

"Just wanted to say hello. I like to get to know folks. Answer any questions they might have." He stuck a big brown hand through the window. "I'm Tal Bliss, the resident trooper."

Mitch shook it. "So you're the welcome wagon?"

Bliss smiled at him. "Yessir. Something like that."

"That's very nice of you. I appreciate it." Mitch decided it would be more neighborly if he got out and joined him. He did so—and immediately felt utterly dwarfed. Tal Bliss was at least six foot four, and that was without the big hat. With it, the lawman was a calm, soft-spoken giant.

"You're a good deal younger than I imagined," he said to Mitch, waving at two old characters in a Jeep as they passed by. "When I heard you were a widower I was expecting an older gentleman."

"Believe me, it came as something of a surprise to me, too."

"I lost a lot of my friends—and myself—in 'Nam," Bliss said quietly. "Never did think I'd heal. The hardest part was being patient." His eyes drifted over to the nearby salt marsh, where an osprey was wafting on the breeze, circling. "This is a good place for it. You picked a good place."

"I'm glad to hear that," said Mitch, who was not expecting to have this conversation with this particular stranger.

"Dolly's an old, old friend, you know." Bliss kicked at the hard dirt with the toe of his boot. "We grew up together."

"She seems very nice."

"She is," Bliss affirmed, coloring slightly. "She's about the nicest person I've ever known."

"How well do you know Bud Havenhurst?"

"Quite well," he replied. "Why?"

"Because I do have a question that you might be able to answer." The rugged trooper peered at him intently. "Sure thing."

"When I was signing the lease, he said he hoped I wouldn't be sorry. And Dennis at the hardware store said that I was a brave man. Is there something about Big Sister that I should know?"

Bliss took off his big hat and turned it over in his hands, examining it for a long moment before he leveled his eyes at Mitch. "You might want to ask Dolly about this."

"I'm asking you."

Bliss puffed out his cheeks. "Very well. Maybe it is better this way. Have you met a fellow named Tuck Weems?"

"Kind of. I said hello, he didn't."

Bliss smiled faintly. "That's Tuck, all right. He grew up on Big Sister. Tuck's father, Roy, was the caretaker. The two of them and Tuck's mom, Louisa, lived out there in your little carriage house. Right after we got out of high school, when Tuck and I were serving in 'Nam, well, Roy went over the edge. Blew poor Louisa's head off with his shotgun. And then did the same thing to himself. It happened right there—in your carriage house. And it was Dolly who found them. A horrible, horrible thing for that lovely seventeen-year-old girl to walk in on ... Anyway, the house has been vacant ever since. No one has lived there—until now. You're the first. I suppose Dolly didn't say anything to you about it because she doesn't like to dwell on it. You see, Dolly's extremely delicate. Fragile, you might say. And these are tough times for her. She got hit pretty hard when her new husband pulled up stakes on her." The trooper paused, his eyes searching Mitch's face. "I sure do hope you'll be considerate of her feelings."

Mitch cocked his head at him curiously. "How do you mean?"

Bliss swallowed uneasily. "I just would hate to see some fellow come to town and take advantage of her again."

"Again?"

"Niles." The trooper spat out the name as if it were a dirty word. "He swooped down on her, flattered her, manipulated her, stole her from Bud. And just look how things turned out. She got her poor heart broken. I don't want to see that happen again. Can you understand that?"

Mitch understood, all right. The trooper was telling him to stay away from Dolly. Not that he was the least bit interested in her. Hell, she was practically old enough to be his mother. What Mitch didn't understand was in what capacity Bliss was delivering this warning. Was he speaking to him as Dorset's resident trooper—a public servant empowered to preserve and protect the family's interests? Or was he speaking to him as a man who happened to be in love with Dolly himself and wanted no rivals for her affections? Mitch didn't know. But either way, his answer was the same: "You're making yourself quite clear."

The trooper's face creased into a smile. "That's good. I'm glad we understand each other, Mr. Berger." Then he tipped his hat at him and strode back to his cruiser and took off, leaving Mitch there with his head spinning.

His dream cottage was a death shack.

As he headed back across the narrow bridge, the island looked different to him now. It wasn't a carefree Yankee eden. It was sinister. And his little cottage gave him the creeps. He could feel the death in the air the second he walked inside. The ceiling seemed lower, the walls closer together. The quiet was no longer soothing. It was ominous.

Shaken, Mitch grabbed himself a Bass Ale, went back outside and sat on one of his garden chairs in the late-day sun, wondering if he could still be happy here. Could he forget what had happened? Why not? He was trying to cut himself loose from his own past, wasn't he? Was this not the same thing? No, it wasn't, actually. He wasn't trying to forget that Maisie had ever existed. But he *was* trying to live in the present, not the past. And that part wasn't so different, was it?

Mitch didn't know. He only knew that his feelings about this place would never be the same.

He was still sitting there an hour later when he saw a Ford pickup pull up. Tuck Weems. He had come to mow the lush green expanse of lawn that grew between Dolly's place and the carriage house. Mitch waved to him. Weems didn't wave back. Business as usual. As he sat there watching Weems unload his big mower, Mitch saw Dolly coming along the gravel path toward his house, smiling at him shyly. It was not hard for Mitch to picture her as a lovely, light-footed young girl with a tennis racket in her hand and an easy smile on her lips. No, it was not hard at all. She was wearing a pair of trimly tailored gray slacks and a black cashmere sweater with a plunging V-neck. She carried a small jar in one hand, a rusty old horseshoe in the other. As she got nearer, he could smell tart, lemony perfume.

"I've brought you a house-warming gift, Mitch," she said graciously, holding the horseshoe out to him. "It's an old New England tradition. One hangs it over the front door, pointing upward, and it's supposed to bring good luck. It's one of our own shoes—I found it in the barn."

"Why, thank you," Mitch said, hefting it in his hand. "Please sit. Can I get you something to drink?"

"Thank you, no," she said, sliding into his other garden chair. "But you could . . . That is, I'm having some people in and I simply cannot get these pimientos open." She pronounced it pim-ee-entos. Mitch had never heard anyone pronounce it that way before. At least not anyone who wasn't trying to do Noel Coward. "I tried warm water. I tried one of those cursed ergonomically advanced jar openers. Utterly useless. The thing seems cemented shut. Would you please try?"

"I'd be happy to."

The jar opened for him right away. It wasn't easy, but wasn't that hard either.

"Bless you!" she exclaimed gratefully. "It is *so* nice to have a man around sometimes. I've been terribly remiss in not inviting you over for a drink. We must do that some evening."

They sat there in silence a moment, watching Weems work. He did nothing to acknowledge their presence there.

"You haven't done much entertaining since you've been here," Dolly mentioned, glancing at Mitch with a raised eyebrow. "That's not to say I've been studying your every move out my window with binoculars, but do you not find yourself terribly lonely?"

"Not terribly, no."

"But it *is* hard, is it not?" she persisted. "Adjusting to the absence of joy in one's life. When one has grown used to it, I mean."

"Yes, it's very hard."

She nodded to herself. "I don't believe it's humanly possible to experience joy by oneself. It takes two. I suppose one does come to appreciate the smaller pleasures. And to accept them. But there are so many nights I just cry myself to sleep asking myself why." She broke off into silence. "You probably understand this better than most people."

"I'm sorry to say I do."

Her eyes locked on to his imploringly. There was tremendous strain in hers. She seemed very tightly wound. In fact, she seemed as if she were on the verge of cracking. "No one has ever told me he didn't want me anymore. I suppose that's a silly thing for a person my age to say . . . To go all these years without ever being rejected by anyone. I-I'd been very lucky, you see. I just didn't know *how* lucky. Now I do. That's what I keep telling myself—*you were very lucky, Dolly. Take comfort in that*." She broke off, her small breasts rising and falling. "Oh, dear, I shouldn't be going on like this. You must be sorry you ever met me."

"Not at all. In fact, I was just thinking how glad I am."

"You're a very sweet man. Are you wanting for anything, Mitch? Is there anything you need?"

"Just some answers, I guess. I met Trooper Bliss today . . ."

"Yes, I know. He told me."

"Why didn't *you* tell me?"

"It was a long time ago, Mitch. I didn't think it would matter anymore. Particularly to someone who wasn't here at the time. Why, does it . . . ?"

"I don't know, to be truthful," Mitch answered. "Does it bother *him* that you've rented the place out?" Referring to Weems.

"One can never tell with Tuck," she replied. "He's rather closed off that way. When I informed him of my intentions, he simply nodded and walked away." She gazed across the lawn at him, her face softening. "That's Tuck. He's been this way since we were small children."

Mitch wondered about that first kiss Dolly had told him about. He wondered if the boy had been Tuck. "Exactly where in the house did it happen?"

"Upstairs," she replied, her voice hollow and distant. "I found them in bed together, dead. It was . . . quite awful." Abruptly, Dolly climbed to her feet, her eyes avoiding his now. "If you wish to leave, Mitch, I'll understand. But I sincerely hope you will not."

And with that she marched back to her house with her jar of pimientos.

Mitch went inside and hung his horseshoe over the door.

He liked it here. He wanted to stay. He was going to stay. This was home now.

The only real problem with the little house was the strong, persistent smell of mildew downstairs. Mitch had a detailed online chat with his newspaper's home repairs columnist on the subject. She felt his trouble was poor air circulation down in the crawl space, and recommended two courses of action. Mitch rolled up his sleeves and got to work.

First, he located the air vents in the little house's foundation. There were four of them, each approximately one-foot square. Sure enough, they'd been boarded shut to keep cold air and small animals out. Mitch pried the boards out with a pry bar—instantly unleashing a dank, dungeony odor—and installed breathable wire mesh in their place.

The next step was to roll out a vapor barrier of 6-mil plastic over the moist, exposed earth down in that dark crawl space. Since there was only about eighteen inches of clearance down there, this meant Mitch had to spend most of a day slithering around on his belly with a flashlight in what he quickly discovered was the preferred habitat of mice, black snakes and large, curious spiders. In some areas, such as over by the fireplace, the space was so shallow that his head would whack into the floor joists if he tried to raise his nose up out of the dirt. Mitch was not especially claustrophobic—he was not, say, Charles Bronson in *The Great Escape*. But it was not pleasant to be facedown in that confined, filthy space, rolling out the plastic, cutting it to fit, securing it in place with rocks and bricks. It was not pleasant to have a living rodent scurry over him, lose its footing on his head and scrabble around in his hair, screeching. It was not comforting to know that his only way in and out of there, the kitchen trap door, was a good twenty-foot slither away. It was slow, tedious work. But Mitch did have nearly half of the house done when he heard footsteps outside on the gravel path, coming toward the house.

They entered the house, clomping slowly and heavily on the wood flooring directly over Mitch's head.

"I'm down here!" he called out. "The crawl space! Hello . . . ?!"

The footsteps moved over toward the kitchen, more determinedly now. And Mitch heard a sharp noise. Something slamming shut—the trap door.

Instantly, it got even darker down there.

"Hey, what's going on!?" he cried out as the footsteps rapidly retreated, running from the house on the gravel path. "Hey, come back!"

Mitch wriggled his way furiously back around the main water lines to the trap door and tested it. No good. The brass transom catch was like an old refrigerator door—self-locking. And the mechanism was topside. So were the hinges. All that faced him was the door itself. He tried prying the door open with his scissors. He shoved at it with all of his might. No use. It was good and locked.

His next response was to slither his way over to the nearest of the air vents, thinking maybe he could kick out the wire mesh and escape that way. No use either. The air vent was way too small for him to squeeze through.

Now the realization hit Mitch—he was trapped down there. Briefly, panic seized him. His pulse quickened. Beads of sweat formed on his forehead. But he steadied himself. Breathed in and out slowly and deeply, reciting the words: *I must not panic. I cannot panic.*

He recalled that he could see Dolly's garage from one of the vents. He would call to her from there. That's what he'd do. He slithered his way across the length of the house toward it, the beam from his flashlight growing feebler by the minute, only to discover that her car was gone. She was out. Damn. The other houses? They were too far away to be within earshot over the steady rippling of the receding tide.

He determined this by screaming "HELP!" at the top of his lungs until he was hoarse.

He finally gave up. Lay there on his stomach, enraged. Why had someone done this to him? What manner of asshole would find this funny? He would like to meet and strangle said asshole.

Mitch stayed there by the air vent. He remained calm. There was nothing to be afraid of. When the black snake slithered its way over toward him and coiled itself between his legs, he did not freak out. Black snakes were not poisonous. He knew this from Camp Tacaloma. Still, he lay there tensed and motionless, until finally it decided to move on.

He had been locked in down there for more than three hours when at last he heard the rattle of Dolly's Mercedes diesel drawing near. He had never been so glad to hear an engine in his life. She pulled into her garage with a splatter of gravel and shut it off. He raised his face to the wire mesh and called out to her.

She was removing shopping bags from the trunk. She turned around at the sound of his voice, smiling. And then frowning. Clearly, she was baffled to discover she could not see him. He called out "Crawl space!" to her several times before she finally started her way toward the carriage house, her face a mask of confusion.

"Good heavens!" she cried out when she located his semi-contorted face pressed up against the wire. "What are you doing down there, you silly man?"

"I'm locked in, Dolly."

"You most certainly are not," she said, with utter conviction.

"I assure you I am."

"Why, how absurd!"

"I could not agree more. Will you please let me out?"

She came in at once and unlatched the trap door, bathing the area under the kitchen in light.

"It must have blown shut," she called to him as he slithered his way toward her.

"Not a chance," he groaned as he climbed back up into the kitchen, his muscles aching, his face and hair caked with earth. Spiders and a host of other insects fell from his clothes. "Someone deliberately did it."

"Who?"

"Someone with a sick sense of humor. I couldn't tell you who."

"How do you know this?"

"I heard footsteps."

Dolly immediately froze, all color draining from her face. Briefly, Mitch thought she might faint. "Y-You heard what?" she gasped, her voice scarcely more than a whisper.

"I heard footsteps," Mitch repeated, watching her curiously.

"No, you didn't!" she snapped with sudden vehemence. "That can't be. It must have been your imagination. It *must*." And with that Dolly Seymour turned on her heel and darted out the door to her own house, leaving him utterly confused.

It was *not* his imagination. Someone had purposely locked him in down there. He'd heard the footsteps. This was a fact. But who, some kid? There *were* no kids on Big Sister. So who, then—Tuck Weems? Was this his way of telling Mitch he wasn't happy to have him living there? Why had Dolly gotten so upset when he mentioned hearing footsteps? What was up with that?

Mitch didn't know. But he did have his first nightmare that night.

He dreamt that he was down there in the crawl space, only now it felt as if the whole weight of the carriage house was pressing down on his chest. Pressing down on him so hard that he could barely breathe. He was all wet, too. Water was seeping down through the floorboards onto him. Only when he tried to wipe it from his eyes he discovered it wasn't water. It was the blood of Roy and Louisa Weems. And it was all over him. In his mouth. In his nose. In his . . .

He awoke with a yelp, heart racing, his body drenched with sweat. As he lay there, panting, Mitch heard something—the crunch of footsteps outside on the gravel path. And he wasn't dreaming now. This was real. *Someone was out there* . . . Mitch tiptoed over to the staircase. Slowly, he descended into his moonlit living room. He paused, listening. Hearing the blood rushing in his ears. Hearing the waters of the Sound lap against the rocks. Hearing more *footsteps*. There was an outdoor light over the front door. He flicked it on. He threw open the door . . .

And he came face to face with two deer who were munching on the azaleas planted next to the house. Startled, they went galloping off, hooves clip-clopping on the gravel.

Mitch let out a huge laugh and shut the door and went back to bed. He lay there, breathing in and out. Through the skylight over his head, the moon was full, with a pearly ring around like in *The Wolfman*. As he lay there gazing up at it, Mitch ached for Maisie's presence next to him in the bed. A person wasn't gone if she lived on inside of you. And Maisie did live on inside of Mitch. He could still hear her. He could still see her.

The only thing Mitch could not do was hold her.

In the morning, he decided he simply could not put it off any longer. The house was in decent shape. It was time to tackle his book. He had a ton of good material. A collection of hidden treasures like *Silver Lode*, the much-overlooked 1954 Allan Dwan Western in which John Payne uttered the immortal lines: "If you can kill one man the second one's not so hard. The third one's easy." He had a salute to the largely forgotten exploits of the Three Mesquiteers, a trio of thirties Republic Pictures sagebrush cutups—dim-witted Ray Corrigan, daffy Max Terhune (a ventriloquist who rode around on horseback with a dummy) and handsome young John Wayne. Not many fans knew about this particular chapter in the Duke's early film career—his Three Mesquiteers roles were usually not included in his filmography. Just the sort of thing Mitch loved to unearth and write about. He made himself a fresh pot of coffee. He sat down at his desk in front of the windows. He juiced up his computer. He got started.

And he got somewhere. He was focused. He was passionate. He was in the groove again. As Mitch's fingers flew over the keyboard, his brain leaping from one sharp observation to the next, he came to the happy realization that it was finally happening:

He was healing.

After a couple of good, productive hours he got up and punched the power button on his stack, feeling the blue Stratocaster come to life in his hands, its six silver strings humming. He closed his eyes. He played. Good hard chops first, laying down Stevie Ray Vaughan's "I'm Crying." Then, when he was in there, Mitch started riffing off of it, bending it, soaring way, way up there where it was sweet and fine. Fingers squeezing out the notes. One set of toes curled around the wa-wa pedal, the other around the tube screamer. Mitch Berger was not gifted. He knew this. But he had the love and the hurt and the power. Oh, God, he had the power.

He didn't realize he had company, too, until he opened his eyes and discovered Dolly standing there, looking positively pie-eyed. "My Lord," she exclaimed. "I could not imagine what that noise was."

"I'm sorry if I bothered you," Mitch apologized. "I'll turn it down."

"No, no. It's quite all right. That's not why I've come," she said hurriedly. She was in a dither of some sort. Positively rattled. "Oh, dear, I do hope I am not annoying you, because I *know* how you writers need your privacy and ordinarily I would not intrude. But, you see, there's this *fox* in my rose garden. And it's, well, quite dead. And I simply don't know what to do about it. I tried phoning Tuck but he's not answering his phone and every other man on island is gone for the day so I was wondering if you would be so kind as to . . ."

"Yes, of course," Mitch said quickly. "I'll take care of it right away." He put on his shoes and grabbed his work gloves and followed her back to her garden, stopping to fetch a shovel from the barn.

Dolly had a lovely garden. There were peonies and foxgloves, wild geranium, irises, bleeding heart. Everything was in bloom at once. It was an explosion of controlled chaos. Her rose garden was set apart by low, carefully cropped boxwood hedges. A brick path crisscrossed it and a copper birdbath anchored its center. Next to the birdbath lay the dead fox. It was red. It was staring right at him. Flies were buzzing around it, but it did not smell too bad yet.

"It must have been searching for water, poor thing," Dolly said hoarsely. "It's probably been living in our woods."

That was where Mitch buried it—in the wooded area between her place and the big summer house. He dug two feet down in the soft soil and slid it in and covered it over, tamping the soil down with his feet and laying a flat, heavy stone over it to keep other animals out.

Dolly was so grateful she invited Mitch over for a drink that very evening to meet his fellow islanders. "It's the very least I can do," she said. "It would be terribly impolite of me not to."

Mitch politely declined. He ranked among the socially lost even when he was at his best. Right now he was far from his best.

But Dolly would not take no for an answer. "You must get out and meet people, Mitch," she clucked. "It's not healthy to spend so much time alone. You *will* come. I insist. It's casual."

Casual, on Big Sister, turned out to mean blazer and no socks. Mitch got it backwards—he wore socks and no blazer. He was also, seemingly, the only guest who arrived at Dolly's cocktail party sober.

He had not been inside her house before, aside from the laundry room off of the garage. He'd been expecting an interior to match the old house's immaculately restored exterior—a house filled with cherished antiques and family heirlooms, floors of wide-planked oak, walls lined with oil portraits of departed pilgrim ancestors. Such was not the case at all. Dolly's parents had rebelled and gone contemporary in the fifties. Laid down harvest-gold shag carpeting over the old plank floors. Thrown coat upon coat of paint over the paneled walls. Converted the fireplaces to gas logs. Hung gold lamé drapes over the old casement windows. Installed a breakfast nook in the kitchen of avocado-colored vinyl. Most of the furniture, which was newish, was covered in persimmon-colored chintz.

Dolly, who was drinking martinis, seemed as giddy as a little girl on roller-skates. Bud Havenhurst was downright jolly, too. It was Bud who tended the bar, which was set up on a sideboard in the study, complete with ice bucket and tongs. It was Bud who made the introductions.

The first islander Mitch met was Bud's tall, young tennis-playing wife, Mandy. Mitch found her to be even more striking upon close encounter. Mandy Havenhurst had long, creamy blond hair, big blue eyes, lusciously plump lips and a dazzling smile. Her short, sleeveless white linen dress handsomely offset her tanned, toned arms and legs. She was not fashion-model pretty. Her jaw was a shade mannish, her nose rather broad and flat. But she was a very attractive woman, and certainly no older than thirty.

Her handshake was firm, her manner direct. "You're the heavy metal guitarist?"

"Blues, actually. Just loud."

"And you have a place in New York?"

"Yes, I do," he replied, sipping his Bushmill on the rocks.

"So do we. Nothing fancy—just a little pied-à-terre." She spoke in rushed bursts and didn't move her mouth when she talked. "I'd be lost without it. I spend as much time there as I can. The city is so alive. But I don't have to tell you that. I read your reviews regularly. I almost never agree with you. But you write so well."

"Thank you, I think . . ." Mitch was already sorry he had come. He was out of practice. He felt tongue-tied and awkward.

Or maybe it was just that there was something so decidedly MGM Technicolor about the whole scene. The ice bucket and tongs. The Dave Brubeck album tinkling softly in the background. The vast assortment of retro hors d'oeuvres that Dolly had prepared—pigs in a blanket, chicken livers wrapped in bacon, miniature egg rolls. Mitch half-expected Gig Young to come tottering through the doorway in a plaid vest, hiccoughing discreetly.

But it was Redfield and Bitsy Peck who arrived next. Dolly's older brother did not resemble her in the least. He was a darkly colored, craggy-faced man with a massive head, barrel chest and uncommonly short legs. His trouser size, Mitch reflected, must have been 36-20. And, unlike Dolly, he was extremely reserved.

"You're the heavy metal guitarist?" he asked Mitch, his voice a mild murmur.

"Blues, actually. Just loud."

"Do you gun, Mitch?"

"Do I what?"

"Gun. Hunt. Do you hunt?"

"No, I don't."

"Too bad. Have to thin out the deer periodically or they take over the whole island. Can never get anyone to help me." Red Peck then wandered over to the window and sipped his drink, gazing out at the Sound. He was, seemingly, out of conversation.

Bitsy was warm and bustling and full of enthusiasm. It was she who explained to Mitch why her husband was gone so much—Red was a pilot for United, specializing in the New York to Tokyo route. She also told him that they had two children, a son who was finishing up his sophomore year at Duke and a daughter, a dancer, who lived in San Francisco. Bitsy was a short, round, snub-nosed woman with freckles and light brown hair that she wore in a page-boy. She had on a denim jumper, a turtleneck, tights and garden clogs. She was friendly and motherly.

And she and Dolly appeared to be soulmates. They immediately started burbling away about each other's flowers, Dolly coming up for air just long enough to mention that she had to take more things out of the oven. Mitch asked her if she needed any help. She allowed as how she did. And so he joined the two of them in the kitchen, where they immediately lit into Mandy's outfit.

"If the poor dear's going to wear her dresses that short," observed Dolly, "then she should really do something about the backs of her thighs, don't you think?"

"I do," Bitsy concurred. "She's not sixteen. Then again, maybe men don't notice or mind the pronounced wattling. Do they, Mitch?"

"She's a good-looking woman."

"Well, if you're going to spout baloney like that you can go back to the study with the men," Bitsy said merrily.

"Mitch is planning to revive Niles's vegetable garden," Dolly informed her as she slid a sheet of egg rolls out of the oven.

Bitsy let out a squeal of delight. "Outstanding! I can get you started whenever you're ready, Mitch. I have dried chicken manure. I have bunny dung. I have the hugest compost pile in the state. They call me the Compost Lady. You're welcome to as many wheelbarrow-loads as you can handle!"

"That's very nice of you."

"Now tell me what you want to plant," she commanded him.

"I was thinking about tomatoes."

"Oh, excellent!" she exclaimed. "I am doing several heirlooms this year, but I also have Sweet One Millions and a few early disease-resistant varieties. Your timing is perfect. The soil temperature is ideal. And if you move fast you can still get your cukes in. I have a whole forest of lettuce you can have, too. The season's running a bit late this year." She paused to sample an egg roll, nibbling at it delicately. "Tell me, did your wife garden?"

A sudden tidal wave of emotion came crashing over Mitch. His Adam's apple seemed to double in size, eyes stung, chest tightened. It still happened to him sometimes when Maisie came up unexpectedly. "Yes . . ." he responded hoarsely. "Yes, she did." Then he excused himself and fled for the powder room.

Only there wasn't one. No bathroom downstairs, period. He finally found one at the top of the stairs. It was the master bath, complete with claw-footed tub and festive wallpaper featuring horseless carriages and men wearing goggles and long duffel coats. Mitch rinsed his face and gazed at his reflection in the mirror, breathing in and out. His eye strayed over to a cluster of prescription pill bottles on the top shelf of a white wicker unit next to the sink. It was, he observed, a full-fledged dispensary of mother's little helpers. Dolly Seymour had prescriptions for Prozac, for Valium and for Vicodin, also known as housewife's heroin. Dolly also had a prescription for lithium, which was serious medicine for serious manic-depression. This was, Mitch reflected, one hurting lady. There was a bottle of Relafen, an anti-inflammatory, that was in Niles Seymour's name. Also a bottle of Urispas, a prostate medication. The man had left his pills behind when he flew the coop. And Dolly had kept them. Mitch found this mildly curious.

Mandy Havenhurst was seated on the stairs when he came back down, blocking his way. Her skirt was hiked up very invitingly on her thighs. From where Mitch was standing, there was not a thing wrong with them.

"You didn't have children?" she asked, tossing her long blond hair at him provocatively.

"No, we didn't." Mitch was trapped there on the steps. He

couldn't go around her. He couldn't go over her. He sat down on a step above her and said, "We weren't ready."

"I'm so ready I could bust. I'd like to have at least two. Maybe three. But Bud keeps saying he's too old to be a father all over again."

Mitch nodded, wondering why she was telling a complete stranger this.

"I'm in the city a lot," she went on. "We should go to a museum together or something. I know *nobody*. And Bud will *never* go in. He's afraid of New York, I think. He grew up out here. Everyone he knows he's known since childhood. I can't imagine that, can you? Knowing all the same people your whole life?"

"No, I can't."

"Don't get me wrong—I love it here. But it can be *so* insulated. I'd go stir-crazy if I had to be out here full-time." She hesitated, glancing up at him through her long eyelashes. "What I mean is, it's nice to meet up with someone who's *real*."

"Thank you," he said, suddenly aware that they were not alone.

Bud Havenhurst was hovering in the doorway, jealously watching the two of them. Dolly's ex-husband was positively coiled with tension, his eyes agleam. He reminded Mitch of Claude Rains in *Notorious* any time Ingrid Bergman got near Cary Grant. Clearly, Bud could not believe that this lovely blond trophy was his. Clearly, he did believe that every other man wanted her as much as he did. Did Mandy encourage this belief by being just a bit too attentive toward younger, available men? Mitch wondered. Because they did seem to be playing some kind of a game. She was staring right back at her husband now, her chin raised, a look of brazen challenge on her face.

I do not want to get mixed up in this, Mitch said to himself.

"Freshen your drink, Mitch?" Bud asked him tightly.

Mandy had to let him pass now. He joined Bud in the study. There was a love seat and a pair of matching armchairs in there. Also a desk with a computer and printer on it.

"I wanted you to know, Mitch, just how great I think it is to have some new blood out here," the lawyer said as he mixed his drink. He sounded very edgy. And he was gripping the glass so tightly Mitch thought it might shatter in his hand. "I hope you didn't think I was being rude to you the day you came to my office. I'm just very protective of Dolly. We all are. Niles Seymour put her through hell." He handed Mitch his refilled glass, peering at him carefully. "Fine girl, Mandy, don't you think?"

"She seems very nice."

"I'm a lucky man," Bud acknowledged, beaming. "There are some mornings when I wake up . . . Hey, boy, I can't believe how happy I am."

Mitch heard jovial voices coming from the entry hall now. Young Evan had arrived with his companion, Jamie. Evan was in his mid-twenties, tall and slender and tanned, with wavy black hair and Dolly's delicate features and blue eyes. He wore a gauzy shirt unbuttoned to his stomach, jeans and leather sandals. Jamie was about fifty, trimly built and fashionably turned out in a blue blazer, yellow Sea Island cotton shirt and white slacks. Mitch was positive he looked familiar, but he couldn't place him.

"So you're the heavy metal metal guitarist," Jamie exclaimed, pumping Mitch's hand.

"Blues, actually. Just loud. I guess I'll have to amp down."

"Not on our account," Evan assured him.

Jamie nodded in agreement. " 'To each his own, said the old woman as she French-kissed the cow.' An old expression of my dear mom's, slightly embellished by myself. Welcome to B.S., Mitch. I'm a huge fan of your work. For one thing, you actually know what you're talking about—which is shockingly unusual. *And* you are not personal or mean. So many critics these days just want to land a zinger. They don't realize how much words can hurt."

"Sure they do," Mitch countered. "That's why they do it."

"You'll have to come see our lighthouse," said Evan. "It's way cool. Second tallest on the Southern New England Coast. The Block Island Lighthouse is taller by ten feet."

"I'd love to. Is it used for anything anymore?"

"Absolutely," Jamie replied cheerfully. "It's a great place to get high."

Now it clicked—it was the drug reference that did it. "I just realized something," Mitch said. "You're Jamie Devers."

"It's true," Jamie confessed, smiling. "I was."

Better known to the world as Bucky Stevens, the resident little cute kid on *Just Blame Bucky*, which ranked as one of the classic fifties family sitcoms, right up there with *Father Knows Best, Leave It to Beaver* and *The Donna Reed Show*. In his heyday, Jamie Devers had been one of the biggest stars on television, a round-faced little munchkin with freckles and a cowlick and an amusingly adenoidal way of saying, "I didn't dood it." But, as so often happened, he outgrew his cuteness. And the show got cancelled. Jamie Devers grew a beard and got mixed up with the Peter Fonda–Dennis Hopper Hollywood drug scene of the late sixties. Got himself busted several times. Then disappeared from public view altogether. Until he'd surfaced a few years back with a highly controversial tell-all memoir, which alleged that during his prepubescent heyday he had regularly been sexually abused by a secret gay fraternity of male studio executives, agents and actors. His scathing memoir, entitled *I Dood It*, also claimed that the actress who'd played Bucky's television mom had carried on a long, secret love affair with a black L.A. Dodgers outfielder. The book had become a huge bestseller and thrust Jamie back in the limelight for a brief time. Now he was out here, living on Big Sister with Evan Havenhurst and dealing in antiques. He seemed at peace. He was certainly fit and cheerful.

"Do you sail?" he asked Mitch.

"No, I'm a city kid, through and through. I can't even swim."

"Not a problem—that's why they have life preservers. I can't swim either. Child stars can't do anything. Hell, I didn't learn how to tie my own shoelaces until I was ..." Jamie paused, glancing down at own his feet. "Actually, I still don't know how to." He let out a huge guffaw. "You'll have to come out for a sail sometime with us, Mitch. You'll enjoy it. And I promise you we'll even wear clothes."

This comment did not go over well with Bud, who immediately stalked off, red-faced.

Evan let out a pained sigh. "Jaymo, why must you rub his nose in it?"

"Sorry, Ev," said Jamie, patting his hand. "The Bud man's just such a prig I can't help myself."

Evan went to fetch them drinks, leaving Mitch with the one-time star.

"Still doing any acting, Jamie?"

"Boyfriend, I never *was* an actor," he replied, with no trace of bitterness. "Being a child star means being *you.* When you get to be older, and you find out they now expect you to play a role, you discover you never really learned how. And you have no real life experiences to draw upon, since you've had no real life." Evan returned now with glasses of wine for each of them. Jamie thanked him and turned back to Mitch. "In answer to your next question: No, I never watch the reruns. It was all a lie. Bogus people living in a bogus world. In fact, we don't even own a TV. That's all behind me now. So is Tinsel Town. Beverly Hills is the only ghetto in America where the rats don't live in the walls. Being here, I have achieved peace for the first time in my life." He glanced fondly at his handsome young companion. "Poor Evan still has the bug, I'm afraid. That's how we met—he was in an acting class that I was teaching in New York. I've been doing my best to talk him out of it. That's absolutely the only thing Bud and I see eye to eye on."

Evan had brought hors d'oeuvres that needed heating. He excused himself to go take care of them. Mitch and Jamie drifted into the study, where Bud and Red sat talking. The subject was Niles Seymour and what a bastard he was.

"It wasn't enough that he broke Dolly's heart," Red was saying, his voice a low murmur. "He had to leave her high and dry, too. That's the detestable part."

"Unforgivable," agreed Jamie, sipping his wine.

"He cleaned out their joint checking and savings accounts," Bud explained to Mitch. "He even liquidated their stock portfolio. Well over a hundred thousand dollars altogether. *And* he used their joint Visa card to buy two airplane tickets to St. Croix—before Dolly could get around to freezing it."

Mitch nodded, wondering why they were suddenly being so open with him.

"Has he filed for the divorce yet?" Jamie asked Bud.

"No, but *she* will," Bud replied. "On the grounds of desertion."

"I call it outright theft," Red fumed. "He should be in jail. The man is a no-good con artist."

"I wouldn't call him no good," Jamie said. "I'd call him damned good. He's handsome. He's charming. And he's as persuasive as hell. Convinced Dolly to put his name on everything, didn't he?"

"We can't touch him, Red," Bud admitted glumly. "Niles had a legal right to that money."

"But the money in those accounts was *hers*," Red said insistently. He had grown considerably more loquacious with a couple of stiff drinks in him. And, like Bud, he was very protective of Dolly. "Those investments were *hers*. They do *not* belong to Niles Seymour and that . . . that . . . *bimbo*."

"Who is the other woman?" Mitch asked.

"We don't know," Bud answered, reaching for his scotch. "Some little redhead he knew in Atlantic City before he met Dolly, apparently. All we can say for certain is that one day she showed up at the Saybrook Point Inn and the next day Niles, his car and every penny Dolly had to her name were gone."

"We spotted them together," Red mentioned. "Bud and I. We'd docked at the inn after a sail for a bite of brunch. And there they were having a cozy breakfast together in the dining room. She was exactly what you'd expect from Niles—young and sleazy. A thorough tramp."

"Dolly found a Dear John letter on the kitchen table the next morning," Bud added. "Bastard didn't even have the nerve to face her. Just cleared out."

"What does he do for a living?"

Evan came in now with a platter of quesadillas. He lingered, refilling his father's scotch and Jamie's wineglass.

"He sells things," Red answered. "Menswear, cars, yachts . . ."

"And himself," Bud added bitterly. "Above all, Niles Seymour sells himself."

At the mention of the name Evan abruptly slammed the wine bottle down and went fleeing back to the kitchen.

"Evan doesn't like to talk about him," Jamie explained to Mitch quietly. "He murdered Bobo, you see. We loved Bobo. She was our baby. Most traumatic experience of Evan's life, watching that poor little dachsund writhe in pain in his arms, unable to do a thing to help her. The vet did an autopsy—said someone had fed her ground meat laced with arsenic. We could never prove it was Niles, but we have no doubt. He's the one who was always complaining about her barking." Jamie's face tightened at the memory. "He used to call us the Queers. Was always leaving us nasty little notes that began: 'Dear Queers.' If we left a trash can out. If we had people in for drinks . . . I think he believed we were having gay orgies. He's a truly horrible person."

"None of us were particularly sorry to see him go, Mitch," Red said. "It was almost as if he went out of his way to antagonize every single person on this island. Kept pushing me to build luxury condos out here. He wanted to bulldoze the woods, have plans drawn up. *Condos* . . ." Coming out of Red's mouth it sounded like the single dirtiest word in the English language. "Can you imagine?"

"He put the moves on Mandy repeatedly," Bud spoke up angrily. "She was not the least bit interested. But he wouldn't leave her alone. I finally confronted him about it. Do you know what that bastard said to me? He said, 'Don't blame me if your wife is a common slut.' I popped him one right in the nose. First time I'd hit someone in thirty-five years."

"Niles used to smack Dolly around," Red recalled. "I saw the bruises. So did Tuck Weems, who threatened to strangle him. That put a solid scare into Niles—Tuck not being the stablest individual around. Niles reported Tuck to Tal Bliss."

"Did Bliss arrest him?" Mitch asked.

"No, that's not Tal's style," Bud answered. "He just told Tuck that it would be best if he didn't work here on Big Sister anymore. Now that Niles is gone, he's back. Dolly insisted. She's always been fond of Tuck."

Red stared morosely into his empty glass. "I must confess there's one thing that greatly concerns me . . ."

"What's that, Red?" Bud asked.

"What'll happen when Niles comes back. Because he *will* be back—just as soon as the money runs out."

"Never," Bud snapped. "That's totally unthinkable."

Jamie said, "I agree with Red. The bastard *will* come crawling back. What's more, Dolly will take him back."

"After what he did to her?" Mitch said. "How could she?"

"Oldest reason of all," Red replied. "She still loves him."

They fell into grim silence. Outside, ominous clouds were rolling in over the Sound. The sky was growing dark.

"Understand you got yourself locked in your crawl space yesterday, Mitch," Bud said offhandedly.

"Yes, I did. Someone closed the trap door on me."

"Damned foolish thing to do," muttered Red.

"Who did it?" asked Jamie.

"No idea," said Mitch. "All I know is I heard footsteps. Heavy footsteps."

"I see . . ." Bud glanced uneasily over at Red, who seemed a bit uncomfortable himself. "May I ask—how did Dolly react to your little misadventure?"

"Rather strangely, now that you mention it. She maintained I *hadn't* heard any footsteps. She was quite insistent about it, actually."

"Well, she would be," Red said heavily.

"What do you mean by that?" Mitch asked.

Red gazed out the window at the approaching darkness. "Not that it's anything you should be concerned about—because, well, we are talking about someone who was clinically deranged—but Tuck's father, old Roy Weems . . ."

The madman who had shot his wife and himself in Mitch's

bedroom. Mitch leaned forward in his seat. "Yes . . . ? What about him?"

"In the weeks leading up to the incident," Red Peck said, "Roy kept claiming he heard footsteps."

Now was when Mitch had his second nightmare.

This one was a doozy. This time Mitch was back in Dolly's study with those three men. Only now their eyes were red and their teeth very sharp, like the vampires in those garish Hammer Films horror flicks with Christopher Lee and Peter Cushing. And Maisie was in this one. In fact, she was one of them. She was trying to kill him. To get away from her he fled back down into the crawl space—only they followed him. They all did. Their eyes glowed at him in the darkness. And they had him surrounded. And they were edging closer and closer and . . .

He awoke screaming. His heart was racing. His T-shirt was drenched with sweat. And his little house was shaking. A wicked storm had blown in. The wind was howling. Lightning crackled in the sky. Thunder rumbled. And the Sound had come to life, pounding angrily against the rocks.

As Mitch lay there in the darkness, listening to this, he heard footsteps again. At first, he felt he might be letting his imagination get the best of him. But he wasn't. These footsteps were real. And they were *in* the house. Downstairs. Now they were *on* the stairs. He could hear the stairs creak. Each creak was a footstep, each one louder than the last. Someone was moving steadily, stealthily toward him in the darkness. Growing closer. And closer . . .

"Who's there?" Mitch demanded to know.

Silence. Only silence.

He fumbled for matches. Lit his hurricane lamp, bathing the upstairs loft in a golden light.

Dolly Seymour stood there at the top of the stairs.

She wore a long white nightgown and an utterly blank expression. She was barefoot. She was shivering. She stood with her hands clasped behind her, rather like a child posing for a class picture.

Except she was no child. She was a mature, lovely woman. And her nightgown was very nearly sheer. Mitch could make out the fullness of her breasts, the rosy hue of her nipples, the darkness of her pubic hair.

"What is it, Dolly?" he asked her huskily. "Are you all right?"

She didn't answer him. Just stared at him, her gaze eerily unfocused. She seemed to be in a kind of trance. Was she sleepwalking? Drugged? He couldn't tell. Her lips were moving, a low murmur coming out of her mouth. But no words. At least, none he could comprehend.

He raised his voice. "Dolly, can you hear me?!"

"The mother," she said in a soft little sing-song voice. Saliva bubbled from her lips.

"What about the mother?"

"The mother is *hurt.*" Now she started across the loft toward Mitch, unclasping her hands, raising one of them over her head.

She held a carving knife in her hand. A long carving knife. And she was coming right at him with it.

Mitch clambered from the bed and grappled with her, wrestling the knife from her hand. Dolly relinquished it with little resistance. Their brief struggle seemed to rouse her from her trance. She blinked her eyes several times now. And she looked around at the loft, wide-eyed. Then she let out a gasp of utter horror and fainted dead away in Mitch's arms. He stood there holding her for a moment. He thought about putting her right to bed here in his bed. But then he thought better of it. He carried her sideways down the narrow stairs, hugging her to his chest, feeling the aliveness, the animal warmth of her in his arms and his hands. He carried her out his open front door into the darkness, the wind howling, the trees rustling. Fat raindrops were beginning to patter down. Soon it would pour. He started down the gravel path with her toward her place. It was a long way to carry someone but she was as light as a feather. He made it through the laundry room door with her and managed to flick on the kitchen light. Several drawers were open, the contents strewn on the floor as if the place had been burgled. He carried her up to her bedroom and set her down gently on her bed. He turned on the nightstand light. Dolly was stirring now, her eyes flickering. Her tiny hands and feet were frozen. He began rubbing them for her.

That was when she came to. She panicked at the sight of him there. "Why, Mitch!" she cried, pulling her nightgown tightly around herself. "Wh-What are you doing here in my . . . ?"

"You were wandering in the night, Dolly. You were in my house."

"That's not possible!"

"I assure you it is. You came all the way upstairs to my room."

"Oh, dear." She swallowed, reddening. "I'm so sorry, Mitch. I do sleepwalk from time to time. I-I'm sorry to have put you to so much trouble."

"Not a problem. That's what neighbors are for."

"Thank you for being so kind." Her eyes softened now, her gaze holding his. She reached out for his hand and took it, gripping it tightly. She seemed very frightened and alone at that moment, very vulnerable.

And, suddenly, Mitch was keenly aware of just how awkward the silence was becoming. He remembered how she had felt in his arms. He realized how long he had gone without a woman. But he was also aware that it was a genuinely bad idea to go down this road. So he said, "Can I get you anything—a glass of water, another blanket?"

"No, no," she said quickly. "I'm fine. I'll be fine. I'm just so sorry I bothered you. Imagine what you must have thought . . ." She yawned. She suddenly seemed overwhelmingly sleepy. "Good night, Mitch," she mumbled, burrowing under the covers. "And thank you."

Mitch shut off the light and went back downstairs, only to discover he was not alone.

Bud Havenhurst was standing there in the kitchen in a silk bathrobe, glowering at him. "I saw the light," he said to Mitch accusingly. "Just exactly what do you think you're doing here?"

"She was sleepwalking. She came into my bedroom. I brought her home."

"Do you honestly expect me to believe that?"

"I *honestly* don't care what you believe," Mitch shot back. "But that's what happened. I didn't invite it. I didn't enjoy it. And I sure as hell don't appreciate where you and your dirty mind are going. So back off, understand?"

"You're right, you're right," Havenhurst said hurriedly. "You're absolutely right. I had no call to . . ." He ran a hand over his face, slumping against the kitchen counter. "I was out of line. My apologies."

Mitch stood there studying him. "Are you always up at three in the morning watching your ex-wife's house?"

"Old habits die hard. I learned to sleep lightly when she and I were married."

"Meaning what, she does this often?"

"Look, she's fine, all right?" Bud said wearily. "Everyone's fine. So just go home."

Mitch didn't budge. "That woman nearly stabbed me in my own bed."

Bud drew his breath in. "She had a *knife* with her?"

"She did."

"I wondered, when all I saw all of the drawers open . . ." A horrible thought seemed to cross his mind now. "You aren't planning to call Tal Bliss about this, are you?"

"I will if you don't tell me what the story is."

"Fair enough," Bud agreed reluctantly. "Dolly has *episodes*. They come and go. There have been stretches where she's fine for three, four years. And then—" He snapped his fingers. "She's off to the races again. No one knows why. The shrinks at Yale–New Haven never could come up with anything concrete. 'It's an inexact science,' was how they kept putting it. Care for a glass of milk, Mitch?"

"No, thanks."

"I think I may have one." He fetched it from the refrigerator. It came in a glass bottle from a nearby dairy in Salem. He poured himself some and sipped it thoughtfully. "This storm might have set her off. Wind scares her. Always has. Or she might still be upset about Niles. Hard to say. Apparently it all dates back to when she found the bodies of Louisa and Roy Weems. Did she speak at all? Did she say anything?"

"Just one thing: 'The mother is hurt.' "

Bud nodded gravely. "That would be Louisa Weems, Tuck's mother. Dolly was seventeen years old, Mitch. A sheltered and sensitive young girl. It was more than she could handle. The brutality, the horror. She was severely traumatized by it. It made her . . ." He broke off, pained by the memory. "She became a different person. She'd been a carefree, sunny girl up until then. Always laughing, full of fun. After that, she went into a dark depression. Had to be hospitalized for months, under heavy sedation. There was even talk of electro-shock therapy. Fortunately, she pulled out of it before that became necessary. But she's still very, very delicate. Still needs to go on her medication from time to time. And she . . . she still acts up in the night sometimes. So I keep an eye out."

"Did she ever attack *you*?"

"No, never," he said quickly. "But she did go after Evan once. Or she tried to—with a steak knife. I stopped her in time, thank God, and we sent him away to boarding school. As long as it was just we two, I always felt I could control the situation."

"What about after she married Niles Seymour?"

"He was told about it. Red told him. As far as I know, there were no episodes. Dolly was happy with Niles," Bud added with ill-disguised bitterness. He finished his milk and rinsed out the glass, sighing heavily. "Well, now you know all of the family secrets, Mitch. I'd appreciate it if you'd keep this to yourself. No need for anyone around town to know about it, right?"

Mitch stared at him a moment. Appearances. Gossip. That's all that was on the man's mind. All that he was worried about. "They won't hear about it from me," Mitch said.

"I appreciate that," he said, looking around at the mess. "I'll take over from here. Good night."

The rain was starting to come down in windblown gusts as Mitch scampered back to his place. He found the bread knife on the floor next to his bed and put it away in a kitchen drawer. He had just climbed back into bed when it truly began to pour outside, the rain furiously lashing the house, gale force winds buffeting it. Mitch felt as if he were in a ship in an angry sea. After one particularly loud clap of thunder he heard a pop and Dolly's porch light went dark. Downstairs, his refrigerator had gone silent. The power was off all over the island. Mitch burrowed under the covers, feeling curiously calmed by the violent storm. It made sense. It was real. He slept.

The worst of it was gone by morning, but it was still raw and drizzly out, the sky and the Sound an identical shade of pewter. He could hear a foghorn from somewhere in the distance. No boats were out. Not one. And his power was still off, meaning he had no heat and no water—both the oil burner and his well pump required electricity. He climbed into his heavy wool robe and built a huge fire in the fireplace against the damp and the cold. His stove ran on propane, so he was able to light a burner with a match and boil some bottled water for coffee. He was huddled before the fire with a cup of it, feeling very groggy after his adventurous night, when the power finally came back on. He showered and shaved and dressed. He made himself some scrambled eggs and slab bacon and toast. He was just finishing up the dishes when he heard the clatter of a garden cart out on the gravel path.

It was Bitsy Peck, bustling along in bright yellow Gore-Tex bib overalls and green rubber rain boots, her cart loaded down with tray upon tray of seedlings. The woman had brought Mitch a small nursery. He went outside to greet her.

"Good morning, Mitch!" she burbled at him excitedly. "We seem to have Big Sis all to ourselves this morning. Red left at five A.M. for New York. Mandy hitched a ride with him. The boys are at their shop. Bud's at the office. And Dolly's at the dentist. I understand she paid you a little visit last night—she's totally aghast. Embarrassed beyond belief. Afraid you might have gotten the wrong idea. That was quite some Nor'easter, wasn't it? I do hope someone warned you that we almost always lose power. All it takes is one hiccough and poof. I can live without the lights but no shower, no toilets, no way." She came up for air, puffing slightly. "I've been up since four, in case you're wondering why I'm chattering away like a magpie."

"This is incredibly nice of you," Mitch observed, sorting through the trays of seedlings.

"Nonsense," she clucked. "After a storm is *the* best time to plant. I can help you get started—unless you have something else you need to do right now."

He needed to work on his damned book. But he was thrilled to have such a good excuse not to. Besides, she seemed downright anxious to get at it. She'd even brought her own fork and spade. A true garden zealot. "There's nothing else I need to do," Mitch assured her. "Let's get cracking."

The vegetable patch that Niles Seymour had tended was out behind the barn. This was the sunniest spot on the property when the sun happened to be out, which it was not. It was roughly twelve by sixteen feet. A crude, homemade chicken-wire fence served as an enclosure.

"That's to keep the rabbits out," Bitsy informed him as she nudged the rickety gate open. "Although, to be perfectly honest, nothing can keep them out if they want in."

The patch was in a state of serious neglect—lumpy, furrowed and weedy. Wild berry bushes and small volunteer trees had begun to take hold. Bitsy knelt and pierced the muddy earth with a trowel, inspecting its composition with an expert eye. She fetched her spade and dug deeper, sifting the dense soil through her fingers, muttering under her breath. She reminded Mitch of Walter Huston studying a gold vein in *The Treasure of the Sierra Madre*.

"As my son Jeremy would say," she concluded, "it's totally bogus."

"Bogus how?"

"All Niles did was dress the top layer, that's how. If you go down six inches it's thoroughly compacted. Look at this—there's zero drainage. Nothing will take root here. Nothing. Either he hasn't a clue how to garden or he's just plain lazy. Probably a bit of both." She leaned back on her ample haunches, sighing. "Mitch, we're going to have to double dig."

"What does that mean exactly?"

"Going down two spade-lengths. Removing the rocks. Enriching the soil with compost and manure, adding peat moss for drainage. Then, and only then, can we plant."

"I didn't realize it would be so much work," Mitch said doubtfully.

"This is what proper gardening is, my young friend. Soil preparation is *everything*. We can take your truck to my place for the organic matter. But first . . ." She thrust a chubby index finger in the air. "We dig!"

A nut, Mitch reflected. This woman was a nut.

He went to the barn for a shovel and a fork and returned with them. She was already at it, turning soil like a demon.

And so they dug. Soon they began hitting rocks. Some of these were small. Some could be loosely classified as boulders. They piled them just inside the fence, Mitch quickly working up a sweat in the damp morning air. Fine pinpoints of perspiration formed on Bitsy's upper lip, but she was surprisingly fit for such a round woman. Downright tireless. And raring to gossip.

"You are probably filled with a million questions after last night," she said gaily. "In answer to what is no doubt your first one, Mandy is the only one on this island who has any real money. The girl's filthy with it, actually. Her family started a brewery in St. Louis back in the eighteen-hundreds. What the poor dear hasn't got is any social class. The women in town loathe her—she wears too much gold and not enough clothing. She didn't go to Miss Porter's. She didn't graduate from Smith."

"Did you?"

"Sure," Bitsy said offhandedly. "Believe me, if you met her father you would think he drives a truck for a living. That's why she married Bud."

"She seems to want kids," Mitch said, puffing.

"Desperately," Bitsy confirmed. "Or so she says. I'm never quite sure whether I believe her. She's one of those women who is always telling people what she thinks they want to hear. I also suspect she

85

has a young hunk of a boyfriend in New York. Bud only keeps that apartment at her insistence."

"He watches her like a hawk."

"Why do you say that?" Bitsy asked eagerly. "Did she hit on you?"

"Not really. I doubt I'm her type."

"Don't sell yourself short, Mitch. You're a very nice-looking young man."

"Are *you* hitting on me?"

"Stop that!" she commanded, howling with laughter. "Now, as for Jamie and Evan, Jamie *will* play the village queen role just a teensy bit—to rile Bud, mostly. But he's a good-hearted man. And he's been *so* good for Evan, who was just the lostest little bunny before Jamie came along."

"Did Bud have a hard time accepting Evan's gayness?"

"As you can well imagine," she affirmed. "Bud has a hard time accepting *anything* that isn't what he knows. Actually, Bud has been something of a puzzle to me. He's still so devoted to Dolly. And acts so crushed by what happened. Yet he *let* Niles steal her away from him."

Mitch's shoulders were starting to ache from driving the spade into so many chunks of granite. "He did?"

"Of course. A good woman like Dolly isn't *lured* away from her husband. She has to be *driven* away. Bud didn't want her anymore. When Niles came along, she was feeling unloved and unattractive. Believe me, it can also get a bit lonely out here. Look at my own situation. Red makes four flights a month to Tokyo. He's four days on—two days to get there, two days to get back—then he's three days off, asleep mostly, the poor lamb. And then he's gone again. Poor Red was such a disappointment to his parents. They wanted him to carry on the Peck political legacy. But he doesn't like giving speeches. Or mingling with strangers. He likes peace and quiet. His cockpit. His little island. We're hoping our boy, Jeremy, will show a taste for public life. He *is* talking about law school after he . . . Oh, beans!" Her spade had collided with yet another solid object. It didn't give off the sharp clank of metal upon stone. This was more of a dull thud. "I was afraid of this," she said.

Mitch leaned on his spade, catching his breath. "What is it?"

"Tree root." She gazed around them with a critical eye. "One of your garden's worst enemies, Mitch. It will hog all of the soil's moisture and nutrients."

"Is it from that oak?" There was a fine old one over next to the barn.

"No, they have a tap root—straight down. It's probably that mulberry over there. I'll fetch my pruning saw. We'll make short work of it." She went waddling off toward her place, swiping at the mud on her overalls.

Mitch started digging out the soil from around it so they could get a clear shot at it—when suddenly the smell hit him. It was powerful. It was putrid. It was so sickening he gagged and very nearly threw up.

The solid object was not a tree root at all. It was somebody's leg.

CHAPTER 6

IT WAS A THIRTY-MINUTE drive straight south on Route 9 from Meriden to Dorset. Des had worked a case down there once before. A sixteen-year-old named Ethan Salisbury had smacked his mother upside the head approximately one hundred times with an aluminum baseball bat, stuffed her body into the trunk of her BMW and dumped it into Uncas Lake. It had not been pretty. Des had the charcoal sketches to prove it. The Salisbury murder had garnered quite a bit of attention. They were bluebloods. They had lived in a $1.8 million home with a sauna and a pool. Things like that weren't supposed to happen to people like that in places like that. But they did.

The same way dead bodies weren't supposed to be unearthed in the vegetable patch on Big Sister Island. But one had been.

Des marveled at the historic village's lushness and calm as she steered her unmarked Crown Victoria slicktop cruiser toward Peck Point. It was so quiet she could hear herself breathe. And so spotless it had the sanitized unreality of a theme park. There was no graffiti, no trash. There was no ugliness whatsoever.

At least none that showed.

As she eased on past the Dorset Academy of Fine Arts, her gaze lingered longingly. There was no postmodern fakery at DAFA. They still believed in the same rigorous, classical training that produced the Renaissance masters. Years and years of study on the human anatomy, on perspective, on materials. It was a private dream of hers to study there someday. Make that a fantasy.

There was a barricade at the end of Peck Point. Here she encountered a horde of cruisers and television news vans. The island itself, which was accessible by a wooden causeway, was shrouded in dense fog. It seemed distant and faintly ominous. It reminded her of the view of Alcatraz across San Francisco Bay.

Tal Bliss, Dorset's seasoned resident trooper, had taken the initial 911 call. He had immediately called the barracks in Westbrook. They sent out several uniformed troopers to seal the area. They had also contacted Major Crimes.

The instant Des stepped out of her cruiser she was assaulted by news cameras from Connecticut's four local television stations, 3, 8, 30 and 61. The reporters shoved microphones in her face, crowding her up against her car, demanding answers. They were in a constant ratings battle with each other. And nothing stirred up their blood like a violent crime in a town of wealthy white people.

"*Lieutenant, do you have the victim's identity?*"

"*Lieutenant, we go on live at noon!*"

"*We need an update, Lieutenant!*"

"*Lieutenant, what can you tell us?!*"

Des's heavy horn-rimmed glasses had come sliding down her nose a bit. She pushed them back up, pausing to compose herself before she responded. She had learned from previous experience that if she did not she came across as too hostile. Also her voice had a tendency to bottom out on her when she was nervous. Brandon used to say she sounded like Don Cornelius. "I can tell you very little at the present time," she stated, blinking into the lights. "As you can see, I have only just arrived."

"*When can you give us a statement?*"

"*We go on live at noon!*"

"*Can you give us something between and twelve and twelve-ten?!*"

"*We need a statement!*"

"Now will you please let me do my job?" Des asked them patiently. It was not easy to remain polite with them. They were just so damned insistent. And so positive that nothing, but nothing, was as important to anyone as their own on-air needs. It was perfectly natural that they felt this way. Virtually everyone on the planet conducted their public and private lives around television. And their demands did have to be met. Still, if you were not firm with them they would engulf and devour you whole. "Please step aside *now*!" she barked.

And they let her by. Nobody liked to be around an angry sister. Not one who had a gun.

Tal Bliss met her at the edge of the wooden bridge, as imposing a figure as ever in his wide-brimmed hat, tailored uniform and polished boots. Des had worked with him on the Salisbury case and respected him. He had handled himself like a professional. He had treated her with courtesy. He was a good resident trooper, comfortable with his size, his badge and his domain. He knew this place. He knew these people. The resident trooper program was a blessing for the smaller Connecticut towns that did not have their own police force. In exchange for his around-the-clock presence, the town paid half of his salary.

"Welcome to Big Sister, Lieutenant," he said, tipping his hat to her.

She smiled at him and said, "Hey back at you, Trooper. And how is Busta Rhymes?"

"Renamed him Dirty Harry, if you don't mind."

"Not one bit."

"And he's fat and ungrateful, in response to your question."

She let out a laugh. "Well, he *is* a cat. Bake anything good lately?"

Des had not been shocked to learn that Bliss had served two tours of duty in Vietnam. He carried himself like an ex-marine. But it had come as a surprise to find out that he'd studied for a year at the Cordon Bleu in Paris and was considered the finest chef in Dorset.

"I've rediscovered the quiche. I'll have to make you one sometime."

"And I'll have to be there to eat it," she said to him, ducking under the yellow crime scene tape and out onto the wooden bridge.

"I don't seem to see you down around these parts unless it's something grizzly, do I?"

"That what this is?"

"Gentleman smells none too sweet, I assure you. Victim was Niles Seymour, age fifty-two, estranged husband of Dolly Seymour. Everyone thought he left town a few weeks ago with a younger woman. It appears he never left at all. He's been down there for quite some time, as you will see. Anything I can help you with before we head on out?"

"How's the security here?" she asked, glancing at the mechanized barricade. It took an I.D. card to raise it.

"They've never had any trouble," he replied. "If the system is tampered with in any way, the private security firm is out here in ten minutes."

"Any tampering recently?"

"Negative. Sometimes the local kids stick chewing gum in the card slot for kicks. The Point's one of their after-dark hangouts. They like to get high out here. I periodically chase them away. But it's been quiet lately."

"Anyone besides the residents have an I.D. card?"

"Just Tuck Weems, the caretaker. No one else, Lieutenant. Not even the postman—they pick up their mail at the post office. Although I should point out the tidal situation to you. Right now it's in, and the water's plenty deep and treacherous, as you can see . . ."

She glanced over the wooden railing at the water. It was swirling and foaming on the rocks. Treacherous was right.

"But at low tide," he continued, "it's possible to *walk* out to Big Sister. If someone's on foot there's no stopping him. Except there's been no trouble with prowlers for quite a few years. For one thing, whatever they steal they have to lug all the way back to shore with them, on foot, over very slippery rocks. For another, those houses have an awful lot of big windows. You can't exactly sneak up on the place."

"You're saying an outsider didn't do this, correct?"

Bliss glanced at her uneasily. "In my opinion, it's highly unlikely we are dealing with a career criminal here. I'd say he was killed by someone he knew. Either someone he buzzed in or a fellow islander—although I must tell you I find the latter possibility extremely hard to imagine. I've known these folks my whole life."

They started their way across the causeway toward the island. It got damper and colder the farther out they got. Des was sorry she had not thought to bring a sweater. Power lines straddled the narrow wooden bridge, she observed. Connecticut Light and Power did not string lines out to private islands for just anyone.

"You'd better tell me about them," she said, shivering.

"Dolly Seymour is a Peck," he said with obvious pride. "As in Peck Point. We are talking about the bluest of the bluebloods, Lieutenant. A true lady. Although I suppose that's considered something of a pejorative term nowadays."

"Not by me it isn't," Des said, wondering how long it would be before she felt the hot breath of Captain Polito down the back of her neck. Not long at all.

"The word around town," Bliss continued, "was that Niles left Dolly a Dear John letter, cleaned out their accounts and took off for the Virgin Islands—leaving a whole lot of bad feelings behind."

"The other woman's name?"

"No one seems to have any idea. She wasn't a local girl."

"Who found his body?"

"The tenant of Dolly's carriage house, Mitch Berger. He and Dolly's sister-in-law, Bitsy Peck. They were digging up the garden when they encountered it. She was able to recognize him."

"I'll be needing a complete list of who lives out here," Des said to Bliss.

"I can give you that right now. Bitsy and Dolly's brother, Redfield, live in the summer cottage. Dolly's ex-husband, Bud Havenhurst, lives in the guest cottage with his new wife, Mandy. He got the house as a settlement after Dolly left him for Niles. And their son, Evan, lives in the lighthouse-keeper's house with his companion, Jamie Devers. Jamie's one of our local celebrities, but he keeps a pretty low profile."

She frowned at him. "Jamie Devers?"

"He was a big television star back in the fifties—*Just Blame Bucky*." On her blank stare he said, "Before your time, I guess . . . God, I'm getting old."

"It doesn't show one bit," she assured him. "You are still a fine-looking gentleman."

"Forget it," he snapped, instantly on alert. "I won't take another one."

"But they're so much happier when they have company."

"Dirty Harry is plenty happy," he insisted, smiling at her faintly. "In fact, given the choice, I'd trade places with him in a second."

They had crossed the bridge and were out on the island now. It was perfectly, incredibly lovely—Des could imagine someone like Martha Stewart belonging here. She could not imagine herself or anyone she had ever known living in such a place.

A trio of blue and white Major Crime Squad cube vans were parked in the gravel driveway outside of the big yellow house. A dozen crime scene technicians in dark blue windbreakers and light blue latex gloves were already on the job. They were top-shelf people. And prepared for anything—each cube van came fully equipped with all fifty-two items of gear recommended in the guidelines drawn up by the National Medicolegal Review Panel in the wake of the O.J. case. Prior to that, unbelievably, no unified system of on-site death investigation had existed among the nation's three thousand jurisdictions. Some of the items, like bodybags, were obvious. Others, like insect repellant, were less so.

The vegetable patch was behind an old barn. Soave was there, muscles bulging inside his shiny black suit. The technicians were there. And the body of Niles Seymour was there. It was not a pretty sight or smell. Saponification had begun, his fatty tissues reacting with the salts in the soil and turning to a soapy consistency. Bloating had caused the pressure points in the skin to split open, his eyes and tongue to bulge. His clothing was rotting away from his flesh.

Crime scene photos were being taken. Des would need extra copies of these. She would need to sketch this.

"He was shot twice, loot," Soave informed her, carefully smoothing his see-through moustache with his thumb and forefinger. "Chest and neck."

"The slugs still in him?" she asked, feeling her stomach muscles tighten involuntarily. She had a hot, bilious taste in the back of her throat.

"The one in his chest is."

"This the primary scene?"

Soave shook his head. "There's not enough blood under him. Man was already dead when he was buried here."

"Do we have a line on the primary scene?"

"Not yet," Soave grunted. "And this one's a mess—the gardeners tromped all over it."

Nonetheless, a forensic archaeologist was launching a dig. He and his assistants skimming off thin layers of moist dirt. Carefully sifting it for evidence. Depositing it on drop cloths. It was no different from a historic dig. Except that in this case the history was very recent. And living.

Meanwhile, a forensic entomologist was collecting samples of the insects and egg masses that had colonized Niles Seymour's decaying corpse. The body could not be removed until he was done. The extent of insect development—along with the soil temperature, amount of moisture in the soil and the state of the victim's decomposition—would tell them approximately how long Niles Seymour had been down there. The type of insects might also help them determine the location of the primary crime scene.

Des had seen enough. She motioned for Soave to join her. The two of them and Bliss moved back toward the driveway.

"Tenant also smeared his muddy prints all over the spade and fork he found in the barn," Soave mentioned sourly. "That don't look too promising neither."

"Any of the islanders own guns?" she asked Resident Trooper Bliss.

"Red hunts a little," he replied, scratching his chin thoughtfully. "Jamie keeps a pistol for protection, I believe."

"Rico, I want uniformed troopers to search every house out here for weapons," she said, knowing perfectly well that the odds of the murder weapon being around were slim to none. But she had to look. She couldn't *not* look. "Make sure you get permission first. If you don't get permission, then—"

"We have to get a warrant," he broke in, a defensive edge to his voice. "I *know* that, loot."

She knew that he knew it. She also knew that it was her responsibility to remind him anyway. She was the ranking officer on the scene. If she failed to remind him, and the chain of evidence was compromised because of it, it would be her fault. *Be accountable*. If there was one thing the Deacon had drummed into her, it was this. "Have them search every outbuilding and shed, under every rock. Then meet me back here. We got to take statements from the family."

"Right." Soave went heading off, his arms held stiffly out to his sides in the classic bodybuilder's strut.

"Is that deluxe conference room at town hall still available?" Des asked Trooper Bliss. It had been her command center for three days and nights after the Salisbury killing. She could still remember the smell of the place—musty carpeting, moth balls and Ben-Gay.

"It is," he affirmed. "I'll see that they're ready for you. How else may I be of assistance?"

"You can tell me who else besides his wife had it in for Niles Seymour."

"Everyone," Bliss replied bluntly. "Niles was not a popular fellow."

"Any blue chip prospects?"

Bliss took off his wide-brimmed hat and examined it carefully for a long moment. "Tuck Weems," he said, running a big brown hand over his bristly gray crew-cut. "He accused Niles of roughing Dolly up a couple of months back when he found some bruises on her arms. He, well, threatened to kill Niles. I got involved at that point. Cooled things down—at least I thought I had. She declined to file any charges against Niles. Assured me there was no need to worry, that the two of them were working things out. Dolly and Tuck, they were tight when they were kids. He grew up out here. Tuck's not a bad fellow. Just has a slight problem with authority. And more than his share of personal demons. His father killed his mother and himself when Tuck was in 'Nam. Happened out here, in the carriage house. And it was Dolly who found them." He glanced over at the big yellow house, his face a grim mask. "So, you see, this is not the first time there's been a violent death out here."

"When you say he and Mrs. Seymour were tight, do you mean they were lovers?"

"I wouldn't hazard a guess on that," he replied carefully.

The resident trooper was protecting his own now, Des observed. Clearly, he was very loyal to these people. How loyal?

He put his hat back on and squared his shoulders. "Tuck has a place up at Uncas Lake. I suppose you'll be wanting to question him right away."

"Is he likely to run?"

"No, I don't believe so."

"Then he'll keep," said Des, who liked to fully acquaint herself with the principals before she rushed to judgment. "There a new man in Mrs. Seymour's life?"

"No man in her life, as far as I know."

"Tell me about this tenant. What was his name, Berger?"

Bliss nodded. "He's a New Yorker, I'm sorry to say."

She glanced at him curiously. "Meaning what—he's a total pain?"

"No," Bliss said grudgingly. "He *seems* like a pleasant enough fellow . . ."

Des frowned, sensing that the resident trooper was trying to give her a small nudge in the tenant's direction.

"I mean he's a media person," Bliss explained. "Writes for one of the big newspapers there."

"Okay, I hear you now." She had learned from the Salisbury case that people in Dorset were strongly averse to publicity. They were especially proud of the fact that the vast majority of New Yorkers could not even find Dorset on a map.

"Dolly just rented him the place two weeks ago," he added.

"Could he figure in?"

"Figure in, Lieutenant?"

"Romantically. He and Mrs. Seymour."

"He's quite a bit younger than Dolly, not that that necessarily means no." Bliss shrugged his shoulders. "Who knows what goes on between two people? I certainly don't."

"Was he acquainted with the victim?"

"Not to my knowledge."

"Doubtful he has anything to do with it, then," Des mused aloud. "Besides, why dig up the body himself? Why incriminate himself?"

The trooper nodded in solemn agreement. "And Dolly did give him explicit permission to dig there. I can't imagine *her* doing so if she knew Niles was down there."

"Agreed. Not unless she wanted him found."

The trooper furrowed his brow at her, perplexed. "Why would she want that?"

"I don't know. I don't know anything. I just got here. What do we know about this woman who Seymour was supposed to have run off with?"

"Very little. Bud Havenhurst and Red Peck spotted the two of them having brunch together at the Saybrook Point Inn."

"This was when?"

"Six weeks ago—a Sunday. They described her as young and a bit cheap-looking. The following morning he cleared out and was never seen again. Until now, that is."

Des made a note to check on this woman at the inn. "And what do we know about Seymour's background?"

"He showed up here three years ago from Atlantic City, where he'd been selling time-share condos," Bliss replied with arid disapproval. "I don't know where he was before that. Or what he was doing."

She would have to find out. The time-share business attracted some seriously low-life characters. No telling who Seymour may have crossed swords with. Or what else he had been into. Possibly, it was his past that had followed him out here. Because there was the matter of the money—he had, supposedly, cleaned out their bank accounts before he disappeared. Where was it? Possibly, she reflected, he had owed it to someone. Possibly they had induced him to withdraw it and then had killed him so as to cover their tracks. She would have to follow the money trail. Match up the date of the withdrawals with the date he had disappeared. And the means of withdrawal could prove to be critical. Had he done it in person? If so, there would be witnesses at the bank. If not—if he had done it electronically—there would not be. In fact, the withdrawals might have been done by anyone who knew the correct PINs. His widow, for example. She had the means. Possibly a jealousy motive. But could she have acted alone? Not likely. Seymour was killed somewhere else. No way she could have moved him to the garden and buried him by herself. An accomplice, then. But who?

"Do you want me involved from here on in?" asked Bliss, cutting in on her thoughts. Ordinarily, the resident trooper yielded now to Major Crimes and resumed his regular duties.

"Damned right I do." She had found him to be an exceedingly valuable liaison to the community. He knew the players. He was one of them. "If you don't mind, that is."

"I don't mind at all."

"Where's Mrs. Seymour right now?"

"She's upstairs resting. Her doctor's been out to see her. You'll discover that Dolly is, well, not a strong individual. I would suggest you tread lightly. Which is not to say you wouldn't . . ."

"I hear you, Trooper."

"As for the rest of them," he said, "Bitsy Peck, Bud Havenhurst and young Evan were gathered in Dolly's kitchen last time I looked. Red Peck is about halfway to Japan right now. Mandy Havenhurst's in New York City and Jamie Devers is up at the Great White Whale, his antique shop. The tenant's in the carriage house."

"I do believe I'll start with him," Des said. "When Sergeant Tedone returns, why don't you two set up shop in the kitchen? Give him any assistance he might need while he takes statements. I'll be along soon enough."

"Right." He tipped his hat at her politely and went striding off toward the house.

The front door to the little carriage house was open. She tapped and when she heard a response stepped inside. It was a wonderful little house. But it wasn't the exposed, hand-hewn beams or the huge fire crackling in the stone fireplace that caught her initial attention. It was the *light*—windows, windows everywhere. And nothing but unobstructed views of the Sound. Even on a raw gray day the place was drenched with the purest of natural light. What a studio this would make. Not even in her wildest dreams could Des imagine such a studio.

It was so magnificent that it took a moment for her to notice its occupant.

He was standing in front of the fire, sipping a mug of coffee and staring into the flames. He was a large-sized man, not fat but definitely soft around the edges. He wore a rumpled navy-blue wool shirt and baggy khakis. And when he turned to look at her, there was something unusual about his eyes that Des noticed immediately.

Mitch Berger had the saddest eyes Des had ever seen on any creature that was not living at the Humane Society, its wet nose and furry paws pressed to the door of its cage.

"Mr. Berger, I'm Lt. Desiree Mitry of the Major Crimes Squad, Central District. I have some questions."

"Yeah, sure," he said hoarsely, crossing the room toward her. He was taller than Des by an inch or two. And a good deal wider. "I'm sorry if I'm . . ." He ran a hand through his uncombed hair, clearly distraught. "I guess I'm still a little shook. It was the smell more than anything. I-I wasn't prepared for that, you know? I mean, I've seen that kind of thing in a lot of movies. So I was somewhat conditioned. But the stench . . . I guess I understand now why Smell-o-vision never really caught on in a big way. It's still *there* in my nostrils. I just can't seem to get rid of it."

"Have you got any oranges around?"

"I think so. Why?"

"What you do, you cut off a piece of the peel and rub it in between your fingers. Then sniff 'em. There's an essence in the oil. Fix you right up."

"Thanks, I'm going to try that." He immediately started for the kitchen. "Can I cut you one, too?"

"I'm okay, thanks."

"I guess people like you get used to it."

"People like me never get used to it. I don't like to see anything get dead. Not even a cockroach."

"I guess you've never lived in New York."

She let out a polite laugh while her eyes got busy flicking around the room, taking in the contents. He was a musician. There was an electric guitar and colossal stack of amps. There was a computer. Books and papers. Most everything else in the place looked like it came from a junk shop. All except for the two framed pieces of art that hung from the walls. Over the fireplace there was a framed photograph of Georgia O'Keeffe when she was an old, old woman. Her intricately lined face was as worn as an ancient streambed. It was the face of someone who had known triumph and defeat, love and loss, joy and pain. It was the face of someone who was still hanging on. A survivor's face.

"Great portrait, isn't it?" Mitch Berger said, returning with his orange peel. "I look at her every day and say to myself, 'If Georgia can make it, I can make it.'" Now he rubbed the peel between his fingers and sniffed at them, rather like a large, inquisitive rabbit. "It belonged to my wife," he added.

"You're divorced?"

"No, she died."

"I'm so sorry," she said, making a mental note to check the date and circumstances of his wife's death.

The other piece of art, which hung on the wall to the kitchen, was a computer-generated drawing comprised of horizontal lines that seemed to grow incrementally in width the farther they moved from the center. "And that one?" she asked him.

"That's the Fibonacci Series," he replied. "Last thing my wife designed. She was a landscape architect." He tossed the orange peel into the fire and turned and gazed at Des with his wounded puppy eyes. "So are you a homicide detective?"

"Something like that."

"You must encounter a lot of horrible things."

"We are not a kindly animal, Mr. Berger. We can be especially cruel to the ones we love the most." This particular nugget of hard-edged wisdom she had learned in the bedroom, not the streets. She smiled at him now, looking around. "I am loving this house."

"Isn't it great? There's a sleeping loft upstairs, if you want to take a look."

The bed was unmade, but she paid little notice to that. What she noticed were the skylights. Even more light. She could not imagine what it would be like to live here. Sketching every morning by the dawn's pure light. Jogging on the private beach. Compared to this, her house was like being locked inside a cave.

"Yum, I could get used to this way fast," she commented as she descended the narrow staircase.

"So bring your sketchpad with you next time. Stay a while."

She stiffened, narrowing her eyes at him. "You just said what?"

"You do sketch, don't you?"

Des cocked her head at him, hands on her hips. A pose she did not like. It was strictly Aunt Esther on *Sanford and Son*. She crossed her arms instead and said, "Now how did you know that?"

"The charcoal under your middle fingernail. You dig your nail into the stick. My wife did that, too. Same nail."

She glanced down at it. It was barely noticeable. This was one very observant white man. Scarily so.

"I'd like to see your work sometime," he said with genuine interest.

"It's just something I do for myself," she responded guardedly.

"That's generally the best stuff, don't you think?"

She let his comment go by, at a loss for how he had suddenly made her feel so off balance and exposed. She did not like this feeling. She did not like it at all. She edged over nearer to the fire.

"Can I get you a sweater?" he asked, following her. "Nice warm sweater?"

"Naw, I'm fine."

"You are not. You're shivering. It can get really damp out here. Gets right into your bones. How about a cup of coffee?"

"I'm *fine*, Mr. Berger." Now he was making her feel girlish and helpless. Something else she really did not like.

"Suit yourself. But if you catch cold, don't blame me."

"I never get colds," she said sharply, seizing back control of the interview. "I understand you work for a newspaper."

"That's correct," he said, flopping down in a worn armchair.

"You planning to write about the discovery of Niles Seymour's body?"

He shook his head. "I'm not that kind of writer—I'm a film critic."

"Is that right? I don't believe I've ever met a film critic before." She showed him her dimples, anxious to get him talking. "How does someone end up in that line of work?"

"I get asked that fairly regularly," he replied. "I don't know how. Or why. I only know that something very unusual happened to me the very first time I walked into a movie theater."

"That was what, Mr. Berger?"

"I discovered that I come alive in the dark," he said. "Not so much like a vampire but more like an exotic form of fungus. A darkened movie theater is my natural habitat. I spent my entire childhood there. Everything I know in life I found out in movie theaters. James Cagney showed me what nerve was, Cary Grant charm, Audrey Hepburn grace. Marlene Dietrich taught me how to bend the rules. Robert Mitchum taught me how to break them." He paused now, glancing around at his little house of light. "This place here, this is not me. My being on this island is what screenwriters call Imposed Behavior."

"Imposed Behavior?" she repeated. "What does that mean?"

He stared at her blankly. "You never heard of Imposed Behavior?"

"What I'm saying."

"That's when a character purposely makes himself do something that goes against his nature because, for some vital personal reason, he thinks he needs to. Like when Joel McCrea became a hobo in *Sullivan's Travels*."

"Never saw it."

"You *never* saw it?" he exclaimed excitedly. "God, are you in for a treat! It's one of the great screwball comedies of all time. And then it becomes unbelievably sad. And then it becomes unbelievably funny again. Preston Sturges directed it. That scene in the black church near the end, when they roll the cartoon, I sob uncontrollably every time."

Des raised an eyebrow at him. "I'm standing here thinking I've never met anyone like you before."

He smiled at her. "Already we have something in common—I've never met a woman who's a lieutenant in the Major Crimes Squad before. I really like your locks. You probably hear that all the time."

"All the time," she said brusquely. He was trying to do it again—turn the conversation back on her. "Were you acquainted with Niles Seymour?"

"Never met him. Heard a lot about him, though."

"Such as?"

"Such as he was a virtual prick. Everyone on Big Sister hated him."

"Including Mrs. Seymour?"

"He ran off on her, didn't he? Or at least she thought he had."

"Were you acquainted with Mrs. Seymour before you moved in here?"

"Yes, I was."

Des raised her chin at him. "For how long?"

"I met her several days before—when she showed me the place."

She stared at him stonily. Now he was jamming her. "Are you two involved?"

"I'm not involved with anyone," he stated quietly.

"Uh-hunh. In the short time that you've been here, has anything struck you as curious or out of the ordinary? Anything at all?"

"Well, yeah," he replied, leaning forward in his chair. "A couple of things."

"Such as . . . ?"

Mitch Berger told her that someone had purposely locked him in the crawl space under the house. He opened the trap door for her and flashed a light down there. It was a dark, shallow earthen pit. A horrible place to be confined in.

"Maybe Seymour's killer was trying to get me to leave," he suggested. "Scare me off because *he* was scared I'd dig up the garden and find the body. I *did* ask Dolly if I could have a garden when I first looked at the place. There's no telling who she . . ." He trailed off a moment, scratching his head. "Bud Havenhurst . . . Of course!"

"What about him?"

"He was dead set against me moving in here. He even told me that he'd tried to talk Dolly out of renting me the place."

"Interesting," she said, nodding her head. "And what about Tuck Weems? Would he have known that you intended to dig up the garden?"

"Most likely. This is the kind of place where if one person knows something everybody knows it."

"You said there were a couple of things, Mr. Berger."

"Seymour's prescriptions. He left them behind. I noticed them there in Dolly's bathroom. I thought it was a little strange. If you had left town for good, wouldn't you have taken your pills with you?"

"Which bathroom was this?"

"Top of the stairs." After a moment's hesitation he added, "Dolly is on some serious medication."

"Such as?"

"Such as lithium . . ."

Des waited, watching him carefully now. He had more to tell her. She sensed it. She *knew* it. "Something else, Mr. Berger?"

He started to respond but instead shook his head at her, unwilling to spill it.

She wondered what it was. And why he'd clammed up. But she did not press him, convinced that she would get no more out of Mitch Berger, New York film critic, at the present time. She merely thanked him for his time and started for the door.

"Do you think one of the islanders killed him, Lieutenant?" he asked her.

"I don't do that."

"You don't do what?"

"Spitball."

"But you must have a gut feeling."

"I must. I do. Only I don't share my gut feelings with members of the working press."

"But I told you—I'm not a reporter. I'm just curious."

Des paused at the door, gazing at him intently. "Mr. Berger, what we have here is a situation where someone has lost control, okay? It has been my experience that when an individual loses control once he or she may very likely lose control again. Consequently, my advice to you is this . . ."

"Yes, Lieutenant . . . ?"

"Don't be curious."

He didn't react. Just stared gloomily into the fire. God, he was a mournful specimen. She couldn't be positive, having only known him for twenty minutes, but there was a distinct possibility that Des had just met the loneliest man on earth.

"Mind if I ask you something personal?" she asked, treating him to her maximum-wattage smile.

"No, not at all," he replied, glancing at her curiously.

"Have you ever thought about sharing your home and your heart with a nice warm cuddly individual of the feline persuasion?"

"What can you tell me about your husband's departure last month, Mrs. Seymour?"

"I can . . . tell you next to nothing, Lieutenant," Dolly Seymour replied in a soft, halting voice. "I-I found his letter on the kitchen table when I came downstairs that morning. And . . . And . . ."

"And . . . ?" Des pressed her gently.

"And he was *gone*."

Niles Seymour's widow lay limply on her bed under an Afghan throw, a moist tissue clenched in her small fist, her blue eyes red and swollen from crying. She had been given a strong sedative to help her cope with the shock. It had made her a bit dreamy and slow on the uptake. But she was able to respond to questions. She was a slender, frail-looking woman with a child's delicate face and translucent skin.

Her bedroom was not especially elegant. It was small and the ceiling was quite low. The furniture was of the ordinary department store variety. Bud Havenhurst, her patrician lawyer and ex-husband, hovered attentively in a chair next to the bed. Tal Bliss loomed just inside the doorway, hat in hands. Des sat at the foot of the bed.

Downstairs, Soave was parked at the breakfast nook taking statements from the son and the sister-in-law.

"What did this letter say, Mrs. Seymour?"

"That he was . . . not worthy of me. That he was leaving."

"You still have the letter?"

"Possibly. I can't remember." After a long moment, she added, "No one knew."

"No one knew what, Mrs. Seymour?"

"How kind and gentle he could be. How he could make me laugh."

Des instinctively disliked this woman. Dolly Seymour was rich, white, privileged and weak—a mewling little porcelain figurine. Des resented such women. But she was also aware that there might be more to her than met the eye. Could be Dolly Seymour was not as helpless as she seemed. Maybe she was a cold, calculating schemer who got what she wanted by *acting* that way. Maybe she was a manipulator, a user. Maybe she was even a murderer. "Did your husband ever attack you, Mrs. Seymour?"

Bud Havenhurst stirred slightly in his chair at the mention of this.

"Attack me?" Dolly repeated.

"Strike you. Physically abuse you."

"Why, no. Never."

"You sure about that?"

"She's quite sure," Havenhurst answered for her, his voice icy.

"He arrived here from Atlantic City?"

"Yes," she replied. "We met at the country club."

"And before that? Where was he born and raised?"

"He was a Southie," Dolly replied fondly. "He came from South Boston. His father was a construction worker, his mother a beautician. He developed his love of fine things from her. And his grooming. He always took such wonderful care of his hands. He came from nothing, you see. Never even went to college. But he understood people. He understood style. Style meant the world to him."

She glanced around at her bedroom. "He always wanted to redecorate this room. He loathed it."

"I'll need to see your credit card records, Mrs. Seymour," Des said. "Bank statements. Any and all account information, please."

She didn't respond. Did not, in fact, seem to hear her. She was still gazing around at the bedroom décor. Her lips were moving, but no sound was coming out.

"I think I can help you with that, Lieutenant," Bud Havenhurst cut in discreetly. "Perhaps if we moved downstairs? Dolly's really got to get some rest."

"Very well," Des allowed.

He closed the curtains and turned off the bedside lamp, pausing to stroke his ex-wife's forehead gently. Then they left the room and went down to the study. Havenhurst seated himself at the desk. Des took a chair, watching him skeptically. He was a lawyer. Therefore, she assumed that every word out of his mouth was a lie. Bliss parked himself in the doorway once again, stolid and silent.

The Dear John letter that Niles Seymour had left Dolly was in the top drawer of the desk. It was on a sheet of common copier paper, folded neatly in half. Des cautioned Havenhurst not to touch it—it might contain latent fingerprints. She sent Bliss out for tweezers. She used these to lift it from the drawer. It was a short letter. It read:

Dearest Dolly—I should never have come into your life. You are too fine. And I am too greedy. I must leave you for another now, my darling. Try to remember me fondly. All my love, Niles.

The letter was not handwritten. It had been computer-generated and printed out.

"He didn't sign it," Des observed.

"Why, no. Is that so important?" Havenhurst's eyes widened. "My God, what am I saying? Of course, it is. That never occurred to me before—when I thought he had run off on her, I mean. I just chalked it up to his utter rudeness. But now that we know he never . . . Niles didn't write this at all, did he?"

"Whoever killed him did it, most likely. Chances are, Seymour was already dead."

"*Anyone* could have written it. Anyone with access to their computer." Havenhurst glanced at it there on the desk, his shoulders slumping. "Assuming it was done here."

"We'll try to match it up," she said. "Dust it for prints. Maybe we'll even find it on the hard drive. Although I'm doubting that whoever did this was stupid enough not to delete it."

Bliss went back out to notify a crime scene technician.

Havenhurst remained seated at the desk. "She never locks her doors. It could have been anyone on the island."

"Um, okay, about those credit card and bank statements . . . ?"

Dolly Seymour's ex-husband seemed very far away for a moment. Des found herself wondering where he was. Then he shook himself and opened another drawer. "You'll find their receipts and records here. Seymour's own things are out in the barn—old papers, letters. There isn't much, but . . ."

"Thank you. We'll look at those, too." She sat back in her chair, crossing her long legs. "Why did you try to talk Mitch Berger out of moving in, Mr. Havenhurst?"

"He was a stranger," the lawyer responded mildly. "I knew nothing about him. Still don't, for that matter."

"You sure it wasn't something else?"

He raised his chin at her. "Such as?"

"Such as that you knew what was buried in that garden."

"Absolutely not," he said, bristling at her. "And I would advise you *not* to throw around such reckless and slanderous accusations, Lieutenant. You are *not* handling a drive-by shooting in Hartford's North End. You are *not* dealing with the disenfranchised, the disempowered or the destitute. You are dealing here with individuals of great influence. The cream of our society. And you will behave accordingly, or suffer the consequences. Is that understood?"

No two ways about it, Des reflected unhappily. She would be feeling Captain Polito's hot breath very soon indeed. "I am well aware of where I am, Mr. Havenhurst," she evenly. "I am also aware that a murder has taken place here among your fine, rich cream. I have a job to do. I intend to do it. And I expect you to cooperate. Is *that* understood?"

"Proceed," he snapped.

"Mr. Berger alluded to certain events that have taken place since his arrival. He seems to feel someone was trying to scare him away."

Havenhurst sighed glumly. "He told you about Dolly's episode, I take it."

Des kept her face a blank. "As a matter of fact, he didn't."

Havenhurst got up and went over to the window. He was obviously annoyed with himself for volunteering this.

"Perhaps you would like to," she suggested.

"Very well," he said heatedly. "Dolly occasionally . . . She wanders in the night. She's not a well woman, Lieutenant. It's important for you to understand that. It goes back to an incident that happened here quite a number of years ago."

"The Weems shootings?"

He glanced at her sharply. "I suppose Tal Bliss told you."

"He said Mrs. Seymour found them."

"Hell of a thing for her to experience," Havenhurst recalled. "She went into a serious clinical depression directly after that. There were suicide attempts, several of them. She had to be hospitalized. We almost lost her, Lieutenant. She remains, to this day, an extremely vulnerable creature. If I seem perhaps a bit overly protective toward her, that is why."

"I understand, Mr. Havenhurst."

"No, you *don't* understand," he insisted vehemently. "Because there's more to it than the simple fact that she found the bodies. Certain details were not included in the newspaper accounts. It was possible to keep such things from the public in those days. But as I've no doubt you will soon dig up the official report for yourself, I'll tell you right now what you will find in it."

"And what is that, Mr. Havenhurst?"

"She was raped, Lieutenant," the lawyer answered bitterly. "Roy Weems, the Peck family's own caretaker, forcibly and savagely raped my Dolly. She was a virgin. A carefree, sunny, lovely seventeen-year-old virgin. And that bastard took that away from her forever. He—" Havenhurst broke off, pausing a moment to compose himself. "We believe that his wife walked in on it . . . happening. And that she threatened to have him arrested. So he shot her. And then turned the gun on himself. And that poor Dolly witnessed the entire thing."

Des frowned. "You say that you *believe* she witnessed it . . ."

"That's correct," Havenhurst affirmed, nodding. "We have never known for sure. Not really. You see, Lieutenant, Dolly retains no memory of the incident. To this day, she remembers nothing about it whatsoever."

It was a small convoy of cruisers that headed up the Old Boston Post Road toward Uncas Lake. Resident Trooper Bliss, who knew where they were going, took the lead. Des followed in her car. A third state trooper brought up the rear as precautionary backup.

Soave remained behind on Big Sister to attend to the Seymours' computer and business records. He had, he informed Des, learned very little from the victim's stepson, Evan Havenhurst. As for the sister-in-law, Bitsy Peck, Soave reported, "Loot, I never heard someone talk so much and say so little in my whole life." He still had to take a statement from Jamie Devers. And the island was still being searched for weapons. Two of the islanders remained at large. Redfield Peck, who was still en route to Tokyo, and Mandy Havenhurst, who had not yet returned any of the calls placed to the Havenhursts' New York apartment. According to her husband, she had intended to spend the day at the Metropolitan Museum of Art.

In reality, there were two Dorsets, Des reflected as she drove. One was the Dorset of the Pecks and the Havenhursts, the old money WASP gentry who'd long ago claimed the lush meadows and pastures, the precious Long Island Sound frontage, the village's power structure and its upper social rung. The other Dorset was made up of the people who plowed that gentry's driveways and mowed their lawns and pumped out their septic tanks. Some of them held low-end factory jobs at the Electric Boat submarine plant in Groton. Or toiled as chambermaids at the mammoth Indian reservation casinos in Uncas. Most of these lower-rung people were crowded into the mildewed cabins and cinder-block ranchettes that were squeezed, shoulder to shoulder, around Uncas Lake. The fetid, sulphurous lake was situated five miles inland from the shore. The soil was rocky here, the roads narrow and dark. Kids in dirty diapers rolled around unattended on scraggly front lawns. Dogs roamed loose, sometimes in packs. Idle men sat on their front porches drinking beer in the middle of the day.

There was a name for white people such as these. They were called swamp yankees.

Bliss slowed his cruiser way down when he turned off of the Post Road and started his way through their squalid enclave. The resident trooper knew the territory well. He knew it because he lived here himself.

He pulled up in front of a seedy cottage where a rusty pickup with no tires rested up on blocks in the driveway. An ancient sofa was set out in the weeds out front, surrounded by empty beer cans. He parked and got out. Des did the same. She heard music blaring from somewhere, a dog barking, a baby crying. She could smell spaghetti sauce. And feel a million eyes watching them through windows up and down the street. As always she felt the same mix of anger and intolerance that smoldered within her whenever she was in such a neighborhood, whatever its racial or ethnic make-up. She simply could not understand how people could sit around all day doing nothing with their lives.

The third trooper remained back at the corner of the Post Road, a shotgun mounted to his dashboard.

She and Bliss strode up to the front porch together. The sound of a television blared through the screen door. Bliss knocked on it. A girl's voice called, "It's open—come on in!"

The room was stuffy and reeked of cigarette smoke and soiled diapers. A slovenly, rather bovine-looking girl of no more than eighteen lay sprawled lazily on the sofa, drinking a diet soda and watching one of those trashy daytime talk shows. A naked baby, a boy, dozed peacefully next to her on a blanket. The girl wore a tank top and cut-offs. She had red hair and fair skin and a small, mean face. Her bare arms and legs were soft and sprinkled with freckles. Her feet were pudgy and dirty. She painted her toenails black and wore rings around two of her toes. Also one in her right nostril. She exuded a certain ripe concupiscence in spite of her chubbiness. By age thirty, Des reflected, she would be jowly and jiggly, a pig. By forty she would be an old woman, her tits hanging down like a pair of accordians. Right now, she was just about the same age Dolly Seymour had been when Tuck Weems's father had raped her.

The girl eyed them warily as they stood there in the room with her. But she did not stir from the sofa. Or turn down the volume on the TV. "Whoa, it's the resident trooper man," she said in a mocking voice.

On the sofa next to her, the baby continued to sleep peacefully.

"Darleen, isn't it?" Bliss said pleasantly.

"Yeah, so what?" she shot back defiantly. "Who's *she*?"

Des told her.

"You can think of her as my boss," Bliss added, by way of explanation.

"No way," Darleen exclaimed. "That is so weird. No offense or nothing. I mean, it just is, isn't it?"

"We're looking for your father, girl," Des said.

The girl's eyes went back to the TV. "My father's been dead for fifteen years, ma'am," she said sullenly. "If you're looking for Tuck he's not around. And I haven't seen him since . . ." She trailed off into silence for a moment. "Why, what did he do?"

"Where is he, Darleen?" Bliss asked.

"How should I know? God, can you *believe* these people?" She meant the ones on the TV—two women who had wrestled each other to the floor and were throwing punches. The show's host was egging them on. "Can you *believe* somebody would go on TV and actually *do* that over some man? I mean, why would they do that?"

Because cows like you actually sit here all day and watch it, Des said to herself. This was the truly remarkable part. "Darleen, Tuck may be in a lot of trouble. I'm not saying he is. I'm saying he *may* be. He's wanted for questioning in connection with a murder, okay?"

Darleen's eyes widened. "*Murder?* No way . . ."

"If we don't find him, and talk to him, then I'll have to alert every trooper in the state to be on the lookout for him," Des told her. "Believe me, that will not be a good thing. He will be considered a dangerous person. And I cannot promise that he will not be hurt. All we want to do is ask him some questions. If you care about him, you'll help us."

Darleen took a long drink of her soda, considering this. "What makes you think I care?"

"You had his baby, didn't you?" Des asked.

"What's that got to do with anything?" She reached for a cigarette and lit it.

Des stared at her intently. At the way her soft, childlike hands shook. And her knee jiggled. She was talking plenty hard and tough, but was clearly frightened. She had a baby to take care of. She had no job, no education, and no skills—other than the obvious one. Tuck was her meal ticket, her comfort zone, her home. And now she could see that disappearing right before her eyes.

"Look, I don't know where he is, okay?" Darleen said finally. "I haven't seen him since yesterday."

"He didn't come home last night?" Bliss asked.

Darleen shrugged.

"Does he stay out on you regularly?" Des pressed her.

The girl shrugged again, although this time her nostrils flared slightly. Evidently, Tuck Weems was not a one-teenager man.

"Where's he been working lately?" Bliss asked.

"Nowhere."

"Big Sister?"

"I guess."

"Lock 'n Load still his regular hangout?"

Darleen didn't answer. She'd gone mute.

Des and Bliss exchanged eye contact. They were not going to get anything more out of this girl.

"Thank you for your help, Darleen," said Des, who felt it was her duty to add, "Girl, exposing your baby to secondhand smoke is a serious health risk. It can lead to ear infections, respiratory disease, even heart disease. You do know that, don't you?"

"I am a *really* good mother, ma'am," Darleen snarled in response. "Why don't you take care of your own business, hunh?! Why don't you *leave*?!"

They did just that. Went out the door and down the steps toward their cars.

That was when Des got the call. It came from Soave, who got it by way of the Westbrook Barracks.

The rain-soaked body of a fully clothed adult white male had just been found behind the dunes on a remote stretch of Dorset town beach called Rocky Neck. He had been shot twice. He had been dead at least twelve hours. And he had been positively identified as Tuck Weems.

CHAPTER 7

MITCH'S IDYLLIC ISLAND PARADISE was different now.

It was no longer secluded. It was no longer peaceful. There was no way it could be. Two local men had been shot dead. *The New York Post* was now calling Dorset "the murder capital of Connecticut's Gold Coast." *Inside Edition*, the syndicated tabloid news show, had delivered up Big Sister to the entire nation on a platter: "The blue blood is flowing," declared their breathless correspondent. *Dateline*, not to be outdone, had unearthed the sordid murder-suicide of Tuck Weems's parents, complete with grainy thirty-year-old local news footage of troopers with mutton-chop sideburns. *Entertainment Tonight* had gotten into the act, too, by sniffing out the celebrity angle—Big Sister's own Jamie Devers.

In fact, there were so many reporters clogging the entrance to the bridge that it was hard for Mitch to get off the island. He ventured out only because he needed groceries. Also a few things at the hardware store, where he found out from Dennis that the villagers bitterly resented how Niles Seymour was being portrayed as one of them by the media—which he was not—while Tuck Weems had been labeled as a low-life, when he was actually a decorated Vietnam vet whose family had lived in Dorset since the early 1800s.

The villagers particularly resented the presence of so many news vans and cameras and microphones. They considered it a gross intrusion on their privacy. In Dorset, the only offense that ranked worse than invading someone's privacy was selling your land to a developer.

Lacy sent Mitch a tart one-line e-mail message from the office: *Still think you can be left alone?*

To which Mitch replied: *I'm doing my damnedest not to think.*

His paper's Connecticut correspondent phoned him in the hope of getting Mitch's exclusive firsthand account of how it had felt to dig up Niles Seymour's body. Mitch didn't want to talk about it. "Sure, I understand," the correspondent retorted, thinking Mitch wanted the story for himself. He did not. He wanted no part of it. He didn't like this real-world invasion. He didn't like that his photograph had been in all of the newspapers. He thought about going back to the city until the whole mess blew over. But he didn't want to do that either. So he stayed and tried to work on his book. Only now it seemed hard to get excited about a sagebrush ventriloquist on horseback.

So he was slouched in his easy chair, chasing doggedly after Hendrix's "Little Wing" on his Stratocaster, when Lieutenant Mitry returned to question him for the second time.

She did not bring her sketch pad. She did not knock. She just stood there in his doorway, smiling at him sweetly. "I learn something new every day, you know that?"

"Oh yeah? What did you learn today?"

"Well, I had no idea that Don Ho ever covered Jimi Hendrix's songs."

"Gee. Thank you, large."

"Hey, don't get me wrong, Mr. Berger. I hear 'Tiny Bubbles,' I go to pieces."

"I'll remember that, Lieutenant. Now what can I . . . ?" Mitch trailed off, frowning. "Wait, what was that noise?" he demanded suspiciously.

"What noise?" she said innocently.

"Meowing. I distinctly heard meowing."

"Oh, that's Baby Spice," she said, retrieving a nylon cat carrier from the front porch. There was a small, wide-eyed kitten inside, predominantly gray, and extremely anxious to be let out of jail. "She's free of worms and ear mites. She's had all of her shots. And she comes with a certificate for one neutering, free of charge. She's my best girl. All she needs is somebody to love her."

"Lieutenant, I told you I wasn't interested in taking in a stray cat."

"You sounded wavery."

"I did not," Mitch insisted. "Look, I had one when my wife was alive. That was then. I don't want to go there again, okay?"

"No, it's not okay. You can't take it out on the entire cat population that your wife died of cancer."

Mitch peered at her, startled. He hadn't told her anything about Maisie's cancer. She had been checking up on him.

"We're living in the here and now," she went on. "This is *today*. And today Baby Spice needs a home."

"Did you *have* to name her Baby Spice? I mean, that's really nauseating."

"So I'm not good with names. I know this about myself. Call her Ashley. Call her Heather. Call her any damned name you please. Just take her. You won't regret it. She's the sweetest little thing. She's excellent company. And it's a proven fact that a cat's soothing presence helps reduce a man's blood pressure."

"There's nothing wrong with my blood pressure, or at least there wasn't."

"Just try her out for a few days, okay?" She was already barging her way upstairs to his room with the carrier. "It doesn't work out, I'll take her back. No harm, no foul."

"You're really going to do this to me, aren't you?"

"You've got that right."

"And my feelings don't enter into it at all?"

"Not one bit," she affirmed. "Now I'm going to release her up here in your bedroom. They like to get acclimated in a small, contained space. She may stay up here a few days. When she's feeling ready to come down, she will. I've brought you a week's supply of food. And I've got a litter box in my trunk. All we need is some native sand." Mitch could hear her cooing softly to the kitten now. "Lookie, lookie . . . She just loves your bed."

"How touching."

The lieutenant charged back downstairs and went into his kitchen to fill a saucer with water.

"Just out of curiosity, do the authorities know about you?"

"I am the authority," she replied, carrying the saucer back upstairs. Then she returned, empty carrier in hand. "And you may as well know this—when it comes to cats, I am utterly ruthless."

Mitch did not know what to make of this woman at all. There was something disconcerting about the pale green eyes behind those thick horn-rimmed glasses. Her gaze was so direct, so calm, so lacking in guile or deceit, that he found himself flummoxed by her. Then again, maybe it was just that he had never been alone in a room before with someone who was licensed to carry a loaded semi-automatic weapon. Mitch's experience with the police was extremely limited. His apartment had been broken into once. That was it. He had never been involved in a serious crime.

The lieutenant had. She tracked down killers for a living. She was obviously tough. She was obviously bright. She was obviously a marshmallow when it came to stray cats. She was also someone who did not like to reveal anything personal about herself. Clearly, she'd been bothered when Mitch had noticed the charcoal under her fingernail. Beyond that, Mitch could not read her. Which would not have been of any great concern to him were it not for two undeniable facts.

Fact number one was that she suddenly seemed to be running his life.

Fact number two was that she was good-looking. She was very good-looking. Her skin was smooth and glowing. Her smile, when she flashed it, did warm, strange things to the lower half of his body. And her figure was positively breathtaking. She was a big woman, at least six feet tall, but lithe and loose-limbed and light on her feet. She also happened to possess one of the top half-dozen cabooses he had ever laid eyes on, right up there with Cyd Charisse, Sheree North and Emily Rosenzweig, the girl who had sat in front of him in tenth-grade Biology at Stuyvesant High. Not that the lieutenant was showing it off. Her clothes were downright mannish. She wore no jewelry either. There was no wedding ring.

She was gazing intently at his right bicep now. It was a warm day and Mitch was wearing the complimentary red T-shirt that had been included in the press kit for *Amityville: The Evil Escapes*. "What does that mean?" she asked, referring to his *Rocky Dies Yellow* tattoo.

"It's the headline from *Angels with Dirty Faces*." On her blank look he added, "I guess you're not into old movies. It's one of the best films Cagney ever made for Warner Brothers. A true classic. It's got Humphrey Bogart, Ann Sheridan, Pat O'Brien, the Dead End Kids. Direction by Michael Curtiz . . . What does yours say?"

"My what?"

"Your tattoo."

"What makes you think I have one?" she demanded.

Mitch shrugged his shoulders.

. "It says *The Answer*," she responded grudgingly.

"Are you?"

"On my good days."

"And where do you have it?"

"Somewhere you'll never, ever see it," she said, sneezing.

Mitch shook his head at her. "I told you you'd catch a cold."

"I don't get colds," she objected, dabbing at her nose with a tissue. "It's mold spores. I'm allergic to them."

"Then we'd better get out of here—this house is mold city." Mitch flicked off his amp stack and started for the door. "Let's get you some fresh air."

"Mr. Berger, I do happen to be here on official business."

"Uh-huh. Like Baby Spice is official business. C'mon, let's walk."

She wavered there uncertainly, her feet set wide apart. Clearly, she was ill at ease on Big Sister.

"Look, I'll make this easy for you," he said. "I am taking a walk. If you want to ask me any questions, then I suggest you walk with me. Do you need to use the bathroom before we go?"

"I'm fine, Mr. Berger," she said curtly.

"I wish you'd call me Mitch. How about Kleenex? Can I get you some more Kleenex?"

"Let's walk," she snapped irritably.

They walked, taking one of the narrow paths lined with beach roses down to the beach. It was a bright, beautiful day. The salt air was clean and fresh. Gulls and cormorants soared overhead. But the tide was in and there was almost no dry sand to walk on. Mitch paused to pull off his chunky Mephistos and his sweat socks. Reluctantly, she did the same with her polished black brogans and gray cashmere dress socks. She had, without question, the longest, narrowest feet Mitch had ever seen.

"My God, what size shoe do you wear?"

"Twelve and a half double-A," she replied, frowning. "Why are you asking?"

"Has anyone ever told you that your feet bear a striking resemblance to a pair of skis?"

"Um, okay, anyone ever tell you that yours look just like piglets?" she shot back. "Fat and pink and hairless?"

"Hold on," Mitch cautioned. "I think there was a racial subtext to that remark."

"There was not," she insisted, nostrils flaring.

"Was."

"Man, do you ever stop flapping your gums?"

"As a matter of fact, I do. When I'm working I have to be silent for hours and hours at a time."

She glanced at him, nodding. "Okay, sure. And then as soon as the lights come up the gas just billows right on out of you. Consider me schooled. Next time I question you, Mr. Berger, it's going to be in the dark."

"That's fine by me, just as long as you bring the popcorn. Extra butter, if you don't mind."

"I don't mind one bit," she said, flashing her smile at him. "I'm not the one who has to look at you with your shirt off."

They walked, her dreadlocks swinging, her stride uncommonly long. His own was plodding and rather heavy. He had to work to keep up with her.

"You ever date a woman named Torry Mordarski?" she asked him.

"I don't think so—the name doesn't ring a bell. How long ago are we talking about?"

"In the past few months."

"Oh, then it's definitely no. Why, who is she?"

"*Was* is the operative verb tense. She was a single mother in Meriden. We found her murdered in the woods up there six weeks ago."

"And . . . ?"

"And the thirty-eight slug that killed her matches up exactly with the slugs we took out of Niles Seymour and Tuck Weems."

He glanced at her in surprise. "That wasn't on the news this morning."

"We don't tell them everything. Same way you didn't tell me everything."

"What's that supposed to mean?"

"It means you didn't mention Mrs. Seymour's episodes in the night," the lieutenant said with flinty disapproval.

"I felt it was the family's job to tell you. Besides, I promised Bud I'd keep it to myself."

"And you're a man who can keep a secret."

"I guess. Never gave it much thought—I don't get asked very often."

They plowed their way past the lighthouse in the direction of Big Sister's private dock. Jamie and Evan were working on their sailboat. Bud was working on his boat as well. Mitch supposed that this was what you did when you had a boat—you worked on it. Especially when you couldn't leave the island without being assaulted by the media. Mitch waved to them. All three of them waved back, watching him with frank curiosity as he strode past with the lieutenant.

Overhead, a news chopper hovered, filming the island for the evening news. Mitch was beginning to get an idea what it must be like to be a Kennedy.

"So the same person who killed Niles Seymour and Tuck Weems also killed this Torry Mordarski woman?"

"Same *weapon*. Not necessarily the same person."

"But probably, right?"

"Most likely."

"Have you found the weapon?"

"Not yet. We did find one freshly dug hole in the woods near Mrs. Seymour's house, but all we unearthed was—"

"A dead fox."

She nodded, peering at him.

"I buried it for Dolly the other day." Mitch furrowed his brow, confused. "Well, I don't understand."

"What don't you understand?"

"How Torry Mordarski and the two dead men connect up."

The lieutenant explained it to him. She told him that Torry had been seeing an older man named Stan, an elusive figure who had covered his tracks carefully and was the prime suspect in Torry's murder. She told him that the description of Stan fit Niles Seymour to a tee—although a coworker who had once caught a glimpse of Stan failed to recognize Seymour from his photo. She told him that Torry Mordarski matched the description of the young woman Bud Havenhurst and Red Peck had seen with Niles Seymour at the Saybrook Point Inn the day before he disappeared. All except for the hair color—Torry had been a blonde, not a redhead. The inn had no record of Niles Seymour or Torry Mordarski having been registered there the night of April 17. But they did have a record of one Angela Becker of Lansing, Michigan, having registered there. She had paid cash for the room, so there was no credit card trail to follow. However, since it was standard hotel policy to photocopy the driver's license of any guest who chose to pay with cash, the inn did have that on file. And Angela Becker's driver's license was a fake. In fact, Angela Becker was a fake. There was no such person living at any such address in Lansing, Michigan. Angela Becker's age, height, weight and hair color—red—matched the woman who Bud Havenhurst and Red Peck had seen with Seymour. And the photocopy of her driver's license picture bore a fuzzy resemblance to Torry.

"So you think this Angela Becker person was actually Torry?"

"I do."

"Why use a fake ID?"

"Not so unusual. Seymour was a married man. They worry about leaving paper trails behind for divorce lawyers to find."

"I see," Mitch said thoughtfully. "So if Torry Mordarski was the woman who they saw with Seymour, then that means Seymour was her elusive boyfriend, Stan. And someone got jealous and killed both of them. And then turned around and killed Tuck Weems when Seymour's body was found. Which makes no sense to me at all. Not unless . . ." Mitch paused, nodding his head at her. "Okay, now I know where you're going with this."

Lieutenant Mitry raised an eyebrow at him. "Where is that?"

"You're thinking Dolly is the killer. She found out that her husband was having an affair with this young babe up in Meriden. So she lured Torry into the woods and shot her. Then she came home and shot Seymour. Tuck Weems, her loyal family caretaker, helped her bury him. Maybe he even got her the gun, too. Then *she* wrote the Dear John letter she claimed Seymour left her. Everything would have been fine if I hadn't dug up the body . . . Do you know yet how long it was down there?"

"Preliminary reports from the coroner and forensic entomologist estimate four to six weeks. It plays," she concurred. "Go on."

"Okay, so now she was afraid Weems might talk. Or maybe he threatened to blackmail her. So she met him out at the beach and killed him to cover her tracks. He *was* killed there, wasn't he?"

"He was. And his truck was parked nearby."

"Then it all fits together neat as can be. All except for one thing."

"And what's that?"

"Do you honestly think that nice lady killed three people?"

"I don't think anything, Mr. Berger. I'm strictly trying to get at the truth."

"But she gave me permission to dig there!" Mitch argued heatedly. "No *way* she'd do that if she knew the body was there."

"Maybe she didn't know," the lieutenant countered calmly. "Maybe Weems didn't tell her where he buried it."

"But she left his prescription medicines right out there in the open in her bathroom. If she *had* killed him, if she *had* wanted it to look like he ran away with another woman, wouldn't she have destroyed them?"

"I would have," she conceded. "But that's just me."

"Besides, if Dolly did kill him, then where's all of that money of hers he supposedly absconded with? The man's not gone. The money is. Who took it? Where is it?"

"We don't know that yet. We're still following that particular trail."

"But she'd still have it, wouldn't she?" Mitch persisted. "If she were the killer then she wouldn't be broke, would she? She wouldn't have needed to rent the carriage house out to me, would she?"

"Those are good questions. I can't answer them."

They strode in silence for a moment, Mitch's chest beginning to heave, his brow streaming perspiration. This woman did not believe in a leisurely stroll. A power walk was more like it.

"What else have you found out?" he asked her, puffing. "That you haven't given to the media yet, I mean."

"Mandy Havenhurst has had herself some brushes with the law. It's on the record. Press will be onto it by tomorrow."

"What kind of brushes?" Mitch asked curiously.

"Got busted in an upscale St. Louis suburb in 1994 for attempting to murder her live-in boyfriend. Poured kerosene over him while he was asleep and set him on fire."

"Jesus!"

"Jealous rage, apparently. He suffered extensive second-degree burns, but refused to press charges. Her father paid him off. She cleared out of St. Louis fast and resurfaced in Martha's Vineyard. Where, in 1996, she rammed her new boyfriend's Jeep through the sliding-glass doors of his cottage and pinned him and the woman she'd caught him with up against a wall. Same story—no one pressed charges. It would seem," the lieutenant concluded, "that she doesn't like it when her man strays on her."

"I wonder how she feels about Bud being so attentive toward Dolly," Mitch said, remembering his 3:00 A.M. confrontation with the lawyer in Dolly's kitchen. "That can't make her happy."

"Wouldn't think so."

"That's very interesting," Mitch said, gasping for breath. Lieutenant Mitry wasn't even breaking a sweat. "Anything else?"

"We're beginning to construct a profile of Niles Seymour. And it's not ultra-flattering. He was your classic career low-life. Always skating right on the edge of the law—selling time-shares in half-built retirement villages, stocks over the phone to unwitting widows. Real boiler-room stuff."

"Makes you wonder why Dolly fell for him."

"She was alone and vulnerable. Easy prey for a man who she'd ordinarily know was bad news."

"This sounds like the voice of personal experience."

"Well, it's not," she snapped, abruptly closing that avenue of conversation.

Nonetheless, Mitch found himself wondering why Lt. Desiree Mitry was speaking with him so candidly. Was this some form of cop game she was playing on him? Was she trying to entrap him into incriminating himself? Was he a prime suspect in her eyes? It hadn't occurred to him that he might be. But he could imagine no other reason why she was talking with him this way. "Am I on your radar, Lieutenant?"

"My radar?"

"Do I need to start looking for a lawyer?"

"No, I wouldn't think so."

"That's good, because I happen to hate lawyers. They have no moral compass, no sense of personal responsibility, no conscience, no—"

"Before you go any further I should tell you that I used to be married to one."

"Well, then I'm not telling you anything you don't already know, am I?"

She glanced at him in astonishment. "No, you aren't," she said softly.

So her husband had thrown her over for another woman, Mitch surmised. Briefly, they fell silent, Mitch convinced that he was going to suffer a massive heart attack if he tried to keep pace with this tireless gazelle any longer. He pulled up and flopped down on a beached driftwood log, wheezing. "Are you ever going to tell me what I told you?" he asked, squinting up at her.

"Which is what?" Her eyes were scanning the sailboats out on the Sound.

"How you ended up doing what you're doing."

She shrugged her shoulders. "Graduated from West Point. Got downsized at the end of the Cold War. Went for a master's degree in criminology. Took the state trooper exam. End of story."

"You got the highest test score in the history of the state, didn't you?"

She narrowed her pale green eyes at him suspiciously. "How did you know that?"

"Dunno," Mitch confessed. "I just did." Same as he knew that she was holding something back. He wondered what. He wondered why.

"Uh-hunh," she said doubtfully. "And what else do you know?"

"That you don't like what you're doing for a living."

She let out an exasperated sigh. "What I don't like, Mr. Berger, is the way you keep doing *that*."

"Doing what?"

"Acting like you know me."

"It just comes out. Strange things like that happen sometimes between two people. It's a brain-wave thing. In fact, I happen to know exactly what you're thinking at this very moment."

"Which is . . . ?"

"If that somewhat largish white fellow makes one more personal comment about me I'm going to hit him over the head with my Glock so hard he won't even remember his name."

"Okay, this time you are way wrong," she said, smiling at him. "It's a Sig-Sauer."

"So I don't know very much about guns."

"You're better off. But keep on busting me and you will get on my bad side."

"Which means what—I get another cat?"

"It could happen."

And with that Lieutenant Desiree Mitry resumed walking, her stride even longer and more purposeful than before. She was a good fifty yards away by the time Mitch made it back up onto his feet and started after her.

Bud Havenhurst was fiddling with the trailer hitch on his Range Rover in the courtyard outside of Dolly's house when the lieutenant drove off in her cruiser. His presence was by no means accidental. He was strictly hanging around there so as to pump Mitch.

"What did she want?" the lawyer asked him with elaborate casualness.

"I'm really not sure," Mitch answered truthfully.

"Hey, boy, do you play golf?"

"A bit. Why?"

"I wondered if you'd let me drag you out to the club today," Bud said genially. "We could have a spot of lunch. Play a round. Best place in town to hide out from the press corps."

"I don't have any clubs."

"You can use Seymour's—they're in the barn."

"They're evidence, aren't they?"

"Of what?" Bud's gray eyes twinkled at him playfully. "Is it a date?"

Mitch thought about it, studying Bud Havenhurst carefully. The man's hearty good cheer seemed forced. He acted rattled and unsteady. He had shaved poorly. Perhaps he had something on his mind. What it was Mitch could not imagine. But he was intrigued.

So he said, "You're on—just as soon as I check my bed."

He headed back to his little house and went upstairs, treading softly, to look in on Baby Spice. A truly awful name. He'd have to change it, if he kept her. If he could *find* her. She was not on the bed, in the bed or under the bed. She was not behind the little dresser where he kept his underwear and socks. That was it for the sleeping loft—there was nowhere else to hide. He called to her gently. Listened for a little squeak of response, a rustling, anything. But there was nothing. Mitch had learned long ago that there's nothing on the face of the earth that's harder to find than a cat that doesn't want to be found. And this one did not.

So he left her in peace, wherever she was. He was curious to see the country club. It was very exclusive. Three recommendations and full board approval exclusive, according to Dennis at the hardware store. Places that hard to get into fascinated Mitch.

He even put on a clean polo shirt.

Not that the Dorset Country Club turned out to be much. Eighteen rather flat, weedy holes. Two tennis courts that no one seemed to be using. A swimming pool that was cracked. A drab, circa-1957 vinyl-sided clubhouse furnished with mismatched plaid sofas and a worn, threadbare rug. There was a card room where a number of retirees were passing the afternoon with their eyes closed and their mouths open. There was a dining room. There was no bar. In lieu of one they had a storage cupboard with lockers where members could keep their private stock under lock and key. They carried it to their tables themselves.

Bud Havenhurst produced a half-empty bottle of twelve-year-old Glenmorangie and poured himself a stiff one. Mitch declined his offer. After taking a long, grateful gulp Bud said, "You would be surprised how many members buy bottom-shelf A and P store-brand whiskey and transfer it into expensive single malt bottles."

"Why would they do that?"

"Appearances, Mitch," Bud answered bluntly. "In Dorset, it's always about appearances."

There were about forty or fifty members having lunch in the dining room that afternoon. Still, it was so quiet in there that Mitch could hear the gentle clicking of forks against loose dentures from across the room. Nobody stared at Bud or made a fuss. But a number of people did stop by their table to pat the attorney on the shoulder and murmur sympathetic things. All of them asked after Dolly. None of them asked after Mandy.

"What's good here?" Mitch asked, glancing at the menu.

"Not a thing. In fact . . ." Bud leaned forward so as to lower his voice to a whisper. His breath smelled sour, as if he were rotting on the inside. "The Friday night New England Boiled Dinner is downright *repulsive*. To save on overhead we take turns waiting on tables ourselves. Half of the corn on the cob—which is truly the only edible thing—ends up rolling right onto the floor." He sat back in his chair, gazing down his long narrow nose at Mitch. "That's your famous Yankee frugality for you. Cheapness is what it really is. I ought to know—I handle their business affairs. These people part with a dime like it's their last precious asset on earth. And I'm talking about folks who are millionaires many times over. *'Never touch the principal.'* That's the credo handed down by every Yankee granddad on his deathbed. And, believe me, these people were raised to respect their elders."

They ordered club sandwiches and iced teas. Bud helped himself to another scotch, gulping it down nervously. He was decidedly ill at ease. Frightened, even. Mitch wondered why. Was the man afraid that he might be the killer's next victim?

"I wanted to tell you how much we all appreciate how you've respected our privacy, Mitch," Bud said, his eyes firmly fastened on the tablecloth.

"It's my privacy, too."

"Still, I imagine one could make some real money for disclosing family secrets. Cash for trash—that's what they call it, isn't it?"

"They do."

"Yet you've resisted that. Been extremely discreet." Bud cleared his throat. Now his eyes were focused somewhere over Mitch's left shoulder. "Even with regards to the lieutenant. It's admirable. We're all grateful, Mitch."

The club sandwich lived up to Bud's advance billing. The toast was cold, the bacon undercooked, the turkey processed. It came with a side order of potato chips. Mitch popped one of these into his mouth. It was stale. He chewed on it, waiting for the lawyer to continue. Mitch was positive this was about more than gratitude.

Bud ignored his own lunch. "There's something highly confidential I would like to discuss with you, Mitch," he said in a low, urgent voice. "You see, I am a man in desperate need of help. Can I count on you, Mitch? Can I trust you?"

"Of course. But what's this all about?"

"Not here," Bud whispered, glancing furtively around at the other members in the dining room. "Out on the course. We'll talk out there." He glanced at his watch. "Our tee time's in ten minutes. Eat up—if you can."

The Dorset Country Club's first hole was a relatively short par four. But the player's tee shot had to carry over a pond. Which, to Mitch's point of view, was not very friendly at all. He invited Bud to drive first so he could get in a few extra practice swings. He hadn't played in over a year. And had taken only a handful of lessons from club pros at the various resort hotels where the various film festivals were held. That was what Mitch generally did to unwind at festivals since he did not gamble, chase women or hang out in bars. He had a wild, unrefined swing. When he connected he really connected. When he did not he really did not.

Bud's swing, on the other hand, was grooved, compact and accurate. His tee shot carried the water hazard easily and landed smack dab in the middle of the fairway. Not much distance for a man of his size. But no embarrassment either. Safe. That was his game.

Mitch had long ago gotten over the fear of making a fool of himself on the course. He stepped up to the tee. He gripped it. He ripped it. Cleared that water hazard with ease, too—on his fourth try. His first three drives dribbled into the pond and sank without a trace.

"Nice one!" Bud exclaimed when Mitch finally connected. "Straight and true!"

Mitch gathered up Niles Seymour's bag and marched down the cart path after it. It felt odd to be playing with a dead man's clubs. Knowing that Seymour's sweat had dried on the very same hand grip that Mitch was now clutching. He'd even found Seymour's worn, crusty glove in a side pocket of the bag. Which he'd chosen not to wear. A scorecard was stuffed in there as well. Seymour had shot an 87 his last time out. Mitch wondered if he'd cheated. He figured he had.

The course was deserted. No one was ahead of them or behind them.

As they walked toward their tee shots Bud Havenhurst took a deep breath and blurted out, "It's about this missing money of Dolly's, Mitch. Niles had nothing whatsoever to do with it. *I* did, the truth be told."

"Exactly what are you telling me here?" Mitch asked him. "You embezzled Dolly's savings?"

"Absolutely not," Bud answered vehemently. "I *secured* them. I had the idea Niles was preparing to leave. When I saw him with that woman, I mean. If a married man is planning to stick around he does not carry on with some babe in public. Not around here he doesn't. It's a kind of unwritten rule. Hence, I was deeply, deeply concerned for Dolly's financial welfare. The man was a naked opportunist—I felt certain he was about to clean her out and run. So, strictly in the interest of shielding her assets, I did something a shade unethical. . . ." He paused now to play his second shot, a 5-iron. Again, he played it safe, laying up just short of the green so as to avoid the sand trap. "I have power of attorney," he continued. "I have the PINs to her checking and savings accounts. Also a key to her safety deposit box, where the stock certificates were kept. I liquidated everything. And hid it where Niles couldn't get at it—in my own safety deposit box. That's where it is at this very moment. Every penny of it. It's not for me. I swear it's not. It's for Dolly. But I did it without her prior knowledge or consent. She doesn't even know it's there. And now the state police are looking into it. And I could be disbarred. Christ, I could even go to jail."

Mitch shanked his own iron shot badly. It didn't go more than ten yards down the fairway. But he nailed it on his next try. It went streaking straight at the green. It went streaking straight *over* the green. They resumed walking, Mitch shaking his head. "Why don't you just tell Dolly? Why *didn't* you tell Dolly? The poor woman thinks she's broke."

"That's a fair question, Mitch," Bud allowed, sticking out his big chin. "In response, I can only say I had a compelling personal reason—Mandy. She's pathologically jealous of Dolly. And if she were to find out I've jeopardized my career for her, well, let's just put it this way—I don't want her to find out."

"Afraid she'll set you on fire while you sleep?"

The lawyer glanced at him sharply. "Lieutenant Mitry knows about that?"

"She does," Mitch affirmed. "Doesn't it bother you—living with a woman who's so volatile?"

"Mitch, when you get to be my age you won't ask a question like that," the lawyer responded, smiling wanly. "You'll understand that passion is something rare and precious. It was missing from my life for quite a long time. A man will go to great lengths to get it back. Even if that means accepting a bit of . . . uncertainty. With Mandy, I've gotten it back. And I've never been happier."

Mitch wasn't sure whether he believed him or not. The man baffled him. He had seemed so proper, so responsible. Yet the more Bud talked now, the more unhinged he sounded. In fact, if what he'd said was to be believed, the man was pathologically self-destructive. *Was* he to be believed? *Had* he put his career and his second marriage in jeopardy in order to protect Dolly's assets? Or had he cooked up something far more fiendish—and was now merely trying to spin the truth in such a way that would keep him clear of the murders? Just how clever was this man? How good a liar?

"I repeat," Mitch said. "Why don't you just tell Dolly?"

"I've told you—because Mandy will find out."

"Why didn't you think of that when you did it?"

"I wasn't exactly expecting Niles to turn up dead, was I?"

"Well, what *were* you expecting?"

"That he'd turn up in Boca or Vegas or some such hole," Bud said. "I'd tell Dolly I'd managed to put the squeeze on him to cough up or else—not bothering to go into any details. And that would be it."

The lawyer used his wedge now to chip onto the green. His ball rolled within eight feet of the cup. If he holed it, he'd make par.

Mitch didn't see his own ball anywhere. He would have to go hunt for it. "You said you thought I could help you. How? What can I possibly do?"

"I haven't got long, Mitch," Bud answered, his voice rising with desperation. "A day at most. The lieutenant is bound to figure it out. And when she does she will lower the boom on me."

"So why don't you explain it to her? She seems like a reasonable person."

"My thought was that if it came from *you* it might conceivably stay off the books, as it were. Because this *can't* go in her official report. If it does I'll be disbarred. You do understand that, don't you?"

Mitch stared at the man in disbelief. "You want *me* to tell her?"

"Well, yes. You two are friends, aren't you?"

"We are?"

"She's going for barefoot strolls on the beach with you, isn't she? I saw you two together this morning. You seemed very tight."

"She was *questioning* me, Bud. We were walking on the beach because she's allergic to the mold in my house. Or so she claimed. *I* think she has a cold—but that's beside the point. The point is, you were totally mistaken. We aren't friends. In fact, I would go so far as to say the lieutenant actively dislikes me."

Bud's face dropped. "Christ, now I've gone and screwed the pooch. I've told you everything." He ran a hand through his neatly trimmed salt-and-pepper hair, clearly distraught. "Now you *have* to tell her."

"I don't *have* to do anything," Mitch shot back, suddenly feeling himself getting sucked in deeper and deeper.

"I didn't mean that the way it sounded," Bud said hastily. "Oh, beans, I don't know what to say, Mitch. I'm completely at sea. You were my best hope."

Mitch sighed inwardly. *I am lost in a foreign language film. I can't figure out what is going on. I don't understand these people*. "Look, Bud," he finally said to him. "I honestly think the truth will go down a whole lot better coming from you. But if you really want me to, I'll tell Lieutenant Mitry for you."

The lawyer's face broke into a huge grin. "Thanks, Mitch," he exulted, pumping his hand gratefully. "You're the real goods. A true friend. Somehow, I just knew I could count on you."

It was midafternoon by the time Bud maneuvered his Range Rover through the crowd of media people at Peck Point and back out onto Big Sister.

They had played nine holes. Bud shot himself a respectable 43. Mitch holed out with a sparkling 57.

The resident trooper's cruiser was parked outside of Dolly's house. Tal Bliss was helping Dolly and Bitsy unload groceries from the trunk of her old blue Mercedes.

"Anything new, Tal?" Bud asked the big trooper as Mitch hopped out and fetched his borrowed golf bag from the back.

Bliss shook his head. "Just making sure the girls could go about their business."

"We've been shopping," Bitsy burbled brightly. "And it was not pleasant. Those reporter persons—they just will not take no for an answer."

"Say, aren't those Niles Seymour's clubs?" Bliss asked Mitch sharply.

"Why, yes," Mitch replied. "Bud thought it would be okay if I used them."

Bliss pondered this disapprovingly, hands on hips. "Is that so?"

"He's absolutely right, Tal," Bud said placatingly. "I did."

"It's perfectly fine, Tal." Dolly rested a small hand on the trooper's sleeve. "Niles no longer has any use for them."

"Fair enough, Dolly," Bliss said gently. "If you say so."

"How are you feeling?" Mitch asked her. Her eyes seemed a bit unfocused. He suspected she was on tranks.

"I shall be fine, Mitch," Dolly replied. "It was the not knowing—

where Niles was, what he was doing. Now that I *do* know, now that I have some sense of closure, I can begin to . . ." She broke off, her voice choking with emotion. "I don't need to tell you the rest, do I, Mitch? You know what it feels like to lose the one you love."

"Yes, I do," Mitch said quietly, feeling the trooper's steely eyes on him. Bliss didn't seem to like her talking to him so intimately.

"And I *did* love him," Dolly added, her voice soaring with defiance.

"Of course, you did," Bitsy clucked, putting a protective arm around her.

"Everyone assumes I didn't," she said bitterly. "Because *they* didn't approve. They thought he wasn't good enough for me. They thought I was a fool. But Niles Seymour *talked* to me. Niles Seymour *listened* to me. He made me feel wanted and desired."

Clearly, all of this was pointed directly at Bud, whose lips immediately tightened. After a brief, awkward silence, the lawyer elected to bail—got back in his Ranger Rover and eased down the driveway toward his own house.

"Poor Tuck, though," Dolly lamented sadly. "He knew so little joy in his life. And now . . ."

Bitsy steered her inside. Bliss followed with the groceries.

Mitch deposited the dead man's clubs back in the barn and strolled home, where he found a hand-lettered invitation taped to his front door:

Jamie Devers and Evan Havenhurst
present
A Supper Cruise
A sophisticated comedy in three acts
starring Mr. Mitch Berger
Location: The B.S. pier   Time: 6:00 this evening
Boating shoes are a must
A reply is not—you wouldn't dare turn us down!

Well, well. First a lunch invite from Bud. Now this. I am suddenly a very popular fellow on this island, Mitch reflected. What now? What did *they* want? Maybe they didn't want anything. Maybe they were just being nice.

There was, of course, only one way to find out.

He cranked up the old Studey and went riding, high and bouncy, over to Old Saybrook for a pair of boating shoes at Nathan's Country Store, a narrow, old-fashioned general store on Main Street that had worn wooden floorboards and a genuine penny candy counter. It was Barry, the bearded storekeeper, who explained to Mitch why the white-soled Topsiders were a must—ordinary shoes left stubborn black marks on the surface of the deck. This was not something that had ever occurred to Mitch, who also bought himself a pair of green rubber wading boots so he could slog farther out into the tide pools.

Mitch did something else while he was in Old Saybrook. He cruised out past the elegant North Cove waterfront mansions toward Fenwick, the very exclusive colony of shingled summer cottages where Katharine Hepburn was living out her last days. Here, in the shadow of the Old Saybrook lighthouse, Mitch found the Saybrook Point Inn, where Torry Mordarski had spent one night and paid cash. And where Bud Havenhurst and Red Peck had seen her and Niles Seymour breakfasting together. It was a spanking-new, ultra-posh resort hotel with docking facilities for boaters, a restaurant and a health spa. The grounds were immaculate. The brass plates on the lobby doors were polished to a sheen. A community events calendar out front notified passersby of the Lion's Club breakfast later that week. And discreetly advertised *Our famous Sunday brunch—A Shoreline Tradition*. The parking lot was crowded with luxury imports and sport utility vehicles from New York, Rhode Island and Massachusetts. As Mitch idled there, a well-tailored executive with a briefcase came out and climbed into a fancy black Lexus. Four terribly proper old ladies emerged a moment later, somewhat tittery from a long, liquid lunch. A bell-hop brought out someone's bags, eyeballing Mitch's dilapidated truck with snooty disapproval.

Mitch moved on, seriously puzzled. It didn't figure. This was no hideaway. This was no place for a middle-aged married man to stash a young babe. It was a hub of community activity. High profile. High traffic. High class. Why on earth had Seymour brought Torry here? Had the man *wanted* to be seen with her? Why?

There was still no sign of Baby Spice when he got back. Her litter box had not been used. Her food did not appear to have been touched. It wasn't until Mitch fetched a sweatshirt out of his dresser that he finally found her—curled up in there among his clean socks, fast asleep. How she got in there he could not imagine—the drawer was only open a crack. She stirred and squeaked hello at him. He picked her up and put her down on the bed. She had a good deal of light brown mixed in with the gray. And her tummy was almost completely white. Big ears, like a bat. And sharp little teeth and claws, he quickly found out.

Mitch stretched out on the bed with her so they could get acquainted. She immediately scampered up onto his chest, exceedingly perky and playful. She pad-padded around, tumbled off, climbed back up, rolled over onto her back with her paws up, daring him to pet her soft white belly. He began wiggling his hand around under the covers. She pounced on it, yowling, and chased it around the bed. As Mitch lay there, playing with her, he began toying idly with a name. Possibly something with a Western bent to commemorate this book. He ran through his favorites. It was not very fruitful. There were no significant women characters to be had in *The Magnificent Seven*, for example. In fact, there was a paucity of female names, period. Until he got around to *My Darling Clementine*, John Ford's 1946 epic about Wyatt Earp and Doc Holliday. One of the best, in Mitch's opinion. Brilliant black-and-white photography by Joseph P. MacDonald. Clementine Carter, played by Cathy Downs, was Henry Fonda's lady love, the nurse who came out from Boston in search of her wayward fiancé, Doc Holliday. Clemmie, Doc called her. *Clemmie*. She was curled up in the crook of Mitch's neck now, purring like a small motorboat as he petted her. In fact, she was asleep again. She seemed to have two speeds—on and off. She seemed to have a tranquilizing effect, too. Because Mitch soon discovered that his eyes were heavy and his limbs somewhat numb.

Soon, the two of them were out cold together.

There was no sign of Evan and Jamie at the dock when Mitch made his way down there in his new shoes promptly at six. After hanging around a few minutes, he moseyed up to their stone cottage next to the lighthouse. A minivan was parked outside, crammed with furniture. Evan's Porsche was there, too. The cottage's front door was wide open. Mitch found the two of them in the kitchen frantically flinging food and drinks into a pair of ice chests.

"Don't mind us, Mitch, we're *always* late," apologized Evan, who seemed terribly flustered.

The stone cottage was very damp and cold inside. It was also very crowded with antiques. There seemed to be three too many of everything—rocking chairs, weather vanes, end tables, cupboards. Mitch found it almost impossible to fight his way through all of it.

"We're compulsive buyers," Jamie explained. "When we run out of space we take things to our store and sell them."

"I think," Mitch grunted, squeezing his way around a parson's bench, "that it may be time."

Over the fireplace were a number of framed photos of the two of them with their late dachsund, Bobo. The dog's collar and tags were displayed there. The dog's bowl was displayed there. And Bobo was displayed there. On the mantel in an ornate silver urn with her name engraved on it. They'd had her cremated.

"Give us ten more minutes," Evan said to Mitch pleadingly. "Why don't you check out the view from the lighthouse? The key's just inside the front door."

"We have to keep it locked," Jamie said, "or the acne-encrusted indigenous youth sneak out here at low tide and fornicate up there."

"Take the lantern, too," Evan added. "The stairway's pretty dark."

Mitch wrestled his way back through the clutter to the front door, where he found the key and the lantern hanging on hooks. The key popped open the padlock on the lighthouse's massive steel door. The door's hinges creaked ominously as he flung it open—shades of *The Old Dark House* with Boris Karloff. Inside, he flicked on the lantern and found himself at the base of a six-story-high corkscrew. He climbed the spiral staircase slowly and steadily, his footsteps echoing in the narrow, cylindrical tower. He was, he realized, getting more than his share of exercise on this particular day. He was panting by the time he got to the lantern room, where its twin thousand-watt lamps had once served to warn seafarers of the treacherous rocks to be found here. But the lamps and lenses and workings had been removed. Now there was only the empty glass-walled chamber, its bare cement floor littered with cigarette butts and marijuana roaches.

And there was the view. What a view it was. A true 360-degree panorama. Mitch stood there, awestruck, drinking it all in. He could see so far up and down the coastline that he could actually make out its shape as it appeared in maps. In front of him, he could practically reach right out and touch Fisher's Island. Behind him, he could see all the way up the Connecticut River to the old cast-iron bridge at East Haddam. Below him, Big Sister was no more than a lush green meatball in the middle of the sea, a narrow wooden lifeline connecting it to the Point.

Two tiny figures in matching yellow windbreakers were standing at the dock waving their arms up and down at him in some secret semaphore code known only to them. Smiling, Mitch headed back down the corkscrew and joined them, full of appreciative noises.

Their boat was called *Bucky's Revenge*. It was a low-slung J-24 racing boat. It had a cabin down below with a galley and space for four people to sleep. Jamie and Evan were in the process of stowing the ice chests down there.

"I'd better warn you," Mitch cautioned them. "I am the ultimate landlubber."

"You are not alone, Mitch," Jamie assured him. "Evan sails the whole boat by himself. All I do is pretend to steer."

Evan was presently unwrapping the sail bags. First, the bright blue canvas bag around the mainsail, then the green one around the jib.

"Here, put this on," Jamie said, tossing Mitch an orange life jacket. He wriggled into one himself and yanked on the outboard motor starter. When it was putt-putting convincingly he said, "Okay, we can cast off now."

"You want me to untie that rope?" asked Mitch.

"Please," said Evan as he stowed the sail bags down below. "And it's not a rope, it's a *line*."

"Ignore him when he gets nautical, Mitch," Jamie advised drily. "I do."

The line was wrapped around a cleat that was bolted to the dock. Mitch unwound it and jumped back onboard *Bucky's Revenge* and they pulled slowly away, bobbing along on the blue water like a rubber duck. It was quite calm, and there was very little breeze.

Evan raised the mainsail while Jamie manned the tiller, edging them away from the mouth of the river eastward in the direction of Long Island's Orient Point. Mitch huddled in his life jacket watching Evan, who was totally in his element on a sailboat, quick and nimble as a cat. Tying this line. Untying that line. Darting here, darting there. Never wasting a motion. Never losing his balance. It was a pleasure to watch him. There weren't many other boats out now, just a couple of late-afternoon fishermen. As they moved farther out into the Sound, the water grew choppier and the air began to freshen. Soon, the breeze was downright stiff. The sails began to billow and flap. Evan signaled to Jamie to kill the engine. Jamie did. And they were sailing now, scooting right along in glorious, windborne silence, the J-24 trim and swift and sure.

A serene glow came over Jamie's face as he hunched there in his life jacket, hand on the tiller. "This is the best time to come out," he said. "You almost always get a breeze."

"I guess I can see why you left Los Angeles."

"I never left, Mitch. My body is here, but my mind is still there. And it always will be." Jamie had brought along a boombox. He reached down and flicked it on. Now they were cutting through the water to the sounds of "I'm a Believer," by The Monkees.

"Jaymo, do we *have* to listen to your oldies crap?" Evan objected.

"That's the best thing *about* crap, my young friend. It never goes out of style." To Mitch, Jamie said, "Did you know that they went with Mickey Dolenz over me at the very last minute?"

"No, I did not."

"It's the absolute truth. I had the part. They *told* me I had it—for twenty-four blissful hours I was actually a Monkee. And then, just like that, I wasn't. They wanted a new face, was what my agent said. God, I was bitter. It is not easy to be told you're an *old* face when you still can't buy a drink or vote. I was washed up at twenty, Mitch. When I didn't get The Monkees—that's when I knew." He let out a heavy sigh. "That's also when I started getting heavily into drugs."

They seemed to be slowing a little now. Evan took over the tiller from Jamie, but to no avail. "The wind's shifting," Evan said. "Let's come about." He immediately started busying himself with the lines.

"What do I do?" Mitch asked.

"You duck," Jamie ordered sharply.

Mitch did—just as the boom swung directly over his head.

Soon, they were zipping through the water again.

They were approaching a tiny speck of an island—not much more than a heap of rocks with a light tower on it. Cormorants perched on the tower. There was a crude dock. Jamie steered them directly for it, nudging the sailboat up gently next to the piling. Evan hopped out and tied them to it. Mitch hopped out as well, grateful to have something firm under his feet again.

"Do they mind people docking out here?" he asked Evan.

"Does who mind, Mitch?"

"Whoever owns it."

"I own it," Evan said modestly. "This is Little Sister. It became mine when I turned twenty-one." He glanced around at it a moment, hands on his slim hips. "We camp out here fairly often. Sleep under the stars. It's just incredibly peaceful. I'd love to build a cabin out here someday."

They had brought a portable barbeque to grill on. Evan got busy lighting the coals while Jamie uncorked a cold bottle of Sancerre and poured three glasses.

After he had handed them around Jamie lit a cigarette and stretched out on the dock, watching his young lover with a mixture of affection and apprehension. "You may as well know, Mitch, that Evan and I have been spatting. He wasn't planning to go to Seymour's funeral. I told him it was fine by me, since *I'm* not planning to go. Only now he's decided he *will* go, out of respect for Dolly. I think he's being a complete hypocrite. What do you think?"

Mostly, Mitch thought that he did not want to get caught in the middle. "How did you feel about your stepfather?" he asked Evan.

"First of all, I didn't consider him my stepfather," Evan replied angrily. "Just some low-life sleaze she was living with. I honestly don't understand why she married him."

"Possibly, he was exceedingly well hung," Jamie suggested.

"Jaymo, that's my mother you're talking about," Evan said indignantly.

"I know, but she *is* something of a cunning little user, our Dolly," Jamie observed, puffing on his cigarette. "That helpless act of hers, designed to make every man she meets go four paws up. It amazes me it works. But it *does* work. Why, I'll bet she's even hit on our young friend here."

"Not really. All she's done is ask me to open her pimientos for her."

Jamie let out a huge guffaw. "Let me guess—she was wearing something low-cut at the time. Am I right?"

He was, but Mitch didn't feel like touching that one in front of Evan. He sat there perched on a rock, sipping his wine and wondering if Jamie was on to something. *Was* Dolly a scheming manipulator? She certainly did have Bud jumping through flaming hoops for her. Maybe she had persuaded him to raid those accounts for her.

Maybe that wasn't all she'd persuaded him to do. Maybe he had killed for her.

"So spill, you tight-lipped cipher," Jamie commanded Mitch. "What did Lieutenant Mitry say? Whom does she suspect? Dish, damn it."

"Well, there's a third victim. Same gun. Her name was Torry Mordarksi."

"My God," Evan gasped.

Mitch looked at him in surprise. "You knew her?"

"No, no." Evan came over with the wine and refilled their glasses. "But I do remember her murder—it was on the news a few weeks ago. She was real pretty and she had a nice little boy who she was raising by herself. I just thought it was so sad."

"Where did this one happen?" Jamie asked.

"They found her body in the woods somewhere near Meriden," Evan replied.

Jamie stiffened. "No way. Niles bragged to me once that he had a girlfriend up in Meriden . . ."

"He did?" said Evan. "You never told me that."

"He even went into graphic detail about how she used to suck on his dick," Jamie went on, his voice rising angrily. "The crude, homophobic bastard wanted to know if I thought a man could ever be as good at it as a woman." He stubbed out his cigarette, glancing at Evan. "I didn't say anything to you about it because I thought you'd get upset."

"Does the lieutenant know about this?" Mitch broke in.

"Absolutely," Jamie replied. "I told her sergeant person, that short one with the muscles and the fuzzy lip."

"And . . . ?"

"He didn't react one bit. But they never do, do they?" Jamie's eyes gleamed at Mitch intently now. "Let's not kid each other, Mitch. Does she suspect either one of us?"

Mitch sipped his wine uneasily. It had just occurred to him, with a sinking feeling, that he had not been very smart. Here he was, alone on this deserted island with two of the prime suspects. No one knew they were out here together. If they were to murder him and dump his body overboard into the Sound not a soul would ever know. "She knows that you disliked him. But she gave me no indication that you were at the top of her list."

Jamie said, "If Bud Havenhurst had one ounce of nerve he'd be her most logical suspect. Hell, he had more reason than any of us to despise Niles. But I just can't imagine him killing anyone. He hasn't the *cojones*."

Evan poked at the coals. Judged them ready. Put the tuna steaks on the grill, where they immediately began to sizzle. "I agree. Mandy is way more the type. Hot-blooded. High-strung. Tough as nails."

"Okay, what if Mandy was boinking Niles on the side," Jamie speculated aloud. "And when she found out that he was two-timing her with Torry, she killed them both."

"But what about Weems?" Evan wondered. "Why'd she kill Tuck?"

"He found out," Jamie answered. "Saw her burying the body in the garden."

"*Why* bury it in the garden?" Evan persisted.

Jamie had no answer to that one. Stymied, he turned to Mitch.

"Clearly, whoever did it assumed that it *wouldn't* be dug up," Mitch said. "My being there was not part of the original equation. But I do have to admit that the same question has occurred to me. Why the garden? Why not dump Niles out in the Sound somewhere?"

"Bodies have a way of washing ashore," Jamie pointed out.

"Okay, then why not bury him in the woods?"

"Couldn't take the chance of transporting him," Jamie suggested. "He was buried in the garden because he was *shot* near the garden. Must be."

"Suggesting he was killed in Dolly's house," Mitch mused aloud. "Or in her barn."

"Or in your carriage house," Evan added.

Mitch fell silent. That was not a thought he wanted to dwell upon.

"Surely the lieutenant must have *someone* in mind," Jamie said to him.

"Judging by the direction her questions were taking," Mitch said, "it would seem that her leading candidate is Dolly."

"Not a chance," Evan said. "My mother is not capable of doing that."

"No one is, my boy," Jamie said darkly. "Until they do it. Me, I keep thinking about Red."

"What about Red?" asked Mitch.

"He logs four flights a month, right? That means he's *gone* four days a week, every week. Face it, Red's got the perfect setup."

"For what?" Evan asked.

"For a man who's leading a double life," Jamie answered.

Mitch frowned at him, puzzled. "You've lost me. It's not as if he has a romantic interest here—Dolly is his own sister."

"Oh, grow up!" Jamie shot back. "How do you think that blood of theirs got to be so blue?"

"Jaymo, I truly don't believe what I am hearing from you!" Evan erupted.

"All right, we'll forget that one," Jamie conceded grudgingly. "But Red *has* been known to play the protective big brother. Could be he killed Niles for cheating on Dolly."

"But why kill the girl?" Mitch asked.

Jamie considered this. "That's a good question. I don't know . . . Unless *he* was boinking her, too. I mean, let's get real here—could you imagine being married to Bits?"

"I think she's a very nice lady."

"Yeah, yeah, yeah. But just imagine years and years of that abundant, earthy good cheer. Imagine burying your face between those pillowy white thighs night after night—"

"Jaymo, that's my aunt you're talking about!" Evan objected, poking at the tuna. "Hey, I think these are ready, guys. Let's eat."

There was a red onion and mango relish for the tuna. There was black bean salad, cole slaw, cornbread. All of it courtesy of Evan. All of it delicious. They ate on paper plates with their legs dangling over the side of the dock. The sun was setting now. Overhead, the sky was streaked with red and purple. The moon was rising. There were, Mitch reflected, worse ways to spend an evening.

"Maybe that niceness thing of Bitsy's is all an act," Jamie plowed on. "Maybe she's the tramp of the century. She's got plenty of opportunity, what with the kids out of the house and Red gone half of the time. *Maybe* she's even a killer. Have you thought of that?"

"You don't actually believe any of that, do you?" Evan asked him. "I mean, I had no idea you felt this way about her."

"I don't," Jamie assured him with a wave of his hand. "I'm just hypothesizing."

"Well, if you don't start behaving yourself Mitch and I will leave you here. Won't we, Mitch?"

"We will—lashed to the light tower."

There were homemade brownies for dessert. Jamie disappeared below deck in search of them.

As soon as he did, Evan quickly turned to Mitch. "Mother told me you were locked in your cellar on Monday," he said in a low, hushed voice.

"Most of the afternoon," Mitch acknowledged, nodding.

Evan glanced furtively over at the boat, then back at Mitch. "I saw someone's car parked in Dolly's courtyard when I pulled in that day . . ."

"You mean you know who locked me in?"

"Maybe. I thought you might want to know. Who it was, I mean."

"You're right. I did. I *do*. Who was it?"

Evan looked over his shoulder at the boat once more. And then, in an urgent whisper, he told Mitch who it was.

CHAPTER 8

DES RAISED A LONG, smooth leg out of the swirling hot water and examined her bare foot in the light of dawn, rotating her ankle slowly, splaying her toes, admiring the way the water gleamed on her pearly pink toenails. It was, in her critical judgment, a shapely, high-arched foot. A slender foot. A lovely foot.

It was not any goddamned ski.

She lowered her leg back down into the water, groaning. The soothing relaxation of the hot tub was just what she'd needed right about now. Her shoulders and back ached. Her sinuses were inflamed. And she was desperate for sleep—she'd worked straight on through the night. Just came on home, fed the cats and went on Dawn Patrol. Big Willie had inched another step closer to the cage. But he was still too smart for them. In fact, Des was beginning to suspect that the little man was laughing at them.

She reached lazily for her tumbler of chilled orange juice and took a long drink, wiping the perspiration from her face with a wash cloth. "Talk to me about Berger with an E," she murmured across the tub at Bella. "That a Jewish name?"

"It can be," Bella replied, swiping at the perspiration on her own round, flushed face. Actually, Bella's face looked remarkably like a bunched fist when she didn't have her glasses on. "Or it could be German. What's his first name?"

"How do you even know I'm talking about a *he*?"

"If it were a *she* you wouldn't be asking."

"You should have been a detective," Des said, grinning at her.

"I should have been a lot of things. But I just decided to become a fat old lady instead."

"The name's Mitch. He's a New York movie critic."

Bella's eyes widened. "Do you mean *Mitchell Berger*?"

"You've heard of him?"

"He's only the single most respected film critic in America, my dear. And he's definitely one of us. He writes with so much passion, such sensitivity. In fact . . ." She wagged a stubby finger at Des. "Are you sure he's not gay?"

"He's a widower."

"He's a major catch, is what he is. Free passes to every movie in town."

"I don't have time to see every movie."

"Well, I do. And my niece, Naomi, is always looking for something to do. She's a research chemist at Rockefeller University. Face on her like the young Joe Torre, but a very nice girl." Bella peered at her slyly. "So . . . ?"

"So what . . . ?"

"Is he good-looking?"

"All depends on whether your idea of good-looking is the Pillsbury Dough Boy."

"What, he's a *shlub*?"

"If by *shlub* you mean a flesh prince, then the answer is yes." Des drank some more of her juice. "Some kind of weird mental thing is happening. He seems to know what I'm thinking. Like he's up inside my head."

Bella nodded sagely. "Morris could read me like a book."

"Brandon never knew what I was thinking."

"And what does that tell you, my dear?"

Des didn't answer. She didn't want to go there. She'd been there.

"Does he like cats?" Bella asked.

"I'll have to get back to you on that one." She put on her glasses so she could see the clock in the kitchen. "Damn, I'll have to get back to you, period." She climbed out of the tub, naked and dripping.

"Does he know you have that tattoo?"

"He know, he knows."

"Does he know *where* you have it?"

"Doubtless. The man knows everything else." Des wrapped herself in her terrycloth robe and made her way upstairs to shower and dress, the four remaining Spice Girls following her every move like Velcro.

She had no time to retreat to her studio. Not today. She took her sketch pad and charcoal with her. By 7:00 A.M. she was parked out on the bridge to Big Sister with her pad tilted against the steering wheel, stroking boldly in the hazy morning light.

Think only of lines, not of things.

Des was not happy. The case was growing more and more complex on her. The clock was ticking. She had zero margin for error. And she could not get her mind around this place. So she sat here, peering out at the houses and trees, at the rocks that were exposed by the low tide, trying to comprehend it with her charcoal.

Convince yourself you are touching the object.

There was something about these people—their shared history, their family ties, their interconnected lives—that left her profoundly baffled. There was a widow. There was her ex-husband and his new bride. There was a brother and his wife. A son and his lover. One of these people was a three-peater—someone who had coldly and carefully snuffed out an errant middle-aged husband, a young barmaid and the island's caretaker. Which one? Who had wanted all of these folks dead? Why?

See the subject, not the paper.

She had found Niles Seymour's Jeep Grand Cherokee in the long-term parking lot at Bradley International Airport up in Windsor Locks. The lot's automated check-in ticket was dated April 18—one day after Bud Havenhurst and Red Peck reported seeing him at the Saybrook Point Inn with Torry. And the same day Torry's body had been found. There were no latent prints on the ticket. Crime scene technicians were still scouring the car itself. According to United Airlines, Seymour had purchased two tickets to St. Croix for the eighteenth—one in his name, the other in the name Angela Becker. He had bought them a week earlier by calling the airline's 800 number. He had used a Visa card jointly held with his wife.

The tickets were never used.

No latent prints had been found on the Dear John letter he had left Dolly. No trace of the letter had been found on the hard drive of their computer or on their floppy disks. The type-face, a twelve-point Helvetica, did match one generated by their machine. And a sample printout was a perfect match. The letter was, they believed, generated in the Seymours' study. Numerous sets of fingerprints were found on the computer. These were presently being compared to the dead man's.

Des expected she would soon find it necessary to take fingerprint samples from each of the islanders.

She had spent a good deal of the night in Meriden down in the dimly lit basement of the old dormitory next door to the headmaster's house. There were cells down there where the bad boys had once been incarcerated—and tortured if one believed the legends. Which Des most certainly did. Central District's records were stored there now. After pawing through them for several hours, she had found the yellowing thirty-year-old state police report on the Roy and Louisa Weems murder-suicide. The case had been handled with extreme care. The island was an enclave of privilege and respectability. Dolly Peck was an ambassador's daughter. The matter of her sexual assault was on a separate page stamped confidential. A medical examination confirmed what Bud Havenhurst had told her—she had indeed been forcibly raped.

Witnesses had been questioned. One was a witness Des was surprised to find listed there. She had been startled to discover the name of the investigating officer as well. And not at all pleased.

None of this confidential material had appeared in either the *Hartford Courant* or *New York Times*.

She had found their coverage on microfilm at the Dorset Library, a small but growing village institution that had one foot planted firmly in the past and the other dipped tentatively into the future. There was an old building, a charming Victorian with panelled walls, a fireplace and comfy overstuffed armchairs. There was a new building with computer stations and low-slung blond wood counters and recessed lighting. The two buildings flowed into each other but did not exactly interact. It was, Des reflected, very much like Dorset itself.

The newspaper accounts were factual, proper and respectful. They gave no hint of any sexual assault. Or even any possible involvement by young Dolly Peck. There was no insinuation, no innuendo, no speculating by unnamed sources close to the investigation. Times had changed, Des realized. Inquiring minds were much dirtier now, the public way more cynical. They expected the dirty details. And they got them.

So what were the dirty details?

She had almost no time left to find out. The heavy leaning had already begun—thanks to that little weasel Soave, who had gone running directly to big brother Angelo with Jamie Devers's disclosure that Niles Seymour had a girlfriend in Meriden. Soave had *not* told Des, which would have enabled her to find out twelve hours sooner than she had that the two cases connected. No, Soave had withheld his vital nugget, forcing Des to wait until the trace came through on the slug. She was absolutely furious with him. Especially for the way he responded when she confronted him about it at their makeshift command center in Dorset's town hall: He just smirked. And lied to her face. "Jeez, loot," he said. "I thought you knew." Like hell. Naturally, big brother Angelo had told his good buddy, Captain Polito, that the Mitry girl was way behind the curve on the Niles Seymour investigation. As a consequence, Captain Polito had called her into his office to notify her that he was bringing in additional manpower starting tomorrow. Strictly in an advisory capacity, he assured her. Choosing his words very carefully, for fear of stepping on any powerful toes. He did not bother to mention that said additional manpower was another lieutenant who happened to be one of his hand-picked Waterbury boys. What he did say was this was not about rank or egos. "We are all on the same side, Lieutenant," was how he put it. "We are all trying to catch the bad guys."

All of which was true. Except that white males who were chasing the bad guys got at least seventy-two hours before the heavy leaning started. And she was only getting forty-eight. And it was not fair. And it was not right. And, God, she was so tired of their little boy crap. But she did not want to go running to the Deacon about it. She could not. Must not.

As Des sat there stroking the page with her charcoal, she noticed a human figure inching its way in her direction over the rocks and tide pools, subtly altering the composition of her drawing. As the figure got closer she realized it was Mitch Berger, looking a bit like an old-time lobsterman as he slogged along in his heavy dark blue sweater and green rubber wading boots. What was it Bella called him—a *shlub*? He was not a graceful man, for damned sure. He lumbered, his arms held out to his side. When he paused on the slippery rocks to wave at her, he lost his balance and nearly fell over. It also happened he was one truly awful guitar player. No ear. She wondered why she had talked so openly with him when they'd walked on the beach together. She supposed it was because he was observant and bright, because he was not one of them.

No, that wasn't it. She'd talked to him because she wanted to talk to him. Could not, in fact, shut up. It wasn't like Des to confide in a civilian. And her candor may have been ill-advised. Because she had no reason to believe she could trust this chubby, sad-eyed man. None. She'd have to be more careful.

She watched him now as he made his way across the rocks and trudged up onto the island-side entrance to the bridge. He was heading right for her. She closed her sketch pad and stashed it under her seat. She wiped her hands clean on a tissue. She rolled down her window.

"Morning, Lieutenant!" he called out to her, pink-cheeked and slightly winded from his morning hike. "How's your cold today?"

"I told you—I don't get colds, Mr. Berger. How's Baby Spice?" she asked, taking note of the tiny scratches all over his hands.

"You mean Clemmie? She slept like a baby. Made her first foray downstairs at around four A.M. Came right back up. Used her litter box like a champ. Chased this wadded-up piece of paper around for a while. Then climbed up on my chest and and went right back to . . . Hey, what are you laughing at?"

"A man who said he didn't want a cat."

"I'm still not sure," he insisted. "This is strictly a trial."

"Uh-hunh."

"May I see it?" he asked her anxiously.

"See what?"

"Your sketch."

Damn. She had charcoal under her fingernail again. "I don't know what you mean."

He peered at her curiously. "You've never shown them to anyone, have you?" On her tight silence he added, "You're afraid to, is that it?" Not accusing her. His voice was very gentle.

"Like I said, I don't know what you mean."

"It's nothing to be ashamed of, Lieutenant. We're all afraid of something."

"Is that right? What are *you* afraid of?"

"Spending the rest of my life alone."

"You think I'm afraid I'm not talented, is that it?"

"No, I think you're afraid that you *are*."

She shook her head at him, baffled. "Man, your mind's on vacation and your mouth's working overtime."

Mitch Berger said nothing to that. Just continued to peer at her with his wounded puppy eyes. She was absolutely positive at that particular moment that he could read her mind.

"Do you know a lot about art?" she asked him guardedly.

"I know talent when I see it. That's *my* talent. And my job. And I'd really love to see your stuff."

"Why are you so interested?"

"Because I'd like to see what you do to please *you*, rather than to please everyone else."

"Okay, now I'm *sure* I don't know what you're talking about."

"Suit yourself. I thought maybe we were becoming friends. No, hunh?" He let out an unhappy sigh. "Too bad, because you're my idea of a real first-class individual. But I'll just have to tell Bud he was wrong. See, when he saw us together on the beach he thought we were. Friends, I mean. Which is why he asked me to give you a message."

It turned out that Mitch Berger had something for her about Dolly's missing money: Havenhurst had it. He'd quietly squirreled it away on her behalf, fearing that Seymour was about to grab it and run. Or so Havenhurst claimed.

"He figured you'd get on to it real soon," Mitch Berger added. "And possibly get the wrong idea."

"Or possibly get the right one."

"Meaning what?" he asked, frowning at her.

Damn. She was doing it again. "Nothing. Nothing whatsoever."

"I'm becoming one of them now. I've been to the club. I've been sailing. I own boating shoes. Soon, I'll even have my own schoolboy nickname. What do you think of Boopy? Does that suit me?" On her mocking silence he acknowledged, "I'm not really. I could live here for fifty years and to them I'd still be the Jewboy from New York. I think it's more a case of them circling the wagons—you're either with us or you're against us. And I guess they'd much rather have me with them." He stood there for a moment, leaning his generous flank against her car. "How well do you know Resident Trooper Bliss?"

"We have a decent working relationship. Why?"

Mitch Berger hesitated, choosing his words carefully now. "Is there any chance he's involved?"

"He's been helpful to me, if that's what you mean."

"It isn't," he said heavily.

"Exactly what are you trying to tell me?"

"Bliss was out on the island that day I got locked in my crawl space. One of the islanders saw him. It's possible that he's the one who did it to me."

"Why would he want to do that?"

Now Mitch Berger was the one who fell silent.

Des considered this for a moment. Tal Bliss *was* an old friend of

Dolly Seymour. A seasoned veteran at cleaning up local messes. Was there any chance he had tried to clean up this one? That he knew more than he had let on? Was there any chance at all?

Of course, there was.

"Don't you have a movie review or something you should be working on?" she grumbled at him.

"I was planning to take the train into New York this morning, actually," he said. "Have to screen a couple of new mega-movies. Will that be okay?"

"I don't see why not."

"I thought you might say 'Don't leave town.' Or words to that effect."

"If I need to find you, I believe I can."

He grinned at her. "Was that a dare?"

"No, it was an honest response to your inquiry."

"The key to the front door of my cottage is under the boot scraper," he informed her.

"You just said what?"

"Well, I can't take Clemmie with me, can I?"

"Noo . . ."

"Of course, I can't—she's just getting acclimated. And you'll be around the island, right? So I thought you could look in on her later. Make sure she's all right. I'll be back tomorrow morning. Okay?"

Reluctantly, Des said, "Okay." Then she removed her billfold from the inside pocket of her blazer, dug out one of her business cards and handed it to him. "You happen to find out anything else, you can reach me at these numbers. Any hour, day or night. The one on the bottom's my pager number."

"Okay, sure," he said, tucking it into his pocket. "You coming out?" He meant to the island.

"In a while."

"Later, then, Lieutenant." He started away from her car and stopped. "Oh, there was one other thing . . ."

"What is it, Mr. Berger?" she asked wearily.

He grinned at her. "I still can't get you to call me Mitch, can I?"

"What is it, Mr. Berger?" she repeated, louder this time.

"Okay, okay . . . I don't buy a married man like Niles Seymour stashing a girl like Torry Mordarski at the Saybrook Point Inn. It's no place for a secret tryst. If anything, it's a place to go if you *want* to be seen. It doesn't add up. Not if they were trying to keep their affair under wraps."

Des did not say a word to that. She did not say that the same exact thing had occurred to her when she was there. She just nodded and watched him go tromping back out to the island on the wooden bridge.

When he'd made it about halfway across Mitch Berger paused to wave to her. She raised a hand in grudging response. She was still trying to decide just exactly what he'd meant when he called her a "real first-class individual." She didn't know whether to be flattered or insulted. All she knew was that he was no slouch himself. Bachelor's degree from Columbia. Master's degree from Columbia Journalism School. And his late wife had been Park Avenue all the way—the Brearley School, Bennington, Harvard Graduate School of Design.

Watching him disappear, Des realized that her hands were trembling and her stomach was in knots. Which was her body's own unique way of telling her it had just been in close physical contact with someone of surging hormonal interest. Surprised and aghast, Des lunged for her sketch pad. Propped it against her steering wheel. Stared out at the island.

Draw what you see, not what you know.

Des took a deep breath and closed her eyes. Eyes tightly shut, she drew.

CHAPTER 9

A REAL FIRST-CLASS INDIVIDUAL?!

Jesus, how had he said anything so clumsy and idiotic? As Mitch trudged his way back toward his little house on Big Sister, he could not imagine. It sounded like something straight out of the file on an NBA draft prospect, under the category of character: *A real first-class individual.* What on earth had he been thinking? He'd wanted to cheer the lieutenant up, that's what. She'd seemed down. He was trying to say something positive. But he hadn't wanted it to sound too sexually or racially conscious. And somehow he had gotten all tangled up and and, *bam*, out came the scouting report.

I do not know how to talk to people anymore. I am a butthead. I should be locked up.

As he made his way along the gravel drive past Bud and Mandy's house he came upon Mandy, who was busy using a rag to wipe off the pea-green coating of tree pollen and early-morning dew that had formed, paste-like, on the windshield of her MG. Her efforts afforded Mitch a superb view of her taut, quivering behind, which was snugly encased in a skin-tight pair of designer jeans.

Mandy wore a suede shirt and pair of backless sandals with her jeans. When she turned at the sound of his footsteps on the gravel, her unlined face broke into a bright, sunny smile of even white teeth and gleaming blue eyes. "Mitch, good morning!"

"Good morning back at you, Mandy. You're certainly up early."

"Well, so are you, sir."

"I'm off to New York for the day."

In response, she clapped her manicured hands together like a gleeful little girl. "Oh, good! That's what I figured."

Mitch frowned. "You did?"

157

"Absolutely. Why else would you be up and out before dawn? I am, too. Going in to the city today. Assuming it's okay with that black girl."

"Do you mean the lieutenant?"

"Well, yeah," Mandy said, squinting at the unmarked cruiser that was parked out on the bridge. "Why is she just *sitting* out there like that anyway? Is she *spying* on us?" Mandy suddenly seemed very tense, very paranoid. "I find it incredibly inappropriate. This island is supposed to be private. We're not supposed to have strangers *watching* us." Just as abruptly, she relaxed, smiling at him warmly. "You should never wear anything but navy blue, Mitch. That sweater makes you look so handsome and trim."

Trim?! Yeah, right. Move over, David Duchovny.

Mitch shifted from one foot to the other, suddenly very uneasy. Because at the sound of their voices Bud had appeared in the window of his little house. He was watching them. He was watching his lovely and volatile trophy bride talk to an available younger man. Mandy's back was toward the house—was she aware that Bud was standing there, listening in?

Of course, she was. That was why she'd said what she said.

"You're very kind, Mandy," Mitch finally responded. "No one has called me trim since I was . . . well, come to think of it no one's *ever* called me trim."

Now she let out a laugh, a delicious, cascading laugh that was sure to carry halfway across the island.

"It shouldn't be a problem," Mitch spoke up. "You going in to the city today, I mean. The lieutenant said it would be okay if I did."

"Well, that settles it, then," Mandy concluded with a happy toss of her long blond hair. "Which train are you taking in? We can ride in together."

"I haven't decided yet. I have to do some paperwork before I go. Actually, you'd better not count on me. Just take the train you were going to take. If we run into each other, great."

Mandy's plump lips formed a pout. "I sure hope we will."

"So do I," said Mitch, as Bud continued to watch them through the window. *But not if I can help it.* Because there was something profoundly unsettling about this woman. Something that was alluring at the same time that it was frightening. Mandy Havenhurst was clearly accustomed to doing whatever she wanted to whomever she wanted and getting away with it. That gave her an air of recklessness, of danger. The Sharon Stone factor, they called it in Hollywood. Playing with fire, they called it in real life. Guaranteed to stir up the blood. And to make Mitch ask himself questions like: Was it by chance that she'd been out here cleaning her windshield? Or had she spotted him coming across the bridge and purposely bumped into him? Questions like: Was it a coincidence that they were both going to New York today? Or was she going in because he was going in? If so, why?

"What takes you to town, Mitch?" she asked him now. An innocent enough question. So why didn't it sound innocent?

"I have a couple of movies to screen. And you?"

"Personal day," she replied. "Nothing but pampering. A massage and facial, my hair, fingers, my toes, a new black dress at Bendel's . . . I want to look nice for the funeral tomorrow. Bud is furious about it, you know," she said, leaning a slender flank against her sports car.

"Why is that?" Mitch asked, wondering how much of this Bud could hear. All of it, he figured.

"He doesn't think Niles should be buried in the Peck family plot."

"That's Dolly's decision to make, isn't it? She's the Peck."

"Just what I said," Mandy agreed. "She's the Peck. But Bud doesn't see it that way. I think he figured that when the time came *he* would be the one buried next to Dolly. Which, if you stop and think about it, should make *me* really angry."

"Does it?"

"Not really," she said with a shrug. "I don't think about what happens after we're all gone. Hell, I don't even think about tomorrow. Just about *now*. He's also pissed that Dolly wants to foot the bill for Tuck Weems's funeral. Apparently it was just Tuck and some teenaged slut he was living with, and she has zero money. Are you staying over in the city tonight?"

Again, it was an innocent enough question. Yet, somehow, coming from Mandy it was tinged with the promise of illicit, athletic sex. "I'd planned to, yes," Mitch replied.

"Me, too. We should get together tonight. Do you like Thai food?"

"I do. Very much."

"Great! I know a place on Spring Street that will positively blow your doors off. And afterward we can go listen to some jazz."

"God, I'd love to. But I have a pretty tight schedule tonight. A screening, followed by dinner with my editor. Can't do it. Sorry."

She frowned at Mitch prettily. "If I were a bit more insecure I'd think you were blowing me off."

"Not at all," he said. Which was not, in fact, completely true. He could have invited her to the screening with him. The invites were always for two. So why wasn't he inviting her? Simple. Because she was trouble. And her husband was watching her every move. And he was not going to get involved in whatever game the two of them were playing.

"Well, maybe next time," she said wistfully.

"That would be great," Mitch said.

Now was when Bud decided to officially show himself. The lawyer came scuffing out the front door toward them in his silk bathrobe and slippers, smiling tightly at Mitch. Bud's hair was rumpled and he was unshaven. Young men, in Mitch's critical opinion, tended to look more virile when they were unshaven. Not so Bud. The grizzled white stubble on his chin belonged to an aging pensioner. So did the chalky residue of dried saliva that was caked to his lips like Spackle. "Hey, boy!" he called to Mitch in a phlegmy voice. "You're up early."

"We're both going to New York today, sugar," Mandy informed him. "Isn't that wonderful?"

"Yes, it is," Bud said, peering at Mitch long and hard. Mitch peered right back at him. The man looked positively ten year older this morning. Also ten times more desperate. His face seemed hollow-eyed and gaunt, his gaze uncertain—even fearful. It was getting to him. The thin ice he was skating on was definitely getting to him. "Take good care of her, Mitch. And of yourself."

"I always try to," Mitch assured him.

"Make certain that you do." Now there was a degree of urgency in Bud's voice. "I don't believe those numbers, you know."

"Which numbers?"

"The ones that say that crime is down in New York. I think the people who came up with those are the same ones who keep telling us that inflation is under control. If it is, then why does the price of everything keep going up? Do you know what I'm saying, Mitch?"

Mitch scratched his head. "Not exactly, Bud. No."

"I'm saying that New York can still be a dangerous, dangerous place," Bud asserted, his voice rising. The man's fists, Mitch observed, were tightly clenched. "Watch yourself, my young friend. I'd hate to see anything happen to you. It would be a shame. A damned shame."

CHAPTER 10

IT WAS SHORTLY AFTER eight when Des started up her cruiser and eased it across the bridge toward Big Sister.

As she was pulling up in the driveway Mandy Havenhurst, the creamy blond beer heiress, sidled over toward her wearing a buttery soft suede shirt that looked as if it cost her as much as Des earned in a month. Another one like Dolly Seymour, Des reflected. A product of privilege and good looks. Not to mention dangerously unstrung. Face it, the only reason Mandy Havenhurst hadn't served any time for her crimes against the men in her life was that she was rich and she was white. Des wondered how Bud Havenhurst slept nights. Herself, she wouldn't sleep a wink lying in bed next to this particular lemon cupcake.

"Good morning, Lieutenant," Mandy exclaimed, showing her a broad, insincere smile. "Are you here to see me?"

Des shut off her engine and got out. "Not right now, no."

"The reason I asked," Mandy said airily, "is that I was planning to spend the day in New York. But if you wish for me to stay around . . ."

"Go right ahead. Mr. Berger's taking the train in himself this morning."

"Yes, I know. We were hoping to ride in together." Her sultry tone of voice made it sound like she and Mitch had themselves a whole day planned together. Followed by a whole night. Did they? Des wondered. Mandy lingered there, tossing her long golden hair. "Was it my husband you wished to see?" she asked Des offhandedly. But there was nothing offhanded about her blue-eyed gaze. It was piercing.

"I can catch him later at his office."

"Are you *sure* there's nothing I can help you with?" Now she was chewing fretfully on her lower lip. Chewing on it almost hard enough to draw blood. "In reference to my husband, I mean."

The lady wanted to know what Des had on him. Particularly as it related to Dolly Seymour. Des had no doubt about this. She also had no intention of fueling Mandy's pathological jealousy. "Enjoy your day in the city," she said pleasantly. Then Des strode toward the natural-shingled house where Redfield and Bitsy Peck lived, feeling Mandy's eyes boring into her.

The Peck house was the most immense single-family home Des had ever seen. Three full stories high, with wings extending off in every direction and a deep shade porch wrapped all the way around. There were balconies upstairs, sun porches, observation turrets, a widow's walk. The fenced-in garden was also huge. A vast collection of vegetables and flowers and herbs grew there in raised, orderly beds. To Des it looked more like a commercial nursery than it did someone's yard. There was a greenhouse, potting shed, tool shed. There was a composting area with a dozen or more wire bins and two large, rotating steel drums.

Bitsy Peck was in the process of dumping a bucket full of orange peels, egg shells and coffee grounds into one of these.

"Good morning," Des said to her. "I wondered if your husband was back from Tokyo yet."

"Why, yes, Lieutenant," Bitsy replied brightly. "He landed at midnight. Got home just after two. He's here for a couple of days and then he's off again, poor lamb. Four international flights a month makes for a tough, tough schedule. But Red's used to it. I suppose you can get used to just about anything if you have to." Bitsy closed the door to the drum, rotated it smartly three times with a hand crank and then reached for her empty bucket. "Do come in—he just sat down to breakfast."

She bustled back toward the house, humming merrily. Des followed her, wondering how anyone could be so cheerful with all of this killing going on.

It resembled a mountain lodge inside, with Adirondack-style

furniture of oak and leather, polished plank floors and a good deal of paneling and wood trim. The rooms were large and airy. Each one had its own wood-burning fireplace and its own terrific view of the sea. There was no hallway. One room simply led into another. There was a sitting room. There was a dining room. There was a game room with an antique pool table, a telescope and a chess board set up by the windows. It was not a pretentious home by any means. It was comfortable and lived in—a house meant for laughter and fun, kids and dogs. Although it was quiet and still right now.

The kitchen was immense. A giant, battered trestle table was anchored in its center, where Redfield Peck sat finishing his scrambled eggs and toast. He had combed his hair but he had not shaved. He wore a hooded Naval Academy sweatshirt, unpressed khakis and a sleepy expression on his lined, craggy face. That expression turned quickly to wariness when he saw Des standing there in his kitchen. And he seemed to grow somewhat pale. He patted his mouth with his napkin and got politely to his feet. He was no more than five foot eight, much shorter than she'd expected from the breadth of his chest and shoulders. She towered over him.

"There's coffee in the pot, Lieutenant," Bitsy offered. "Can I make you some eggs? Skillet's still warm."

"I'm all set, thanks."

"How about some nice hot tea for that cold?"

"Don't have one. It's just my allergies."

Bitsy snuffed at her disapprovingly. "Lieutenant, I've raised two children. I know what a sinus cold sounds like. You, my dear girl, have a sinus cold."

"Leave the poor woman alone, Bits," Red murmured with a faint smile. "She already has a mother, haven't you, Lieutenant?"

"That I do." Des smiled back at him. "Was wondering if I could go over some things with you."

He swallowed uneasily. "Of course. Why don't we go out on the porch?"

"Yes, do that," Bitsy Peck exclaimed. "I have to get to my garden.

I have weeds, weeds, everywhere. They are *impossible* this time of year. Unless, that is, you need me, Lieutenant."

"No, ma'am, you go right ahead."

And she did just that, humming.

There were kitchen herbs growing in pots out on the porch. There was wicker furniture. They sat in two armchairs facing the water, Redfield Peck's manner studiously calm and careful. He put Des in mind of a doctor who was about to give her a gynecological examination—everything about his body language was geared toward putting her at ease, to conveying competence and professionalism. It was a manner he had no doubt cultivated after years of moving through a cabin full of apprehensive air passengers.

Interesting that he would fall back on it now, she reflected, seeing as how it was he who was about to climb into the stirrups and say *aaah*.

"How may I help you, Lieutenant?" he asked her quietly, folding his large, blunt-fingered hands in his lap. "I'm not a suspect, am I?"

"You're not a suspect in the murder of Tuck Weems. You were out of the country when his shooting took place. This has been confirmed by your airline. But I do have a question for you."

His bushy eyebrows raised slightly. "By all means."

"Mr. Peck, where are you the one week out of every month when you are not where your wife thinks you are?"

Her question did not take him by surprise. He was braced for it. "What do you mean?" he asked coolly, reluctant to volunteer any more than he had to.

"I mean," Des replied, "that for the past year you've been making three flights a month to Tokyo—not four."

"Please keep your voice down." He shot a glance in the direction of the garden, where his wife was crouched stoutly in a flowerbed, weeding.

"Wasn't aware that I was shouting."

"Look, it's not what you're thinking, Lieutenant."

"I'm not thinking anything, Mr. Peck."

"I haven't got some tootsie stashed somewhere that Bits doesn't know about. It's a family matter. A private matter. I've been in San Francisco, as I'm sure the airline can confirm."

In fact, he was averaging a half-dozen employee discount flights per month to San Francisco. Some of these flights originated in Tokyo, others in New York. Many were layovers lasting no more than one night.

Redfield Peck sat back in his chair and crossed his short legs. He gazed out at the Sound. "It's Becca—Rebecca, she's our eldest. Twenty-four now. She moved out there because of the dance community. She dances, you see." He paused, sighing heavily. "And she's gotten herself into some trouble."

"What kind of trouble?"

"Intravenous drug trouble," he replied, his voice choking with emotion. "Becca's a sick, sick girl, Lieutenant. And I've been doing everything I possibly can to help her get well again. Getting her treatment, counseling. Making sure she's using clean needles. God, I am so afraid she's going to get the AIDS virus . . . She *won't* come home. I can't talk her into that. But she can't seem to stay out of trouble either. She seemed to be doing better over the winter but then she got mixed up with some guy and he dropped her and she . . . I fly planes for a living, Lieutenant. I am trained to believe that there is no problem I can't solve. Becca I can't solve. Because there's no solution. There's only today and tomorrow. It's utterly perplexing to me. And it's humbling. And it's very, very lonely." He breathed in and out a moment, wringing his hands. "Her mother doesn't know about it, you see. Any of it. It would *kill* Bits if she found out Becca was on drugs. She didn't want her to move out there in the first place, because Becca was always a bit wild. I talked Bits into it. I thought the girl would be fine—she just needed to grow up a little. And now, well, Bits just wouldn't be able to understand. Or forgive. She's always been closer to our boy, Matt. Matt knows. And Evan, who has always been tight with Becca. But I live in constant fear that he'll tell Jamie, who can be very indiscreet when he drinks. If Jamie were to let it slip to Dolly or Bud, it would immediately get back to her. You can't keep a secret on this island . . . I-I'm hoping to get her cleaned up and home before it's too late. She used to love horses. We could get her one. There was a young man here who was fond of her. And would give anything to see her again. She's a lovely, lovely girl . . ." He pulled her picture out of his wallet and held it out to Des.

It was a snapshot of a slim blond girl in a tu-tu and ballet slippers. She was not especially pretty. She had too many of her father's features. What Des found most remarkable was that it was a picture of her when she was no more than twelve years old.

Redfield Peck had some trouble sliding the photo back in his wallet. His eyes were filling with tears now. "Please don't say anything to my wife about this, Lieutenant," he pleaded, a wrenching sob erupting from his chest.

Des did not like to see men cry. She knew how painful it was for them. She knew this because she knew how painful it was for her. She got to her feet and said, "My interest is in the investigation of these killings. Nothing more."

"Then I-I can count on your silence?"

"I am like money in the bank," she assured him.

Then she left him to his tears. He would have a much easier time if she were not there.

His wife was still digging up the weeds in her flower garden.

"You have got yourself one lovely garden, Mrs. Peck," Des said to her.

"Why, thank you, Lieutenant," she responded gaily. "I do love it so. Every morning when I come out here to play I think to myself just how lucky I am to be around things that are fresh and growing. They make me feel so alive and . . . Oh, beans, those darned birds!" Her eyes had zeroed in on a clump of weeds under the peony bush next to her. "See those shiny green leaves? That's poison ivy. No matter what I do it comes back. The darned birds spread the seeds. And I am *so* allergic to it. Even if I'm wearing gloves I break out like the dickens. Red will have to come pull it out for me."

"Your husband's not allergic to it?"

"My husband can roll around in it buck naked and not get a rash. It's not fair. All of the Pecks are lucky that way. Dolly isn't allergic. Neither is Evan."

"And Tuck Weems? Did he ever help you pull it out?"

"Yes, he did, now that you mention it. I asked him to once when Red was in Tokyo. Tuck wasn't allergic either."

"You folks out here all go to the same doctor?"

"Why, yes. Shoreline Family Practice. Three doctors, actually. Pretty much everyone in town goes there. They're right across from the A and P on Big Brook Road." Bitsy Peck climbed to her feet and brushed herself off. "Do you like rhubarb, Lieutenant?"

"I'm afraid not."

"Well, you must let me give you something to take with you."

Des dabbed at her runny nose with a tissue. "Totally not necessary, Mrs. Peck."

"Nonsense. You absolutely cannot leave here empty-handed. Do you care for these?" she asked, waving a chubby arm at a wildflower bed that was bursting with white geraniums. "That's Geranium Cantabriense Biokovo. It originated in the mountains of Yugoslavia. Aren't they just the loveliest?"

"Yes, they are. Very much so."

"Well, that settles it, then." She went trudging off to her potting shed and came back in a moment with a vase filled with water. "It's a funny thing about geraniums, Lieutenant," she said, cutting some for her with a small pair of shears. "They'll never be as pretty as they are at this very instant. The second they leave the garden they'll start to wither and die. But if they stay here too long they become overgrown and crowd out the other plants. I *have* to thin them out," she explained with a touch of sad resignation. "It's a law of nature that beautiful things have to be shared with others."

Des nodded, wondering whether Bitsy Peck was talking about her flowers or her drug-addicted daughter. She couldn't help but get the feeling that this was the woman's oblique way of letting her know that she actually knew all about Rebecca's problem. That she wasn't nearly as clueless as her husband thought.

Bitsy Peck was no fool. She was just old school.

She deftly arranged a generous fistful of the flowers in the vase and handed it to Des. "For your kitchen table, Lieutenant," she said, smiling at her warmly.

"Thank you."

"The morning haze is lifting," she observed, gazing out at the Sound. "It's going to be a nice day."

"Yes, it is," Des agreed. "It's going to be a very nice day."

"I've already told your sergeant *all* of this," Jamie Devers said to Des in total dismay. "At least I think I did. I can never be totally sure, you understand."

"Why's that, Mr. Devers?"

"I've lost a lot of gray cells along the way," he responded. "You know those things they told us about how drugs would fry our brains? They were all true." Now an alarmed expression crossed the former child star's face. "Oh, God, I've just confessed to habitual recreational drug use. Forget I said that, will you? It was the sixties, Southern California. *Everyone* inhaled."

"It's forgotten, Mr. Devers," she assured him as they strolled along together. "Hey, I am digging on your shop."

"I'm so glad." Jamie was relieved to change the subject. "If you see anything you like, don't be bashful."

Great White Whale Antiques was housed in a drafty old barn up in Millington, a small country hamlet in the rolling hills north of Dorset. The shop was eclectic and cluttered. He and Evan Havenhurst offered a little bit of everything. Colonial furniture. Weathered Victorian garden ornaments. Rugs, quilts, paintings. There were some very expensive pieces. There were some that bordered on tag sale junk. At the moment, Evan was at an estate sale up in Farmington. There were no customers around.

"We positively freeze our buns off in the winter," he confided. "There's zero insulation—and nothing but a wood stove. But it's fun. And it keeps us off the streets."

"You have any trouble with mice?"

"Yes, we do. They scare the old ladies to death."

"What you need is a barn cat." Maybe two. Rob and Fab would be perfect.

"Please don't get the wrong idea, Lieutenant," Jamie said. "I really don't mean to be difficult. I just don't see why I have to go through it all again. It seems so unnecessary."

"It's necessary." Des could no longer be sure Soave was feeding her everything.

He folded his arms, looking at her curiously. "Well, what is it you need to know exactly?"

"I need to confirm where you were the night Tuck Weems was shot."

"As I told your sergeant, I was camped out on Little Sister. Went out there after Dolly's cocktail party for Mitch. Evan and I often spend the night out there."

"You two were together?"

"Of course. I can't sail the damned boat without him."

"Can he sail it without you?"

"Evan can sail anything. He's part pirate. Why do you ask?"

Des didn't respond. Couldn't respond. Because a certain object *had* caught her eye over by a china cupboard in the corner. It was a truly fantastic object. In fact, she had never seen anything quite so beautiful. Slowly, she approached it.

"Lovely, isn't it?" Jamie enthused, gazing affectionately at the painting. It was an Impressionist landscape of a lush green meadow streaming with morning sunlight. "It's a Bruestle. George M. He was a fairly prominent member of Dorset's art colony at the turn of the century, best known for his well-ripened greens. The meadow's located off of Ely's Ferry Road. It's still there."

"It's very fine. Only what I'm beaming on is the easel." She could not take her eyes off the artist's stand that the painting was displayed upon.

"You do have a keen eye, don't you? It was Bruestle's. His son Bertram, who was a fine painter in his own right, used it for years. I bought it from the estate of his widow. It was custom-made by a local cabinet maker. Solid oak, with brass fittings. Truly one of a kind. Works like a charm."

"Is it for sale?"

"Dear girl, everything here is for sale, including the barn, the land under the barn and me. It's perfect for displaying things on, isn't it? A sampler perhaps?"

"I'd want to use it."

He cocked his head at her in surprise. "You paint?"

"I draw a little," she said uneasily.

"How interesting. I would never have guessed." Jamie thumbed his chin judiciously. "It's yours if you'll give me exactly what I paid for it—eight hundred."

Des shook her dreadlocks at him. "That's way out of my price range."

"All right, make it seven-fifty," he said with nimble ease.

"Not a chance."

He waved her off. "Nonsense. I believe that when someone loves a piece, they should have it. And I can tell from the glow in your eye that you love this one. I insist that you take it home. We'll work something out."

Des glanced at him sharply. "That would not exactly be appropriate."

"No, of course not," he agreed hastily. "What am I saying? Christ, now you must think I'm trying to *bribe* you. God, I am hopeless when Ev's not around. I just blither on and on, slipping and sliding and . . ." He broke off, puffing out his cheeks. "Why don't you just shoot me right now and put me out of my misery?"

"Mr. Devers, please try to relax."

"You're absolutely right," he said, running a hand over his face. "Let's relax. Let's all relax."

There was an old library table just inside the front door that Jamie and Evan used as a desk. A crystal decanter filled with cognac served as a paperweight. He poured some into a snifter and drank it down in one gulp. He sat down in his chair and lit a cigarette, dragging on it nervously.

There was an armchair across from him. Des sat in it, watching him closely. The man was obviously terrified of her. Was this just vintage sixties paranoia? Or was he actually guilty of something? She made a steeple of her fingers. She rested her chin upon it, gazing at him intently across the desk. "It rained that night," she pointed out quietly.

"What night, Lieutenant?"

"The night Tuck Weems was murdered. There was a truly vicious storm."

"There absolutely was," he acknowledged. "It blew in around three in the morning. Lightning, thunder, the works."

"And you two were camped out in that?"

"Not after it started we weren't. We went below deck, snug as bugs. Actually, too snug. It can get really stuffy down there. And the water was *way* choppy. But that's the vaunted nautical life for you. If you want to be dry you have to be nauseated."

"Did anyone see you?"

"See us?"

"You recall anyone passing near enough to the island to observe that you were docked out there? A fisherman, maybe?"

Jamie Devers considered this. "No one saw us. Not unless they saw our bonfire. We lit one when we first got out there. The rain eventually drowned it, of course. But the Coast Guard might have spotted that. They patrol pretty regularly." He stubbed out his cigarette and immediately reached for another. "Once the storm hit, nobody was out on the water."

"What did you use for firewood?"

He stared across the desk at her, perplexed. "We used firewood, what else?"

"That island's a barren rock pile. Not one stick of wood out there to burn."

"We brought it with us. Logs, kindling, the works."

"Sounds like an awful lot of trouble," she said doubtfully.

"It is," he acknowledged. "But to us, it's worth it."

"When did you return from Little Sister?"

"In the morning, after the storm had passed over and the Sound had calmed. There was virtually no way we could have made it back *during* that storm in a J-24. It's a racing boat. Built very low to the water. We'd have gone down for sure." He smiled at her hopefully. "So, you see, we couldn't have killed Tuck Weems. It's not possible."

"You're right, it's not—assuming you were there."

"We were," Jamie Devers insisted. "I swear it."

Des would have to check this out further with the Coast Guard. And have a trooper canvas the area boatyards to see if anyone could recall spotting their fire. But even if someone did remember it that did not necessarily clear them. The fire was not a guarantee they were on Little Sister when Tuck Weems was murdered. It was not a guarantee of anything. They could have built themselves a huge bonfire as a decoy and then headed right back to Big Sister *before* the storm ever started.

Right now, the only alibi Jamie Devers and Evan Havenhurst had was each other.

Right now, they had no alibi whatsoever.

CHAPTER 11

A POKY LITTLE COMMUTER train called the *Shoreliner* shuttled its way back and forth through the villages and tidal marshes that stretched in between Old Saybrook and New Haven, where Mitch could pick up the Metro North line into Grand Central. It was Metro North that carried the Wall Street warriors in from Fairfield every morning, armed for combat with their matching Burberry's, cell phones and game faces. For Mitch, the trip was about two and a half hours, door to door. The *Shoreliner* was not particularly crowded. He had a two-person seat to himself, which was fine by him. He did not enjoy bumping elbows and knees with someone he did not know. He had bought the morning papers to read. He spread them open and read.

Lieutenant Mitry's superior, Capt. Carl Polito of the Central District Major Crimes Squad, was expressing his support for her in the *Hartford Courant*. "The investigation is proceeding in a swift and thoroughly professional manner," he said. "We have every reason to believe we will have a suspect in custody very soon." To Mitch this sounded remarkably like one of those ringing votes of no-confidence Yankee owner George Steinbrenner gave to his soon-to-be outgoing manager. No wonder the woman seemed uptight—her head was on the chopping block. There was still no acknowledged link-up between the two Dorset slayings and the Torry Mordarski murder. They were, it seemed, choosing to keep that under wraps for now. There was a mention that Niles Seymour would be buried tomorrow in Dorset's Duck River Cemetery. Burial arrangements for Tuck Weems were still being made.

The New York tabloids, meanwhile, were pouncing on the Mandy Havenhurst angle with obvious relish. Her torrid love life, her run-ins with the law. "Beer Baroness Finds More Trouble

Brewing," screamed the headline in the *Daily News*. "Fanning the Flames of Mandy's Passion," shouted the *Post*. Both carried old photos of her. She was practically a teenager in them. Her hair was worn very differently—piled high atop her head. And she wore tremendous quantities of eye makeup. Mitch barely recognized her.

As he was reading, a woman strode down the aisle, stopped and asked if she could join him in his two-person seat. It was Mandy, of course, flashing her dazzling smile at him.

"I had a feeling I'd run into you," she said happily, sliding in next to him and depositing a Ghurka shoulder bag at her feet.

"That's funny," said Mitch. "So did I."

"I wouldn't say the lieutenant sounded totally enthusiastic about me coming in, but she did say it was okay. She's kind of a tight-ass, don't you think?"

Mandy smelled of a heavy, fruity perfume, the kind that Mitch had always associated with the old widows he used to ride up and down in the elevators with in Stuyvesant Town when he was a kid, the *bubbies* with their shopping carts and moustaches and Eastern European accents. Styles must have changed, he decided. Because Mandy Havenhurst was nobody's idea of a *bubbie*.

"The lieutenant came to see you this morning?" he asked her politely.

"No, no. I just bumped into her, is all. She was on her way out to talk to Red."

"She was?"

Mandy stared at him intently now, as if suspecting his words held some secret double meaning. "Yes, she was."

"Hey, did you know you made the papers today?"

"No way, really . . . ?" Mandy drew her breath in sharply when he showed her the headlines. Then she heaved a long, pained sigh. "Lies," she said between gritted teeth. "Nothing but lies. But what can I do—people have been telling them about me since I was thirteen years old. That's what happens to you in this world when you're someone like me. I'm pretty. I'm blond. And my family has money. Therefore, I am automatically considered a bitch—by people who don't even know me. I'm used to it. But it hurts." She turned the tabloids over so she wouldn't have to look at them. "God, I'm so glad I'm coming in to the city today. It'll be impossible out there. Reporters will be calling nonstop. And poor Bud will be wigging out."

"Are you going to speak to them?"

"No way," she said with sudden savagery.

"But if they have the story wrong don't you want to tell your side?" he asked, wondering just exactly what her side might be. The facts in the stories seemed to jibe with what the lieutenant had told him about Mandy's stormy past.

Mandy's response was, "Why bother? Once people make up their minds about you there's not a goddamned thing you can do to change it. No one ever believes me when I tell them that the men I've loved were abusive toward me, both physically and mentally. That I've had to literally fight for my life in order to survive their cruelty. I don't know why I provoke that in men, Mitch. I really don't." Her big blue eyes locked on to his now. "When I love someone, I'll crawl across broken glass on my hands and knees for him. There's *nothing* I won't do. And I'm as kind a person as you'll ever meet. I don't have a nasty bone anywhere in my whole body." She sighed. She ran the tip of her tongue over her lower lip. She said, "I sure wish we could get together tonight."

"Like I said, I'm going to be tied up all—"

"The God's honest truth," she broke in, "is that there's something I have to talk to you about. It's really personal, Mitch. And it's really, really important. Could we meet somewhere *after* your dinner date? Just for a little while?"

Mitch wavered. She was married. She was crazy. She was trouble. But he was also intensely curious. What did she want to talk about? Was it the murders? Was it Bud? He had to find out. He couldn't *not* find out. So he agreed to swing by her apartment at about ten and buzz her. She lived at 20 E. Sixty-fifth Street, a very posh address. They would go out for a nightcap together—someplace quiet where they could talk.

Their train pulled into Grand Central right on time. They separated in the Grand Concourse, near the clock, in a shaft of the bright morning sunlight that streamed in the newly scrubbed windows. As Mitch started to say good-bye Mandy surprised him by throwing her arms around him and giving him a big juicy kiss on the mouth, her pelvis pressing tightly against his own. Heads turned. Wolf whistles sounded. All of the blood in Mitch's body seemed to rush right to his head. "Later," she purred. And then she was off, the heels of her backless sandals clacketing sharply on the marble floor.

Mitch stayed right where he was for a long moment, waiting for some of the feeling to return to the lower half of his body. *No, I really do not want to get mixed up with this woman.*

He found he was way out of sync as he made his way across the floor of the giant terminal. The commuters criss-crossing in front of him were moving with much greater urgency than he was. Sauntering along at his Dorset pace, he kept bouncing off of them, like a human bumper car. But Mitch found this to be a short-lived phenomenon. It took less than thirty seconds for his metabolism to rev back up from small-town slo-mo to Big Apple overdrive. The city's pace simply demanded it. Soon Mitch was darting this way and that, back in the flow, just another one of the hyper multitude.

He made his way down the long tunnel to the subway and caught the shuttle across town to Times Square. There was no faster way to get across town, day or night. When the one-stop shuttle pulled in at Times Square he maneuvered his way across the crowded underground station and down the steep stairs for the number One train, heading downtown. It had been a while since a train had come through. Folks were stacked up ten-deep at the edge of the platform, fanning themselves impatiently. The warm air was heavy and reeked of overflowing garbage cans and unwashed people. Burrowing his way in among them, Mitch found himself missing the crisp, clean, sea air of Big Sister. Also the sheer luxury of having so much space to himself. Here in the city, there was no such privilege. Everyone shared the same island.

When he finally heard the train pulling in Mitch began working his way closer to the edge of the platform so he'd have a shot at getting on. Boxing out was a standard aspect of belowground life in New York. Nothing unusual about this. Until, without warning, Mitch suddenly felt *it*—the ultimate New York nightmare.

He felt someone trying to shove him onto the tracks right in front of the onrushing train.

It all happened so fast that Mitch had no chance to react. No chance to resist. No chance whatsoever. One second he was fine. The next second he was teetering helplessly there on the edge of the raised platform, fighting desperately to hold on to his balance, to his *life*—as the tracks yawned before him and the four-hundred-ton train bore down on him, someone's full weight pressing violently, murderously against him. Brakes screeched. A lady screamed.

Two things saved Mitch's life. One was his unadulterated love of high-caloric sweets, which made him just an exceptionally hard man to knock off of his feet. The other was the immense construction worker standing next to him, who grabbed him by the scruff of the neck and yanked him back at the last possible second as the train shot past him.

"Damn, you got to be more careful, man," he scolded Mitch. He was Jamaican by the lilt of his accent. "Take your time. That's how accidents be happening."

"That was no accident—somebody pushed me!" Mitch cried out, his eyes flicking wildly around at the passengers surrounding him. "*Who?* Did you see *who?*"

"Didn't see nobody, man," Mitch's savior replied gruffly. The other passengers offered him nothing more than blank stares. They were like zombies. The un-dead. "You lost your balance. Too big a hurry."

Now Mitch saw it—a blur of green streaking up the stairs back up to the station. Someone wearing an olive-colored trenchcoat with an upturned collar and a baseball cap with its visor pulled low. Someone he was not able to recognize. He could not even tell if it was a man or a woman.

"Hey!" Mitch shouted at his would-be killer. "Hey, stop!"

The figure sped up. Mitch went after it. Fighting his way through the crowd. Dashing up the stairs in breathless pursuit. He caught sight of his attacker sprinting down a narrow, dimly lit corridor. He broke into a mad sprint of his own across the underground station, running into people and over people, leaving grumbles and curses and spilled purses in his wake. Trying to keep up with that distant figure in green, gasping for breath, his loaded day pack growing heavier and heavier on his shoulders. And he *was* keeping up. Until, that is, he ran smack into a phalanx of slow-moving Japanese tourists in shorts and sandals who were walking, what, twelve abreast? There were small children and elderly grandmothers among them. And, for a brief moment, he could not get around them. That brief moment was all it took for the figure in green to shoot through the turnstiles and up the steps and out into Times Square. *Gone*.

Mitch did go tearing up the steps onto Forty-second Street, his chest heaving, but it was no use. Whoever it was, they had disappeared.

But who was it? And why had they tried to kill him?

He didn't know. He didn't know anything. Except that he was lucky to be alive.

Shaken, he opted for a cab ride home.

Mitch hadn't been to his apartment in over two weeks. It was stuffy and smelled musty. He turned on the air conditioners in the living room and bedroom. Checked his phone messages. Sorted through his mail. Thought long and hard about calling the police to tell them what had happened. Decided not to. Thought about calling Lieutenant Mitry to tell her what had happened. Decided not to do that either. He opened the fridge and threw out whatever had gone to blue in his absence, which was most everything. Made himself some scrambled eggs and stale toast. Sat at the dining table and ate, realizing to his surprise that this apartment didn't feel like home anymore. His little cottage out on Big Sister felt more like home. Mitch had not expected this to happen. Most of his world was here, after all. His books, his tapes, his memories. Then again, he reflected, this had been *their* home. The carriage house was *his*. Maybe that explained it. Still, for Mitch this was a disconcerting feeling. He had never known a time in his entire life when he didn't consider the city to be home.

Sitting there, he wondered how Clemmie was doing.

His afternoon screening was in the 666 Fifth Avenue building, near Rockefeller Center and St. Patrick's Cathedral. Mitch forced himself to take the subway there, even though he didn't much feel like it. He stood well away from the tracks while he was waiting for the train to come. And he kept glancing around the platform to see if anyone was showing too much interest in him. Or furtively looking away. No one was. No one did. He was not being followed. Or at least he didn't think he was.

But he still felt exceedingly jumpy.

He also felt as if he were the only person on Fifth Avenue who had any actual business to conduct there. This was a phenomenon Mitch was still having trouble accepting. Fifth Avenue had undergone a remarkable transformation in the past few years. He almost never came upon businessmen with briefcases anymore. He came upon very few New Yorkers, period. Just tourists, the majority of them foreign, wearing cameras and sensible shoes. The shops along the avenue reflected this. The fine B.Dalton's bookstore in the ground floor at 666 was now a store devoted to the sale of NBA merchandise. And the fabled Scribner's bookstore across the street was now a Benetton.

The screening room was up on the ninth floor. It was small—two dozen plush seats for two dozen plush critics. Mitch knew all of the people who were slouched there, pale and round-shouldered. They were his compadres from New York's other daily papers, from the local TV stations, from *Time* and *Newsweek*, from the network news and entertainment outlets. They were his fellow fungi, that rare breed of folks whose passion for the movies actually equaled his own. All of them had an opinion about Mitch. Some of them looked up to him. Some of them envied him. A few of the older, second-tier reviewers downright hated him for having attained so lofty a berth at such a tender age. It had taken Mitch a while to get used to this, but he had. He exchanged cordial greetings with one and all. Caught up on the latest news—what was hot, what was not. And then the lights dimmed and Mitch took a seat by himself with his press kit, feeling that same stirring of excited anticipation he always felt when he was about to see a brand-new film for the very first time.

This one, its studio's major $160 million Fourth of July weekend release, was all about evil aliens inhabiting the body of the president and first lady. Fortunately for mankind, first daughter Heather noticed the difference. And knew how to operate a ray gun. It was painfully awful, Mitch felt. He was not alone in this. Several very distinguished New York film critics started talking back to the screen. One even stormed out in the middle. Mitch would never do either of those things. Movies were his religion. Every film, no matter how awful, was sacred. And every theater was a temple.

But he did find himself drifting away, his thoughts straying toward how contrived and false Hollywood's big-budget thrills seemed compared to what real life had had to offer him lately. How devoid of genuine personal consequences such films were. How mindless and predictable and safe. Real life? Real life was not predictable and it was not safe. And there were no stunt doubles or feel-good Spielbergian moments to soften its blows. Real life was Maisie rotting away before his eyes. Real life was the sound of that shovel colliding with Niles Seymour's leg.

Real life was that someone had just tried to kill him. But who? And why? Did he know something? What, damn it?

After it was over, Mitch headed back downstairs, momentarily disoriented by the late-day sunlight and the bustling cab traffic that greeted him out there on the avenue. Blinking and yawning, he trudged his way westward to his second screening, this one in an editing lab in a Times Square office building. All in a day's work.

Mitch hated what had happened to Times Square. His Times Square was the spiritual cradle of the Jim Brown double bill, the Sonny Chiba triple bill and the peep show that never quit. It was garish, grotesque and glorious, an aging streetwalker with smeared lipstick and runs in her stockings. Mitch had always adored it. It was real. It was vulgar. It was New York.

The new Times Square was clean, safe and bogus—a processed cheese food theme park. Disney started the transformation when it cleaned up the New Amsterdam Theater so tourists would come see *The Lion King* roar on Broadway. And then pause afterward to shop at the smiling, happy Disney store, a giant shopping mall emporium festooned with billboards hawking the studio's latest fun-filled family classics. Seemingly overnight, the genuine Times Square had been morphed into a Disneyfied version of Times Square—a soulless, fresh-scrubbed, crime-free urban tourist zone. All that was missing, Mitch felt, was a hologram of Gene Kelly, Frank Sinatra and Jules Munchin dancing down Eighth Avenue in their sailor suits.

His second screening was the new Bruce Willis, which he found to be very much like the old Bruce Willis. If pressed, he could have written his entire review in five choice words: *More broken glass, less hair.*

Afterward, he met Lacy at Virgil's, a boisterous two-story barbecue emporium on West Forty-fifth. Lacy came loaded with some choice office gossip—one of the paper's editorial page columnists was sleeping with one of its Washington correspondents—and neither her husband, who was the managing editor, nor his wife, who worked for CNN, knew about it.

"If that's the case, then how do *you* know about it?"

"Because I'm the one who *used* to be sleeping with him," Lacy shot back, washing down a huge mouthful of pulled pork with a gulp of Dos Equis. Mitch's editor was needle-thin, yet she ate and drank like a longshoreman. She could also chow down on barbecue while wearing white linen and not get a single drop of sauce on herself. He didn't know how she did it. Any of it. "But enough about newsroom yakahoola," she said. "I am way more anxious to hear about you, young sir. Tell me what it's like to be mixed up in a true life murder."

"It's revealing," he answered, chewing thoughtfully. "Fear has a way of bringing out the things that people ordinarily do their damnedest to hide about themselves. Human nature, I guess. We drop our guard. Say things to other people—people such as me—that we wouldn't ordinarily say."

"Such as . . . ?" Lacy asked eagerly.

"What I'm discovering is that you've got this privileged, sheltered little enclave—let's call it old money's last bastion, because that's literally what it is. And on the surface it's all so beautiful and carefree and perfect. But, underneath, these people are just incredibly unhappy, messed up and obsessed with keeping up appearances." He paused to sip his beer. "Dolly's husband, Niles Seymour, didn't belong there. They didn't approve of him. He wasn't one of them. And so one of them took him out. All three murders, I'd swear, spring from that single fact. And a single pathological fear."

"Of what?"

"The outside world," Mitch replied. "That's what this is all about, Lacy. It's not about some evil Freddie Kreuger lurking in their midst, sadistically picking off his victims one by one. It's about the future. It's about change."

"*You've* changed," Lacy observed, studying him carefully. "What's her name?"

Mitch frowned at her. "Whose name?"

"The woman you've met."

"I haven't met anyone."

"Oh, yes, you have."

"Lacy, I haven't met anyone."

"Trust me, I know about these things," Lacy assured him. "Other people's love lives happens to be the only subject I'm truly an expert on. In every other way, I am a complete fraud, as you and I both know." She delicately dabbed barbecue sauce from her mouth with her napkin and reached for her alligator handbag. "I'm very happy for you, my child. Mother approves. And now I have to go. My Wall Street titan will be asleep, limp dick in hand, in precisely one-half hour. The madman gets up at five A.M. Can you imagine?" She rose to her feet, snatching up the check. "You should do a piece on this for the Sunday magazine, Mitch. You really should."

"Maybe I will. When it's all over."

Mitch lingered for a few minutes after she was gone, finishing his beer. Several young career women were seated together at the bar, drinking and laughing. One of them was quite pretty, with shiny eyes and a brilliant smile. She noticed that he was looking at her.

And returned his gaze, steadily and frankly. Mitch looked away suddenly feeling very alone.

He had never missed Maisie more than he did at that moment sitting there by himself in Virgil's.

The night air was breezy and fresh. He strolled across town to the Havenhursts' apartment with his hands in his pockets, enjoying it. The theaters were beginning to let out. The sidewalks were swarming with animated, excited people. Policemen on horseback patrolled the streets. Vendors hawked pretzels. It was life in New York at its finest—something that Mitch never grew tired of.

Still, he glanced over his shoulder every once in a while to see if he was being followed. He was not.

He reached the well-tended brownstone on East Sixty-fifth Street just after ten. He buzzed, as he'd said he would. But Mandy didn't come down. Instead, she told him through the intercom to come on up. He did. The building was elegant and spotless inside, with ornate hallway lamps, charcoal-gray herringbone wallpaper, and a banister of polished hardwood. There were two apartments to a floor. The Havenhursts' was on the third floor, in back, and it had to run them at least three thousand dollars a month.

"We rented it furnished," Mandy said in reference to the décor, which had the *just so* look of a Bloomingdales showroom display. "Don't you just hate it?"

"Not at all," said Mitch, although the gold-veined mirror over the ornamental fireplace did strike him as a bit overwrought. So did the screechy Michael Bolton CD Mandy was listening to. "I thought we were going out."

"I didn't feel like getting dressed again," she said offhandedly. "You don't mind, do you?"

"I guess not."

In fact, what Mandy was wearing was outrageously sexy. A white, gauzy, see-through summer shift that buttoned all the way down the front. She'd left the top two and several of the bottom ones undone, and near as Mitch could tell she didn't have a stitch on underneath. Her bare legs were shapely and shiny. She was bare-foot, her toenails freshly painted the same shade of crimson as her fingernails. Her newly trimmed hair seemed an even creamier shade of blond than it had that morning.

Mandy was a very desirable woman. But she was still married to Bud Havenhurst. And she was still no one who Mitch wanted to get mixed up with.

She was drinking white wine. She offered him some. He accepted it.

"This is nice, isn't it?" she said, pouring him a glass. "Getting away from that island, I mean. I spoke to Bud on the phone this afternoon. He said the press had been calling all day long, wanting to talk to me. I am *so* glad I'm here. It is *so* narrow out there. It is *so* impossible to hide."

And she was, Mitch suddenly realized, *so* drunk.

"I didn't tell him you were coming over," she added, handing him his glass.

"Why not?"

"He would not understand. He just gets terribly jealous."

He sipped his wine. "What was it you wanted to tell me, Mandy?"

Mandy stared at him, dazed and dumbfounded. "Don't believe in wasting time with small talk, do you, Mitch?"

"It's been kind of a long day."

"Well, then have a seat," she commanded, waving him over toward the sofa. "Relax."

He sat on the sofa, but he did not relax. She turned off the music and curled up next to him, one bare leg folded underneath her.

"It's about the night of Dolly's cocktail party," Mandy began. She suddenly seemed edgy and distracted, as if she were trying to listen to a radio broadcast in the other room. Only no radio was playing. "The night when the Weems man was murdered, remember?"

"Yes, I remember."

"Well, Bud did not come to bed that night," she revealed. "Truth of the matter is, he was not even home."

"Where was he?"

Mandy took a sip of her wine. "With her," she said to him over the rim of her glass.

"Dolly?"

She nodded her head, slowly and gravely.

"What are you saying exactly?"

"I'm saying that he and that bitch are still sleeping together," Mandy replied, her voice now low and menacing.

"How do you know this?"

"I *know* because he slips out in the night on me all the time. I've followed him to her place. I've *seen* him."

She wasn't necessarily telling Mitch anything he didn't already know. He knew that Bud kept an eye on Dolly in the night. He'd run smack into the lawyer in her kitchen. "Go on," he urged.

"He didn't come home that night until almost five in the morning. And when he did he was wet—and I mean *soaking* wet. Not from running next door in the rain. But from being out in it for a long, long time."

"I see . . ." Mitch considered this for a moment, wondering where else Bud had been on that stormy night. Where had he gone *after* Mitch was safely back in his own bed? For that matter, where else had Dolly gone? Mitch had no idea. And his mind was racing now. Because the two of them could have killed Weems together. "Did you tell Lieutenant Mitry this?"

Mandy lowered her eyes and gave a brief shake of her head.

"Why not?"

She didn't respond, other than to shake her head again.

"Why are you telling me?"

Now her blue eyes met his. And she did not seem the least bit drunk. She seemed cold sober, her gaze piercing, her body tensed. "Because I want there to be trust between us."

"Well, sure. Trust is important between friends."

"Is that what we are . . . friends?" she asked him imploringly. "People who can say anything to each other? No shame? No fear?"

"Absolutely, Mandy. We're friends."

She untensed now, smiling at him. "Good, I'm *so* glad. Because there *is* a favor I wanted to ask of you. It's kind of a humongous one . . ."

Mitch sipped his wine. "Name it."

"Do you remember me mentioning how much I want to start a family?"

"Two or three little Havenhursts, as I recall."

"Well, Bud can't anymore," she said matter-of-factly. "His sperm count's too low or something. Actually, I'm not sure what it is, since he refuses to go see a fertility specialist. In fact, he's dead set against the whole idea of starting a new family with me. And so what I thought was . . ." She trailed off, swallowing. "He'll *believe* it's his baby, Mitch. And he'd never find out the truth. I swear I'd—"

"Whoa, freeze frame!" Mitch broke in sharply. "What are you saying—that you want to have my test tube baby?"

Mandy frowned at him prettily. "Why, no, Mitch. I'm saying I want to go to bed with you."

"Whew," he gasped, fanning himself. "Is it getting weird in here or is it just me?"

"I'm perfectly serious, Mitch."

"You *can't* be serious!"

"Do I look like I'm kidding?"

"Well, no, but . . ."

"Save my marriage, Mitch," she pleaded. "Save me. Make love to me." Her voice was a soft purr now. And she had moved very close to him on the sofa, her hand caressing his chest. "I am *way* serious." She took his hand and guided it along her bare leg, her skin like electric velvet to his touch. "And *way* good." Now she moved his hand under her shift . . . up, up, up . . . *there*. "And *way* ready," she whispered. Which she most definitely was.

Briefly, Mitch could not believe this was happening to him. Utterly amazing. Also utterly out of the question. He snatched his hand away from hers and got up and crossed the room toward the faux fireplace, Mandy's eyes following him.

"You barely know me," he said hoarsely.

"I know plenty," she countered. "I know you've got brains. You scored at least fourteen hundred on your SAT exams, am I right?"

"Well, yes, but that doesn't necessarily equate with—"

"You're smart. I want someone with smarts. I'm a big, healthy girl, a good athlete, pretty. Between us, we've got all the bases covered. Our kid would be great, Mitch. Pure dynamite."

Mitch cleared his throat, swallowing. "Look, I'm very flattered. And I think you're incredibly attractive. But there's something you have to understand about me . . ."

"What is it?" Mandy wondered anxiously.

"I haven't slept with anyone since my wife passed away. And when I do—if I do—I want it to be someone who I'm seriously involved with. I want it to be special. Can you understand that?"

She let out a sad laugh and got up and came over to him. "Of course, I do. You're a romantic. I think that's wonderful. Quaint and sweet and wonderful. I really do. Only answer me this . . ." She set her wineglass down on the mantle, then whirled and slapped Mitch across the face as hard as she could, an open-handed blow that stung like fire. "What am I, a goddamned bag lady?! Do you *know* how gorgeous I am? Do you *know* how many men want me?! How dare you say no to me?! What are you, some kind of fag?" Now she hurled herself at him, pummeling his chest and shoulders with her fists, kicking him, kneeing him.

The woman was out of control. The woman was totally mad.

Mitch tried to subdue her. He grabbed her by her bare arms, gripping her tightly. They wrestled. They grappled. They fell to the floor with a loud thud, her nails raking his face, an animal snarl coming from deep down in her throat. She was coiled and strong, but he was stronger. And he did outweigh her. And now he had her pinned to the carpet with his body. And as the fight slowly began to seep out of her, her eyes grew softer and her body began to shift and writhe and undulate beneath his, her lips pulling back from her teeth, her breathing becoming shallow and swift. She was, Mitch realized much to his horror, intensely aroused by this. She wanted this.

"God, give it to me right now, Mitch," she moaned, her arms and legs entwining around him now, clutching him to her. One bare, perfect breast was fully exposed, her breath was hot on his face, her tongue in his ear. "Give it to me!"

Recoiling from her as though she was toxic to the touch, Mitch scrambled to his feet and fled out the door, Mandy screaming curses after him at the top of her lungs. He caught a cab home. His driver didn't seem to notice—or care—that he was bleeding from his face, neck and hands. His lip was swollen and numb. His shirt was torn. He felt as if he had just been mauled by a tiger. He *had*. She *was* a tiger. Also a card-carrying lunatic. And the knife cut both ways—if Bud wasn't home in bed the night Weems was murdered, then she had no one to vouch for her own whereabouts either. What if *she* and Niles Seymour had been an item? What if Niles had tried to break it off with her after he took up with Torry? What if Mandy had murdered them both? She did not exactly cope well with rejection, Mitch now felt safe in saying. And she was certainly capable of it. What if Weems found out and had to be done in, too? Mitch could believe it. He could believe all of it.

Mitch took the longest, hottest shower of his entire life when he got home. But he still did not feel clean. He applied antibiotic ointment to his scratches, an ice pack to his lip. He helped himself to a pint of Häagen-Dazs chocolate-chocolate chip. Popped *Angels with Dirty Faces* into his VCR. Turned off all of the lights in the apartment and sat there in the darkness, watching Cagney trade spunky, crackling barbs with Ann Sheridan.

And, slowly, life began to make sense again. And it was fair and it was just and it was fun. And, for the umpteen-millionth time in his thirty-two-year life, Mitch Berger remembered why they made films and why he loved films and why it was that they purposely had nothing whatsoever to do with real life.

After a while he dug out Lieutenant Mitry's business card and called her pager number. She got back to him in exactly two minutes, her voice alert and anxious.

"I'm sorry if I woke you up," Mitch apologized, it being 1:30 in the morning. "But I thought I ought to check in."

"Not a problem, that's why I gave you my number," she responded, her voice partially drowned out by an entire choir of cats meowing in the background. "Sporty, you behave now, girl. No!"

"Just exactly how many cats do you own?" Mitch asked, his words somewhat slurred by his fat lip.

"Not a one. They own me. And if you're wondering about Clemmie . . ."

"I'm not. But seeing as how you mention her . . ."

"When I stopped by this afternoon I found her curled up downstairs in your easy chair. The girl's just moved right on in. Pretty soon she'll be making microwave pizza, talking to her girlfriend on the phone . . . Now what have you got for me? And please, God, make it good."

"Well, somebody in a green trenchcoat did try to push me onto the subway tracks today."

She fell silent.

So silent that Mitch said, "Hello . . . ?"

"Where was this?"

"Times Square."

"Did you report it to the transit police?"

"And say what?"

"What you just said to me."

"No, I didn't."

"Why the hell not?"

"Because whoever it was got away. And no one else saw anything. Who knows, it could have been a random act, some subterranean loon . . ."

"Uh-hunh," she said doubtfully.

"Then again, I should also point out that Mandy Havenhurst and I had just parted company a few minutes earlier."

"You're saying it could have been her. She. Mandy."

"Well, yeah," Mitch acknowledged, fingering his fat lip.

"She was wearing a trenchcoat?"

"Well, no. But she was carrying a good-sized shoulder bag."

"Um, okay, there's one other possibility—Bud Havenhurst."

"What about Bud?"

"He wasn't around today."

"She told me she spoke to him on the phone."

"Maybe she did, but she didn't speak to him at his office. Or at their house. Because he wasn't at either one of those places all day. He wasn't in town, near as I can tell."

"You think he might have followed me in?"

"Her, more likely—if I know men."

"Do you?"

"I can check with the conductors on the *Shoreliner* tomorrow," she said, deftly slipping his jab.

"What if he drove in?"

"Then he's very clever," she admitted. "Are you all right?"

"Why, don't I sound all right?"

"No, you sound like Elmer Fudd," she said, stifling a yawn. "Have you been to the dentist or something?"

"No, I've just paid a round-trip visit to Mandy's dark side. She came on to me this evening, big time."

"And . . . ?" The lieutenant's voice seemed a degree or two chillier now.

"And I told her I wasn't interested, right?"

"How would I know? You're the one telling the story."

"Okay, I told her I wasn't interested."

"Fine. You told her you weren't interested. And . . . ?"

"And she tried to claw my eyes out."

"Well, that certainly fits with the girl's history."

"I did find out something interesting from her, though. While she was still in full cuddle mode, I mean." Mitch filled the lieutenant in on what Mandy had said about Bud being elsewhere, and wet, the night Tuck Weems was murdered—taking care to point out how this meant Mandy had no one to vouch for her own whereabouts either.

"Interesting," she concluded. "Sounds like you've had yourself quite a day."

Mitch allowed as how he had. And then she was yawning again.

And the cats were yowling. So he said, "I'll let you get back to sleep. Sorry I woke you. What does it say anyway?"

"What does what say?"

"The T-shirt you're wearing."

"Man, how do you know I'm wearing a T-shirt?"

"I just do. Why, have you got a problem with it?"

"With what, the way you keep acting like you're up inside my head?"

"I guess this means yes."

"No . . . Just trying to understand you, that's all."

"Well, that's it right there, Lieutenant. I'm trying to understand you, too."

"Why?"

"Why not?"

"Man, that's a riddle, not an answer!"

"I don't know why, okay? Only that nothing in my life makes any sense right now. And it seems important to understand something. Or someone."

She was silent a long moment. "It doesn't say anything."

"What doesn't?"

"My T-shirt. It's blank. No message. None. Good night, Mitch." She hung up the phone before he could get out one more word.

He threw the dead bolt on his front door and climbed into bed. It wasn't until he'd turned off his bedside lamp, punched his pillow two times and closed his eyes that he realized she'd finally stopped calling him Mr. Berger.

CHAPTER 12

DES LAY THERE STARING at the ceiling while the four Spice Girls chased each other blissfully around the bed, scampering over her, rumbling, tumbling. Their energy was boundless. So was their ability to amuse themselves. Their whole universe was right here inside this house. And, within its carpeted confines, they were totally content.

Damn, she envied them sometimes.

She had not been asleep when Mitch Berger called, even though she'd been awake nearly forty-eight hours straight and her body was exhausted. But she could not shut down her mind. It had kept right on searching and rewinding. Sorting through Big Sister's residents, one by one. Reviewing what she knew about them. Focusing on what she didn't know. And now she had a new fact to throw into the mix: Someone had tried to take out Mitch Berger.

Why? How did eliminating him link up to the three murders? Was Mandy responsible for it? If so, why had she let him leave her place alive tonight? How did *that* make any sense?

Des lay there, wondering. Same as she wondered how that man knew what she was wearing at this very moment.

Sighing, she reached for the phone again and dialed the number she knew so well. It rang twice before she heard the familiar rumbling voice at the other end.

"I need to see you," she said, instead of hello.

"I'll put the coffee on," he said, instead of good-bye.

There had never been any wasted words between the two of them.

Des dressed hurriedly. Every cat in the house assumed it was happy meal fun time—if she was up, then that spelled food. Not knowing when she'd be back again, she gave in to them. Working her way from room to room, bowl to bowl, stepping her way patiently through her furry entourage. Big Bad Voodoo Daddy, her mud room resident, was in particularly cheery form at two A.M.—he merely glowered at her, a low, baleful moan coming from deep down in his throat.

Des had half a mind to stuff him in a carrier and drop him on Mandy Havenhurst's doorstep with a short, sweet message taped to his chest: *"From me to you, bitch."*

She paused in her studio to examine the sketch she'd started working on before she went to bed. It was a sketch of Mitch Berger. She'd cut his grainy black-and-white photograph out of the *Hartford Courant*, pinned it to the easel and studied it long and hard. Then she'd drawn what she had seen. Reducing him to shadows and shapes. Abstracting him, deconstructing him, *finding* him. Now she unclipped the portrait and slid it into her portfolio.

Then she grabbed her keys and jumped in her slicktop, steering it down Hemlock Hollow in the silent darkness to Amity Road, which took her to the Wilbur Cross Parkway. She headed in the direction of New Britain, the home of Stanley Tools and the Pontiac Trans Am capital of Southern New England. Des didn't know if there was any connection between these two facts. Probably. There were a few overnight truckers out on the road, flying. Her presence there slowed them right on down, since absolutely nobody in the state of Connecticut drove an unmarked Ford Crown Victoria sedan except for a trooper. When somebody spotted her, they eased right off the gas. If she slowed to 30 in a 65 mph zone, they would, too. No one dared pass her. No one.

Kensington, her destination, was a working-class suburb of the Hardware City. The small, neat house was located in a neighborhood of small, neat houses belonging to school teachers, nurses, postal workers and other hardworking people.

Strivers Row, Brandon used to call it mockingly.

Des knew it simply as the place where she had been raised.

The porch light was on. And Buck Mitry was seated at the kitchen table in his flannel bathrobe, patiently drinking his coffee. He was good for ten or twelve cups a day. Used to be a heavy smoker as well, but gave that up as a twenty-fifth anniversary present to Des's mother, who had then proceeded to leave him for her high school sweetheart, an Allstate claims adjustor down in Augusta, Georgia. "I am reborn," she had told Des at the wedding. "I have rediscovered laughter and joy." Buck remained behind in the house alone—like father, like daughter. He was a big, rangy man with a furrowed brow, graying hair and wire-rimmed glasses. His hands were immense and blunt-fingered. He had been a fine athlete as a young man, even played first base in the Cleveland Indians organization for two years out of high school until he met Des's mother and decided to get serious. He took the state police exam in 1968, when they happened to be looking for a few good, black troopers. He had risen slowly but steadily through the ranks. And now, at age fifty-six, he was the deputy superintendent— the highest-ranking black man in the history of the state. He got there by being honest, steady and careful. He got there by getting along. No flash, no dash. Buck Mitry believed in proper procedure. He believed in saying please and thank you. He believed in shined shoes, muted ties and dignified charcoal-gray suits. He owned eight such suits, all identical. Always, he had been guarded with his emotions. Des, who was his only child, had never once seen her father lose control of his temper. To the best of her knowledge, no one else had either.

That was why they called him the Deacon.

"Correct me if I'm wrong," she said to him, hands on her hips, "but isn't that the same robe I gave you for Christmas back when I was *twelve*?"

"Quality never wears out," he said, smiling at her faintly. "You got a cold?"

"Allergy."

"Sounds like a cold."

"It's an allergy."

She kissed him on the forehead and poured herself some coffee and sat down opposite him, hearing steady, determined crunching noises coming from the direction of the back door. Cagney and Lacey, the two stray cats Des had talked him into adopting, were nose down in their kibble bowls. They, too, thought it was time for breakfast.

"Why'd you go and do that to your hair?" he asked, eyeing her dreadlocks critically. "What is it, some kind of a statement?"

"No statement. It's just hair."

"Doesn't look professional," he grumbled at her. "And the powers that be think you've become a Rastafarian."

"They are seriously behind the times."

"They are in charge."

"It's just hair," Des repeated, louder this time.

"So why don't you wear it normal?"

"This *is* normal, Daddy. The Anita Hill look was chemicals. And when my head looked like the business end of a felt-tip marking pen, that was chemicals, too. Now I look like *me*. And it's my head, thank you, so let's just drop the subject, okay?"

They dropped it, Des gazing across the table at him in anxious silence. The two of them were not especially close. No one ever got close to the Deacon, not even Des's mother. If she had she wouldn't have fled elsewhere in search of joy.

"If this about Captain Polito I can't help you, Desiree," he spoke up. "Polito runs his own squad his own way. And if he wants to bring in further supervisory manpower, that's his business."

"That's not why I needed to see you," she said quietly.

He sat back in his chair, big hands folded before him on the table, waiting for her to continue.

She took a sip of her coffee, followed by a deep breath. "I want to see Crowther."

His eyes widened at the mention of the one man, the only man in the Connecticut State Police who outranked him—Superintendent John Crowther. "What about?"

"Some unanswered questions from his past."

"Which unanswered questions, girl?" he asked sternly. "And don't you be giving me any double-talk. I want it straight up. I want it specific."

"The Weems murder-suicide on Big Sister Island thirty years ago. Crowther was the investigating officer."

"So . . . ?"

"So the bodies were found by a seventeen-year-old girl named Dolly Peck who had recently been forcibly raped by the male victim. So this girl's grandfather happened to be a U.S. senator. So this girl now goes by the name Dolly Seymour and is smack dab in the middle of three more murders that practically have me chewing my own foot off. She's the linchpin, Daddy, then and now. I've been looking through Crowther's official bio. The man's career just took off after the Weems case. He went from sergeant to captain in the blink of an eye. I am talking *zooom*. And it so happens that his report is full of holes. So is Dolly Seymour's memory—she claims to remember nothing of what happened that day. I have to find out what he left out."

He got up and refilled his cup, his face stony. "You want to rattle the man's cage, is that it?"

"Absolutely not. I could care less about the politics. All I care about is this investigation. Here and now. What's happening *now* isn't adding up. If I can find out what really went down thirty years ago, maybe it will."

"And if it doesn't?"

"I am under the gun. I need results. I can't help it if the trail leads me to him, can I?"

He considered this for a long moment before he said, "Have you gone through Polito on this?"

She ducked her head, her mouth tightening.

"Uh-hunh," he grunted. "Because he'd tell you to drop it. And that's exactly what I'm telling you to do. Don't go there. You don't accuse the superintendent of falsifying a report and concealing information. You'd be committing political suicide."

"I told you, this isn't about politics."

"Girl, *everything* is about politics," he said, shaking his head at her. "That is the *reality* of the situation. And if you don't accept it you will get ground into dust. Crowther is one tough SOB. You do not want to go one-on-one with him. What do you think is going to happen— you'll twitch your fine tail at him and the man will spill something he's been holding onto since Richard Nixon was in the White House?"

Des could feel her face burning now. She said nothing.

"Do you honestly think he's going to jeopardize his whole career to help you put away a rich white woman he didn't put away thirty years ago? Not a chance. All that'll happen is you will make yourself one powerful enemy. Probably end up back in uni, staked out at a speed trap outside of Killingley. Is that what you want? Explain yourself, girl. What is going on here?"

Des got up and went over to the sink, aware of his eyes on her. Clearly, he was baffled by her. She had never given him much reason to be. She had always been the good daughter. Good grades. Good manners. Never got into drugs. Never brought home a thug. Hell, her idea of running away from home was going to West Point. She'd taken the right job. Married the right man—or so they'd all believed. Never once had she been the wild child. Never once had she rebelled.

And now, standing here in this small, spotless kitchen of this small, spotless house, Des suddenly felt herself suffocating. Every nerve ending in her body seemed to be crying out for spontaneity, for *life*. "I don't know what's going on here," she replied softly.

"Well, Desiree, you'd better figure it out. And soon. Because there is zero room for doubt in our business." He watched her intently over his coffee cup. "Tell me, what's his name?"

"Whose name?"

"This man who has thrown you for a loop."

"No man has thrown me anywhere," she shot back, bristling. "Why do you immediately assume it's a man? Why can't it just be me?"

"Little late for us to be having this conversation, isn't it?"

"Are you talking about late in the evening or late in life?"

"Like I said," he responded, "it's late."

She rinsed out her cup and sat back down at the table across from him. "So what do I do now?"

"Your job."

"You just told me that the one man who might be able to help me is off limits."

"*That's* your job," he affirmed. "To get results, no matter what. If it were a smooth, easy ride, nothing but cherry pie, they wouldn't be

198

paying you. You'd be paying them. That's the truth, girl. That's the real world." He trailed off a moment, his broad chest rising and falling. "Deal with it. Or find yourself a new world to live in."

The Havenhursts, Bud and Mandy, lived in a doll-sized version of the big summer cottage where Redfield and Bitsy Peck lived. The shutters and front door of the little house were painted colonial blue. The window boxes were bursting with pansies. Two cars were parked out front in the gravel drive, a Range Rover and an old MG convertible.

One tabloid news crew was parked at the entrance to the bridge. Otherwise, all was quiet.

No Studebaker pickup was parked outside of Mitch Berger's carriage house. Des pulled up in her slicktop and got out, buttoning her blazer. The stiff morning breeze out on Big Sister was distinctly chilly.

She used his spare key to check up on Baby Spice, a.k.a. Clementine. This time Des found her upstairs in Mitch's half-open T-shirt drawer, fast asleep. The little vixen barely stirred at the sound of Des cooing at her. Doubtless she had spent the wee hours exploring her new universe. She still had plenty of food and water. Her litter box had been used. Des cleaned it out, yawning hugely. What she really felt like doing was shucking her clothes and jumping into that nice warm bed.

The man's clothes closet was downstairs. Des opened the closet door, figuring now was as good a time as any to find out. A wool shirt Mitch Berger had been wearing the first day she met him was hanging from a hook. She removed it and buried her face in it, inhaling his aroma. Instantly, she felt a fluttering sensation all the way from her tummy to her toes. Followed by a sense of giddy lightheadedness. Briefly, she thought she might faint.

And this was with a stuffed-up nose.

Damn, damn, damn.

She hurriedly returned the shirt to its hook and went back out to her cruiser and popped the trunk, staring down at what she'd

brought with her. It lay there atop her first-aid kit, flares, blanket
and other emergency gear. She hesitated a moment before she
removed it. She could not believe how nervous she was. Her hands
were actually shaking. She took it inside and laid it on his desk. She
locked up and slid the key back under the boot scraper.

Then she knocked on the Havenhursts' door.

It was Mandy who answered it. She had on a plum-colored Izod
shirt and khaki slacks, her long blond hair pulled back in a tight,
tight ponytail. In fact, everything about her seemed pulled taut. Her
flesh was drawn across the bones of her face like the skin over a
snare drum. The cords in her neck stood out, fists were clenched,
knuckles white.

"I didn't expect to find you here, Mrs. Havenhurst," Des said,
surprised.

"Why wouldn't I be here?" Mandy responded sharply, her eyes
icy blue pinpoints. "This is my home, Lieutenant. I live here."

"I understood you were in New York."

Mandy stared at her with utter contempt. "You 'understood' I
was in New York?"

"Mr. Berger happened to mention it."

"Is Mitch back?" she asked casually, shooting a not-so-causal
look over Des's shoulder at his house.

"No, we spoke on the phone."

"Oh, I see. Well, I drove back late last night with Bud. We picked
up my car at the station."

"Your husband was in the city yesterday, too?"

"He was," Mandy replied, smiling tightly. It came off more like a
grimace. Actually, Mandy's face was starting to remind Des of one
of those sun-bleached animal skulls that people find out in the
desert and hang as wall ornaments in their homes.

"You and Mr. Havenhurst went in together?" she persisted, wondering if this creamy, twisted blonde was ever going to invite her
inside.

"No, we went in separately—our schedules didn't quite match
up." Mandy raised her chin at Des, her nostrils flaring. "I don't

mean to be pointy, Lieutenant, but I'm not exactly accustomed to having my comings and goings put under a microscope by law enforcement officers."

"Most impressive," Des said, smiling at her approvingly. "I mean it—you've got what my friend Ms. Bella Tillis calls *chutzpah*. But you and I both know that you have an extensive police record, so let's not pull each other's curls, allright?"

"Whatever Mitch told you about last night isn't true!" Mandy declared, her voice rising, cheeks mottling. "He got the wrong idea about me. About us. He came after me. And he wouldn't take a firm *no* for an answer. And he—"

"Mr. Berger told me next to nothing," Des said coldly. "I'd suggest you do the same, unless you're looking to press formal charges."

"Why, no. I was simply trying to—"

"Good. Because I am not someone who you want to be talking to about this. I am not your sister. I am not your friend. And I am for damned sure not Doctor Laura. Now is your husband in? I'd like to ask him some questions."

Mandy finally let her inside. It was quaint and snug, with low ceilings and lots of country antique furniture. Arrangements of dried herbs were on display everywhere, just like in *Country Living* magazine. It reminded Des of that inn in rural Vermont she and Brandon stayed in once. All that was missing was the pervasive smell of potpourri. There was a parlor and a dining room. The airy farmhouse kitchen opened onto the back porch. Bud Havenhurst was slumped at a wicker table out there with a cup of coffee, his back to the panoramic view of Long Island Sound.

It occurred to Des that only someone who had lived on Big Sister a very long time would sit facing the house, not the water.

He wore a starched white shirt, striped tie, dark slacks and even darker circles under his eyes. He seemed very tired and drawn. The smile he gave her was a weak one. "Good morning, Lieutenant," he said, climbing politely to his feet. "Sorry if I'm not fully awake yet. We got back quite late last night. Please, sit."

Des did so, facing the view. A couple of fishing boats were

already out, and a work boat was chugging its way across the Sound toward Plum Island.

"Do you need me here, sugar?" Mandy asked him from the kitchen doorway. "I want to get some things at the market."

"You go right ahead, hon." He made a big fuss out of escorting his young wife out, doting on her, kissing her good-bye. He seemed excessively clingy. Des found herself wondering if this was for her benefit. She heard the little MG start up with a throaty roar and speed off in a splatter of gravel. Then Havenhurst came back and sat down and said, "Now, then, Lieutenant, how may I help you?"

"I tried to see you at your office yesterday. You weren't in."

"Some things came up that required my presence in New York."

"Your wife and Mr. Berger rode into the city themselves yesterday morning."

"That's right. She told me she ran into him on the train. I drove in a bit later in the day."

"Why didn't you and she go in together?"

"It was something of a last-minute thing on my part," he answered vaguely. "A financial matter."

"Can anyone confirm what time you arrived?"

"The fellow at the parking garage I use, I imagine."

Des nodded, well aware that for twenty dollars your average parking lot attendant would swear under oath that he had seen Elvis pull up in a pink Cadillac—with Marilyn Monroe seated next to him in the front seat.

He rubbed a thumb carefully along his big, thrusting chin, as if to test his morning shave. "It's on Second Avenue and Sixty-sixth Street. And I still have the ticket stub somewhere, I think. But, frankly, I'm having trouble seeing how my visit to New York has anything to do with matters that concern you."

"It concerns me," Des explained, "because someone tried to shove Mr. Berger in front of a subway train yesterday morning in Times Square. He claims it happened shortly after he said good-bye to your wife."

Now Bud Havenhurst went silent on her, his face a stone cold blank. The man conveyed nothing. It was just like sitting across the table from a lawn statue. *Lawyers*. They were worse than born liars, she reflected bitterly. These bastards were trained at it by high priests.

She elected to move on. "Let's talk about your ex-wife's missing money."

"Mitch spoke to you about that?" Bud asked her uneasily.

"He did."

"And you understand why I did what I did?"

"I understand *bupkes*," she said sharply. "Maybe you believed you were acting in your ex-wife's best interest. But I'm not prepared to say whether what you did was legal or ethical or proper. Or whether a Connecticut State Bar Association grievance panel will find probable cause for misconduct. Or whether a judge will suspend your license to practice law." She paused a moment, the better to dangle her bait. "Of course, if you're prepared to give some *news* I can *use*, then that's another matter entirely . . ."

Bud Havenhurst suddenly became very interested in the view. He even got up and went over to the porch railing so he could get a better look at it. "Such as?"

"Such as it occurs to me that you are in and out of Mrs. Seymour's house . . ."

He turned back to face her. "It used to be my house," he said quietly.

"Did you write that Dear John letter?"

He shook his head emphatically. "If I had done that, then I'd be Niles Seymour's murderer. And I'm not."

"You weren't home in bed the night that Tuck Weems was murdered. Where were you?"

Havenhurst didn't respond. Just went into statue mode again.

"Were you with your ex-wife? Were you sleeping with her?"

He heaved a pained sigh. "No, Dolly wouldn't have me again in a million years," he replied, his face expressing a curious mix of longing, frustration and hopelessness. He was an older man besotted with a volatile and promiscuous younger woman. Yet he clearly remained attached to his first wife. Maybe he just didn't know what, or who, he wanted. Maybe he was just a fool—he *was* a fully grown adult male after all. "I just looked in on her," he explained. "To make sure she wasn't wandering. She does, as I believe I've mentioned to you."

"You didn't mention that you were soaking wet when you got home. How did you get so wet, Mr. Havenhurst?"

"I walked on the beach."

"In the middle of a violent rainstorm?"

"I like to walk in the rain. I find it therapeutic."

"Are you in need of therapy?"

"Everyone is in need of therapy."

And these were supposed to be the happy people. Had their own damned island. If they weren't happy, who was? "Did anyone see you?" she asked.

"No, of course not."

Just as no one could recall seeing his son, Evan, and Jamie Devers docked out on Little Sister Island having themselves a bonfire. She had checked with the Coast Guard. She had checked with the boat-yards. Nothing. Everywhere she turned it came up nothing.

Havenhurst abruptly glanced at his watch. "I really have to be getting to my law office, Lieutenant. A number of my later appointments got pushed up to this morning because of Niles Seymour's funeral this afternoon. Are we done?"

"Not a problem," Des said agreeably. "I wouldn't want to keep you from your appointments. The big wheel of justice must keep on turning." She climbed to her feet and treated him to her maximum-wattage smile. "But, counselor, I would not be saying we're done."

CHAPTER 13

"HONEY, I'M HOME!" MITCH called out as he came charging in the door.

And bright-eyed little Clemmie was right there, slipping and sliding her way across the wooden floor to greet him. She seemed kind of clumsy for a cat, in his opinion. In fact, she was so adept at tripping over her own feet that Mitch was starting to think she might have a future as a starting wide receiver for the New York Giants. He picked her up. Petted her. Told her how much he'd missed her, managing to discover yet again just how sharp her young teeth were.

He could not believe how happy he was to be back. To smell the sea air. To be in his little house on Big Sister Island. He could not believe it.

The lieutenant had been there some time earlier that morning. Mitch knew this because Clemmie's litter box was clean. Also because the lieutenant had left a highly prized possession of her own behind on his desk.

Her portfolio.

She had set it there without fanfare. No note. No fuss. Just *wham*, here it is. This, Mitch concluded, was the woman's style.

Inside, he found two dozen charcoal drawings that had been torn out of a sketch pad and loosely gathered. Mitch was not sure what to expect. The only time he'd observed her at work she'd been parked out on the bridge sketching what he'd assumed to be a landscape. He didn't know what her art would be about. Had no idea what it would show him.

What it showed him was pure horror.

Faces that were smashed and contorted and frozen. Innocent

lives that had been destroyed by violence and hate and the evil that men and women do to each other. What it showed him, one drawing after another, was the soul of an artist. Lieutenant Mitry was trying to cleanse herself of the destruction she saw in her daily life. To capture it. To understand it. And she had—her drawings jumped right off the page. They were breathtaking in their visceral impact. They were positively haunting. Leafing through them, Mitch was reminded of the tabloid crime photographs of Weegie. But there was more to the lieutenant's drawings than that. Within them, Mitch found both the noirish foreboding of Edward Hopper and the violent spiritual anguish of Edvard Munch, the great Norwegian impressionist who gave the world *The Scream*. Within them, he found a vision that was uniquely her own.

Dead people. She drew nothing but dead people. All except for the last one Mitch came to. This one was a portrait of a living man whose face was a wretched mask of pain, his eyes hollow and etched with sorrow. As Mitch stared at it, he realized with a shudder that it was a portrait of himself.

He immediately gathered her drawings back up, jumped in his pickup and headed for Dorset's graceful, tree-lined historic district. Several cruisers, marked and unmarked, were parked out in front of the white, wood-framed town hall. Also a television news crew van. Mitch left the portfolio on the seat of his truck and went inside, where he was nearly bowled over by the smell of musty old carpeting. The office of the first selectman, the village's equivalent of a mayor, was just inside the front door. His desk was positioned out in the middle of the room and his door was open. A quaint old Yankee custom—anyone who wanted to speak his or her mind just had to walk in, sit down and start talking. Right now, that anyone was a freshly minted J-school grad who looked remarkably like an eleven-year-old child wearing Lesley Stahl's clothing and hair. A cameraman was stationed in the doorway, capturing their conversation on video, the lights from his camera bathing the office in artificial brightness. The first selectman, a wheezy white-haired man with an extremely red nose, looked very unhappy.

Lieutenant Mitry's temporary command center was located down the hall in the conference room. Here Mitch found a hive of activity. Four uniformed troopers talking on telephones, two more pecking away at computers. Files and evidence reports were stacked everywhere. Lieutenant Mitry was locked in grim conversation with her short, muscular sergeant. It was he who noticed Mitch first.

"Help you?" he grunted, eyeballing Mitch's fat lip with chilly suspicion.

"I'll take this," she broke in quickly, crossing the room toward Mitch. "What have you got for me?"

"Something out in my truck that you left behind."

Her gaze narrowed, her almond-shaped eyes studying his anxiously. "I'll be back in a sec, Rico," she said.

They went out the door together.

"Quite some number Mandy did on your lip," she observed, as they strolled out into the sunshine, the midday sun glinting off her freshly oiled dreadlocks. "You look like you were in a head-on collision."

"Don't kid yourself, Lieutenant—I was."

"Funny, she didn't have a scratch on her."

"That's because I'm a gentleman."

"That's not what *she* said."

Mitch frowned. "Why, what did she say?"

"Bud Havenhurst was in the city yesterday, too," the lieutenant mentioned, sidestepping him.

"I thought he hated the city."

"He may hate it, but he was there."

"Interesting. Find out anything else?"

"The forensic entomologist discovered no insect life on Niles Seymour's remains that's inconsistent with the life found on Big Sister."

"Meaning he was killed on the island?"

"Meaning there's nothing to indicate he wasn't," she replied. "Toxicology turned up a little something on Tuck Weems—the man was flying high when he died."

"Marijuana?"

"And booze. Blood alcohol level of point two-six percent—more than twice the legal limit. I'm doubting he could have driven his truck down to the beach in that condition."

"What does that suggest to you?"

"That he split a fifth of Jack D on the beach with his killer before he got himself done."

"In the pouring rain?"

"Okay, in the front seat."

"Did you find a bottle anywhere?"

"Nope."

Now Mitch opened the door of his truck and removed her portfolio and handed it to her. "I'm sorry, but it is my duty to inform you that you're a fraud."

"Just exactly what do you mean by that?" she demanded.

"I mean you're an artist, not a cop."

She leaned her long frame against the truck and sighed, hugging the folio to her chest. "Please don't be doing a number on my head right now, okay?"

"I'm totally serious. You should be doing this full time. You have to. Your technique needs refining, and you need to start thinking about color, although there's a lot to be said for how the black and white captures the immediacy of a news photo. But just think of what's in store for you. Look at Munch's career. He got into nature painting, etching, printmaking, lithography . . . He also had a nervous breakdown in 1908 but, hey, that was him. Besides, he was Norwegian. The point is, you have a gift."

"How do you know?" she asked, squinting at him uncertainly.

"I just do. But if you don't believe me, let's march on down the street to the Art Academy. They've got world-renowned artists teaching classes there. Classes you should be taking. We'll show your portfolio to them. Come on," he said, grabbing her by the wrist.

"Let go of me, Mitch."

"They'll tell you the same thing. I'm positive."

"And I said let go!" she cried, wrenching her hand free of his. "I *really* don't like people tugging at me."

"Well, you'd better get used to it, because I come from a long line of great American tuggers. And I would *kill* to have one tenth of your talent. Christ, don't you realize just how gifted you are?"

She stood there in wary silence, her eyes probing his. At that moment, she reminded Mitch of a big cat that suddenly found itself on unfamiliar turf—feet wide apart, hackles raised, ready to run. Or to strike. Depending on what happened next.

"Tell me something," Mitch said to her in a low, calm voice. "Exactly why did you decide to show it to me?"

"I'm beginning to ask myself that same question."

"Okay, I think I know why you did."

She let out a brief laugh. "Somehow I had a feeling you would."

"You were hoping I'd tell you that you were no good—so you could forget about the whole thing. Not a chance. I won't do it. You *are* good. And you know it. And you're scared to death. I don't blame you, believe me. Talent is a very frightening thing."

"Now why do you say that?"

"Because if you have it, you have to do something with it. You owe it to yourself. Wasting talent is one of the deadly sins. Maybe it didn't make the Bible's top seven, but it's right there at the top of mine. You *must* study and work and grow. And that's where it gets scary. Because the people closest to you will think you've gone a little nuts. They will not understand why you've quit your job—"

"Wait, who's quitting her job?"

"And they for sure will not approve, because it's impulsive, impractical, selfish and all of those other things we're taught not to be when we grow up. There's big-time risk. Most of us never take that kind of a risk our whole lives. But most of us don't have your kind of talent. Am I getting through to you, Lieutenant? You are *not* a cop. You are leading somebody else's life." He broke off, watching her closely. She looked shaken. In fact, she looked like she was about to be sick. "I'm not telling you anything you haven't already thought of, am I?"

She considered this for a long moment before she said, "Nice words. Every single one of them."

"But . . . ?"

"What makes you think there's a *but*?"

"I hear a *but*."

She glowered at him. "*But* art doesn't pay the bills."

"You'll get by."

"You're dreaming. This is real life—not some Robin Williams movie where everybody hugs everybody at the end."

Mitch shook his head at her. "If you don't watch out you are going to make me really angry at you."

"Why, are you a big Robin Williams fan?"

"Don't play games with me, Lieutenant!"

Her eyes widened at him in surprise. "You're totally serious about this, aren't you?"

"Totally," Mitch confirmed. "And unless you're prepared to be as serious about it as I am I don't ever want to discuss it with you again."

"I don't take well to bullying," she warned him.

"I'm *trying* to encourage you."

"Well, *try* a different way before that lip of yours suddenly starts bleeding again." Four helmeted school girls on rollerblades went teetering past them on the sidewalk, giggling. She watched them. She seemed bothered and distracted. "Look, I don't mean to be ungrateful. I appreciate you saying what you said. I've just got a lot on my mind right now, okay? Something I have to do. And I'm not looking forward to it."

"Do you want to talk about it?"

She hesitated before she gave him a shake of her head.

"May I ask you something personal?"

"What is it?"

"Why did you draw me?"

She immediately tensed, clutching her folio tightly. "It was . . . an attempt to try to understand a certain situation."

"What situation?"

She ducked her head, didn't answer him. She seemed very uncomfortable.

"Are you saying that you think I'm dead inside?"

"No, no," she said hastily. "Not at all. It was more about me than about you. I-I probably shouldn't have shown that one to you." She raised her eyes to his. "I'm sorry."

"No need to apologize. None at all. You don't ever have to . . ." Mitch swallowed, his Adam's apple suddenly feeling as if it were the size of a musk melon. He gazed at her. She gazed back right at him, her eyes large and lustrous behind her horn-rimmed glasses. "I'm genuinely honored that you chose me to show your work to, Lieutenant," he said. "It's an experience that I'll never forget." Then Mitch got in his truck, started it up and eased away from the curb, glancing back at her in his rearview mirror.

She remained there on the curb, watching him pull away. She was still standing there, watching him, when he went around the bend by the public library and was gone.

CHAPTER 14

AN ATTEMPT TO TRY to understand a certain situation?!

Jesus, how could she have said something so stiff, so impersonal, so outright lame? Des could not imagine as she piloted her slicktop up the Post Road toward Uncas Lake. Hell, compared to her the IRS sounded positively warm and fuzzy. What on earth had she been thinking? She'd wanted to tell him she was trying to sort out her feelings, that's what. But she hadn't wanted to spring that particular f-word out into the open air and so she got all bollixed up and *wham*, out came the Notification of Pending Audit.

I do not know how to talk to a man anymore. I am hopeless.

Des slowed her cruiser way down as she rolled past the seedy cottage where Tuck Weems had lived. He was scheduled for burial that day, same as Niles Seymour. Same minister. No doubt a lot of the same mourners. Dolly Seymour would be there, for one. That rusty pickup was still up on blocks in his driveway. No other vehicles were parked there. There was no actual sign that anyone was around.

Des kept on going past more shacks and bungalows, wondering if Mitch Berger were right. *Had* she wanted to hear that she was no good? She didn't know. All she knew was that her life was starting to feel as if it were spinning out of control. It was a most unfamiliar feeling. It made her slightly dizzy.

The road began to climb steeply as it snaked its way around the lake. The resident trooper's house was perched high on a hill overlooking the water. Tal Bliss had served two tours in the jungle in Vietnam. Sunlight and fresh air were a priority for him now. She deduced this from the way he'd added on a second storey with walls of glass and a wooden deck suspended all the way around. From the road, the place looked like a firefighter's lookout station in the mountains.

His bedrooms were downstairs. The kitchen, dining room and living room were up on the second floor, the better to watch over his domain. He kept the house very neat and clean. Particularly his professional kitchen, which gleamed.

"My one and only indulgence," he confessed, as he poured Des coffee.

There was a center island with a double sink and well-used copper pots hanging from a wrought-iron holder bolted into the ceiling. The countertops were granite, the cupboards pickled-pine. The range was a stainless-steel Jenn-Air with a down-draft vent, the refrigerator a top-of-the-line Sub-Zero. No walls enclosed Tal Bliss's kitchen. It opened right out into the sun-drenched living and dining area.

On the stereo, Miles and Trane were putting the moves on "Kind of Blue," filling the house with everything that was sweet and pure.

Dirty Harry, an immense orange-and-white male tabby, was out on the deck applying his death stare to a squirrel in a nearby cedar tree, his body poised, his tail swaying back and forth. The squirrel was chittering at him in derision. Down below, two men in a kayak were making their way slowly across the shimmering blue lake.

Lunch had been the resident trooper's idea. When Des had mentioned that they needed to talk he had extended the invite. And she had accepted. When Tal Bliss offered to cook you something you did not say no. He wore a denim apron over a spotless white T-shirt while he was preparing it. Right now, he was finishing a fruit salad, his big tanned hands moving swiftly and expertly as he sectioned a pink grapefruit and halved strawberries. A quiche was baking in the oven, smelling marvelous.

"You shouldn't have gone to so much trouble."

"No trouble at all, Lieutenant," he assured her. "I already had the pie shell on hand. I make a half-dozen of them at a time and freeze them. Just hope you like sage. I've fallen in love with it this year and am trying it in *everything*." He tossed fresh blackberries and a cup of toasted walnuts into the salad, and began chopping up some mint. "We should really have ourselves a spicy Bloody Mary with this meal. Damned shame we're on duty."

"Damned shame."

"Oh, I got a call from Bud Havenhurst," he mentioned offhandedly. "Regarding what happened yesterday in New York."

Somehow, this did not surprise Des.

"He felt a bit more at ease talking to a man about it, I guess," he explained. "So I listened."

"To what?" Des sipped her coffee.

"Apparently, Mandy gave Mitch Berger some form of playful shove on the subway platform as a train was pulling in. All in fun, was how Bud described it."

"And just exactly what's so damned fun about it?"

"Bud said that she considers danger to be a powerful aphrodisiac," Bliss replied, coloring more than a little. He wasn't so comfortable talking to a woman about this either. "She feels when someone has been mortally frightened that he or she is more susceptible to achieving a heightened level of sexual arousal. It seems she intended to seduce him later that evening. And this was simply her idea of . . ."

". . . Foreplay?"

"According to Bud, she would have pulled Mitch back if there was even a remote chance he might fall." Bliss had a pained expression on his face. He was hating this. He paused to check on his quiche in the oven. It was done. He removed it and placed it on a rack, fragrant and golden brown. "She was strictly playing a game."

Des shook her head at him skeptically. "Are you trying to kid me, Trooper?"

"Why, no, Lieutenant."

"Good, because there is no such thing as *playful* when it comes to pushing an unsuspecting individual in front of an oncoming train. They teach kindergarteners that. And when an adult in full command of her faculties does it, that's called reckless endangerment. In Mandy Havenhurst's case it might even qualify as assault with intent. She has a *track record* for inflicting bodily harm on men. I mean, come on, this is *so* not sane."

"I know, I know," Bliss agreed quickly. "Believe me, I'm not excusing it. Or condoning it. I'm merely reporting what Bud told me. And you'd better get ready, because there's more." He hesitated, clearing his throat. "Bud was there when she hit on Mitch at the apartment."

"What do you mean he was there?"

"I mean he was listening in the bedroom the whole time. Watching, too, I imagine. Another little game they play. It . . . excites both of them."

"They get off on making each other jealous—is that it?"

"Precisely."

"And what does he . . . ?"

"He tells her he's still sleeping with Dolly."

"Is he?"

"I'm quite confident he isn't." Bliss sighed, puffing out his cheeks. "What can I tell you—it's not my idea of a healthy, normal relationship. But maybe there is no such thing as a healthy, normal relationship. What do you think, Lieutenant?"

"I think that I could be very happy never knowing this stuff about other people."

"That makes two of us," he agreed, smiling at her faintly. He removed his apron and wiped his hands on a towel. The stomach under his T-shirt was flat and hard. He was in excellent shape for a man over fifty. "Shall we eat?"

They ate out on the deck at a redwood table. The quiche was delicious—its crust flaky, the sage-scented filling of egg, bacon and gruyere rich and savory. And the fruit salad somehow managed to be sweet, tangy and nutty all at the same time. The man was truly gifted. Des told him so.

She did not tell him that she had almost no appetite.

Dirty Harry moseyed over and sniffed her ankles desultorily, offering no sign that he recalled it was she who had rescued him from out behind that bar in Ansonia, where drunks were throwing beer bottles at him. She who had nursed him and fed him. She who had given him a loving home for nearly three months until she had placed him with Bliss. Not so much as a hello. Not that Des expected any gratitude. He was, after all, a cat.

The kayakers were still making their way across the lake. The sound of their carefree laughter carried extraordinarily well off of the water. It seemed as if they were only a few feet away.

"What can I help you with?" Bliss asked her as he cleaned his own plate.

"Mitch Berger claims that somebody locked him in his crawl space a few days before he dug up Niles Seymour's body. To scare him off, possibly."

The resident trooper helped himself to some more fruit salad, his solemn face revealing nothing.

"One of the other islanders recalls seeing your cruiser out there on the afternoon in question. I wondered if you might have observed anything. Seen anyone near his carriage house. Anything like that."

Bliss munched on his salad thoughtfully. "Not that I recall."

"Mind if I ask what you were doing out there that day?"

"I'd swung by to look in on Dolly. She wasn't home, as it turned out."

"You often do that?"

"Drop in on her? Sure. She's gone through some tough, tough times. And we're old friends. And she's . . ." He trailed off, grimacing slightly. "Oh, hell, there's no sense in my being cute about it. The truth is that I've been carrying a torch for Dolly since we were eight years old."

"Does she know that?"

He let out a dismal laugh. "I think it's painfully obvious to everyone—including her. Sad to say, I've never been much more than good ol' Tal to her. First, there was Bud. Her class of people, unlike me. Except that he was never worthy of her. Bud Havenhurst's a weakling. Someone who needs a babysitter."

"I'd hardly call Mandy a babysitter," said Des.

"I would," he countered. "To me, she's a woman who exists solely to feast upon a man's frailties. Bud's little more than a blubbering child with her around." Bliss gazed out at the lake for a moment, his face hardening. "And then Niles Seymour blew into town. A truly low-class individual, if ever I saw one. But a charmer when it came to women. You know how the story goes from there." His eyes met hers across the table. "We've both got a lot of good years left. We could be happy. I could make her happy. But who knows—some things are meant to be, and most things aren't." He put down his fork and patted his mouth with his napkin. He was a very tidy eater. "What else can I help you with, Lieutenant?"

"You told me that Tuck Weems's parents were killed when you two were serving in 'Nam . . ."

"Correct." His eyes narrowed at her ever so slightly.

"Only you didn't tell me that *you* were actually home on leave when it happened. It was you who found Dolly and the victims in the carriage house. You who phoned it in. I found your name in Crowther's report."

"I know I didn't," he conceded. "It's not something I like to talk about. Or think about. Not if I can help it. I just . . . What is it you'd like to know?"

"What you saw."

"It was a long time ago."

"Maybe. Maybe not."

Bliss gazed at her curiously before he shrugged his broad shoulders and looked down at his hands. "We were supposed to play tennis on their court out there on the island that day," he began. "Mixed doubles. She and Bud versus me and some girl Dolly was trying to pair me up with. She was constantly fixing me up with her friends. They were always big girls, horsy girls . . ." He broke off, sighing. "Bud hadn't gotten there yet. He was late. Or maybe I was just early. I often was. It gave me a chance to be with her. No one else was around. Her parents were in Bermuda."

"What about her brother, Redfield?"

"Red was at the Naval Academy," he replied. "I'd just gotten out of my car when . . . It was her screams I heard first. I'd never heard anyone scream like that before. I ran toward the sound. And I found her out there in the carriage house on her hands and knees at the bottom of the stairs, her clothing ripped to shreds, blood all over her—their blood, her own blood. She was scratched up pretty bad. Her nose was broken, shoulder dislocated. And she was in shock.

Kept mumbling the same thing over and over again: 'The mother is hurt. The mother is hurt.' And I can . . ." Bliss ran a hand over his face, his chest heaving. "I can remember the sound of the dripping."

"What dripping?"

"The blood from upstairs. It had soaked through the floorboards of the loft and it was dripping right down onto the living room rug. I went up there. Up to the sleeping loft. And I found them up there together. Tuck's mom was facedown on the bed with one side of her head blown off. Roy was propped up against the headboard next to her, still clutching his shotgun. After he'd shot Louisa he'd fired up through the roof of his own mouth. The wall behind him was covered with his brains and his blood. There was *so* much blood . . . I phoned the police from the kitchen. Then I tried to make Dolly comfortable until they arrived. But it was a long, long time before she got over it. In fact . . ." He reached for his coffee mug with an unsteady hand. "I don't believe she ever has. Not really."

"Anything more to it than that?" Des asked.

The resident trooper was far away for a moment. Lost in the horror. Then he shook himself and said, "Such as what, Lieutenant?"

"Is it possible that it didn't go down as you described?"

"I can't imagine what you mean."

"I mean is there anything that happened that day thirty years ago, anything at all, that could possibly shine a light on what's happening now?"

"Louisa Weems walked in on her husband raping Dolly Peck," Bliss said, a harder edge creeping into his voice. "They fought. He shot her. And then he shot himself."

"Okay, but how do you know this? What I mean is, if Mrs. Seymour remembers nothing of that day, if the victims were already dead when you got there—how do you know it went down that way?"

"Because there's no other way it could have happened. Everyone said so—Crowther, the coroner, the district prosecutor. There was no doubt in anyone's minds. And no attempt to cover anything up."

"I wasn't saying there was."

"You didn't have to. Your eyes did it for you." The resident trooper's own eyes were glaring across the table at her. "Crowther did his job. It was all by the book. And in answer to what is no doubt your next question, the superintendent and I have no relationship whatsoever. He wouldn't know me from a hole in the ground. There's nothing there, Lieutenant. Nothing at all." He abruptly got up and began clearing the table. "Now, is there anything else I can fill you in on?"

"Yes, there is," she replied, helping him stack the dishes. "We ran a check at the Dorset Pharmacy to see if anyone filled a prescription in recent weeks for Diprolene, the brand name for betamethasone dipropionate. Your name showed up. Doctor Knudsen of the Shoreline Family Practice wrote you out a prescription for it on April the nineteenth. You filled it that same day. Diprolene is prescribed for patients who've suffered a severe allergic reaction to poison ivy."

"That's absolutely right." Bliss headed back inside with the dishes. Des followed him. "I was hiking in the woods up by the Devil's Hopyard with the Boy Scouts. Came in contact with it up there. I'm highly susceptible. When I get it, I get it but good—hands, face, everywhere." He began piling things in the kitchen sink, glancing at her curiously. "Why are you interested in that?"

Des was not liking this. Tal Bliss had invited her into his home. She had eaten his food. At this particular moment she would have given anything to be somewhere else—such as in her studio with a piece of charcoal in her hand . . . *"You are leading somebody else's life."* . . . "The reason I'm interested," she said slowly, "is that your outbreak occurred the same day Torry Mordarski's body was found in the woods by Laurel Brook Reservoir. There was some nasty poison ivy at that crime scene. Two tekkies got it bad."

"I see," he said, clenching and unclenching his jaw muscles. "Mind if I ask you where you are going with this?"

"Trooper, I am trying to get my mind around what's going on."

"And what do you think is going on?"

"If I knew, I wouldn't be asking you questions."

The resident trooper stood there in brittle silence a moment. "Questions like—Does a fellow officer who has been in love with a victim's widow since he was a child know more about that man's murder than he's telling me? Questions like—Is he shielding someone? Is he in over his head? Does that about cover it?"

Des remained silent. She was waiting for his answers.

"Lieutenant, may I be candid with you?"

"Please, by all means."

"These are good people here. Good friends. Don't step all over the ashes of their ruined lives just so you can make a name for yourself in Hartford. I won't allow it, do you understand?"

"Not entirely. But I'd very much like to."

A trace of uncertainty crept into the resident trooper's eyes. Briefly, Des sensed him wavering. She thought he might give in to her and spill it—whatever *it* was. But he would not. Could not. And, in a flash, that flicker of doubt was gone. All she could read in his eyes now was unyielding resolve and righteous anger.

"If you'll excuse me, Lieutenant," he said coldly, "I've got a couple of funerals to get ready for." He strode heavily toward his front door and flung it open wide. He was throwing her out, politely but firmly.

"I'm sorry if I've offended you," said Des. "I respect you and the work you do. Sometimes I have to do things I'd rather not do."

"I can appreciate that," he said curtly, his back stiff, his eyes daggers.

"Thanks for lunch."

He stayed there in his doorway, grimly watching her as she got in her slicktop. She wondered what it was that he was holding back from her. Wondered if it was he who had tidied the Laurel Reservoir murder scene. Someone had. Just as someone had driven Niles Seymour's car to the long-term parking lot at Bradley Airport, making sure to leave no traces anywhere on the vehicle. He was a big man with big hands. She wondered what size shoe he wore. Might he wear a size eleven or twelve?

As she eased her car slowly down the hill Des decided to pull over at the house where Tuck Weems had lived. She got out and tapped at the screen door.

Darleen was watching a soap opera now, a can of Budweiser in her hand, her baby gurgling next to her on the sofa. The redheaded girl's eyes were puffy from crying. Otherwise, the scene was exactly the same as before—dirty dishes and ashtrays piled on the coffee table, the smell of dirty diapers fouling the air.

"I'm Lieutenant Mitry, Darleen. I was here the other day with Trooper Bliss."

Darleen's gaze was somewhat unfocused. Des would likely find the remains of a joint in one of those ashtrays if she cared to look. Which she did not.

"I'm, like, I remember you," the girl responded, still way more interested in her TV show than she was in Des. "What do you want now?"

"To see how you're doing."

"What for?" demanded Darleen, going from zero to ultra-defensive in nothing flat.

"I'm concerned, that's what for. Do you have any family who can be here for you?"

"Tuck was my family." Her eyes never leaving the TV.

"That's what I mean. How will you and your baby get by now?"

"That ain't none of your business, bitch!" Darleen snarled at her. "And don't you dare try to take my baby away from me, y'hear? Or I'll mess you up so bad nobody will *ever* want you!"

The phone rang. Darleen got up off the sofa and went flouncing off to the kitchen to answer it.

Des stood there a moment in that dingy living room looking down at the baby. More human wreckage that the killer had left behind. First Torry's little boy, Stevie. Now here were two more children—helpless, clueless, lost. Des took two twenty-dollar bills out of her billfold and tucked them under the beer can Darleen had left on the table. Then she went back outside to her cruiser.

She was just getting in the car when she heard the gunshot.

It came from above the lake.

It came from the direction Des had just come from—Tal Bliss's house.

She floored it madly back up the hill. She encountered no car on its way down. She saw no one on foot.

His front door was wide open. She slammed on her brakes and jumped out, her eyes zeroing in on the shrubs that surrounded the house. Then flicking across the road at the neighboring houses. Not a leaf stirred. Not a curtain moved. She went in slowly with her Sig drawn and her back to the wall. Her mouth was dry, her heart racing. She called out his name. She got no response. Only silence. The stereo was off now. It was so quiet in there she could hear the blood rushing in her ears. And the house still smelled of the quiche he had baked for them. She called out his name again. No response.

The resident trooper was a very tidy chef. He had put all of their dishes in the dishwasher, refrigerated the leftovers, wiped off the counters, swept up the crumbs. He had written a short, succinct note and left it on the counter under a paperweight of polished stone, his lettering neat and precise: *"I did what I thought was right. Just as I am doing now."*

And then Tal Bliss had blown his brains out.

He was seated out on the deck at the redwood table where they had just eaten, weapon still clutched in his hand. It was not his service piece. It was a .38 caliber Smith and Wesson revolver. Des had no doubt that it was the same weapon that had killed Torry Mordarski, Niles Seymour and Tuck Weems. None.

Dirty Harry rubbed up against her ankle now, a low yowl of protest coming from his throat. Des gathered him up in her arms and took him downstairs and closed him in one of the bedrooms. Then she went out to her cruiser to phone it in.

Tal Bliss was tidy, all right. Except that he had left his mess behind for her to clean up. Des was so damned mad at him that she could spit.

CHAPTER 15

THE VILLAGE WENT INTO deep, heartfelt mourning over the death of its long-time resident trooper.

Flags were flown at half-staff at town hall and the fire house and the barber shop. Voices at the market were hushed. Tears were shed, hugs exchanged. Tal Bliss, Mitch discovered, had been one of those rare individuals who virtually everyone seemed to look up to. He was a big brother, a father figure, a friend. Above all, he was one of their own.

And everyone had a story to tell about him.

Dennis shared his when Mitch stopped by the hardware store to pick up two quarts of oil for the truck: Back when Dennis had been something of a wild child, Tal had pulled him over one night at three in the morning. Both Dennis and his high-school girlfriend were high on pot—and holding. Instead of busting them, Tal Bliss had escorted them home, confiscated the dope and never said a word about it to their parents. "He knew we were good kids," Dennis recalled fondly. "He just wanted to make sure we didn't screw up big-time."

This, according to Dennis, was Tal Bliss. Not the deranged killer who had taken three lives before he took his own.

The gun he had used on himself turned out to be the same one that had killed Torry Mordarski, Niles Seymour and Tuck Weems. And he had owned a pair of size-twelve Timberland hiking boots that were an exact match for a shoe print that had been found at the Torry Mordarski murder scene. These were proven facts. But beyond that, no one really understood why Bliss had done what he did. All that he'd left behind in the way of explanation was his two-line handwritten suicide note. Everything else died with him. No one *knew* anything—except that when Lieutenant Mitry had begun to close in on him, Tal Bliss had chosen to take his own life rather than face the music.

A Lieutenant Gianfrido had been put in charge of wrapping up the investigation. Lieutenant Mitry had been placed on paid administrative leave, pending the results of an Internal Affairs investigation to determine whether she had violated correct procedure. The lieutenant took a lot of heat from her own people in the *Hartford Courant*. Unnamed sources high up in the state police questioned whether she'd been "too eager." They so much as implied that Tal Bliss would still be alive if she'd waited to question him in official surroundings. Included other officers in the interrogation. Apparently, no one else knew she was meeting with Bliss.

The *Courant* also dug into her background. This was how Mitch learned that Desiree Mitry was the daughter of Deputy Superintendent Buck Mitry, the highest ranking black officer in the history of the state of Connecticut. Mitch wondered why she hadn't mentioned this to him. He wondered why she felt it was important not to.

He wondered how she must be feeling.

He wanted to call her up and ask her. But he didn't. He felt quite certain that he was the last person in the world she'd feel like hearing from right now. *He* had pointed her in the direction of Bliss. Still, her plight troubled him deeply. The woman's career was in serious jeopardy. Virtually everyone in Dorset felt she was a cold, heartless glory seeker. And Mitch felt more than a little responsible.

He also found himself thinking about her morning, noon and night.

The tabloid press invaded Big Sister in full battle dress again. The islanders were besieged. Couldn't leave. Couldn't answer their phones. Not that they had anything to say to the media. All they wanted them to do was go away. The whole village did. The minister of the Congregational Church spoke for the entire village when he said, "Dorset is a family, and we believe in keeping our troubles within the family."

As it happened, the only card-carrying member of the working press who had any genuine access to the story was Mitch himself. When he'd first discovered Niles Seymour's body, Mitch had had zero interest in writing about it. He'd just wanted to forget. But the Tal Bliss suicide changed how he felt. Possibly it was the reaction of the villagers—their homegrown hero's spectacular fall from grace had left them profoundly confused and shaken, their image of themselves and their serene little world utterly shattered. Mitch likened it to one of those cases when a couple of teenaged kids in a small, stable bible-belt community suddenly show up at school one day with AK-47s and begin wiping out their classmates. People want to know why. They take long looks at themselves in the mirror, wondering whether such shockingly monstrous behavior is inside of them, too.

Mitch noticed it when he went to the grocery store. He could see the self-doubt in their eyes, hear the fear in their voices. He found this response disturbing and fascinating. So when the Sunday magazine editor phoned him, at Lacy's suggestion, to see if he'd like to do a piece, Mitch reversed himself and said yes.

Possibly, it was his own way of looking in the mirror.

But first he wanted to make sure that Dolly was okay with it. He strolled down the gravel path to her house and found her having tea in the breakfast nook with Evan. In profile, their delicate features looked nearly identical. Both mother and son seemed defeated and downcast. Still, she greeted Mitch with a cheery smile and insisted that he join them for a cup. He did so, sliding into the nook next to Evan.

"We were just talking about poor Tal," she told Mitch, her voice quavering with emotion. "What I keep thinking is if only I had *known* what was going on inside that mind of his. Perhaps I could have influenced him somehow. In a positive direction, I mean. Surely I could have prevented all of this from . . ." Dolly shook her head, gazing down into her teacup. "If only I had known."

"But you didn't know," Mitch pointed out. "So you mustn't beat yourself up. You're not responsible for what he did."

"He's right, Mother." Evan reached across the table for her hand. "You know he's right."

"I know that he's *not*," said Dolly, her porcelain-blue eyes puddling with tears. "I know that Tal Bliss killed three people because of me. I know that I shall have to carry this around for the rest of my life." She dabbed at her eyes with a tissue and said it again. "If only I had known."

"My paper wants me to write about it, Dolly. Seeing as how I do have a rather unusual point of view. And I'd like to do it. But I'll tell them no if you aren't comfortable with the idea. This wasn't part of the deal when I signed the lease," he added, smiling at her.

Dolly glanced across the table at Evan, her mouth tightening. "Why on earth would I object, Mitch? I think it's a simply wonderful idea."

"You do?"

"Absolutely. Because you're not a tabloid gossip monger—you're a clear-eyed and sympathetic individual. Someone we all trust. Please do it. It's the only real chance we'll have for a fair, honest portrait to come out."

Mitch had not been expecting this response from her. He'd been positive that she would be much more interested in seeing the whole matter buried and forgotten. But he should have known better, he now realized. Because if there was one constant about his life on Big Sister it was that he really, truly did not understand these people. "Do you feel the same way, Evan?"

"I do," Evan replied softly, running both of his hands through his wavy black hair. "And I must tell you that I'm feeling a bit responsible for what happened, too. I'm the one who saw Bliss parked out here that day. I'm the one who told you about it. I didn't have to. I could have kept quiet."

"Instead of kicking yourself," Mitch said, "just be thankful he didn't decide to handle the situation differently."

Evan frowned at him curiously. "Like how?"

"By killing you so you couldn't tell anyone, that's how. He could have gone after you, Evan. And me. He could have killed me instead of just trying to scare me. We should both consider ourselves lucky to be alive. And leave it at that."

And so Mitch Berger, the most influential film critic in America, found himself at work on a real-life story of sex, murder and suicide in a small New England town.

Lacy e-mailed him that evening to say: *"Welcome to the fun-filled world of participatory journalism. This may be the start of a whole new you."*

To which Mitch replied: *"It's the same old me. The world's getting weirder, though."*

Way weirder. When word got out about it, no less than seven A-list Hollywood producers, each of them anxious to curry Mitch's critical favor, called his literary agent to find out if he was interested in signing a development deal.

Mitch politely declined.

A special memorial service was held for Tal Bliss at the white steepled congregational church. It was bright and airy inside the lovely church, with two stories of windows to let in the sunlight. It was crowded, too. The whole village seemed to be in attendance. The islanders certainly were. Red and Bitsy Peck were there. Bud and Mandy Havenhurst. Dolly, Evan and Jamie Devers. Mitch was there, too. The rest of the media were kept out by burly young state troopers.

Bud delivered a stirring eulogy about how he had looked up to Tal Bliss since they were little boys, and how he would always remember just how fair and decent Tal was. "This is the way I choose to remember my friend," he said in a strained voice. "This is my right." The red-bearded minister spoke at great length on how within each human being there is strength and there is weakness and that these two forces are constantly at war with each other. Tal Bliss, he concluded sadly, just happened to lose his war.

One elderly white-haired woman sat by herself on the aisle sobbing loudly throughout the ceremony. Mitch asked Bitsy who she was.

"Why, that's old Sheila Enman," Bitsy replied, gazing over at her fondly. "Gracious, she must be pushing a hundred and thirty by now. She ran the volunteer ambulance corps for years and years. And before that, she taught English over at the high school. Tal was her pet. He's been keeping an eye on her for the past few years, poor dear."

Later that afternoon, Mitch jumped into his truck and headed up Route 156 into the farm country, where the air smelled not of the sea but of moist, freshly turned earth and cow manure. The corn was getting up now, and the dogwoods and lilacs were in full bloom. Hawks circled slowly overhead, searching for prey. Sheila Enman lived on Dunn's Cove in an old mill house that was built right out over the Eight Mile River at the base of a twenty-foot waterfall.

"My great-granddaddy built it," the old woman explained as they stood on her front porch watching the white water race over the polished rocks and directly under them. "I've lived here since I was a little girl. Back then, we generated our own electricity—for this place and a dozen others down river. There were no paved roads here. We raised most of our own food. And I went to a one-room schoolhouse, grades one through eight. But those days are gone. Too damned bad, you ask me. People were happier back then. Look around you, Mr. Berger. No one's happy now. Got too little time and too damned many credit cards."

Sheila Enman was the kind of hard-nosed character who was known around the village as a cranky Yankee. Mitch liked her right away. She was feisty. She was opinionated. She was totally no-bull. Her blue eyes were clear and alert, her hair a snowy white. She wore a ragged old yellow cardigan, dark blue slacks, ventilated orthopedic shoes and reading glasses on a chain around her neck. Her age didn't seem to have slowed her mind down one bit. Just her stooped, big-boned body—she needed a cane to get around.

"It's my bad hip," she sniffed. "Doctors keep saying they want to give me a new one, but that just seems so wasteful, don't you think? I'll be ninety years old next month. Someone younger would get a lot more mileage out of it. But enough about that—it's really not a very interesting story. Now how can I help you? You said on the phone you're living in Dolly's old caretaker cottage . . . ?"

"That's right," said Mitch, pulling his eyes away from the waterfall, which he found positively hypnotic. "And I'm writing an article about what happened. I'd like to know more about Tal Bliss. I understand you two were close."

"Knew him his whole life," she confirmed, her eyes misting over.

"What sort of a kid was he? Can you describe him for me?"

"I can do you one better than that, Mr. Berger. I can show you."

"Do you mind if I tape our conversation?" Mitch had brought along the microcassette recorder that he used for the interviews he occasionally did with directors and stars.

"Hell, no. I got nothing to be ashamed of. Take a seat, stay awhile."

There were two rockers out on the porch. He sat in one while she hobbled inside, her cane thumping on the wooden flooring. He set the recorder on the table between the two rockers and flicked it on. She came thumping back a moment later, balancing a tray on one arm. There was a plate of homemade oatmeal cookies on it, two glasses of milk and an old, slim high school yearbook.

"Can I help you with that?" Mitch offered, climbing to his feet.

"You stay right where you are," she commanded him. "I don't keep doing things for myself I'll end up in a wheelchair over at Essex Meadows, sitting in a puddle of my own urine and not even minding." She managed to set the tray down without spilling any of the milk. She sat in the rocker next to him with a heavy grunt. She opened the yearbook.

Mitch sampled a cookie. It was chewy. It was good. It was very good.

"Don't be bashful, son," Sheila said, urging another one on him.

The front page of the yearbook proudly noted that the Dorset Fighting Pilgrims were the 1967 Shoreline Champs, although it did not say of what. *"There is pleasure in doing,"* was the senior class motto. Sheila began leafing her way through page after page of group photographs, her hands knobby and misshapen. They were photos of neat, well-groomed teenaged girls and sturdy, short-haired boys, all of them smiling, all of them white. It was a Wonder Bread world that bore no resemblance whatsoever to the roiling, multicultural city that Mitch had grown up in. It was a world as alien to him as Sheila's rural childhood of dirt roads and one-room schoolhouses.

"That whole bunch is in here somewhere," the old woman murmured absently. "All except for Redfield, who graduated two years ahead of Dolly. The ambassador and Mrs. Peck tried to enroll her at Miss Porter's up in Farmington. She didn't care for it, though. Came back home after one year. Girl's not happy if she strays too far from the nest. Neither is Bud. They're two of a kind that way . . . Ahhh, here they are," she exclaimed, handing the open book over to Mitch.

There they were, all right, frozen in time for their senior class pictures. There was Dolly Peck, just as Mitch had imagined her—a slender, pretty girl with a nice smile. There was Bud Havenhurst, with his thrusting jaw and air of WASP superiority. And broad-shouldered Tal Bliss, wearing the same crewcut he went to his grave with. And Tuck Weems, who sported slicked-back hair and a somewhat mocking grin. They were all there, alongside thumbnail profiles of their campus accomplishments, complete with inside jokes:

Dolores Sedgewick Peck (Dolly) . . . "Oh sure!" Prom Queen. Senior class vice president. Varsity field hockey. Civics club. "You're not going to beleeeve this . . . !" Most Gullible. Peanuttiest. Pet Peeve: Dislikes grouchy people.
Kinsley Twining Havenhurst (Bud) . . . "Hey, boy!" Prom King. Senior class president. "Guys, who put the mouse in my briefcase?" Chess club. Debating society. Varsity tennis. Most Likely To Succeed. "Seriously, guys . . ." Yale bound.
Talmadge Huffman Bliss (Tal) . . . "Help you across the street, ma'am?" Dudley Do-Right. Never seen without Tuck.

Co-captain, basketball varsity. All Shoreline, junior and senior years. Most Courteous. Eagle scout. Vietnam bound. **Tucker Adair Weems** (Tuck) . . . "What are YOU looking at?" Dudley Do-Wrong. Never seen without Tal. Captain, baseball varsity. Co-captain, basketball varsity. All Shoreline, junior and senior years. Best Excuse Maker. "Who said you could sit on my GTO?" Vietnam bound.

Mitch helped himself to another cookie and a sip of milk. "I hadn't realized that Tal Bliss and Tuck Weems were such close friends," he observed, leafing his way through the yearbook to the varsity basketball team. There they stood, shoulder to shoulder with their teammates in their Pilgrims jerseys, looking strapping and confident.

"Oh, sure, those two were like Mutt and Jeff when they were growing up," Sheila recalled, rocking back and forth in her chair. "Two sides of the same coin—one good, one bad. Although Tuck wasn't really, truly bad. Just wild. Had a troubled home life. Alcoholic mother, abusive father. He hated them both. Loved his fast cars and his *nasty* reputation." She gazed out at the waterfall for a moment. "The girls went crazy over Tuck. Why, he could charm them right out of their knickers without so much as a wink. Poor Tal, he was always the shy one."

"Did the two of them stay good friends through the years?"

"Yessir, they did," Sheila replied, nodding. "Never did let Dolly come between them."

Mitch gazed at the old woman intently. "What about Dolly?"

"Now that one *is* an interesting story," she replied, munching on a cookie. "You see, from day one Dolly's socially correct beau was *always* Bud Havenhurst." Sheila's voice dripped with scorn at the mention of his name. "Her folks liked Bud. Bud was the 'right' sort. Decent and upstanding. You ask me, he was about as thrilling as a bowl of my warm tapioca pudding—"

"Wait, you make your own tapioca pudding?"

"Been known to," she said, her eyes twinkling at him with amusement. "Why, do you like tapioca, Mr. Berger?"

"Like isn't a strong enough word for it," replied Mitch, who was drooling just at the thought of it. "But I interrupted you. You were telling me about Bud."

"A weasel from the word go," she stated firmly. "I never have trusted him with my personal affairs—and I don't care *where* he went to law school. Young Dolly, she liked him well enough. But she was *mad* for Tuck Weems. Crazy in love. Tuck was everything Bud wasn't. He was the son of hired help. He was rude. He was greasy. He was Dolly's walk on the wild side."

"And how did Tuck feel about her?"

"Couldn't be bothered with her," Sheila replied. "Not when most every other girl in town would do whatever he asked, if you understand what I'm saying. A few married women, too, or so it was said. Dolly just wasn't his type. Too proper. But Dolly would not take no for an answer. This was a girl who was used to getting her way. She chased after him shamelessly. And made Bud insane with jealousy. Some said Tuck went to Vietnam just to get away from that girl. Not me, though. It was to get away from his folks." Sheila broke off, her face darkening. "After they died, he became much more sullen and withdrawn. The war may have had a little something to do with that, too. And the drugs. He used them heavily, I'm told. Lived up at the lake. Went his own way. Dolly, she settled down with Bud. And eventually she talked Tuck into coming back to work out on Big Sister, which folks in town thought was real kind of her. And maybe Tuck did have some feelings for her after all. Tal did mention to me that Tuck was none too happy about the way Niles Seymour was treating her."

"I wouldn't expect Tal was too pleased about it either."

Sheila eyed Mitch shrewdly. "You're right, of course. A crying shame if you ask me. That poor man could have made some nice girl a good husband. He would have been a fine father. He just loved kids to death. But no, he just hung on and waited for Dolly. And waited and waited."

"She's a pretty special lady."

Sheila glanced at him in surprise. "Do you really think so?"

"Don't you?"

"Don't take my word for anything, Mr. Berger. I'm just a buggy old woman. But do take a good look at the evil that has happened around that woman. Look at how many lives have been ruined. Ask yourself how that happens. Ask yourself why."

"I've been asking myself a lot of things lately," Mitch confessed. "What I don't seem to have are many answers."

Mitch did have a theory of sorts—that the resident trooper had flown into a jealous rage when he found out that Niles Seymour was two-timing his beloved Dolly with Torry. Possibly, he had confronted Seymour over it. Possibly, a fight had broken out that led to Bliss using a gun on him. Possibly, Bliss had then eliminated Torry so she wouldn't start asking questions around town. This would explain why Seymour was buried on Big Sister Island while she was murdered at the Laurel Brook Reservoir in Meriden. Bliss may have lured her there with the promise of a message from Seymour. Then, to cover his tracks, he had made it look like the two of them had run away together—the Dear John letter, airline reservations and so on. That much added up.

But the murder of Tuck Weems did not. Mitch hadn't the slightest idea why Tal Bliss had lured his best friend down to the beach in the rain and shot him. No one did.

"I still can't believe Tal did it," Sheila spoke up suddenly. "I guess I can't accept it either, because he was such a good, caring man. He drove me to church every Sunday. Picked up my groceries for me. Fixed things around the place. Never asked if they needed doing. Just *did* them. He was also, and I don't mean this in a negative way, not very imaginative. He was more what you'd a call a point A to point B sort of a fellow. I think that's why he enjoyed spending so much time in the kitchen. He had his instructions all laid out in front of him and as long as he followed them, step by step, something good would come out of it. Something that would make other people happy. What I mean to say is . . ." Sheila paused, considering her next words carefully. "I don't believe Tal could have dreamt this whole scheme up all by himself."

"Are you suggesting that he and Tuck might have been in on it together?"

Sheila beat a hasty retreat. "Oh, I wouldn't know about that. And I am not one to speculate about the dead. It's just that Tal got to be like family to me. I like to think I knew him. And one thing he would never do was court trouble. Or run from it, either. If he did wrong, he'd take his punishment like a man."

Mitch leaned forward in his rocker now, studying her. "You don't believe he committed suicide either. You think someone shot him and made it look like a suicide."

Sheila Enman didn't respond to this. Just let it slide on by, rocking back and forth on her porch in front of the waterfall.

"Mrs. Enman, Tuck Weems was already dead and gone when Tal Bliss shot himself. If it wasn't suicide, if Tal was *murdered*, then that means a third person was in on it with them. Someone who's still walking around. *Who*, Mrs. Enman?"

She didn't seem to be hearing Mitch anymore. She was lost in her grief.

"Mrs. Enman?!"

"Mercy," she finally said in a reedy, faraway voice. "Who will shovel my driveway for me now?"

CHAPTER 16

"TAL BLISS WAS MY first," Des announced as they rocketed down Rimmon Road in Bella's Jeep Wrangler, empty pet cages rattling around in back. It was dusk—dinner hour at the A & P Dumpsters on Amity Road. "I never killed someone before."

"You didn't kill this one," insisted Bella, her round double chin practically resting on top of the steering wheel as she drove. "It was his own doing."

"If I hadn't gone to see that man, he'd still be alive today."

"You don't know that, Desiree."

"Yes, I do," Des said somberly. "I do know that."

"Sweetheart, you must not hold yourself responsible for what he did," Bella said scoldingly. "You'll make yourself *meshugah*."

"What's *meshugah* mean?"

"Crazy."

"I heard that." Des nodded to herself. "Yes, indeed—in Dolby Sound."

She had spent an entire day and night in the Internal Affairs building next door to Major Crimes being grilled by a lieutenant from Hartford who she did not know. The man was not hostile. The man was not sympathetic. The man simply wanted the facts. He had already spoken with Soave who, in spite of the unwritten code, had made virtually no attempt to help cover Des's bootay. Not that she had expected him to. Not after the way he'd sold her out once already . . . *"Why did you keep your sergeant out of the loop?"* the I.A. lieutenant wanted to know. *"There was time pressure,"* she replied, leaving it at that. She was not going to whine to I.A. that she didn't trust him. *"These things happen in the heat of an investigation."* But the man clearly did not feel right about this. Nor did he like that she had failed to go through I.A. channels before looking into the personal medical history of a fellow officer. *"But I didn't search his medical file,"* Des objected. *"And I didn't know before the fact that I'd find his name on that pharmacist's list. How could I know that? I simply asked him about it, that's all. I asked him about a lot of things. How was I supposed to know he'd blow his brains out? Man, I was just doing my damned job."*

Except they were not going to let her do that job anymore. Not for a while, anyway. She was on the shelf, pending the findings of an official Department of Public Safety review panel. Or at least that was the formal way of putting it. Here was how the Deacon put it when he gave her the news, his voice low and solemn: "This case has generated too much heat, Desiree. The superintendent doesn't want you within ten miles of it until it's good and cooled down."

Translation: They were paying her to go away.

Soave could not quite manage to look her in the eye when she came back to the Jungle to gather up her things. No one could. Not big brother Angelo, not Captain Polito, not Gianfrido, Polito's hand-picked boy from Waterbury. No one had a comforting or encouraging word to say to her. No one had a thing to say to her. It was as if she had ceased to exist.

The last thing Des did before she cleared out was take down the CATGIRL FROM HELL sign from her cubicle.

There had been television reporters waiting outside her house. She had brushed past them without a word, locked her door, closed her shutters. Thwarted, they had tried interviewing her neighbors. A huge mistake, because Bella had been only too glad to hold forth for them: "Why don't you goddamned vultures cover the *news* for a change?" she demanded at the top of her lungs. "Our public schools are crumbling. Affordable health care is a fantasy. And all you're interested in is destroying decent people's lives!"

They cleared out right after that.

God, Des wished she had that woman's *chutzpah*.

She had spent this, her first full day of forced leave, getting physical. She ran three miles. Did two circuits with twenty-pound dumbbells on the pressing bench in her guest room. Mowed the lawn, pruned bushes, weeded beds, raked. She vacuumed the entire house. Cat hair, mostly. She got down on her hands and knees and scrubbed the kitchen floor. But it was no use—she remained profoundly shaken. Counseling had been offered to her. She had declined it. She had her own form of therapy.

"What did your father have to say about all of this?" Bella honked at the slow-going Toyota in front of them. The traffic on Rimmon was sluggish, folks heading out for the evening.

"Almost nothing."

"You don't sound surprised."

"Only because I'm not." In the world according to the Deacon, no special allowances were made for family. He would not intercede. He would not play favorites. "All he wanted to know was whether I went by the book."

"Did you?"

"Bella, they can spin it any damned way they want. They have the benefit of twenty-twenty rearview vision." She would get her job back, she felt sure. They couldn't fire her over this. But from now on, there would be an asterisk next to her name. The fast track would be muddy. She was tainted now. Damaged goods.

"Screw 'em," Bella fumed. "If I were you, I'd quit."

"And do what?"

"Whatever makes you happy. You're young, you're bright, you're gorgeous—what do you need those bastards for?"

"And do what?" Des repeated, even though she knew perfectly well what. Except that it was simply not in her nature to walk away from a fight. She was not a quitter. Never had been. "Do you know what I'm saying?"

"No, dear, I do not."

"If everyone did exactly what they wanted, then the fabric that holds our society together would completely unravel and the whole world would go straight to . . ." Des broke off, aghast. "Damn, now I'm sounding just like the Deacon."

"You're not your father, Desiree. Or anyone else. You're you."

237

Des gazed over at her fondly. "I'd pay good money to see you go twelve rounds with him, know that?"

"Not a chance," Bella scoffed. "He wouldn't stay on his feet more than seven rounds." She pulled *bumpety-bump* into the A & P parking lot and began easing the Jeep around back to the Dumpsters. "So did he call you?"

"Did who call me?"

"Mitch Berger. As if you didn't know who I meant."

She shook her head. "Wouldn't expect him to."

"Really? I would. Maybe he's shy. Is he shy?"

"Not so I've noticed. And, for your information, it's not like that—him and me, I'm saying."

Bella let out a whoop. "Tie that bull outside, as we used to say on Nostrand Avenue."

"And just exactly what does it mean?"

"It means, my dear, that you are full of you-know-what," Bella replied as she pulled up and killed the engine.

Big Willie was lurking there in the bushes, acting like he wasn't waiting for them. God, he was mangy. Looked like he'd gotten himself in yet another fight, too. The dried blood that was caked around his left ear hadn't been there early that morning.

Des and Bella baited their cages with the jars of strained turkey and stationed themselves a safe distance away, strings in hand. Big Willie moved in closer, crouched low to the ground. Looked at them with his one good eye. Looked at the cages. He inched closer still. Looked at them. Looked at the cages . . . Des talking to him softly, telling him it was all going to be okay.

It was, she reflected, uncanny how after all these weeks Big Willie chose *now* to come in from the cold. It was almost as if he sensed that Des was hurting. Or maybe he just knew that this was one moment when she really and truly did not need any more aggravation in her life. Whatever it was, this was the night Big Willie crept nearer . . . and nearer . . . and finally went all the way inside the trap as Des slammed it shut behind him.

They had him. He hissed. He yowled. He hugged the ground,

swatting at them. Damn, he was mean. Like a little caged lion. But they had him at long last.

"Big Willie is in the house!" exulted Des, triumphantly high-fiving Bella.

"You go, girl!"

Dr. John would have to check him over in the morning. Until then, they quarantined him in Bella's garage—Des had a full house right now with Dirty Harry being back in residence. But Des had no doubt that once the vet gave Big Willie a clean bill of health he would end up with her. He was her kind of he-cat. Although she would have to find Dirty Harry a new home first. Where?

Des had herself a hot shower and a cold Sam Addams, good and tired from her day of physical activity. She heated up Bella's stuffed cabbage and wolfed it down. Then she went in her studio for her therapy.

She had two photos of Tal Bliss pinned to her easel. One was his official I.D. photo, the one that had been distributed to the media. It was a standard head-on portrait of a lawman, gaze direct, his jaw strong. Tal Bliss had been the living image of a state trooper—brave, determined and fair. He had an honest face.

The other picture was a crime scene photo of him slumped at his redwood picnic table with most of that face gone.

Des stared at it long and hard, slowly reawakening her senses. Summoning up the smell of bacon and sage in the air. The sound of laughter from the kayakers out on the lake. The sunlight streaming through the trees and onto the deck. Remembering how at peace Tal Bliss had seemed, standing there in his kitchen making fruit salad in his spotless white T-shirt and apron. Remembering her horror, her anger. Remembering . . .

Now she began to draw him in vine charcoal, stroking boldly and rapidly. Gesture drawings at first, one after another. Placing Tal Bliss on the page. Finding her major contours and shapes. Locating her light source, her core shadows. Then she began to get more specific, gradually taking away with her kneaded eraser, squinting as she searched for the values in his shattered face, the cast shadow of the gun on his chest. After two hours she had a drawing that was beginning to work on a technical level. It was three-dimensional. She had her information down, her shapes and values. What she did not have was her emotion. The drawing was not alive yet. It merely sat there, cold and remote.

Draw what you see, not what you know.

She switched to a hard graphite stick, focusing less on values and more on lines. To free herself from what she *knew*, she turned his photograph upside down and tried drawing it that way. An exercise she had once been taught. She drew a portrait of Tal Bliss with her left hand. Another with her eyes closed. She drew for hour upon hour, deep into the night, until the floor around her was heaped with discarded drawings. But it still didn't work. She could not make it work. Exhausted and frustrated, she hurled her stub of graphite stick against the wall.

She didn't believe it. That was why.

Tal Bliss was no killer. He was an old-school cop—a good, decent man who lived to serve. Tal Bliss had believed in the code. He was prepared to put his own life on the line to protect someone else. That was his job. That was his duty.

Des got up and went into the bathroom to wash the charcoal from her hands, her mind beginning to race ... What if ... Jesus, what if *that* was what really happened? It sure made a hell of a lot more sense, didn't it? What if Tal Bliss hadn't committed those murders at all? What if he had shot himself to spare the life of the woman he loved? What if he had been protecting Dolly Seymour?

Des didn't know the true story. But she did know that her portrait of the man wouldn't come to life until she did. Nor would she be able to rest. Not until she knew what happened. She had to know what happened.

She was staring long and hard at her reflection in the bathroom mirror, wondering what on earth she was going to do about this, when her phone rang.

CHAPTER 17

THE SANDWICH BAG FULL of oatmeal cookies that Sheila Enman had pressed upon Mitch as he left was empty by the time he reached the army of TV reporters who were staked out at Peck Point, desperate for a chewy morsel of their own.

Mitch barreled his pickup right through them and out onto the bridge, paying scant attention to their shouted queries. His head was still spinning. *Had* Tuck Weems been in on it with Bliss? *Was* there someone else—a *third* person? Or was Sheila Enman merely an addled old lady who refused to believe her beloved boy was capable of such monstrous behavior on his own?

Mitch wondered. He most definitely did.

He played back the tape of their conversation when he got home, Sheila's voice firm and strong over the cascading waterfall . . . *"I don't believe Tal could have dreamt this whole scheme up all by himself."*

Listening to her. And wondering some more.

He cranked up his computer and got to work. He'd put a lot of thought into his opening paragraph. He felt pretty sure he had it:

I think that many of us have a yearning for the joyous and pastoral New England scene. It is the stuff of Currier and Ives, this scene. And Norman Rockwell. The feel-good Yuletide bathos of Frank Capra's It's a Wonderful Life *is poured all over it like Vermont maple syrup. But I am here to tell you that the reality does not quite match the fantasy. In fact, it is not even close.*

Mitch had his opening, all right. What he did not have was the rest of it. And it was bugging the hell out of him.

By now, the sun was getting low over the sparkling blue Sound, casting long shadows through his living room windows. The tide was out so Mitch went for a walk among the tide pools. One question kept nagging and nagging at him as he plodded along in the wet sand among the crabs and oysters: *Why?* He could not shake it. It was there as he heated up some three-day-old American chop suey and scarfed it down. *Why?* And while he watched a few choice minutes of *Hombre*. The stagecoach scene early on where it slowly begins to dawn on the other passengers that Newman is a halfbreed. Ritt's camera never leaves his riveting blue eyes. *Why?* When Mitch flicked on his Stratocaster and went chasing after "It Hurts Me, Too," the old Elmore James blues number, it was still there:

Why had Tal Bliss killed his very best friend in the whole world?

Say Sheila was right. Say he and Tuck Weems *had* pulled off the murders of Niles Seymour and Torry Mordarski together. Why would he then proceed to eliminate Tuck? Had the two old friends had a falling-out? Had Tuck threatened to expose him? Was this simply a case of Bliss covering his own tracks? Or had *another* conspirator shot both of them? Someone who was now walking around, free and clear?

It didn't make sense. Well, it made some sense but not absolute sense. Maybe because Mitch was searching for a proper villain like Richard Boone in *Hombre*. But this was no Western, its morality clearly etched. This was real life—complex, interwoven and exceedingly murky. And these were real people. Real people did not necessarily have intelligent reasons for the way they behaved. In fact, they might very well have no reasons at all. At least none that were sane or rational.

Mitch arrived at this unhappy conclusion after several hours of lying in bed in the darkness with his wheels spinning. Clemmie was curled up on his chest, purring away. He stroked her soft fur gently, gazing up at the half-moon through his skylight. Take Niles Seymour—why did he show up at the Saybrook Point Inn flaunting his young girlfriend for everyone to see? The man had even told Jamie Devers about her. Why does a married man who's cheating on his wife do that? Why be so reckless and foolish?

Baffled, Mitch roused Clemmie from her sound sleep and went

downstairs to put on milk for cocoa. It being chilly he built a small fire in the fireplace and lit it, the kindling crackling in the quiet. He fixed his cocoa and sat in his easy chair with it, gazing into the flames. After a moment he heard small plopping noises—Clemmie venturing downstairs after him, step by step by step. She let out a squeak to announce her wee presence in the room, then leapt up into his lap. After a few minutes of pad-pad-padding she curled up and fell instantly back to sleep.

Unlike Mitch, she did not have a lot on her mind.

Questions. He had so damned many of them . . . If there was a third person, who was it? Bud Havenhurst? The man's timing *was* awfully fortuitous. After all, he had chosen virtually the same precise moment to raid Dolly's funds as Tal Bliss had chosen to murder Niles Seymour. Bud's explanation was that when he'd seen Niles and Torry together at the inn he felt certain Niles was about to skip town. And so, faster than you can say Rouben Mamoulian, he cleared out her accounts to protect them from the man's evil clutches. Was that believable? Or did Bud know more than he'd let on? He and Red Peck had been together that day at the inn. Both of them had seen Niles with Torry. This made them the only two people who ever had, didn't it? Hadn't Lieutenant Mitry said that none of Torry's friends or coworkers ever saw Stan? Because if that were the case, then that would mean . . . Wait a minute . . .

Mitch suddenly sat up in his chair, awestruck. Slowly, he found his gaze drawn over toward the wall—at the art that was hanging there, aglow in the dancing golden firelight. The more he kept looking at it the more the pieces started to fall into place. Ghastly, horrible place. They fit. Sure they did. All of the pieces fit. He had his answer. But how to prove it? How to prove any of it?

Now Mitch jumped to his feet, dislodging Clemmie. She blinked up at him quizzically, unable to comprehend anything that might be more significant than her natural rest. Mitch raced to the phone. He'd tracked down the lieutenant's home number when he was thinking about calling her. Now he dialed it, his heart pounding. She answered on the second ring.

"Did I wake you up?" he asked her, not bothering with hello.

"Why, no . . ." Her voice sounded guarded and cool. "I was drawing."

"Good for you. How is that coming? Have you thought about what we talked about?"

"I *have* had a few other things on my mind, Mr. Berger."

"What happened to *Mitch*?"

"How did you get my home number, *Mitch*?"

"I went to journalism school, remember? They teach us things like that."

"And did they teach you how to tell time? It's four o'clock in the morning."

"You said I should call if something came up."

"That was then. I'm on the shelf now, in case you haven't been paying attention. So if you don't mind . . ."

"I do mind. It wasn't fair. What they did to you. What they said about you in the papers. It wasn't fair."

"It's never fair. If I *hadn't* achieved some measure of closure, they would have said I was in over my head. Either way, I end up as toast. Your classic lose-lose situation." She fell silent briefly. "Actually, there was something I've been meaning to tell you. Tal Bliss told it to me before he died . . ."

It was about that day in New York, when Mitch had almost been pushed in front of the subway train. Bud Havenhurst had informed the resident trooper that it was Mandy who had done it. That it was a sex game with her. With the two of them. Bud had even been in the apartment later that night when she'd tried to seduce Mitch.

Mitch considered this news for a long moment, his emotions teetering back and forth between anger and just plain revulsion . . . *No, I really do not understand these people* . . . Finally, he said, "I don't buy it, Lieutenant. Well, *maybe* I buy that Bud was hiding there in the apartment. After all, why make up anything so sick? But I don't buy the rest of it."

"Neither do I," she concurred. "The numbers simply do not add up. Mandy Havenhurst weighs in at, what, a hundred and twenty pounds? One-twenty-five? And you must weigh—"

"A lot more than that," Mitch conceded quickly.

"She couldn't have pulled you back in time. Not even if she'd wanted to. She's not strong enough. Only a good-sized man could do that."

"Which means one of two things," Mitch mused aloud. "Either Mandy really did intend to kill me or Bud lied to Tal Bliss about who was responsible. What do you think?"

"I think that I'm all done thinking," the lieutenant replied wearily. "Man, what in the hell do you want, anyway?"

"I don't think this case is closed. I don't buy that either. And I can't believe you do. Surely you're not satisfied."

She let out a short, bitter laugh. "Satisfied? That is one strange way of putting it."

"Okay, fine, I'll put it to you another way—you don't believe Tal Bliss did all of this by himself, do you?"

"The case is closed, Mitch."

"You're not answering me. What do you *believe*?"

"I *believe* in evidence."

"So do I. That's why I called. I have a very important question to ask you: Is there any chance that Bliss didn't shoot himself?"

She fell silent for so long that Mitch said, "Hello . . . ?"

"What, you mean like was he murdered?" she finally responded. "Not a chance. I got there in two seconds flat. I saw no one leaving the scene. And the coroner found nothing to indicate a struggle. The man's clothes were clean. The man's skin was clean—other than the powder burns on his face. The only prints on the gun were his. And the handwriting on the suicide note was his. No, it was suicide. Bank on it."

Mitch thought this over carefully. Sheila *could* be wrong about that element. But that didn't necessarily blow his theory out of the water. There was another explanation. An even simpler one.

Now it was Lieutenant Mitry who plunged into the silence. "Exactly where are you going with this, anyway?"

"You said Torry Mordarski registered at the Saybrook Point Inn under an assumed name."

"Correct. Angela Becker was the name on the driver's license."

"Did anyone see Angela Becker and Niles Seymour together?"

"Well, yeah. Bud Havenhurst and Redfield Peck did. And they positively identified Angela as Torry from Torry's photos. This is old news. You know all of this."

"No, I mean, did anyone *else* see them together?"

"Such as who?"

"Such as a chambermaid or room service waiter. Another guest in the dining room."

"I don't remember. Why, is it important?"

"Ultra."

"Then let me get my notes, okay?"

Mitch waited anxiously while she fetched them. He could hear her footsteps as she returned. Hear a whole lot of meowing, too.

"I'm showing no other corroborative testimony," she said, leafing through her notepad. "That's a no."

"So Bud and Red are the only ones who saw them together?"

"That's a yes. What of it?"

"Where are you going to be tomorrow, Lieutenant?"

"I'm driving to Newport in the morning."

"Pick me up on your way. I'm coming with you."

"Um, okay, I don't recall inviting you."

"But don't come anywhere near Big Sister. I don't want people to know we're still in contact. I'll be waiting for you in the parking lot of the Super Stop and Shop in Old Saybrook. What are you driving?"

"My usual ride, but—"

"Fine. Shall I look for you around ten?"

"Give me a reason. Give me one good reason."

"I can give you two. There's a place in Newport called the Black Pearl that's supposed to serve the world's best New England clam chowder. And we have to talk."

"About what?"

"Not what," Mitch corrected her. "Who."

She drew her breath in, exasperated. "Okay, *who*?"

"Yogi Berra—as in it ain't over till it's over. Good night, Lieutenant."

Mitch hung up the phone and flicked on his computer. A plan was forming in his mind. One that was ingenious and daring and foolproof. He began to write, setting the wheels of his plan in motion. As his fingers flew over the keyboard he realized he was so excited that he could barely sit still.

It would work. Mitch knew it would work.

He knew it because he had seen this movie before.

CHAPTER 18

MITCH BERGER'S HIGH RIDING, kidney-colored Studebaker pickup truck was not exactly hard to spot in the half-empty Stop & Shop parking lot. The man himself was seated there behind the steering wheel, drumming it nervously with his fingers when Des pulled into the empty space alongside of him.

He climbed out and got in next to her, looking rumpled and unshaven. His hair was uncombed, his sad puppy eyes red and puffy. "Morning, Lieutenant. How's your cold?"

"It was never a cold. And I feel a whole lot better than you look, if you want to know the truth."

"I didn't sleep very well last night."

"Why all of this secrecy?" she demanded as the two of them sat there in her cruiser, engine idling.

"It's important that no one on the island see us together."

"You told me that already. What you didn't tell me was why."

"I've never been in a police car before," he spoke up, glancing around at the interior with keen, sudden interest. "You don't have an on-board computer?"

Des shook her head. "Mobile data terminals cost major bucks. And we're a big public agency. The bigger they are, the slower they are at keeping current. The IRS is still using equipment that's twenty years out of date."

"Well, that's comforting."

"The only agency using equipment that's even older is the FAA."

"Well, that's not," Mitch said, his fingers busily probing the dashboard. "What's this thing?"

"My radio."

"And what does this do?"

"Stop touching my damned stuff, will you?!"

"Sorry, I'm a little wired this morning," he said. "Kind of grouchy yourself, aren't you?"

"I have excellent reason to be," Des huffed, easing her car out onto Route 1 in the direction of the I-95 on-ramp.

Mostly, she was anxious. When Mitch had said there might be more to the Tal Bliss suicide, she had had to find out what it was. She desperately wanted there to be more—something, anything that would make her feel less responsible for his death. She also knew, down deep inside, that she had agreed to let Mitch tag along because she wanted to see him again. Although now that the man was sitting there next to her she could not imagine why. He was pudgy. He was strange. He dressed like a high school chemistry teacher. Plus he was edgy and annoying and way, way white.

Damn, girl, what were you thinking?

She steered them onto the highway, heading north. Newport was about an hour and a half ride up the coast, much of it through drop-dead gorgeous little shoreline towns like Mystic and Stonington and Watch Hill, Rhode Island, which had the distinction of being home to the oldest merry-go-round in America. She settled into the right lane at a comfortable 60, a lengthy procession of cars and trucks falling cautiously into line behind her, and said, "Okay, you're on. Talk at me."

"You first," he insisted. "Why are we going to Newport?"

"*We're* going because Superintendent Crowther is the lunchtime speaker today at the annual convention of the Northeastern Association of Forensic Scientists. I can buttonhole him afterward. Otherwise, the man's totally not accessible. Not unless I snag him outside his house, which would not be appropriate. It would be like I'm stalking him."

"And this isn't?"

"I have to talk to him," Des said firmly.

"Why, what does he know?"

"What actually happened to Roy and Louisa Weems. The real story behind their deaths. The real story behind Dolly Peck's rape."

"Wait, Dolly was *raped*?"

"By Roy," Des affirmed, glancing sidelong at him. "Tal Bliss found their bodies. Crowther was the investigating officer. His report was full of holes. That's why I have to see him. I have to find out what he knows."

"We both do." Mitch rubbed his hands together eagerly. "Hot damn, my article just got a whole lot better."

"What article?" she demanded sharply. "You didn't tell me about any article."

"I'm writing a piece for my paper's Sunday magazine."

"I thought you weren't that kind of journalist."

"I'm usually not. But this sort of thing doesn't usually happen to me. So when they asked me, I said yes. Why, do you have a problem with it?"

"Hell, yes. When I agreed to let you tag along I didn't realize you were acting as a member of the news media."

"You're not going to kick me out of the car now, are you?"

"I'm thinking about it," she fumed angrily. "I sure as hell am."

They rode on in charged silence. They were nearing Stonington, the one-time Portuguese fishing village near the Rhode Island state line that was now a yachter's paradise. Lush green pastures and wetlands surrounded it, the Sound glittering in the distance. There were certainly worse places to be ditched. But it was still a long way from home. And the gentle blue morning sky was streaked with red along the horizon. A storm was due to arrive before nightfall.

"Look, I'll fill you in on as much as I can," Des said finally. "But I have to see the man alone. And you are not quoting me as a source on this particular aspect of the case. I am already in enough trouble. Deal?"

"Deal. Only, what makes you think he'll talk to you?"

"He'll talk to me."

"Why, because your father is deputy superintendent?"

"That's got nothing to do with anything." She could feel Mitch's eyes on her.

"How come you didn't tell me about him?"

"Did you tell me about your people?"

"No," he conceded. "No, I didn't."

"So why should I be telling you about mine? Besides, never mind about me. You're the one who's up now. Talk at me."

"Not a chance," he said, crossing his arms in front of his chest. "If I tell you what I know before you talk to Crowther, then I'm handing you my only leverage. You'll have zero reason to fill me in."

"Um, okay, our relationship is deteriorating by the second here . . ."

"We haven't got a relationship—not when it comes to business. First you talk to Crowther. Then I'll talk. For now, let's just enjoy the scenery. Beautiful part of the country, isn't it?"

Des promptly pulled over onto the shoulder and came to a stop, seething.

"Hey, isn't this illegal unless it's an emergency?"

"Oh, it's an emergency, all right," she said as they idled there, cars whizzing past them. "I'm about to call nine-one-one to come save your sorry ass."

He grinned at her maddeningly. "You probably hear this all the time, but you're really quite lovely when you're angry."

"Stop jamming me, doughboy!"

Mitch's eyes widened. "*Doughboy?* Am I detecting a slight racial subtext here again?"

"What you're detecting is your face on the verge of coming into full frontal contact with my fist!"

"Lieutenant, I'm just trying to do my job," he explained patiently. "It's not a nice job. I know that. Reporters are not nice people. I know that, too. But this story is something I need to do in order to get this horrible nightmare out of my system. You can understand that, can't you?"

"Maybe I can," Des allowed, studying him. "But I have to tell you—I liked you a whole lot better back when you were . . . what did you call yourself, mildew?"

"I think the word I used was fungus. And that makes us even."

"Is that right? How so?"

251

"I prefer you as a starving artist. So let's just call it a draw, okay?"

"You can call it whatever you damned please. To me, you're nothing but a raw dog now—somebody's who's strictly out for himself. But I'm fine with it. These eyes are wide open." She resumed driving, her eyes on the road, back straight, both hands gripping the wheel.

Neither of them spoke for a long while.

It was Mitch who finally broke the quiet. They were in Rhode Island by then. "Okay, maybe I overplayed my hand a little," he conceded.

"No maybe."

"Then again, maybe you're just trying to make me feel guilty so I'll show you the cards I'm playing."

She let that one slide on by. Just drove. And waited.

"Allright, I'm playing the Fibonacci Series," he finally revealed.

Des furrowed her brow at him. "Wait, wait . . . That was the name of the picture hanging on your wall, wasn't it? The one with all of those lines."

He nodded. "My wife's design plan. It's a variation of the Golden Section—one of the basic systems of proportion dating back to antiquity."

"Mitch, why are you talking at me about geometry?"

"I'm not talking at you about geometry, Lieutenant," he said quietly. "I'm talking at you about people."

And with that Mitch Berger shut down on her, same as he had the first time she interviewed him in his carriage house. She would get no more out of him. Not now, anyway.

Damn, what was he talking about?

At Hope Valley Des got off I-95 and onto Route 138, a two-lane rural road that snaked its way through low, fertile farm country before it hit Narragansett Bay. A bridge took them over its narrow West Passage to Jamestown, where the tollbooths for the Newport Bridge were. It took them out over the bay's broad East Passage and into Newport, the scruffy colonial seaport that New York robber barons had turned into their summer playground at the end of the nineteenth century. These days, yachters were drawn to its marinas. Tourists came to gawk at the gargantuan Bellevue Avenue mansions and to stroll the historic waterfront, where the streets were narrow and the traffic impossible.

Des turned right at the bottom of the exit ramp and followed the signs for downtown Newport, passing in between two vast cemeteries before she turned right onto America's Cup Avenue. Her destination was the Doubletree Inn out on Goat Island, an old naval installation that was situated out in the harbor across from Market Square. The Goat Island connector road was just past Bridge Street. There was a small park at the mouth of the connector road. Benches overlooked the shipyard and the neighboring district of immaculately restored three-hundred-year-old houses that fronted on Washington Street.

Des glanced at her watch. It was just past twelve-thirty.

"I can find the Black Pearl from here on foot," Mitch said. "I'll be waiting for you there, spoon in hand."

She pulled over at the park and rolled down her window. The breeze was cool and tangy with the scent of the bay. Soft gray clouds were beginning to form in the western sky beyond the Rose Island lighthouse.

"Look, I owe you one," she said. "I'm sorry I called you doughboy."

"Not to worry, I'm a pro. It won't affect our negotiations."

"That's not why I'm sorry."

He gazed at her curiously. "Just exactly how often do you get that angry?"

"Never. Well, almost never."

"That's too bad."

"Why do you say that?"

"Because the next time it happens I just might have to kiss you. I really don't think I'll be able to stop myself." He opened his door now, smiling at her brightly. "Good luck, Lieutenant. I hope the superintendent is in a talkative mood today. In fact, I hope he can't keep his mouth shut." Then Mitch Berger slammed the car door shut and went galumphing off down Washington Street in the direction of the wharves.

Des watched him go, feeling as if she'd just been plunged headlong into one of her recurring bad dreams, the one where she suddenly found herself boarding an airplane without any luggage or even any idea where the plane was going or why she was getting on board.

But this was no dream. This was really happening. She and Mitch Berger. The two of them. Even though it made no sense. None.

He was more than three blocks away, nothing more than a distant blob on the sidewalk, before Des was able to stop shaking.

The Doubletree Inn was hunkered at the northernmost tip of Goat Island, the better to see Newport Harbor from. Apart from the awesome view, it was a standard issue convention hotel—fairly new, fairly big and about as charming as a military supply depot.

Des left her slicktop in a loading zone and went inside. The lobby was small and low-ceilinged. There was a piano bar. There was a gift shop. There were potted palms. A long corridor led to the ballrooms. She followed the arrows.

Registration tables were set up in the ballroom foyer, where a couple hundred lab rats from all over New England were milling around with soft drinks in their hands and name tags on their chests. Many of these forensic scientists were shes. The crime lab had long been considered law enforcement's kitchen—it was okay for women to excel there. Once a year, they got together to network and to attend workshops on subjects like Capillary Electrophoresis Analysis and Headspace Gas Chromatography. Display booths had been set up in one of the ballrooms by the makers of lab microscopes and cameras.

Her timing was good. The annual awards luncheon had just let out.

The man himself was standing in the ballroom doorway in a navy-blue suit and gleaming black wingtips, shaking hands with the commonfolk and being charming. John Crowther was sixty starched and straight-laced, a family man, a church-going man, a Brylcreem man. He was very good at being charming. He was also good at being open-minded, approachable and caring. In reality, he was none of these things. He was a mean, vindictive son of a bitch, a consummate political in-fighter, a man who was always on his toes, ready to deliver a punishing blow. He was also known to be someone with his eye on the governor's mansion.

When he spotted Des standing there on the edge of the crowd, he welcomed her warmly. Introduced her around. Then steered her smoothly away from the others and murmured, "I've been expecting you, Lieutenant."

"You have?" she said, surprised. "Why is that?"

"You're Buck Mitry's daughter, that's why," he replied, the politician's public smile never leaving his narrow, rather pinched face. "You've been knocked off of your horse. You don't like it. Not one bit. Neither would the Deacon. Although I'd be willing to wager my entire pension plan that he doesn't know you're here. And, believe me, I have one helluva pension plan."

"Sir, the reason I am is that we have to—"

"Not here!" he cautioned her, waving at the conventioneers as he led Des across the foyer and away from them.

The superintendent found the two of them an empty banquet room and shut the door behind him, immediately dropping the smile and the charm. "I know perfectly well why you're here, Lieutenant," he said to her brusquely. "And I have nothing to tell you. Not one thing."

"You don't have to tell me anything, sir," Des said. "Tal Bliss did—before he shot himself."

Superintendent Crowther stared into her eyes, long and hard. "You wouldn't be wearing a wire, would you?"

"Of course not."

He raised his chin at her imperiously, looking her up and down. "I shouldn't think you'd be transmitting. You'd need backup, and if there's a soul who's more alone at this moment I can't imagine it. But if I were you I'd certainly have considered a tape recorder." She had. "Not that I'd be that stupid." She wasn't. "Still, I'm going to have to pat you down, young lady," he concluded with steely resolve.

"That's fine, sir." She removed the lightweight navy blazer she was wearing and held her arms out to her side. "You go right ahead and pat."

He checked over her blazer first, expertly inspecting the lapels, the pockets and the lining. Then he started in on her, carefully turning back the collar and placket of her blouse, his fingers probing her stomach, her sides, the small of her back, the waistband of her slacks, her thighs, calves, ankles. He searched her scalp and dreadlocks as if he were checking her for head lice—all the while staring deeply and coldly into her eyes. Des stared straight ahead, her gaze neutral. West Point had trained her well for this particular head game. She could tolerate this, although she could barely breathe and her heart was pounding so hard she was positive he could hear it in the sound-proofed silence of the banquet room.

His own eyes were eerily opaque and dead. The superintendent never so much as blinked.

Finding nothing, he handed her back her blazer and said, "You're running a bluff, Lieutenant. Bliss told you nothing about what happened on Big Sister Island thirty years ago."

"I wish that were the case, sir. But it's not."

He turned a dining chair around and sat down at one of the bare banquet tables, swatting at a scrap of harvest-gold carpet lint on his knee. He took out a pack of Parliaments and lit one with a disposable lighter, inhaling it deeply.

"There's no smoking in here." Des motioned to the sign over the door.

"Arrest me, why don't you." He glanced around for an ashtray. Finding none, he flicked his ash on the carpet. "Go ahead, then," he said impatiently. "Say what you came to say."

Des took a seat. She was not the world's most gifted natural-born con artist, so she had prepared her pitch carefully. "What Tal Bliss told me," she began in a low, steady voice, "is that when he arrived at the murder scene, young Dolly Peck was seated on the stairs. She was sobbing uncontrollably. She was incoherent. And she was clutching that shotgun in *her own two hands*."

Superintendent Crowther said nothing to this. Merely sat there puffing on his cigarette and watching her, the light from the ballroom's chandeliers gleaming off his shiny, stay-put hair. His eyes remained utterly expressionless.

Des plunged ahead: "Bliss told me *he* took the shotgun away from her and positioned it in Roy Weems's dead hands so it would look like Roy shot himself. Which was exactly how it went down— even though that wasn't what happened. It was really Dolly who killed Roy. The bastard raped her and she shot him for it, right there in his soiled bed. His wife, Louisa, was working in the main house. She came running when she heard the gunshot. And when she came up those stairs Dolly shot her, too." Des halted for a reaction out of the superintendent. Still nothing. But he didn't deny it. Not any of it. "You walked into a real, first-class mess, sir. Dolly should have gone down for their murders. Well, maybe not Roy's. Maybe that was self-defense. But Louisa? Not a chance. The reality, however, was that Roy and Louisa Weems had no chance. They were yankees. Dolly was an ambassador's daughter. A rich, troubled girl who was clearly headed for a good long stay at a mental hospital no matter what you did. So you tidied up their mess for them. There was no mention about finding her prints on the gun. No mention of conducting any kind of a test to determine whether she had fired that gun. Even the matter of her rape was kept sealed. You simply let her go, even though you knew she did it. Everyone knew."

Superintendent Crowther took one last pull on his cigarette before he ground the butt out against the heel of his shoe. He laid it on the table and clasped his hands together in his lap, raising an eyebrow at her. "What do you want from me, Lieutenant?"

"The truth, sir. That's all."

He let out a grim laugh. "*The truth*? I've been in law enforcement for thirty-five years, and if there's one thing I've learned it's that *the truth* is whatever someone wants it to be. O. J. Simpson was telling *the truth* when he said he was busy practicing chip shots on his front lawn while someone else was cutting up Nicole and Ron. Bill Clinton was telling *the truth* when he wagged his finger at us and told us he never had sexual relations with that Lewinsky woman. Did Dolly Peck kill Roy and Louisa Weems? You want *the truth*? Maybe she did. I don't know. I never knew."

"You put her back out on the street."

"I did what I was told to do by the powers that be. I was a scared, confused kid, just like you are at this very minute. I'd just gotten married. I was living from paycheck to paycheck. And that girl was a *Peck*. I don't have to tell you that the wealthy elite get treated differently than everyone else. For crying out loud, that's how they *stay* the wealthy elite."

"How tight were you and Tal Bliss?"

He glanced at her curiously now. "Why, what did he say about it?"

"That you weren't."

"Then why ask me about it?"

"He became a state trooper when he got back from 'Nam, that's why."

"Well, it wasn't any kind of a payoff, if that's where you're heading," he said. "Tal was bright and competent and they were happy to have him. I did try to offer him my counsel on occasion. To me, he was wasting his time as a resident trooper. But he ignored me. The job in Dorset was all he ever wanted."

For the simplest of reasons, Des reflected. So he could look after Dolly.

"Let's stop dancing around, Lieutenant," Superintendent Crowther blustered, abruptly seizing back the conversation. "Who else knows about this story Bliss supposedly told you?"

"No one."

"The Deacon?"

"No one."

"Internal Affairs?"

"No one."

"You came right to me?"

"I came right to you."

"Okay, here's what I believe, Lieutenant," he said. "I believe that you're either incredibly smart or incredibly stupid. Because your handling of this case is presently under investigation by I.A. And one word from me that you've shown up here, peppering me with wild accusations, and you will no longer be in the employ of the Connecticut State Police." He paused, stroking his chin thoughtfully. "I like to think I know your father pretty well. And he's not stupid. So I'm going to give you the benefit of your genes. I'm figuring that you've come directly to me because you want to cut a deal. You're thinking I'll be grateful to you—so grateful I'll somehow help you out of this mess that you presently find yourself in. Does that about cover it?"

Des said nothing to that.

Crowther narrowed his eyes at her piercingly. "Then again, this could all be a scam on your part. You climbing way, way out on a shaky limb. And me sitting right here with a chain saw in my hand. Which is it, young lady?"

"I'm trying to find out who killed Torry Mordarski, Niles Seymour and Tuck Weems," she answered quietly.

"Tal Bliss killed them," Crowther said easily. "It's clear. It's clean. It's closed. Why can't you accept it, Lieutenant? I have. Everyone has."

"I can't accept it because if Dolly murdered those two people thirty years ago she may have murdered again. And if Tal Bliss knew that, he may have taken his own life to protect hers."

"I don't buy it," he said dismissively. "That's too high a price for anyone to pay."

"He would have paid it. He'd loved Dolly since he was eight years old. If it meant shutting down my investigation, I have no doubt that he would have paid it. None."

Crowther got up out of his chair and began to pace around the room with his hands in his pockets, distractedly jangling his coins and keys. He finally came to a stop, gazing at her sternly. "Do you want to know what I think?"

"Yessir, I do."

"I think I'm not going to tell anybody we had this conversation. I think you're a good officer who got a raw deal. And I think this flap with I.A. will blow over. In fact, I'm prepared to guarantee it will."

Outwardly, Des's expression remained guarded and serious. Inwardly, she was doing cartwheels. Because she wasn't wrong. Not about any of it.

"When it does," he went on, "I want you reassigned to my team. Politically, it will be good for both of us. I can help your career. And you can help me in the minority community. You come across very well. You're an extremely telegenic, well-spoken young lady. I especially like your hair."

"You do?" Des absolutely could not believe they were talking about her hair.

"I do," he said earnestly. "It conveys that you're someone who's new and modern. Someone who understands what's going on out there." Now the superintendent smiled at her tightly, as if it were causing him great pain. Possibly, it was. "So you see, Lieutenant, where the rubber hits the road, we both want the same things."

"Do we?" she asked him challengingly.

He narrowed his eyes at her again. "Don't we?"

"I really don't know, sir. Because I don't believe this case is closed. I believe the murderer's still out there, walking around. And I believe you know it, too. And that's the part I will never, ever be able to accept."

Now Superintendent Crowther glared at her, a vein in his temple beginning to bulge. "Let me spell something out for you, Lieutenant," he said in a low, menacing voice. "If you're not my friend you're my enemy. And you don't ever want me for an enemy. Do you understand?"

"Perfectly. Thank you for your candor, sir. And your time. Good day." Des started for the door.

"Where do you think you're going, young lady? We're not done talking—!"

She left him there in that banquet room. She didn't stop. She didn't look back. She just marched back down the long corridor to the lobby with her head held high. She was elated. She was smiling. She was definitely smiling.

But the hair would absolutely have to go.

"Awesome move on your part," Mitch Berger said admiringly as he sat there across the table from Des, hunched over his soup. "You've got Dolly for the Weems killings. You've got the head guy of the entire state police admitting to a thirty-year-old cover-up. This is major stuff. There's only one problem with it."

"What's that?" she demanded.

He reached for a hunk of bread and tore into it, chewing with his mouth open. "Dolly didn't kill Niles Seymour or Torry Mordarski or Tuck Weems. I'm positive."

The Black Pearl was on Bannister's Wharf in what had once been a sail loft. There was a formal dining room called the Commodore's Room. And there was the casual and boisterous tavern, where she'd found Mitch slurping up his third bowl of fragrant New England clam chowder, a napkin tucked into the collar of his shirt. When the man ate soup he sounded remarkably like a drain unstopping. There was a huge basket of bread and a schooner of beer in front of him. He seemed positively starved.

Des ordered coffee when the waitress appeared.

Mitch was aghast. "No chowder? You've got to have the chowder. It's a sacrilege not to. Tell her it's a sacrilege," he commanded the waitress.

"You'll go straight to hell, honey," said the waitress, nodding.

"Just coffee," said Des.

The waitress went off to get it.

Mitch peered at her across the table. "You don't eat when you're tense, am I right?"

She nodded reluctantly.

"Me, I eat like crazy. Which I guess explains why you look the way you do and I look the way I do. This is a big difference between us."

"Well, what do you know—we found one," said Des, wondering how he'd look if she cleaned him up. Say, three months on the treadmill. No between-meal snacks, a decent set of threads, proper haircut . . . Then what would she have?

An average-looking white man who's hungry all the time, that's what.

When her coffee came she took a sip, shaking her head at him. "If Dolly Seymour isn't our killer, then why did Tal Bliss go and kill himself?"

"For the very reason you gave," Mitch answered. "He was afraid that you'd unearth the truth about Dolly murdering Tuck's parents. He took his own life so as to short-circuit your investigation. That much is true. But there's much more to it than that. A boatload more."

"What are you telling me—that Bliss *did* kill them?"

"Yes and no."

"Man, don't talk at me in riddles."

"It's like I was telling you—it all comes back to the Fibonacci Series."

"And don't you start gas-facing me about geometry either, because I am *so* trying not to hear that."

"You have to hear it," Mitch insisted. "It's a law. Not your kind of law, but a fundamental principle of proportion based upon—"

"I know, I know. The Golden Section. Which is . . . ?"

"Which is a line that's divided such that the lesser portion is to the greater as the greater is to the whole."

"Which *means* . . . ?"

"The Fibonacci Series is an algebraic variation in which each number represents the sum of the two preceding numbers. So instead of counting out *one, two, three, four, five,* you count out *one, one, two, three, five, eight, thirteen, twenty-one* and so on. Get it?"

Des thought about this long and hard before she said, "No, Mitch. I don't."

"Okay, here it is," he explained. "Two men acting together are capable of doing something that's twice as heinous as a man who is acting alone. When you add a third man you're not just adding another player. You're ratcheting up the disease quotient—*each man's capacity for evil represents the sum total of the previous players combined*. Add a fourth and you're taking a quantum leap over into the dark side. Add a fifth and you've got yourself a lynch mob. It's a law of human nature, Lieutenant. It explains the insanity of mob rule. It explains the atrocities of war. And it explains what happened on Big Sister Island. Hell, it's the only way this whole crazy thing does make any sense."

She gaped at him in disbelief. "You're saying that every man on Big Sister was in on it, is that it?"

"And Tuck Weems, too. Don't forget Tuck—he played a very valuable role." Mitch paused to take a gulp of his beer, swiping at his mouth with the back of his hand. "We can exclude Evan. He wouldn't have fingered Bliss as the man who locked me in the crawl space if he had played any part in this. And we can for sure eliminate Dolly, Bitsy and Mandy. This was strictly a guy thing. The ultimate act of male chauvinism, if you stop and think about it. They felt Dolly was too fragile and misguided to make the right choice, so they made it for her. Are you with me so far?"

"I wouldn't say I'm with you," Des said doubtfully. "But I'm listening."

Mitch leaned forward in his chair, his eyes gleaming at her. "Okay, here's what we know. We know that Bud Havenhurst hated Niles Seymour for stealing Dolly away. We know that Red Peck, her big brother, hated Niles because he was a low-class con man who roughed her up—*and* wanted to build condos on Big Sister. Jamie Devers hated him for killing Evan's dog, not to mention his constant gay-bashing. And Tal Bliss wanted him gone because he wanted Dolly for himself. It was he who recruited Tuck Weems, a man who had already threatened to kill Niles for beating up on Dolly."

"But why would Tuck come rushing to her defense?" Des objected. "Dolly's the one who murdered his parents."

"For which he was exceedingly grateful," Mitch countered. "Tuck *hated* his parents. His father was abusive. His mother was an alcoholic. The only real structure in his life was Tal Bliss. They'd been best friends since they were kids. Totally inseparable. Did you know that?"

"No, but so what?"

"We'll call our boys the Fab Five—better that than the Garbagemen, which is what they were. Together, they took it upon themselves to rid Big Sister Island of a man who they regarded as utter human garbage. Alone, not one of them had the nerve or the cunning to pull it off. As a group, they were able to achieve staggering heights."

Their waitress came by now to refill Des's coffee. Des stared down into her cup, her head spinning. "Um, okay, how do you know this, Mitch?"

"Because it's what happened. That's how I know it."

"That's not even close to good enough. You have to give me a reason to believe."

"Not a problem," he said easily. "Let's play it out, starting with Torry's married boyfriend, this shadowy Stan person who none of her friends ever saw. We've been supposing all along that Stan and Niles Seymour were one and the same. And that's exactly what we were supposed to think. It's what they *told* us to think. Jamie *told* me that Niles told him he had a girlfriend in Meriden. *Bam*, we immediately jumped to the conclusion that the girlfriend was Torry. Bud and Red *told* me they saw Niles and Torry together at the Saybrook Point Inn. *Bam*, we assumed that they in fact had. Why wouldn't we? Even though, as you may recall, I said I thought it seemed like a very odd place for a married man to stash his girlfriend."

"Agreed. Way too public. Only, she *was* there."

"I know that," Mitch acknowledged. "But no one from the hotel ever saw her and Niles together. All we have is the word of Bud and Red."

"And you're saying they made it up?"

"Exactly."

"Why would they do that?"

"To make us believe that Niles was dating Torry, that's why. He wasn't. It wasn't Niles who they saw there with her. Niles never even knew the woman. *Niles wasn't Stan.*"

"So who was—Tal Bliss?"

Mitch shook his head. "No, no. He was pathologically shy with women. Dorset's resident cocksman, according to Sheila Enman, was none other than Tuck Weems. Tuck had the midas touch when it came to women. *He* was Stan. He had to be, if you stop and think about it. Jamie's a former child star. Too recognizable. Also gay. Red is away too much. And Bud has a jealous, psychotic wife. That leaves Tuck. That's why he was recruited—to seduce an unsuspecting girl from some low-rent town far enough away from Dorset that no one would connect her death up with Niles Seymour's disappearance."

Des considered this a moment, recalling how Tuck's young live-in love, Darleen, had admitted that he wasn't always home nights. "Keep talking."

Mitch continued: "Their plot was put in motion when Tuck, who now had Torry good and hooked, asked her to check into the Saybrook Point Inn. She paid cash, per his instructions, and used a fake driver's license. Thus enabling the Fab Five to cover their tracks. That's why he had her wear the red wig, too. Poor Torry probably just thought it was good, kinky fun."

"Wait, pull over a minute. Why go to so much trouble? Why not just *pretend* they saw her?"

"Because they wanted documented evidence that Niles had abandoned Dolly for another woman," Mitch replied. "That way Dolly could begin divorce proceedings immediately. Otherwise her case might drag on through the courts for years. His relatives might come crawling out of the woodwork . . . No, no—the so-called other woman had to exist. They needed a disposable Jezebel. Someone like Torry who the law would simply write off as a borderline hooker who got what girls like that get." Mitch paused to take another gulp of his beer. "And it all worked like a charm. As far as the world knew, Niles Seymour had run off with another woman. Meanwhile, your investigation of Torry Mordarski's murder . . ."

"Went nowhere," Des admitted grudgingly.

"Exactly. But what they hadn't counted on was the X-factor—me digging up Niles's body. When that happened they were screwed, because they'd used the same gun to kill both of them . . . But wait, I'm getting ahead of the plot. How do you like it so far?"

"I think it sounds like just exactly that," she replied skeptically. "A plot. As in one of your movies. As in not real."

"Oh, it's real, all right," Mitch insisted, rubbing his hands together eagerly. "Now, then, the Fab Five were good and thorough. When Niles 'disappeared' they made it look as convincing as possible. They left Dolly the infamous Dear John letter. They ordered plane tickets for two. They parked Niles's car at the airport. Bud liquidated Dolly's accounts—supposedly to protect them from Niles—thereby making their case seem all the more convincing. Tuck Weems disposed of Torry, I suspect. And Tal Bliss tidied up the crime scene for him. Who better to make sure that it was spotless than an actual state trooper? Then they sat back and congratulated themselves on a job well done. They had pulled off an elaborate, carefully planned operation to rid themselves of the most odious man they had ever come in contact with. Everyone, most especially Dolly, thought Niles had left town. Only he hadn't. He was buried right there on Big Sister. Don't ask me which one of them shot him. I don't know. I only know that they would have gotten away with it if Dolly hadn't suddenly decided to take on a tenant. That was strictly her doing. They tried to talk her out of it. Even tried to scare me half to death. But they failed. And you know the rest of the story."

"The hell I do," Des said. "Why did they kill Tuck Weems?"

"Maybe he was wracked by guilt," Mitch suggested. "Maybe he genuinely cared about Torry. I do know that he was very, very tightly wrapped. And getting tighter by the day. I wouldn't be surprised if he just plain lost it when Niles's body was found. Bud certainly did—he suddenly had to account for why he'd raided Dolly's accounts. Maybe Tuck threatened to tell Dolly what really happened. Or even to go to the law. And so they had to kill him. That job no doubt fell on Tal Bliss's shoulders. Bliss met his old friend down at the beach. Got him so drunk that he wouldn't feel any pain. And their secret died with him. Everything was cool. Until, that is, you started moving in on Bliss. He couldn't handle it. The guilt. The shame. The suspicion and scrutiny that would fall upon Dolly. So he shot himself, thereby letting Bud, Red and Jamie off the hook. Except they're not. We're on to them." Mitch grinned at her now. "Well, say something, will you? Take your best shot. Go for it."

"Straight up, it's a sweet theory, Mitch," she said slowly. "It plays. But it's not nearly enough to go on. I mean, you can't *prove* any of it."

"I know that," he acknowledged. "That's why I'm taking steps."

"Steps? What kind of steps?"

"Ever hear of a movie called *I Saw What You Did*?"

Des let out a groan. "Oh, God, I have a feeling I'm really not going to like this."

"No, no. Everything's cool. Really. It was a grade-Z black-and-white thriller that William Castle made back in 'sixty-five with John Ireland and a somewhat cadaverous Joan Crawford. Budget of about twelve dollars. Serious shlock. Although, interestingly enough, the screenplay was by William McGivern, the novelist who wrote *The Big Heat*. Which was made into the movie where Lee Marvin threw the pot of coffee in Gloria Graham's face, remember?"

"Man, if you don't get to the point, and fast, I am going to get way ugly!"

"Okay, okay—what happens is these two teenage girls are home one night making harmless prank phone calls. They pick numbers out of the book at random, call people up and say 'I saw what you did.' And then hang up giggling, right?"

"Right . . ."

"Only, by accident, they happen to call a guy who has just murdered his wife. And he totally freaks out because he thinks they saw him do it. And he comes after them to shut them up. Neat idea, right?"

"Right . . ."

"In my case, I go with a note. Something simple and direct: *I am on to you.* I slide it under each of their doors. They freak out. They come after me, thereby showing their hand, and, *bam*, we've got 'em. Perfect, right?"

Des peered across the table at him. "Okay, I've really got to nail something down here right now."

"Not a problem. Go right ahead."

"Are you goofing on me or what?"

Mitch seemed startled by her question. "I'm being totally serious. Why would you think I'm goofing on you?"

"Because this is real life, not a freaking movie!" Des cried out. Heads at nearby tables immediately turned. She lowered her voice. Or at least she tried to. "You *can* tell the difference, can't you? Because they have a technical term for people who can't—they're called *meshugah*!"

"It'll work," he insisted stubbornly.

"Mitch, it's a bad idea."

"It's the only way."

"Mitch, forget it."

"I'm really sorry you feel that way, Lieutenant." He ran a hand over his face. He suddenly looked terribly concerned. "You see, I already did it. I've set the wheels in motion."

"You *what*?!" Out of control. Her life was truly spinning out of control. *"When?!"*

"Last night," he replied, swallowing. "Right after we spoke on the phone. I put notes under each of their doors. Anyone who's innocent will have no idea what it means. Anyone who's guilty is probably plotting my demise at this very minute."

"My God," she gasped. "You *are* insane."

"No, I'm not," he said with quiet determination. "I just happen to like Big Sister. These guys have done something truly awful out there. And they've ruined your career. And I don't think they should get away with it. Any of it."

"And what if they actually try to kill you?" Des demanded. "Have you given any thought to what happens then?"

"Of course. You'll arrest them. I have total confidence in you."

Des took a deep breath and let it out slowly. "Mitch, I want you to listen to me very, very carefully. What you're proposing falls under the legal heading of entrapment. Anything I learned under such circumstances would be considered inadmissable in a court of law. A judge would drop-kick it right out the door. And me with it. I cannot have anything to do with this. I am already under investigation by Internal Affairs. If I am even remotely associated with such a loony-toons stunt, my career in law enforcement will be over and out."

"And you'll have to concentrate on your art, instead. Worse things could happen."

"That's *my* decision to make. It's *my* career, *my* art and *my* life!"

"And I'm not trying to run your life, Lieutenant. Honestly, I'm just trying to help."

"*Why*, damn it? Why are you doing all of this? I mean, how did I get to be so lucky?"

"Because Lacy was right," he explained.

"Who in the hell is Lacy?!"

"My editor. She was positive I'd met someone. I was positive she was wrong. But she wasn't. I *had* met someone. And that someone was you."

All of the air went right out of Des's body. She was speechless, her mouth dry, her heart racing so fast that she felt light-headed.

"I wanted to see you again," he continued. "I wanted to get to know you better. Frankly, this all seemed to me like a perfect convergence of priorities."

She reached for her coffee and took a sip, wondering if he could see how her hand was trembling. "If you wanted to see me again why didn't you just ask me out?"

"You mean like on a date?"

"What I'm talking about."

"Would you have said yes?"

"Well, no . . ."

"There, you see? My point exactly."

"But there are ways for sane adults to behave, Mitch. And this isn't one of them. This is not some old Preston Surtees movie—"

"Sturges. It's Preston Sturges."

"Shut up! You can't just go around throwing yourself in front of a moving car because you want to get busy with the driver." She shook her head at him disapprovingly. "Man, I am *so* not happy that I ever met you."

"That's the nicest thing anyone has said to me in a long time," he said, beaming at her proudly. At that particular moment, Des felt quite sure she knew exactly what he'd looked like when he was a round little boy with grape jam all over his face.

"*Why* didn't you check with me before you did this?" she asked him. "You should have checked with me."

"You're absolutely right," he acknowledged readily. "Next time I'll check with you."

"There isn't going to *be* any next time, fool! Not if you're right— they are going to *kill* you!"

"Will you watch my back for me?" he asked her imploringly. "Will you be there for me.?"

"I just told you—I can't! You *know* I can't!"

"All I know is you have two choices," Mitch Berger said to her in a low, grim voice. "You can say yes or you can say no. Which is it going to be, Lieutenant?"

CHAPTER 19

MITCH KNEW THE STORM was going to be a genuinely nasty one when he got a good look at those gray clouds as he drove back over the causeway in his pickup.

They were converging upon each other from opposite ends of the sky like two big, hulking fighters in a ring. Mitch had never seen cloud formations do that before in his entire life. Thunder rumbled ominously in the distance. The air was heavy and charged with electricity. The wind was gusting. And the surf was so angry that cold salt spray was carrying right up and over the causeway.

He found Clemmie burrowed under his bed covers with her ears pinned back. Cats did not like wind. Or thunder. Cats were not stupid.

Mitch immediately closed all of his windows and filled every pot and pail he owned with water from the tap. He poured oil in his hurricane lamp and put fresh batteries in his flashlight, fetched two big armloads of firewood from the woodpile in the barn, brought his garden chairs inside. It was, he felt, very important for him to behave as if nothing were out of the ordinary.

Even though everything was. Mitch Berger was not an old hand at derring-do. At least, not when he himself was playing a featured role in the adventure. And had no idea how it would play out. Or if he would prove to be its hero or its victim. In truth, he was petrified. But he had not wanted the lieutenant to know this.

It was very important that she not know this.

By now the sky was turning black and fat raindrops were beginning to fall. Thunder shook the entire island. Lightning crackled. And then, with sudden ferocity, the heavens opened up and hail stones the size of pea gravel began pelting his roof.

The electricity went out with a pop right after that, plunging him into the dark of night even though it was only late afternoon.

The phone went out, too.

The hail quickly turned into a hard, driving rain. Mitch made a fire against the damp and curled up in his living room chair to read Manny Farber by the light of his hurricane lamp. He could not concentrate. The words were nothing more than meaningless squiggles on the page. He flung the book aside, lit a burner and made coffee. He drank a cup. He listened to the storm rage outside, the wind gusting so hard that Mitch wondered if it would tear the roof right off of his house. He heard a tree come down somewhere very close by. It was a frightening sound—like someone ripping a piece of canvas cloth—followed a second later by a heavy thud that shook the ground the way a wrecking ball did when it slammed into the side of a brick building. He thought about seeking safety down below in his crawl space, but decided he'd rather be blown all the way to Oz than go back down in that horrible place.

He waited. Inevitably, he got hungry. He heated up the remains of a batch of American chop suey and ate it right out of the pot with a serving spoon. Eight o'clock came, nine o'clock came. The rain came, harder and harder. So hard that it began to stream in under the front door, sparkling and golden in the lantern light. He fetched a mop to soak it up. Then he realized it was leaking in around his living room windows as well. He put a couple of old bath towels down under them to contain it and knelt there with the lantern, checking the floorboards for moisture. It didn't appear to be streaming any farther into the room. Not yet anyway. Satisfied, Mitch stood back up and let out a sudden and wholly involuntary gasp of shock.

He was face to face with them.

Three figures clad in foul-weather gear stood right there on the other side of the window in the pouring rain, staring in at him. Their features were slightly distorted by the beads of water on the glass, but Mitch had no trouble making out who they were.

It was Bud Havenhurst, Red Peck and Jamie Devers who stood

out there. He had not heard their footsteps on the gravel path. Not with all of that rain and wind.

Briefly, Mitch felt as if he'd been bolted to the floor. Here is what he was thinking: *My God, it actually worked.* He hadn't expected it to. Not really. Sure, it had worked in that Joan Crawford movie. But that was not real life. And he really did know the difference, whether the lieutenant believed him or not. *This* was real life— staring at him through the window. And Mitch's first reaction was total panic. He was not sure if he could actually pull this off. He was smart enough, but did he have the nerve?

He honestly didn't know. But after that first jolt of shock had passed, an inner resolve did begin to kick in. Determination coursed through his veins. He felt steady. He felt strong. It wasn't on the level of, say, Popeye after the sailor man had gulped down a can of spinach. But he'd take it. Mitch took a deep breath, strode to the door and flung it open, holding it against the wind with all of his weight.

"Hey, boy!" Bud called to him from out of the stormy darkness.

"Hey back at you!" Mitch exclaimed, a big smile on his face. "Don't you guys know enough to come in out of the rain?"

"May we?" pleaded Jamie. "It's really wet out here."

"Of course." Mitch stepped aside to let them in.

"We were just checking up on Dolly's tree," Red Peck said stolidly as the three of them came tromping inside in their rain boots, the water pouring from them. All three wore shiny yellow rubberized jackets and pants. Bud was clutching a long black Mag-Lite flashlight. "It was that old oak out by the driveway," Red added, shrugging off his rain hood. His hair underneath was plastered flat but dry.

"I heard it come down," Mitch said, his heart racing. "Sounded pretty bad."

"One big limb broke off," Bud said. "But she was lucky—it landed in the driveway instead of on the house. We'll have to take a chain saw to it in the morning, assuming it ever stops raining."

"That's a mighty bold assumption, pilgrim," Jamie cracked with an impish twinkle in his eye. "We saw your lantern light, Mitch. Just wanted to make sure you were okay. See if you needed anything."

So they were going to play games. Fine.

"I'm hanging in," he said, shoving the door shut. "Nice of you to check, though. Can I offer you a scotch for your trouble?"

"You can," said Jamie, rubbing his hands together with eager anticipation.

The other two nodded in agreement.

Mitch fetched four glasses from the kitchen, struggling to keep his calm. He'd positioned his bottle of single malt on a bookcase over by his desk. This gave him an opportunity to do what he had to do—flick on his microcassette recorder—while he was busy pouring. Then he brought them their drinks, the scotch glowing like honey in the lamplight.

Bud and Jamie had removed their slickers and stood over by the fire in their rubberized overalls, looking very much like commercial fishermen unwinding after a long day out on the Sound.

Red had unbuttoned his own slicker to reveal the Browning twelve-gauge that he'd been concealing underneath it. He did not raise the shotgun at Mitch. He held it like a safety-conscious hunter would hold it, with the barrel pointed down at the floor.

"What are you planning to shoot with that, Red?" Mitch asked as he handed him his glass.

"Mitch, that all depends on you," Red responded in a quiet voice.

His three visitors stood there in ominous silence now, gazing cold-eyed at Mitch as the wind howled and the rain tore at his little house. They were no longer the Fab Five. They were the Three Amigos—an aging child star who dealt in antiques, an attorney who dealt in estates and a short-legged airline pilot who had never shot anything more predatory than Bambi. Tuck Weems and Tal Bliss had been the trigger men. With them out of the picture, these three were on unfamiliar turf. And quaking in their boots.

Or so Mitch desperately hoped and prayed.

Bud slid a hand in his pocket and fished out the note Mitch had left for each of them. "What's the meaning of this?" he demanded, looking down his long, narrow nose at Mitch.

"It means just what it says," Mitch replied, pleased by how normal his own voice sounded. "It means that I'm on to you."

Jamie took a swallow of his scotch. "About what, Mitch?"

"All of it, Jaymo," Mitch said. "How you banded together to get rid of Niles. How Tuck seduced Torry. Why you had her check into the Saybrook Point Inn. Why Tal Bliss killed himself." Mitch paused to take in their reactions. Beads of perspiration were forming on Bud's forehead. Jamie's breathing had become shallow and uneven. Of the three, Red seemed the coolest and most in control. This was not good, since it was he who was holding the Browning. "Naturally, I intend to go to the law. Only there's a few things I still don't understand. For starters, why did you bury Niles out here on Big Sister?"

"Don't tell him a thing!" Red barked at the others. "Not one word."

"I don't see any upside in that, Red," Bud countered. "It's not as if he's going to get that chance to go to the law."

"Agreed," Jamie said heavily.

They intended to kill him. Right here. Right now. Mitch swallowed, his eyes falling on the shotgun. Red still had it pointed down at the floor.

"It had to do with the tides, Mitch," Bud said. "If it had been high tide, we would have taken his body away by boat and buried him under the rocks out on Little Sister. Unfortunately, it was low tide that afternoon. The channel from our dock is narrow. It's not uncommon for one of us to run aground. We couldn't afford to take that chance. Not with Niles's body onboard. Therefore, burying him here was our safest option."

"But why did you kill him so close to home?"

"Name a better place," Bud answered. "It's totally private out here. No witnesses. The women were gone for the afternoon."

"We met up with him in the barn," Jamie recalled. "That's where it happened."

"Niles was utterly flabbergasted," Bud jeered. "The bastard couldn't believe it. He thought we were joking."

Mitch took a gulp of his scotch, his hand wrapped tightly around the glass. "Who pulled the trigger?"

"Tuck Weems," Jamie replied. "He shot the girl, too."

Red was still not saying anything. Just standing there in front of the fire with the shotgun. Outside, the wind howled and the rain still poured down.

"It was stupid of him to use the same gun," said Mitch. "That was the one crucial mistake you made."

"Agreed," Bud acknowledged miserably. "But only with the benefit of hindsight. At the time, we had no reason to believe that anyone would ever find Niles's body."

"And Tuck *seemed* to know what he was doing," Jamie added defensively. "He ran the early stages, really. All the rest of us did was loan him our cars for his assignations with that *girl*."

"Torry," said Mitch. "Her name was Torry."

"Tuck didn't want to leave a recognizable trail behind," Bud explained.

"And why did you shoot *him*?"

"Tuck's conscience started gnawing at him," spoke up Red, who'd finally decided there was no point in staying silent. Mitch couldn't decide whether this was a good sign or a bad sign. He suspected it wasn't good. "Something to do with him becoming a father for the first time at age fifty. Poor guy thought he'd seen God or something." Red puffed out his cheeks in disgust. "Suddenly, he wanted to set things right—marry Darleen, become a decent family man."

"He threatened to go to the police," Bud said. "And take the rest of us down with him."

Red nodded. "Not an acceptable option. So Tal Bliss took care of him. Which upset Tal greatly."

"Plotting to kill Niles Seymour didn't?"

"Niles was a cancer," Bud said with savage certainty. "Taking care of him was necessary."

"Just as keeping Dolly's thirty-year-old secret was necessary?"

Bud took a sip of his scotch, eyeing Mitch over the rim of his glass. "So you know about that, do you? Lieutenant Mitry was getting very close to the truth. That's what Tal told me over the phone right before he shot himself. He was afraid that after all of these years poor Dolly would be branded a murderer."

"Well, she did kill them," Mitch pointed out.

"That man *raped* her," Bud argued, his voice choking with emotion. "She was a *virgin* and he *took* that from her! No court of law would have convicted her. But the trial—my God, it would have destroyed her. And she didn't deserve that. She deserved better. She still does. There are very few truly special people on this earth, Mitch. Dolly is one of them."

"And so is Evan," Jamie added fondly. "Like mother, like son. They're too gentle, too *good* for this world, Mitch. People like Dolly and Evan can't make it in life on their own. They need protecting."

"On this particular issue Jamie and I have always been in agreement," Bud said. "They *must* be protected."

"And so must Big Sister," Red said. "This island has belonged to my family for three hundred and fifty years, Mitch. It's our legacy. Each generation is beholden to it. We have a duty to make sure it stays *ours*. Niles didn't see family tradition. All he saw were big, fat dollar signs. Lord knows what might have happened to this place ten or twenty years down the road if he were allowed to remain here. Niles was a problem that needed solving. We solved it."

"Even though you had to kill an innocent girl to do it? You guys don't seem too concerned about sacrificing the life of Torry Mordarski. Or about leaving her son an orphan."

"We needed the girl," Red explained simply. "It wouldn't have worked otherwise."

"I did suggest using Darleen," Bud spoke up. "Checking *her* into Saybrook Point Inn. But Tuck wouldn't implicate her—he actually loved the little cow."

"Did he have any feelings for Torry?"

"Torry was a whore," snapped Red.

"And you three are gutless wusses," Mitch said, shaking his head at them. "You should have killed me when you had the chance. Not that you didn't try, of course. On the subway tracks—am I right, Bud?"

"That was . . . a different matter," Bud responded quietly.

"You didn't drive into the city that day, did you? You rode in on the same train we did."

"Yes," Bud confirmed, reddening. "I sat ten rows behind you the whole way in. You two never noticed me. But I saw you. I saw how she cozied up to you. I saw how she k-kissed you in the middle of Grand Central with all of those people watching. Her body pressed against yours. Her lips . . . I-I lost my head on that subway platform. Utterly and completely. Loving Mandy—it's a disease. A vile, incurable disease."

"And yet you told Tal Bliss that Mandy was the one who pushed me. Why?"

"That was her idea," Bud explained. "She said no one would prosecute her. They never have, never will. But with me it might be different. We had my career to think of. And my reputation."

"You should have killed me," Mitch repeated, glancing around at the three of them. "But the fact remains that *you* didn't kill anyone. You had the Dudleys Do-Right and Do-Wrong do it for you. This time it's different. You actually have to pull the trigger yourselves. And I don't think you can do it. In fact, I'm prepared to bet my life you can't."

They all stood there in charged silence now.

"What is it you want, Mitch?" Bud asked him finally.

"What is it I want?" Mitch thought he heard a door slam somewhere in the distance. But it may just have been the wind. He couldn't tell for certain. "I want Hollywood to make some decent, well-acted movies that are not totally devoid of intellectual ambition. I want to lose thirty pounds. I want to spend some quality time with a certain long, tall brunette. I want—"

"He means," Red broke in impatiently, "what would it take for you to remain silent?"

"None of us are millionaires," Bud cautioned. "And Mandy's

money is bound up in a trust. But I could arrange to transfer the deed to this house to you."

"It belongs to Dolly," Mitch pointed out.

"Not a problem, I assure you."

"If it's money you want," added Jamie, "I could get my hands on a hundred thousand in cash by ten o'clock tomorrow. Another hundred thou by the end of the week. How does that sound?"

"Like a pay-off," Mitch replied. "Look, guys, it's no use. Maybe you honestly and truly think you did the right thing. And for all of the right reasons. But you didn't. And I know it. And I'll be damned if I'll keep quiet about it. Because no one has the right to do what you did. No one. So I guess you'll just have to shoot me, Red. It's a little different than shooting a deer—you aren't planning to eat me afterward. At least I hope you're not. But it's not completely different. After all, I'm just some clueless stranger who got caught in your headlights. So pull the trigger, Red. Go ahead and be done with it."

Now the three of them exchanged a long, hard look.

"I think you'd better come with us, Mitch," Red finally said hoarsely.

"Where to?"

"The dock."

Mitch cocked his head at him curiously. "Why the dock?"

Bud finished his scotch and stared down into his empty glass. "You made a crucial mistake yourself, Mitch. You told us you couldn't swim."

"You're about to fall in, my boy," Jamie explained. "You're about to hit your head on a piling and drown."

"Hell, that'll never play. The police won't buy that I was that reckless or stupid—storm or no storm."

"But they *will* buy that you were suicidal over the death of your dear wife," Bud said. "You told all three of us about it at great length. You've been despondent. Inconsolable, even. And now you shall be joining her."

Red raised his shotgun and nudged Mitch in the chest with it. "Let's go."

Only they weren't going anywhere. The doorway was blocked.

Standing there in the pouring rain was Dolly, drenched to the skin in her flimsy nightgown. Her gaze was eerily unfocused, her hair soaked and stringy, her pale bare feet covered with grass clippings and mud.

In her right hand she clutched a carving knife.

Mitch had heard a door slam, all right. It was Dolly having herself another of her episodes. Same as that night when she had shown up in his bedroom. The storm had set her off. It was the storm.

Saliva bubbled from her lips now. "The mother," she murmured softly. "The mother is hurt."

"The mother is okay, Peanut." Bud started toward her—gently, so as not to startle her. He led her inside out of the rain. "The mother is *okay*."

Dolly responded to the sound of Bud's voice. She even appeared to be coming out of her trance. She blinked her eyes rapidly several times and began to look around the room in puzzlement. She was trying to grasp where she was. Trying to understand. But just when it seemed as if she were about to, Dolly's eyes suddenly bulged in terror. And she screamed. It was a blood-curdling scream. Mitch had never heard anyone scream like that before in his life.

It was the shotgun.

It was the sight of Red standing there holding that shotgun. Except she wasn't seeing Red's face. She was seeing the face of Roy Weems. She was back there all over again, back to that day thirty years before when Roy had raped her at gunpoint in this very house. That day when she had shot him and Louisa. That day she remembered nothing about.

She was back there.

"No, don't hurt me anymore!" she whimpered, her voice that of a desperate little girl. "Please don't hurt me!"

"I'm not going to hurt you, Dolly," Red said, straining to keep his voice calm. Pain etched his face. "No one is going to hurt you. Now please give me the knife . . . Just give me the knife, okay?"

No, it was not okay.

Dolly charged her brother—the carving knife raised over her head and a feral roar coming from her throat.

"No, Dolly!" he cried out. "It's *me*! It's *Red*!"

It was no use. She wasn't hearing him. She wasn't seeing him. It was Roy Weems, the trusted family caretaker, who she was seeing. It was the man who had robbed her of her innocence. And she was ready to kill him all over again.

Bud dove for her, wrestling with her, grabbing her by the wrists. The knife clattered harmlessly to the floor. Only now Dolly lunged for the shotgun, fighting Red for it. Clawing him savagely. Raking him and Bud both with her nails. Then all three of them had their hands wrapped around the gun barrel, gasping, moaning, groaning . . .

Until suddenly it went off with a deafening boom.

And just as suddenly everything in Mitch's universe became tilted and strange and he didn't seem to be standing up anymore. The floor. He was lying on the floor.

And now there were rapid footsteps on the staircase and the lieutenant was standing over him, Sig-Sauer in hand.

"No, no, you're blowing it," Mitch scolded her. "You were supposed to stay upstairs unless the play broke down."

"Guess what—it broke down!" she cried out. "Now let's just hold it, people! Don't anybody move!"

Only somebody was. Jamie was making a dash for the door. He didn't get there—the lieutenant was quicker on her feet. She kicked one of his legs out from under him and threw him to the floor. Jamie landed with a thud and lay there. He did not get up.

Somebody else was sobbing. Dolly. It was Dolly. The others were silent.

Now Lieutenant Mitry was kneeling over Mitch. "How are you?" She seemed terribly worried about him for some reason. "Talk at me."

How was he? He was cold. He was dizzy. Everything seemed to be swirling around him. He'd broken his wrist once when he was ten years old. Fell out of a tree in Stuyvesant Oval. That's how he was. "I'm just great. Did we get 'em?"

She wasn't listening to him. She was too busy yelling into her cell phone. "I don't *care* if it's raining. I need an ambulance *now*." Mitch couldn't make out the rest of what she was saying. Something to do with a *bleeder*.

There was blood. He was lying in a pool of his own blood. He'd been shot, he suddenly realized. Now she was tying a belt around his leg with all her might. He could see the cords in her neck stand out.

"Damn, how did I let you talk me into this?" she fumed at him.

"Simple. If they got away with it you'd never be able to live with yourself."

"I still might not. And who the hell's this long, tall brunette you were going on about?"

"Gwyneth. She's really a bottle blonde."

The lieutenant showed him her dimples. "That a fact? I had no idea."

"Stick with me. You'll learn all kinds of amazing, trivial things." Mitch felt himself getting even dizzier. He was starting to think he might even pass out. "Lieutenant, I've discovered something truly shocking about myself."

"Which is what?"

"I'm really, really good at this."

"Uh-hunh."

"No, I mean it. I was calm. I was cool. I was, dare I say it, *macho*."

"You just keep telling yourself that, macho man. It'll dull the pain."

"Will you take care of Clemmie for me?"

"Not a problem. Anything else?"

"Tapioca."

Her face was very close to his now. "You said what?"

"I want a large bowl of warm tapioca. Tell Sheila Enman, will you?"

The lieutenant's features were starting to get fuzzy. And then Mitch couldn't make out her face anymore. It was Maisie's face he was seeing now. His beloved Maisie. She was right there next to him, reaching out to him, beckoning him to join her. Smiling, Mitch held his hand out to her. She gripped it, her hand warm and strong, just as he remembered it.

Together, the two of them went far, far away.

Mitch woke up in a hospital bed with an immense bandage wrapped around his leg and a pair of Hideki Irabu's used sweat socks stuffed in his mouth. It was daylight. The sun was shining. And he was not alone.

"Welcome to Lawrence and Memorial Hospital in historic New London, Connecticut," Lieutenant Mitry said to him briskly. She was seated at the foot of his bed, dressed in a crisp white shirt and gray flannel slacks. The woman looked bright and efficient and way more alert than Mitch felt. "You've been out for something like sixteen hours. The bullet hit an artery so you lost a lot of blood. Straight up, another fifteen minutes and you might not have made it. But you're okay. No broken bones. You took it in the meatiest part of your thigh. Lot of meat there. Whole lot of meat there. In fact, the doctor said—"

"Okay, you've made your point about the meat, Desiree," interjected the lady seated next to her. She was a roundish little old lady in a faded sweatshirt that was emblazoned with the bygone slogan: E.R.A.-Y.E.S. There seemed to be a great deal of cat hair on this sweatshirt.

"Who are you?" Mitch croaked at her. There was nothing in his mouth after all. He was simply thirsty. He had never been so thirsty.

"Give it up for my girl Bella Tillis," said the lieutenant.

"I am a huge fan of your work, Mr. Berger," Bella exclaimed. "Although I must tell you I still disagree strongly with your negative assessment of *The Truman Show*. I felt that its message about the pernicious pervasiveness of modern media far outweighed the inherent plot weaknesses."

Mitch groaned inwardly. *I am not in any hospital in New London.*

I have died and gone to film critics' hell. "Bella, we've met before, haven't we?" he asked, peering at her.

Bella stuck her lower lip out at him. "I don't believe so, no."

"You ever live in Stuyvesant Town?"

"No, never."

"Wait, I know—you were my Uncle Sid's first wife, am I right?"

"No, dear, you're not."

"We're related," Mitch insisted. "I'm positive we're related."

"Can I get you anything?" Lieutenant Mitry asked him.

"Water, please."

There was a carafe on the credenza next to his bed. She got up and poured some. Mitch could feel his pulse quicken as she stood there close to him. His gaze held hers when she handed him the styrofoam cup, her own eyes growing large and shiny behind her horn-rimmed glasses.

"What's up with that Band-Aid on your arm?" he asked her after a long drink. "Were you wounded?"

"No, no. Just donated some blood, that's all."

"That was nice of you."

"Well, you needed it."

"You mean you donated your blood to me?"

"What I said, wow man."

"You mean *your* blood is coursing through *my* veins at this very moment?"

The lieutenant cocked her head at him curiously. "Why are you making such a big deal about it?"

"Because it means we're members of the same tribe now."

"Get out of here—that's kid stuff."

"It most certainly is not. It's a time-honored truism that dates all the way back to *Broken Arrow*."

"Man, if you're about to start in on old movies again I am way out of here."

Now he became aware that someone else was standing in the doorway.

"You're awake," this someone said.

Mitch's jaw dropped. "Lacy, what on earth are *you* doing here?"

His editor stiffened. "I am deeply offended by your overt display of astonishment. I can nurture. I can donate blood . . . Well, I can nurture. Besides, the press corps is mobbing the parking lot outside and I *need* your article."

"I'll get right on it, boss. Have you folks . . . ?"

"Oh, we've met," Lacy responded tartly. "We've bonded. We've swapped secrets. We've arranged for me to pick up two neutered male tabbies on my way home to the city." She broke off, her lips pulling back from her teeth in a pained grin. "Mrs. Tillis has even been kind enough to share her thoughts with me on the overall decline of our arts coverage."

"I especially hate that dance critic," Bella sniffed. "So smug."

"How did it go with your people?" Mitch asked the lieutenant.

"It went," she answered curtly. "I told them I was there because I'd brought a stray kitten by for you. And I happened to be upstairs with her when the three perps showed. And that turning on the tape recorder was your idea."

"All of which is technically true," Mitch pointed out. Of course, it was also true that he'd sneaked her out there in his truck and that she'd been hiding upstairs, waiting for them to show their hand. "Did they buy it?"

"They did and they didn't."

"Meaning what, exactly?"

"Meaning my case is still under review. And I'm still on administrative leave."

"I'm really sorry, Lieutenant. This is all my fault."

She shook her head at him. "Don't even go there. I had a choice to make and I made it. No regrets. But I *can* tell you this much—if you hadn't pulled through I would be roadkill."

"Hey, I wouldn't be doing so hot, either. How's Dolly?"

"Not great," the lieutenant replied grimly. "She'd always blocked it out. What happened that day, I mean. Now that the truth's come flooding in, she's gone into a severe depression. Her doctor believes she'll be able to deal with it in time. But for now she's downstairs in the psychiatric ward—under a suicide watch."

"Poor Dolly," Mitch said heavily. "Will she be charged in those murders?"

"There's no great desire on the part of the district prosecutor to proceed on that."

"How about the Three Amigos?"

She brightened considerably. "They were arraigned this morning in New London Superior Court. They're being charged with multiple counts of conspiracy to commit murder. Plus the attempted murder of yourself—times two on Bud Havenhurt's part. They're being held without bail."

"Well, this is good news."

"It gets even better—Jamie Devers has already confessed. Man's trying to cut a deal for himself. *And* we found strands of Torry Mordarski's hair in Bud's Range Rover."

"Excellent."

"Indeed," she agreed. "Although it's kind of quiet out on that island. The only two people left are Bitsy Peck and Evan Havenhurst."

"What happened to Mandy?"

"She hightailed it for New York." The lieutenant's voice dripped with scorn. She did not have much use for Mandy Havenhurst. "She's in seclusion, quote-unquote."

"Shall I arrange to have a reporter and photographer tail the little bitch around the clock?" Lacy asked her sweetly.

"Girl, you and I are going to be friends," Lieutenant Mitry said, smiling at her. "Oh, hey, I almost forgot . . ." She reached for a covered Tupperware bowl and presented it to him. "Here's your tapioca. Mrs. Enman was only too pleased."

"You remembered!"

"Damned straight I remembered. A man's last request matters. Although I can't imagine why you'd want to eat this stuff. Looks like a bunch of eyeballs floating around in custard, if you ask me."

"Who asked you?" Mitch demanded. "Besides, what do you know about food?"

"You are so right, Mr. Berger," Bella agreed, shaking a stubby index finger at him. "This girl does not eat. If I didn't watch her dietary intake like a hawk she would simply waste away."

The lieutenant let out a pained sigh. "Okay, now I am definitely out of here."

"You are not," Bella huffed at her. "You will stay here and you will feed this poor man. He needs to get his strength back." She began rifling through the credenza. "Do you suppose there's such a thing as a spoon around this place?"

Lacy said she would try to find one. Or maybe it was the lieutenant who said this. Mitch wasn't sure. He was slipping away again. He was tired. He was so tired that everything was starting to get fuzzy again.

But he didn't join Maisie this time. Maisie wasn't there anymore. She was gone—gone for good. Mitch felt certain of it. She had given him one precious parting gift before she went away. She gave him the Fibonacci Series. And for this Mitch would always be grateful. Because from now on, whenever he thought of his beloved wife, Mitch would be able to smile.

And maybe, someday soon, he might even be able to laugh again.

Epilogue

Three Days Later

"I WANT YOU TO tell the whole story, Mitch," Evan Havenhurst
informed him as he scampered about the deck, raising the sails.
"Every word of it—even the part about Mother and Tuck Weems'
father. Don't hold anything back. Not one thing."

There was a morning mist out on the Sound. The late May air
was soft and warm and held the first promise of summer. Mitch
manned the tiller of *Bucky's Revenge*, huddled there in his life jacket
with his bad leg held out stiffly before him. The throbbing was
beginning to subside. He no longer needed the pain pills and he
could hobble around on it pretty well, although he still tired
quickly. To build up his strength, he'd taken to walking the beach
three times a day—each time a little bit farther than the last.

Going out for a sail had been Evan's idea. The young man
wanted to talk. "Let's get it out in the sunlight," he declared, taking
over the tiller from Mitch. Soon the J-24 began to pick up the breeze
and run with it, its sails taut, the salt spray cold and bracing. "Blow
the cobwebs and the dust off. Let it breathe."

"You're sure about this, Evan?"

"Mitch, I'm totally positive. I need for you to do it. Consider it
part of my healing process, okay? And I *will* heal."

"Sure you will," Mitch said encouragingly.

Not that anyone would have blamed Evan if he'd broken into
small pieces. He'd lost his lover, his father and his uncle in one fell
swoop. And his mother was still on very shaky ground. It could easily have destroyed him. But that hadn't happened. Evan had spent a
good deal of time alone out on *Bucky's Revenge* since that night,
searching within himself for reserves of hidden strength. And

seemingly, he had found them. To Mitch he seemed more take-charge than he had before.

"Mitch, I despise this notion that they somehow felt they had to do it for me," he said angrily as they scudded across the blue water. "I don't need coddling and protecting. I'm not a helpless child. I never asked them to do *any* of that. Nor did my mother. We *never* would."

"I know that," Mitch said. "Everyone does. That was all just a grand delusion—an excuse they made up so they could justify their criminal behavior to themselves. And maybe it worked. Maybe they fooled themselves. But they didn't fool anyone else. So don't take it to heart, Evan."

"Believe me, I won't," he said. "I just have to stay focused. I'll get up every day. I'll run the shop, take care of Mother, manage the island . . . For the first time in my life I'll be responsible for more than just myself. But I'll be okay. Aunt Bits is in my corner. So's my cousin Becca. She's coming back from San Francisco to work in the shop with me. She's had some drug problems, but she's a genuinely cool, twisted person. You'll like her, Mitch. Which reminds me—I hope you'll be sticking around. I mean, I hope this hasn't scared you off."

"I'm not going anywhere," Mitch assured him. "I can't—I already promised Sheila Enman I'd be picking up her groceries for her every week. And I still have my damned book to write."

As the sun got higher it burned off the morning mist and the sky turned blue. It was going to be a bright, sunny day.

A sad smile crossed Evan Havenhurst's handsome face. "My family, to state the obvious, is really screwed up."

"I think all families are. I think that's what earns them the right to be called families."

"I know that now," Evan acknowledged. "And I accept it. Once you do, everything else seems to fall into place. Kind of funny how that works, isn't it?"

Bitsy Peck, meanwhile, had retreated deep into her garden.

Mitch found her in there after he and Evan docked. She seemed to be in the process of installing an entirely new hedge between her vegetables and her perennials. A dozen four-foot-tall holly bushes, their roots balled in burlap, were lined up in a row, waiting for her to finish digging a twenty-foot-long trench for them. Bitsy dug with feverish intent, the sweat pouring from her. One day soon her tears would come, Mitch felt certain. For now she was pushing them away, one spadeful at a time.

As he stood watching her, Mitch could not help but remember the sound of his own spade hitting Niles Seymour's leg.

"It's *Ilex pedunculosa,*" Bitsy burbled excitedly when she noticed him there. "I *finally* found a male. I've been searching for weeks and weeks. A commercial grower out on the Cape had one. You see, the females won't produce those lovely red berries unless you plant at least one male in their midst. They can't propagate."

"I had no idea that plants came in different genders," Mitch confessed.

"Oh, my, yes," Bitsy exclaimed, puffing. "It's a very basic birds and bees kind of a thing, Mitch. Just don't ask me for the scientific details because I don't understand them."

"How can you tell which one's the male?"

"No berries at all. See the third one from the left? That's my little stud bull." She paused to swab her face and neck with a bandanna. "Oh, this is *so* excellent. I have been wanting this hedge for years!"

"How are you making out, Bitsy?" Mitch asked her gently. "Are you going to be okay?"

She immediately resumed her digging, attacking the soil with manic energy. "Of course, Mitch. And so will Dolly. We're a much hardier variety than you men realize. There's absolutely no need for you to worry about me. No, no—I'm not the one who has behaved recklessly and stupidly. I'm not the one who's sitting in a jail cell all by himself at this very minute. I'm the one who's still out here, holding down the fort." She paused a moment, gasping for breath. "Take a look, Mitch. Take a good, hard look at what's happened. And ask yourself this: Which one is the weaker sex?"

Mitch didn't answer. There was no need to answer.

He limped back to his little house, flicked on his computer and got to work on his Sunday magazine piece. Out went his initial, somewhat treacly Currier and Ives lead paragraph. In came a leaner, more muscular opening: *She was a slim, bright-eyed girl with blond hair and a nice smile. She was the granddaughter of a U.S. senator. Everyone called her Peanut. Everyone wanted her—especially the family caretaker. And one afternoon, shortly before she shot and killed him, he had her.*

Now it flowed. Now he had it.

Now he knew.

Mitch was still clicking away at it that evening, Clemmie dozing contentedly in his lap, when he heard a car pull up outside in the gravel driveway. Followed by footsteps and a tap on his door.

It was Lieutenant Mitry. She was casually dressed—a gray Henley shirt and faded jeans. And she was not empty-handed. She held a gym bag in one hand and a cat carrier in the other. An occupied cat carrier. Meowing was taking place in there. Clemmie was immediately intrigued. So was Mitch. So intrigued that it took him a moment to realize that something was radically different about the lieutenant.

"My God, you cut off all your hair!" No more dreadlocks. Her hair was cropped short and nubby now. Way different but no less striking. It accentuated the long, graceful contour of her neck and shoulders. Her bearing now seemed positively regal. A sculptor would have a field day with this woman. "How come?" he asked her curiously.

"I had my reasons," she answered, setting down the cat carrier. Clemmie immediately let out a playful squeak and went nose to nose with its resident, both of them crouching low.

"And who, may I ask, is in there?"

She flashed her wraparound smile at him. "Put your hands together for Dirty Harry. Tal Bliss's cat. I have to move him out now that Big Willie's in the house."

"You brought me a dead man's cat?"

"Hey, you're lucky and you don't even know it—I could have brought you Big Willie. Besides, Harry's a good little mouser. Figured he could show Clemmie the ropes. Cats are happier in pairs, anyway. You don't mind, do you?"

"Would it matter if I did?"

"Of course not. How's the leg?"

"It's fine."

"Glad to hear it." She started across the living room with the carrier, Clemmie in eager pursuit. "No need to get up. I know the way."

She let Dirty Harry out upstairs while Mitch shut down his computer and fetched two beers from the fridge. He handed her one when she came back down a moment later.

"Success," she reported after taking a long, thirsty gulp. "They're already hissing at each other like family."

"Did you eat dinner? I've got some of my famous American chop suey left over in the fridge."

"God, that sounds great, Mitch. But, you know, I'm really kind of full right now."

Maybe it was a gender thing, Mitch reflected. Maybe women simply didn't comprehend the finer points of American chop suey.

The lieutenant had something to tell him. Something heavy. Mitch could sense it. She seemed very uneasy now as she stood at the windows in silence, drinking her beer and watching the sun drop into the Connecticut River. Mitch joined her there, listening to the cats tear around after each other up in his bedroom.

"This case made me realize something," she finally said, her voice low and guarded. "I've been in a kind of a holding pattern ever since Brandon left. And the time has come for me to . . . What I mean is, I've decided I need to make some serious changes in my life."

"Such as?" he asked, watching her carefully.

"I'm putting my house on the market, Mitch. I'm moving somewhere else."

Mitch's heart sank. *I will die. I will not make it without this woman in my life.* After a long moment he said, "I'm sorry to hear that,

Lieutenant. For strictly selfish, personal reasons. But I'm happy for you that you're making a positive move. And I hope we'll be able to stay in touch."

"So do I."

"Do you have any idea where you'll be heading?"

"Yes, I do."

"Where?"

She turned to face him. "Here."

Mitch stared at her, dumbfounded. "I'm sorry, I thought I just heard you say the word *here*."

She looked back out at the sunset. "Um, okay, maybe I'd better explain . . ."

"Well, yeah." Now his heart was racing. "Maybe you'd better."

"I am no longer what you might call the state police's equal opportunity poster child. Which is to say they did not exactly buy my version of how things went down that night."

"They've canned you?"

"In their dreams. If they tried to put me out it would get very messy and very public and Superintendent Crowther does not want that. I know too much. So the Deacon and I have brokered a settlement that allows both sides to come away with something. I've agreed to accept a slight reduction in rank and pay in exchange for a new opportunity that will, I believe, allow me greater time and flexibility to pursue other interests that are more—"

"Okay, plain English would be a *really* good thing right now," Mitch cut in impatiently.

She gave it to him in plain English: "I'm Dorset's new resident trooper."

"You're *what*?"

"The village needs someone to fill Tal Bliss's shoes," she explained, the words tumbling out quickly now. "And that someone is going to be me. I don't think I'll be the most popular choice with the locals. In fact, I'm sure I won't be. But I'm used to fighting uphill battles. And once folks get to know me, I believe I can earn their confidence and their trust. It's old-fashioned, hands-on community law enforcement, Mitch. The real deal. I'll be putting on a uni every day. Dealing with the people one on one. Anything nasty goes down, I pick up the phone and call the Westbrook barracks. But not much does in a town like this."

"Really? That hasn't been my experience."

"This case was way out of the ordinary."

"So let me see if I've got this right . . ." Mitch mused aloud, scratching his head. "You're going to be like Roy Scheider in *Jaws*—except without the shark?"

"Hopefully."

"What about your friend Bella? What'll she do?"

"She's been wanting a smaller house for a while. Now she's looking for one here. She intends to be Dorset's first angry Jewish woman."

"I'm sure that's something the community has been wanting for a long, long time. Your dad is cool with this idea?"

"My father thinks I've gone insane, actually. But he can't comprehend how important my art has become to me. My life will be way more my own now, Mitch. And I'll be like two minutes from the Art Academy. I picked up their catalogue this afternoon. They've got night classes all year around—anatomy, three-point perspective, life drawing . . . I'll actually be able to take them, which there was no way I could do when I was on Major Crimes. I'll be able to give it *prime* time."

"Okay, this part I like."

"Do you really?" Her eyes were searching his face now.

"I do. I like it large. In fact, I've got something for you. Was saving it for the right occasion. I think this qualifies." Mitch hobbled over to the narrow closet underneath the stairs and dug out the old oak easel that Evan had sold him. It once belonged to a renowned local painter named George M. Bruestle and the lieutenant had been crazy about it. Or so Jamie had reported to Evan after she visited their shop.

"Man, what in the hell are you doing with that thing?" she demanded, gaping at it in disbelief.

"I bought it for you."

"Get out of here!" She ran her fingers over it, touching it, stroking it, loving it. Clearly, she was not someone who was accustomed to spoiling herself. "But why?"

"I wanted to see you smile."

"That was one very expensive smile. I hope you got your money's worth."

"Oh, I did. Believe me. Only, can I ask you a personal question, Lieutenant?"

"I'm not a lieutenant anymore, Mitch. I'm a master sergeant."

Mitch shook his head. "I can't call you Master Sergeant. Sounds too much like Master Cylinder from *Felix the Cat*. Plus there are the sexual dominatrix overtones. No, no, I don't think we can go there. What do I call you instead?"

"You call me Desiree."

"Is there any other reason why you chose Dorset, Desiree? There must be other towns around the state that need a resident trooper."

Her eyes shied away from his now. "It's close to the art academy, like I said."

"And that's the only reason you're interested in this place?"

"Man, what do you want me to tell you?"

"What you're thinking."

She went back over to the windows and stared out at the view, her posture rigid. She didn't say anything.

Mitch flicked off the two lamps that were on and crossed the room toward her. He put his hands on her shoulders and gently turned her around to face him. She did not resist. They stood very close, gazing deep into each other's eyes.

"Why did you turn out the lights?" she asked him softly. She was trembling, just as she had been that day in the Black Pearl when she reached for her coffee cup.

"Force of habit. I do all of my best work in the dark. Can I ask you another personal question?"

She gazed back at him steadily. "Go ahead."

"What's in the gym bag?"

"My sketch pad and charcoals."

"What else?"

"My jogging clothes."

"What else?"

"My nightshirt," she said huskily. "Would you like to see my tattoo?"

"Desperately."

"How desperately?"

"What, there's a condition?"

"There is."

"Name it."

"We don't worry about what other people are thinking. We don't ask ourselves whether it'll ever work. We don't—"

"Freeze frame. I'll go you one better—we don't think about it at all. Deal?"

"Deal."

"Shall we shake hands on it?"

Her lips gently grazed his, sending a jolt of electricity through his entire body. "Oh, I think we can do way better than that."

Later, much later, as they lay in each other's arms in the moonlight, Mitch said, "Desiree . . . ?"

"Hmmm-mmm?" she murmured, running her fingers lazily over his bare chest.

"Your tattoo . . ."

"What about it?"

"I had a feeling that's where it was."

To which Desiree Mitry smiled and said, "Boyfriend, I had a feeling that you had a feeling."

Keep reading for an excerpt from David Handler's next
Berger & Mitry mystery

THE HOT PINK FARMHOUSE

Available in hardcover from St. Martin's Minotaur

AUTUMN'S ARRIVAL MEANT THE onset of headless mousey season out on Big Sister Island. Or at least it did in Mitch Berger's little corner of it.

Shortly before dawn, Mitch's rugged outdoor hunter, Quirt, deposited a fresh head-free corpse on the welcome mat of Mitch's antique post-and-beam carriage house and meowed to be let in. And meowed. And meowed. Upstairs in his sleeping loft, Mitch reluctantly stirred. Next to him on the bed, Clemmie, his gray-and-white short hair, did not so much as open an eye. Not even a hurricane could rouse Clemmie. In fact, with each passing day, Mitch was becoming more and more convinced that she had been genetically altered into a meat loaf.

Yawning, Mitch padded barefoot down the narrow stairs into the living room and waddled to the front door, flicking on the porch light to find one orange tabby who was immensely proud of himself and one white-footed field mouse who was missing his or her head.

It definitely took some getting used to as a morning wake-up call.

Quirt immediately made straight for the kibble bowl. The mouse stayed outside. Later, Mitch would bury him. Her. It. A small ceremony, nondenominational. Right now, he put the coffee on, watching Quirt chew his way steadily through his breakfast. Quirt had been a feral stray until he was six months old, same as Clemmie, but the two could not have turned out more different. Quirt remained a sinewy outdoorsman who did not linger inside unless it was raining. On those rare occasions when he would consent to sit in Mitch's lap he'd squirm and wriggle and make this unbelievably strange noise in his throat that sounded more like Gorgo, the monster that rose from the ocean's depths, than it did a pussy cat. Clemmie, on the other hand, never went outside, never stalked anything more threatening than dust and spent so much time in Mitch's lap that he sometimes felt she was attached to him by Velcro.

Mitch had not actually chosen to adopt either one of them. The new lady in his life was one of those kindhearted people who rescued feral strays from supermarket dumpsters and she had, well, forced them on him. But now that they were settled in, he could not imagine life without them.

While his coffee brewed, Mitch shaved and put on a baggy fisherman's-knit sweater, rumpled khakis and his wading boots. Then he poured himself a fresh hot cup, topping it off with two fingers of the rich chocolate milk that came in glass bottles from a dairy in Salem. He stood there sipping it contentedly and watching the purple-streaked dawn sky through the big windows that looked out over Long Island Sound in three different directions. A few fishing boats were heading out. Squadrons of geese flew overhead, honking. Otherwise, it was so quiet he could hear the water lapping at the rocks outside his door.

This was his first autumn in the cottage on Big Sister, a family-held island off Dorset, the historic New England village situated at the mouth of the Connecticut River halfway between New York City and Boston. The summer people were gone now, the kids back in school. The water was bluer and colder, the sky clearer and spiced with the smell of wood smoke. Migratory barn swallows and monarch butterflies filled his trees by the thousands, pausing to feed on insects before they took off again like a cloud for the Carolinas. With each passing day, the afternoon shadows grew longer and longer.

Mitch was the only one on the island who was not a Peck by birth or marriage. Right now, he was also the only one in residence, which meant he could enjoy the rare luxury of playing his beloved sky-blue Fender Stratocaster as ear-splittingly loud as he pleased. There was a decommissioned lighthouse on Big Sister, the second tallest in New England. There were four other houses on the island besides Mitch's, forty acres of woods, a private dock, a beach that Mitch alone used, tennis courts that no one used. A rickety wooden causeway connected it to the mainland at Peck Point, a preserve that belonged to the Nature Conservancy. Paradise. It was a Yankee paradise.

For Mitch Berger, a pure-blooded New York City screening-room rat, it was also a brave new world. He had taught himself to garden. Bought a palm-sized pair of bird-watching glasses and well-thumbed copy of Roger Tory Peterson's *Field Guide to Eastern Birds*, a high-low thermometer, barometer, tide clock, and a rain gauge that was calibrated to one-hundredth of an inch. He yearned for a telescope, too, but worried that he might turn into one of those unshaven old geezers whom he'd seen around town with egg-yolk stains down the front of their Mackinaw bib overalls, the ones who kept bees and railed on to total strangers about the virtues of the flat tax.

Still, he was really looking forward to the Leonid meteor shower on November 16.

At age thirty-two, Mitch was lead film critic for the most prestigious and therefore lowest-paying of the three New York City daily newspapers. He was also the author of two highly entertaining film reference books, *Shoot My Wife, Please* and *It Came From Beneath the Sink*. Mitch loved what he did for a living. He especially loved this time of year in the film calendar. The bloated, over-hyped idiocy of the summer blockbuster season had been put to bed. He had been revived by the quirky talents on display at the Toronto and New York film festivals. And now he had several clear weeks before the Christmas screenings to spend out here on *They Went Thataway*, his woefully overdue guide to Westerns, which explained the discs, files, books and video cassettes that were heaped everywhere.

Last night he had E-mailed news of this to his editor at the paper, Lacy Mickerson. Mitch fired up his G4 and logged on to see if she had replied. She had. Her response began with two well-chosen words: *As if*. Because Lacy knew perfectly well the real reason Mitch wanted to be out there. She continued: *But if you insist on playing small-town boy, how about that Cookie Commerce article?*

This was in reference to the so-called Serious Fun Edict devised by the new executive editor, who was encouraging staffers to branch out into other sections of the paper. The Knicks-beat reporter, for instance, recently got a chance to spend an entire fun-filled day hanging at the U.S. Supreme Court with Ruth Bader Ginsberg. Mitch was being steered toward the food section by Lacy based on something he'd mentioned to her at lunch one day.

His E-mailed response to her on this day: *Still searching for a hook*. Which was newspeak for: *Go away and leave me alone*.

He shut down his computer and started in on his morning chores. Scooped up that headless corpse with a garden trowel and buried it out behind the barn with the others, wondering what an archaeologist would make of this site in five thousand years. Headed down the path to the island's beach with a trash bag. Trudging along the sand, alone except for a family of cormorants, Mitch dutifully picked up the plastic bottles, Styrofoam cups and beer cans that had washed ashore from the fishing boats in the night. People, he had discovered, were absolute pigs.

He returned to his cottage, puffing slightly, and went to work with a rake on the leaves that had fallen in his beds, relishing the physical activity. Mitch was a big guy, just over six feet tall, burly when he was in shape, pudgy when he was not. Since his job called for him to spend every working hour in the dark on his butt, he could morph into the Pillsbury Doughboy if he was not careful. Being out here kept him in tip-top shape. The biceps under his *Rocky Dies Yellow* tattoo positively rippled. Okay, maybe it didn't really ripple, but it *was* a biceps.

He dumped the gathered leaves into a wire enclosure where they would quietly rot into mulch. Then he put on his work gloves and cut back the honeysuckle and wild blackberry vines that were threatening to engulf his whole house. These invasive predators he could not compost, he loaded them into the back of his bulbous, kidney-colored 1956 Studebaker pickup and tied a tarp over them. Mitch paused to cut a generous bunch of fresh white Japanese anemones from his garden, then hopped into his truck with the flowers and went toodling off across the rickety wooden causeway toward town.

The leaves on the old sugar maples that lined Dorset Street were turning a million different glorious shades of orange. John the Barber was out early sweeping the walk in front of his shop. Bill the Mobile Vet was stocking the medicine drawers in his truck outside his house. Over at the Grange Hall a hand-lettered sign announced that performances of the Dorset Players' fall production of *Bye Bye Birdie* were under way. The volunteer fire department was running its annual cow-chip raffle—first prize was a thousand dollars. Lew the Plumber was busy hosing down one of the fire trucks. He waved to Mitch. Mitch waved back. Rita, who worked behind the counter at the drugstore, was taking her morning power walk. She waved to Mitch, too. And, if he had cared to stop, would no doubt have asked him how he was making out with his jock itch.

Outside Center School, the charming circa 1912 elementary school located directly across Dorset Street from town hall, there were countless red SAVE OUR SCHOOL ribbons and green WE CARE ribbons festooning the trees. Center School was the focus of a heated local controversy. There were problems with its ventilation system—kids had complained of mold-spore-related respiratory problems last year, as well as nausea and headaches. Concerned parents, most of them the newer arrivals in town, had denounced the school as a health risk. This group, which called itself WE CARE, wanted Center School to be replaced by a new high-tech school that would be built on forty acres of woods on the outskirts of town and be able to hold twice as many students. Their SAVE OUR SCHOOL opponents, most of them folks who had grown up in Dorset, merely wanted the existing school to be renovated and upgraded.

The issue would be settled in a special election on November 1, when a thirty-four-million-dollar bond issue to finance the proposed school was scheduled for a vote. For a town with a year-round population of less than seven thousand, it was a major financial undertaking. It was also a referendum on the very future of Dorset. Opponents were sure that if Center School got torn down it would strip the village of its small-town character. They also believed a giant new school would open the door to rampant suburbanization. Their mantra: *If the school doesn't grow, the town can't grow.* Proponents argued that those who opposed the plan were living in the past, not to mention cheap, selfish and sadistic for putting Dorset's kids at risk for the sake of a little charm.

The issue was pitting neighbor against neighbor. Tempers were flaring. No one was neutral. The nine-member school board was itself sharply divided—five members were for it, four against. Dorset's longtime school superintendent, Colin Falconer, was against the plan, pitting him directly against its biggest backer, school board president Babette Leanse, a sharp-tongued new arrival from New York. A prominent architect, Babette Leanse was married to Bruce Leanse, the most famous real estate tycoon not to be named Donald Trump. The Brat, the New York tabloids called Bruce Leanse, who was busy bulldozing hundreds of acres of Dorset's farmland and forest to make way for new designer mansions.

Mitch opposed the new school. He liked Dorset the way it was. That was why he had moved here—because it *wasn't* suburbia. But he was aware that he might feel different if he had kids. And, after losing his beloved wife Maisie to ovarian cancer, Mitch was well aware of something else: As hard as it might be to hold on to the past, it's even harder to hold on to the present.

He stopped in at the market to shop for Sheila Enman, a retired schoolteacher who had just turned ninety and couldn't get out much anymore. Mitch bought her a box of Cream of Wheat, milk, eggs, a half dozen bars of bittersweet chocolate and several gallons of the Clamato juice she loved. Also a jumbo-sized tub of sour cream, which she would go through in less than three days. The old girl went through sour cream so fast, Mitch wondered if she bathed in it.

On his way up Route 156 he dropped the stuff off at her house, an amazing old mill house built out over the Eight Mile River directly in front of a waterfall. Sheila had lived there since she was a girl. Her kitchen door was unlocked, her bedroom door shut. She wasn't up yet. Mitch stowed the groceries and put the anemones he'd cut for her in a vase on the kitchen table. She'd left money for the groceries on the kitchen counter, not to mention his payment: a sandwich bag filled with her homemade chocolate chip cookies. Sheila's chocolate chip cookies were the finest Mitch had ever eaten—big and chewy and filled with gooey chocolate chunks. He marketed for her twice a week in exchange for them. Reputedly, Sheila also made a killer lemon meringue pie, but Bob Paffin had that franchise all sewn up. Dorset's white-haired first selectman still shoveled Sheila's walk for her whenever it snowed, just as he had done back when he was in high school, in exchange for one of her pies.

Mitch was discovering that this kind of payment system was the invisible commerce that held Dorset together. Cookie Commerce, Sheila called it. Lacy wanted him to write about it. Mitch was tempted. He had already written a lighthearted piece for the travel section on Dorset, as well as a longer, more sober article for the Sunday magazine on the disappearance of one of Big Sister Island's residents. He found the place quirky and intriguing. And he had always admired the way one of his idols, E. B. White, had written about the life he'd found on his saltwater farm in Maine. Maybe this was something he could do, too. A way for him to grow as a journalist now that he'd ventured out of the movie theater and into the sunlight, stumbling and blinking. Then again, writing about people whom he knew as friends was something entirely foreign to him. He wasn't sure he felt comfortable with that idea. That was why he'd put Lacy off.

That and the fact that he really, truly had no hook.

He jumped back in his truck and continued up the narrow country road to the dump, munching contentedly on one of his cookies as the morning sun broke brightly through the autumn foliage. The cookies were all gone by the time Mitch got there. First he backed up to the brush pile and unloaded his vines and brambles, then he eased the Studey over to the green dumpster where folks deposited their metal items. A picker's paradise. Mitch almost always came home with something choice. In fact, he'd furnished his whole house at the dump—his desk, bookcases, chairs, lamps, lawn furniture—the works.

On this particular morning, he was not alone. Another man had descended the ladder to the bottom of the bin and was sorting his way through the things that people had left behind. He was an old man, well into his seventies, with a scruffy white beard and a wild, uncombed mane of hair. He wore a beat-up black leather jacket, filthy corduroy trousers and work boots. His vintage motorcycle, complete with sidecar, was parked nearby, leather helmet and goggles hanging from its handlebars.

"It's no mm-rr-McDougal's House of Horrors," the old man growled up at him. "But it'll do, wouldn't you say?"

"Excuse me?" Mitch responded, frowning at him.

The old man sported a mouthful of crooked teeth ranging in color from yellow to brown to black. He sounded as if he were gargling lumpy mashed potatoes. Plus he reeked of whiskey. "Well, you're Mitchell Berger, aren't you?" he demanded, staring up at Mitch with eyes that were shockingly clear and blue and lit with intensity.

"Why, yes. Yes, I am."

"Sure you are. Recognized you from mm-rr-your picture. Only writer worth reading in the whole damned paper. Rest of 'em are a bunch of bed-wetters and suck-ups. Well, did you or did you not write that *Abbott and Costello Meet Frankenstein* was your all-time favorite Halloween film?"

"I-I did . . ." Mitch stammered, stunned. It had just hit him. He had not happened upon just any old wino. The old man standing down in that bin was Dorset's most famous and reclusive resident, Wendell Frye, the man who had single-handedly redefined modern American sculpture. Andy Warhol had transformed a Campbell's soup can into art. Wendell Frye had done the same for the automobile hubcap. His towering, breathtaking scrap-metal sculptures graced plazas and parks throughout the world, his name echoing alongside that of Alexander Calder, Isamu Noguchi and Ellsworth Kelly. He was a giant, a genius. He was also someone who hated prying eyes, publicity, critics and virtually anything to do with the art world. Wendell Frye hadn't granted an interview in at least twenty years. If the art critic from Mitch's paper somehow got a chance to meet him she would, well, plotz. And here Mitch was standing in a dumpster talking to him about Abbott and Costello.

"Must have seen that movie fifty times," the old man muttered, fishing an unfiltered Lucky Strike from a rumpled pack in his leather jacket. His hands were huge and knobby and scarred. He lit his cigarette with a battered Zippo lighter and pulled on it deeply, setting off a cough that seemed to rumble up from the pit of his stomach. "I love when they're searching for the mm-rr-monster down in Dracula's dungeon. Those wonderful slimy walls and cobwebs." He seemed quite chatty for a recluse, Mitch couldn't help but notice. "And then when part of the wall swivels around and Bud finds himself in that secret chamber with Karloff."

"Strange," Mitch spoke up.

"It's hilarious is what it is!"

"No, no. I mean it's not Boris Karloff playing Frankenstein's monster in that movie. It's Glenn Strange."

Wendell Frye peered up at him, befuddled. "You're kidding me."

"I never kid about credits, Mr. Frye."

"Christ, don't called me *that*." The great artist seemed genuinely hurt, as if he'd extended his big hand in friendship and Mitch had slapped it away. "It's Hangtown."

"Okay, sure," Mitch said, smiling at him. "As in a Hangtown Fry—bacon, eggs and oysters, am I right?"

"So you know your eats, too," he said approvingly.

"You don't get a shape like mine by nibbling on rice cakes and parsley."

"I sure do love that movie." The old geezer was still talking about Abbott and Costello. "Love dungeons and secret passageways of all kinds."

"If that's the case, then you ought to check out an old Charlie Chan picture called *Castle in the Desert*."

"Is that the one where Douglass Dumbrille wears that mask over one side of his face to cover his scars?"

Mitch raised his eyebrows, impressed. It wasn't often that the name Douglass Dumbrille came up in conversation anymore. Not even in the critic's section on the flight back from Sundance.

Hangtown flicked his cigarette away and went back to pawing through the trash bin. "You mm-rr-might enjoy my house. It's rigged with all sorts of secret passageways and chambers. They used to hide slaves there back in the days of the Underground Railroad. Emma Teasman owned it then."

"The poet?"

"That's the one. My great-grandmother. Mind you, I've made a number of modifications and I've put in . . . Aha!!!" he exclaimed suddenly. He'd found himself a bent-up old rooftop television aerial. It must have been eight feet high when it was intact. It was still plenty large. "A monument if ever I saw one!" he proclaimed, hoisting the ruined aerial up in Mitch's general direction.

"A monument to what?" Mitch grabbed it by the other end and yanked it up onto the ground.

"To when the one-eyed monster was king," Hangtown

replied, starting his way slowly up the ladder out of the dumpster. "It's not anymore. That damned Internet's the big boss now. Point and click. Point and click. Now the nincompoops are buying crap they don't need without even getting up off the sofa. Hate those damned computers. Only good thing about 'em is they killed television—except for 'Celebritydeathmatch' on MTV, of course. Ever watch it?"

"You bet. Martha Stewart removed Sandra Bernhardt's inner organs with an ice cream scoop last time I saw it."

"So you have cable at your house?" the old man inquired slyly.

"Why, yes. Don't you?"

"Nope. Still aren't wired out by us." Hangtown reached the top of the ladder and climbed out, wheezing. He was a big, lumbering old man, at least six feet three, and he had a lot of trouble moving. "I'd love to get me a satellite dish. But then I'd never do a thing except sit and watch old movies all day. Hey, what are you looking for down here anyway, Big Mitch?"

"A bucket to hold my kindling."

"Hell, got some old copper apple-butter tubs in my barn. Fix you right up."

"That's awfully generous of you, Hangtown."

"The hell it is. You'll pay me for it."

"Why, sure," Mitch said hastily. "How much did you have in mind?"

"I need you to take this aerial home for me. Won't fit in my sidecar."

"You've got yourself a deal," Mitch said, glancing admiringly at Wendell Frye's antique ride. "That's quite some old bike."

"It's a 1936 Chief," Hangtown said, as the two of them deposited the aerial on the tarp in the back of Mitch's truck. "Manufactured right up the mm-rr-road in Springfield by the Indian Motorcycle Company. Found her in a barn in Higganum a few years back. Cylinders still had the original nickel plating." He climbed slowly on and donned his leather helmet and goggles, cackling at him. "*Spiral Staircase* was another good one. Remember that eye in the peephole? Man, that's the good stuff! Who was the villain in that?"

"George Brent."

"George Brent! Whatever happened to him?"

"He died."

Hangtown shook his huge white head at Mitch. "Wish people would stop doing that. Makes me wonder if it might happen to me someday."

"You think it won't?" Mitch found himself asking.

"I don't *think* at all, Big Mitch," the great artist roared, kick-starting the bike's engine. It caught right away, spewing clouds of thick exhaust in the morning air. "*Thinking* is what kills you. Christ, didn't you know that?"